BENEFIT OF THE DOUBT

BY NEAL GRIFFIN

Benefit of the Doubt

BENEFIT OF THE DOUBT

NEAL GRIFFIN

A TOM DOHERTY ASSOCIATES BOOK
New York

BENEFIT OF THE DOUBT

Copyright © 2015 by Neal Griffin

All rights reserved.

A Forge Book
Published by Tom Doherty Associates, LLC
175 Fifth Avenue
New York, NY 10010

www.tor-forge.com

Forge® is a registered trademark of Tom Doherty Associates, LLC.

The Library of Congress Cataloging-in-Publication Data is available upon request.

ISBN 978-0-7653-3850-1 (hardcover)
ISBN 978-1-4668-3902-1 (e-book)

Forge books may be purchased for educational, business, or promotional use.
For information on bulk purchases, please contact the Macmillan Corporate and
Premium Sales Department at 1-800-221-7945, extension 5442, or write to
specialmarkets@macmillan.com.

First Edition: May 2015

Printed in the United States of America

0 9 8 7 6 5 4 3 2 1

To my Dad

James Phillip Griffin

1925–2008

I'd like to think this would have made him proud.

ACKNOWLEDGMENTS

I've come to learn that like police work, the publishing industry places great value on dogged persistence. A detective can have the acumen of Sherlock Holmes, but without the application of a good bit of shoe leather, little will come of it. So it is with the aspiring writer. Nothing can take the place of words on the page, except more words on more pages, every day. For that long list of fellow cops and writers, early readers, my family, friends, and all the others who over the years encouraged me to stick with it, you have my deepest appreciation.

And, a good outcome in publishing is not unlike a successful criminal investigation. The measure of success is dependent on the team assembled. Early on, my incredible agent, Jill Marr of the Sandra Dijkstra Literary Agency, was like the first cop to arrive on scene. She found something that looked mildly interesting and, even though many others had just walked by, Jill saw a lead. It needed to be fleshed out, but there was potential. She took a chance and I will be forever grateful.

Emily Heckman, a freelance editor of impeccable skill and straight talk, was my field training officer. She didn't pull any punches in an early assessment of my work and that has made all the difference.

Beat partners are those senior cops still on the job, who look out for the rookies. They're the ones who have better things to do, but still take the time to help out the new guy. My beat partners make up the who's who of crime fiction. Joe Wambaugh, the godfather of the genre, who can and still does bring it. Don Winslow and Jeff Parker, a couple of local SoCal guys who have made the big time but never turned down a chance to provide a word of encouragement. Jon Land, Hank Ryan, Andy Gross; the list is long and formidable. I couldn't have dreamed up a more accomplished group of supporters.

Then there's my boss. The precinct sergeant. The ultimate authority. Melissa Ann Singer, *my* editor at Forge, who has watched over this project from start to finish. She knew what the end product would be and she kept us on course. Like all the best cops I ever worked for, Melissa is "old school" and I wouldn't have wanted it any other way. To Melissa, Tom, Linda, Patty, Emily, Diana, and all the others at Team Forge: I hope we get to do this again, and again and again.

No cop ever goes it alone. There is always a partner. An indispensable one who sits in the passenger seat and listens to all the complaining and grousing. Who shares the victories as well as the setbacks. My wife, Olga Diaz, is my one true partner. An amazingly accomplished woman in her own right, she took the time to cheer me on and stand by me every step of the way. Olga, I owe it all to you.

BENEFIT OF THE DOUBT

Harlan Lee took one last hit off the joint, then popped the glowing stub in his mouth, a habit left over from prison life. He clenched his jaw, pressed his tongue firmly against the roof of his mouth, and took in the odor of burning flesh. From the seat of the stolen car, he fought the nervous inclination to move things along. *Stick with the plan,* he told himself. Either that or just plan on another long stretch of hard time. Then a chill of anticipation started in his chest and pushed out until it bumped up his skin. He checked his watch.

"Okay, lady. Time's up."

Harlan stepped into the crisp moonless night and walked a hundred yards of deserted sidewalk. He hunched his shoulders against the cold and cast his gaze to the ground, doing all he could to convey a sense of the ordinary, but it was a lie. Harlan felt anything but ordinary. Three weeks out and the exhilaration of his newfound freedom remained, accompanied by a rage of confounding intensity.

Seventeen years. The thought swirled through his head in a hazy cloud brought on by the dope. He'd never get past the waste of it.

The anger in it. He'd learned the hard way that prison didn't end when a man walked out. It lingered and gnawed, holding on to the mind. It sure as hell hung around. It was on his skin. It was in his hair. Even his clothes reeked of captivity. Every free moment provided Harlan with another reminder of all the things a man missed by being caged.

There. That's the one. Harlan figured he had ten minutes to work with, maybe twenty. The jack-off had shown a tendency to run late.

The house stood bathed in a white light reminiscent of a guard tower beacon. The front door was unlocked. Inside, the warm air carried odors of garlic and sage. He heard the sizzle of a hot pan and breathed deeper. Salmon. The woman's voice came from what he assumed must be the kitchen.

"Hey, you. You're early for once."

Harlan sensed she had stopped to look up and wait for him to emerge into view. He closed the door and threw the bolt, picturing her smile of anticipation.

"Pour the wine. Dinner's in ten minutes."

Harlan walked into the open kitchen and found the woman studying his unfamiliar shadow.

"I don't answer to 'you,' and I can't say as I much care for wine."

Her head cocked sideways in a moment of confusion that in the blink of an eye changed to terror. She let out a piercing scream that rang in his head and that he thought might have carried outside. Harlan figured her next thought would be more about flight than fight, but instead she kept it simple and reached for a phone on the countertop. *Can't allow that.* Three easy numbers and he'd be fucked. Harlan closed in with several quick steps and raised his arm. He let the gun settle just inches from her face, forcing her to focus on the copper bullets that stared out from the cylinder.

When he was certain he had her full attention, he spoke a chilled warning.

"Shut your mouth and stay away from that damn phone or we'll end this right now."

She pulled her hand back. Harlan looked hard into her eyes and concluded she'd never been closer to a real gun. He took in the scene around him, noticing the nearby candlelit table set for two.

"How cozy." He spoke with a contemptuous nonchalance.

Standing barefoot and stock-still in a thin T-shirt and tight jeans, small hissing noises escaped her throat and grew to quiet sobs. She drew a breath, immediately followed by another and then another. Large, hitching gulps without exhale. She forced herself to speak, and the words conveyed her desperation.

"Look, just take what you want and leave. I won't make any trouble for you. Just . . . just leave me alone, please."

Harlan picked up on the quiver in her voice and the shaking of her hands. She raised her arms a bit and backed away. She had every right to fear his intent.

"I ain't here to steal from ya. And I got no interest in forcin' myself on ya neither."

"Okay, okay. Just tell me what you want. I don't know what I did—"

Harlan cut her off. "I got no quarrel with you. Fact is you shoulda been more particular about your associations."

He saw her fight to get her wits about her, saw the irrepressible shivers that spread over the appealing curves of her body. Harlan read people well and sensed her resignation. She'd suffer any indignity that offered the slightest chance of survival. Were the circumstances different, he might have acted on his base desires, but with a calm detachment, he pressed ahead.

"That boyfriend of yours. Shouldn't he be comin' right along? Mr. William Petite, I believe." He spat out the name with no shortage of spite. "I hear he's had quite the run as a shyster lawyer. Am I right, Rebecca?"

"Did his wife send you? Is that what this is? I won't see him anymore. I swear I won't."

Harlan sensed regret in her words but only the sort felt by most anyone once their offense has been discovered. He corrected her thinking.

"His wife ain't got no part in this and I couldn't give two shits who you put out for. It's just a little something between me and Petite. Not much can be done about you gettin' caught up in the middle."

Harlan looked her over one last time. A damn pretty woman, no doubt. It crossed his mind again that she likely had some skills in carnal affairs, but he gave no thought toward reconsideration. Her path was set.

"Ain't no sense draggin' this out. Take a second and make your peace." Harlan cocked the hammer with a calloused thumb. In the way another man might target a rusty beer can balanced on a fence post, he took quick aim and fired twice.

The small-caliber weapon popped, and he felt the jump of the gun. She threw her hands out as if she intended to catch the bullets in midair, but both projectiles found their way to the meatiest portion of her slender gut. The cotton of her shirt puffed out in a tight circle of smoke, and splotches of red appeared like magic as the lead sliced into her. Harlan figured the hot burrow of the metal tore through muscle and flesh with a good bit of sting, but all the woman could muster was a coarse grunt. She brought her hands to her belly, and he watched the red seep heavy between her fingers. He imagined the blood running wild through her, filling crevices and empty spaces, turning her into nothing more than a human sink.

She looked down to take in her predicament, then fell to her hands and knees. She fought to stay there, arching her back and tensing her body. Her face turned up and she met his gaze. All was lost now and she knew it. In a pleading voice, she begged for a reason.

"Why? Why me?"

Harlan stared back, impassive. Explanation would be meaningless.

She dropped to the floor, landing with her face pressed against the tile, one arm twisted beneath her body. Blood began to pool and form a frame of crimson around her figure. She rolled to her back and struggled to stand but could not.

Harlan closed the distance until he stood directly over her, avoiding the blood. Struggling for breath, her lips parted in a rhythm reminiscent of the bass and pikes he'd caught as a small boy growing up in the deepest forest of Florence County, Wisconsin. He looked down at her face and offered what he believed to be good advice.

"I figure it best you just surrender to it."

Chunks of scarlet blood gurgled thick from her mouth, but she managed to push out a few last words. Her eyes shone clear and hateful.

"Go to hell."

"You first, missy."

Harlan took aim and squeezed the trigger smooth four times. The sacs of silicone that had created the sensual swell of her round breasts erupted an instant before her heart did the same, spraying blood and other fluids in all directions. Each bullet cracked against the tile beneath her, vibrating up through the soles of his shoes. At the first impact, her body jolted like a current had run through it and her face snapped to the left. Her eyes went to a place far enough away that he knew any further violence against her would be a waste. Burnt powder overtook her perfume, and a trickle of wetness grew to a puddle between her legs. He looked down at the dead woman at his feet, giving some consideration to what he had done. He smiled at the ironic nature of his thinking and spoke out loud.

"You are ruthless animal, Harlan. You damn sure oughta be locked up."

The arrangements took seconds, and he made certain not to

improvise. He used a dish towel to turn off the stove—a fire would ruin everything—then gave the scene a quick study. With his affairs in order, he stole a glance into the street before slipping out the front door. At the sidewalk he became a man out for a walk, no cause for alarm in a neighborhood where people often strolled after dark, safe in the heartland of America.

Several minutes passed before the sleek blue import rounded the corner and pulled to the curb. The man parked in his usual spot and walked to the house with a cocksure deliberation that left Harlan irritated at the reminder of the man's haughty arrogance. Back in the car, Harlan cranked the ignition. The engine purred smooth, and he headed into the night wearing a tight but irrepressible grin, warmed by the pleasure that always accompanied the overdue settlement of an old score.

ONE

The digital timer on the treadmill hit forty minutes and Ben Sawyer fought the nagging urge to quit. Tempted to slow to a brisk walk, Ben cursed himself through clenched teeth. He cranked the speed half a point higher, increased the incline, and gave himself a silent ration of shit for being weak. He despised artificial exercise, but the alternative meant dealing with the slush, soft ice, and bone-snapping potholes that scarred the roads every spring. To make matters worse, Ben knew that after a short respite, summer heat would blanket the countryside with a muggy hatred for all things human. The wet, sticky air would be thick with dragon mosquitoes patrolling the skies like military drones in search of easy targets. An endless parade of miserable seasons. If he spent the rest of his life in the earthbound purgatory of Newberg, Wisconsin, he'd use his last breath to curse the goddamn weather.

In the cramped storage room that doubled as the gym of the Newberg Police Department, Ben ran in place while half a dozen patrol officers held what amounted to nothing more than a circle jerk disguised as a workout. He couldn't help but overhear as one officer held the group spellbound with his firsthand account of a bizarre dead body call at an all-night grocery store.

"I'm telling you, fellas, we break the office door down and find the guy slumped over dead, pants around his ankles, and the most imaginative collection of kinky shit I've ever seen outside a porn store."

Graveyard cops are all the same, Ben thought. Young. Aggressive. Mostly male and inevitably vile natured and foul mouthed. As a veteran sergeant, Ben knew they might be crude and tasteless, but street cops from any department had to be allowed to blow off steam.

The officer went on, "And he had this . . . this . . . I don't know what you'd call it . . . this rubber ass thing. I'd never seen one before. Flat on one side so he could prop it up on the desk, two holes in it. And man, I'm not lyin' when I tell ya this. He was buried in that damn thing right up to the hilt."

Expressions of disgust and disbelief were met by a raised hand signifying there was more.

"I bullshit you not, but check this out. The body snatchers show up, right? But they say they ain't gonna take the guy with the man-made attachment. So I draw short straw and I gotta separate him from his . . ."

The officer seemed perplexed, wondering how to explain, but plowed ahead.

"Well, shit . . . I had to yank it off him. I swear it popped off like a champagne cork. And I'll be damned if there wasn't something sloshin' around in there."

This was more than the audience could stand. Profane objections rang out and the crowd backed away, giving the storyteller a wide berth.

"Fuck you guys, I double-gloved. But I'm tellin' ya, the damn thing had some heft to it, must've weighed four or five pounds. Anatomically correct, sure as shit. It was like . . . like a desktop piece of ass." A sweeping gesture of the hand accompanied the last line, followed by gales of laughter, then a question from the audience.

"So was he working or just hanging around to get his rocks off?"

"Oh, he was working all right. Just threw his green apron over his shoulder, lubed up, and got at it. Dropped dead of a heart attack so fast he couldn't even put his junk away, poor bastard." The officer feigned sympathy, then went for the showman's big finish.

"Ya know, I'll bet before he croaked out he was looking through the one-way glass, puttin' it to that ass contraption of his and all the while dreaming about having at one of those sexy little checkout chicks. You think about it, that ain't a bad way to go. I saw a couple I wouldn't mind bending over that desk." A dramatic thrust of the hips emphasized the final point, which was followed by even more laughter. Ben saw high fives go around for everyone but the man in middle, whose objections were met with a hard dose of cop-world reality.

"Dude, it don't matter if you triple-gloved. Your ass is quarantined for life after handling that shit."

Ben shook his head and smiled in spite of himself. *Rough crowd.* But he had to admit it was the perfect cop war story: sex, death, and some no-count civilian schmuck to ridicule. Most candy-ass civilian types would no doubt disapprove of the officer's graphic storytelling. But Ben knew for a fact none of these guys gave a damn that their private conversation about a dead man not yet in the ground might offend the churchgoing populace. Cops figured anybody who didn't want to hear it, didn't have to listen. Ben was in complete agreement.

Okay. Four more minutes. Forget the damn shop talk and get at it.

To fight the monotony, Ben conjured up a mental picture of the sandy shoreline of Crab Cove back in Alameda, when low tide and sunrise came together to create perfect running conditions. The taste of sea salt drifting in on the light breeze, the surf breaking a hundred yards out. He'd do six miles, ending up at the South Shore Café, where he'd spoil himself with a well-deserved twelve-hundred-calorie breakfast and the sports section of the *Oakland Tribune*.

You really know how to screw up a good gig, Sawyer.

Ben was honest enough to accept the blame. He'd been a thirteen-year veteran of Oakland PD. A sergeant in charge of the prestigious Gang Suppression Unit. His star on the rise, lieutenant bars in his future. High-ranking bosses threw his name around as a future commander, maybe even chief. Then it happened. Shitcanned back to Newberg, his childhood home. A place that on the law enforcement career ladder came in about six rungs below mall cop.

Oh, let it go already.

Ben put in his earbuds, turned up the volume on his iPod, and notched the speed up another two points. The rhythmic hum of the treadmill fell in sync with AC/DC's "Highway to Hell," and the antics of his fellow officers faded away. Ben did his best to drown out the internal critic by concentrating on the opening guitar riffs, but the usual insults ran amok in his head.

You're lucky to have any kind of job. How about a few years in prison, you ever think of that?

He counted the impacts of his left foot on the moving rubber surface. Anything to keep his mind a safe distance from the past—but he couldn't stop the emotional drift. Memories flooded over him in relentless, violent waves. Years of street work in Oakland. A band of brothers. Human bonds that could stand any test. Any test, that is, other than twenty seconds of insanity and a convict-turned–urban folk hero named Hector Espudo.

The past took form in a series of staccato sounds and still images, flashing in his mind as isolated moments. Shifting angles and light. A rookie officer's sudden and frantic call over the radio.

"Foot pursuit of 187 suspect. Westbound on Fortieth approaching Broadway."

The crime and location said it all. Every cop in Oakland knew the suspect was Hector Espudo, a convict put back on the street through the governor's bullshit early-release program. A made member of the Nuestra Familia inside the walls and a high-ranking lieutenant of the Norteños street gang on the outside, Hector had been on parole less than three weeks when he got into a beef with an adversary from a rival gang. Hector went at the man with the ass end of a table lamp, and by the time he was done, his victim's face was mashed flat into the orange shag carpet of an Oakland crack house like a pile of stepped-in dog shit. The rival gang put a bounty on his head, and the state of California officially reneged on the early out. Every cop in Oakland was on the lookout for Hector . . . not to mention a couple thousand gang members hoping to get famous.

The next radio transmission was a hysterical call for cover that caused a hundred sirens to scream out at once from all over the city. It was clear the rook had made contact and the fight was on. Sergeant Ben Sawyer was two blocks away and on scene in thirty seconds.

The hell with it, Ben thought. *You really wanna go there? Let's go.* Ben dug deep and pushed the speed of the machine to seven-minute miles. The sights and sounds of Deep East Oakland came clear in his mind.

Ben jumped from his car before it stopped rocking on its chassis. Visible waves of heat blasted up from the asphalt; sirens wailed from all directions, growing closer. Just ahead, an officer lay prone on the sidewalk with Hector's hulking figure on top of him. Hector wore a tight wifebeater T-shirt over a tattooed physique that marked him as a recent graduate of the California penal system. He outweighed the cop by sixty sculpted pounds. As Ben closed in, he could hear the cop's panicked voice, shrill and full of fear.

He's got my gun. He's got my gun.

The music kicked in full force, and Ben opened his gait, taking longer and longer strides, arms and legs moving in a smooth but furious motion. The nearby crew of Newberg officers turned to gawk, but Ben saw only the face of Hector Espudo. Brown, full of hate and determination. Prison-green tattoos of two teardrops inked beneath one eye and the name of his barrio pulsing on his neck, all outlined in a sheen of sweat. As Ben closed in, he saw that Hector's hands were wrapped around the grip of the officer's gun, the barrel pointed directly into the man's chest. The rookie, true to his training, had both hands tight around the slide of the semiauto and his finger shoved behind the trigger, making it temporarily impossible for the gun to fire.

Ben's chest burned and his breath came hard. With any luck his heart would explode and kill the memory forever, ridding him of this constant reminder of lost honor and betrayal.

Ben wasted no time, grabbing the thick, greasy ponytail that ran ten inches down Hector's back, wrapping it tight in his fist and jerking hard. Hector's head snapped back until his face pointed to the sky, blinding him in the intense sunlight. His mouth spewed spit and profanity. The odor of Mad Dog 20/20 mixed with the chemical smell of meth radiated like red heat off Hector's muscular frame.

"*Hijo de puta,* pig motherfucker. I'll kill both your asses," Hector shouted in a coarse, rage-filled voice.

In one fluid motion, Ben slid his gun from the hard plastic shell of the tactical holster he wore and shoved the barrel against the side of the man's head. Ben made sure the contact was hard enough that there would be no mistaking his intentions. A contact shot to the temple or through the top of the skull was justified, but Ben didn't pull the trigger.

"Your choice, Hector: hands off the gun or die."

The second syllable wasn't spoken before Hector's hands came off the cop's gun and went high over his head in a clear display of unconditional surrender. His eyes filled with terror as he looked awkwardly toward the gun that was still poised at the side of his head. His expression said it all. Hector knew this cop would not hesitate to kill him.

It could have ended there, and if it had, Ben figured he probably would have received a commendation for lifesaving. Hell, not only for saving the cop but he even managed to keep Hector alive. Avoiding an officer-involved shooting always gave the department brass something to brag about. Yep. It could have been a great day for the Sawyer legacy. A hell of a war story for the locker room: how Sawyer almost performed a gangbanger street execution with his forty-cal. But it didn't end there. Ben was just getting started.

Ben smashed the Stop button on the treadmill in defeat, his heart pounding defiant and strong, signaling there would be no easy exit. The intense whine of the machine slowed to a steady drone, then went silent. He bent at the waist and drew deep breaths. Large drops of sweat fell from his face to the floor. The reality of Newberg returned.

Two minutes remained of his self-imposed physical torture. Ben restarted the machine and finished his run at a slow jog, emptying his mind of everything but the motion of his arms and legs and the steady thump of his heart. Done, he headed for the showers. An arriving officer looked Ben over and gave nothing more than a nod of his head and a look that said it all. No greeting of respect or friendship. Ben avoided eye contact. He gave no indication he would even want to stop and shoot the breeze. Ben had come to accept his place in this strange world. Outsider. Non-player. *Chief's boy.*

Ben listened to the newcomer join in with the officers already present. He heard the exchange of curse words, insults, and bravado: standard greetings for cops sheltered from public view. He felt the familiar pang of isolation.

In the crude shower room, Ben cranked the water as hot as it would go. Steam filled the stall, and he worked to lose himself in the mist. Ben pushed his head under the water, and a thousand hot needle pricks scalded the back of his neck. He forced himself to relax. It was time to put it all away again. Try to be normal for the entire day that lay ahead. He closed his eyes and spoke in a low voice to the only person that was the least bit interested in hearing anything he had to say.

"Forget about Oakland, Sawyer. This is Newberg."

TWO

Alex Sawyer stood in front of the century-old house, stretched her arms above her head, and drew crisp, spring air deep into her lungs. The morning sun had escaped from the lingering mood of Wisconsin's strongest season, and the warmth felt good against her face. She took in the neighborhood of stylish Victorian homes surrounded by towering oaks, a stark contrast to the California subdivision where she and Ben had lived for more than ten years. That neighborhood had oozed comfortable conformity—five different floor plans, three color palettes, tiled roofs, and postage-stamp yards. The eclectic Old World charm of Newberg fed her Midwestern nostalgia. In that respect it was good to be home.

Alex stepped off the porch, jogging at a brisk pace, and began to mentally map out her day.

With twelve-year-old Jake off to school, Alex knew whatever plans she cared to make had to revolve around the two other men in her life. Then again, dealing with her husband wasn't an issue—Ben had pulled his usual early-morning disappearing act and snuck off to the police department gym before the sun was up. *Won't be seeing him until dinner,* she thought. Alex had done her best, but there was no denying that resentment had begun to set in. These early-morning departures were getting old. *When was the last time we enjoyed coffee in bed? Or how about just sleeping in?* But she felt no anger, more a sense of loss.

He's been through a lot, she reminded herself. Thrown to the wolves by his own department. Tossed aside after almost fifteen years of dedicated service. Forced to come back here and work for his father-in-law. Of course, Ben refused to talk about it. Typical cop. Confront an armed gunman in a dark alley? No problem. Talk about personal issues? No way. *If he ever does open up,* she told herself, *I want to be there for him.* Then again, how much longer was she expected to wait? But her absentee husband was only one of the troubled cops in her life. The other was her most challenging relationship of all.

Four months had passed since Police Chief Lars Norgaard collapsed while giving his update on the state of crime in Newberg to the local Chamber of Commerce. He had been air-lifted to the university hospital in Madison sixty miles away. By the time Alex reached him, her father had slipped deep into a nonresponsive state that lasted for days. He had finally come around, but the initial reports were grim: severe stroke with possible brain damage. Total loss of speech. Greatly reduced motor skills. The best the doctors could offer amounted to "wait and see." Progress had been slow.

Even as she ran, Alex knew her father had likely been awake for hours and was already awaiting her arrival. She pictured him, cross and surly, banging his cane and pointing at a staff nurse or orderly. He'd keep it up until someone wheeled him to the porch. There he'd sit and watch the sidewalk, waiting for his daughter to come into view. But the staff at the Newberg Convalescent Center discouraged visitors before ten and she had time to kill.

With all they had been through, being back in Newberg gave Alex a sense of peace. The isolated prairie town was forty-five miles west of Milwaukee and inhabited almost exclusively by twenty thousand second- and third-generation Swedes and Norwegians. A place where the only social institutions of any significance were bars and churches. It was the town of her childhood. The place she met her husband. Home.

Alex headed into the heart of Newberg's downtown. Owner-operated shops specializing in the niche-market of antiques, crafts, and pottery lined the shady cobbled street. At this early hour none of the stores were open, but Alex decided to slow her pace to a brisk walk and enjoy the window displays and the solitude of near-deserted sidewalks. The aroma of coffee drifted toward her from Newberg's one and only bistro. A moment later she found herself standing inside the empty shop, calling out an inquisitive hello.

A man's voice answered from out of view, "Come on in. I'll be with you in a minute."

The place was clearly in transition. Stacks of aged, hardcover books stood like short towers along the length of a wall. Alex began a quick mental inventory and noted several familiar titles until her eyes stopped on one. She reached out and ran her fingers over the gold embossed letters on the binding. She pulled the book from the stack and opened it gently. The odor of old print and paper, along with the familiar lines of text, took her back in time.

"Find something you like?"

Alex looked up to see a man standing across the store. His voice implied hope for more than a one-word answer.

"*My Ántonia*. Cather has been a favorite of mine since I was a little girl."

He stepped forward to get a closer look. "Yeah, that's a quality printing. I think it's about forty years old. I'm not sure, but maybe it's a first edition."

"No. It was published in around 1918. Way back."

The man looked at her with surprise, and Alex thought she

might have come off sounding stuffy. "Like I said. She's a favorite of mine."

The man smiled. "I'm Louis Carson."

"Hi, Louis. Alex Sawyer." Alex extended her hand and Louis shook it warmly. His grip was firm, and Alex guessed Louis might be five years younger than her. He was a good six inches taller, with a trim physique and jet-black hair worn long and combed back. His jaw was square and covered with two or three days of stubble. For a moment, the gaze of his hazel eyes felt intense and unsettling. Alex drew her hand back and looked away; an awkwardness hung in the air.

She stammered out, "Is this a bookstore or a coffeehouse?"

Louis, apparently clueless of her discomfort, put his hands on his hips and looked around. "Well, I need a customer, so if you're looking for a good read, it's a bookstore. If you're thirsty, I'll offer you some coffee."

"So . . . it's both, then?" She asked, liking the idea.

"Yeah, I guess so," Louis said. "I bought this place about two months ago. Business is okay, but I want to give it something distinctive. The coffee's already great. The previous owner had a first-rate roaster; I won't change that. But I thought it might be interesting to dabble as a bookseller. You know, only the finest coffee and nothing less than classic books."

Louis delivered the last line mocking an advertisement on the radio. He paused and looked around at the stacks of books and the empty seats and unoccupied tables. His voice took on a much less enthusiastic tone. "That's the plan, anyway."

"I like it," Alex said, nodding. "How about I take a cup to go?"

"I'd rather you have a cup to stay." He was still smiling. "That's the idea, you know."

Alex couldn't help but think the attention felt pretty good. "All right," she said. "Make it for here."

Alex looked around at the cramped space. "You might be on to something. Newberg doesn't have a used bookstore. I think the yuppies from Madison who come into town on the weekends will be all over it."

"Good," Louis answered. "I'm glad you think so, seeing that I am a yuppie from Madison." Louis stepped behind the counter and poured out two mugs of coffee as he explained how he came to own a coffeehouse.

"One day I was a financial planner and the next day I wasn't. The job just sort of evaporated. Then I figured out I was better off. Instead of jumping onto another spinning wheel of the rat race, I cashed out my severance and here I am."

"Pretty brave," Alex said. "Tough time to be opening your own business."

"Yeah, but I did my homework. I looked around and found this great town with the only coffeehouse up for sale," he said. "The bookstore angle is just my twist. But I have to tell you, this town is turning out to be a tough nut to crack." Louis returned with two steaming mugs and cleared a small table. He motioned Alex to sit.

"Yeah, us Newbergers can be a stalwart bunch," Alex said. "Mixture of Nordic values and Protestant work ethic. Bottom line, we don't trust anyone born outside the city walls."

"So you're native?"

"Sort of. My husband and I lived out in California for almost fourteen years with our son, Jake. But we both grew up here. Just moved back about a year and a half ago." Alex's comfort level rose, spurred on by adult conversation. She took a sip of the flavorful coffee, then went on. "Actually one year, seven months, and twenty-three days ago, but who's counting."

"The ultimate long and winding road, huh?"

"I swear, in the time we were gone, nothing changed. This place is like Brigadoon." Alex warmed her hands on the mug of coffee and began to tell Louis the G-rated version of the Sawyer saga. She told Louis about Ben being a cop in Oakland—leaving out the juicy conclusion—and that he now worked for Newberg PD. When she mentioned that her dad had spent the last five years as chief of the small department, Alex was pleased to see that Louis didn't raise his eyebrows with the assuming look that said, *Your husband must be a kiss ass*. She didn't stop until she had drained her cup, looked at her watch, and found that an hour had passed. It struck her she hadn't talked to anyone for an entire hour in, well, *years*.

"Oh, my gosh, it's nine thirty already?" Alex stood abruptly from her chair. "I'd better go. I'll be back when I can spend some time on a cup of coffee and a good book."

"I'll look forward to it," Louis said as he stood. "Take the Cather with you."

"That's okay. I've got a paperback copy somewhere. It's been a while, but if I want to find it, I will."

"Cather in paperback? Stop. The book needs a good home. Take it," Louis said, extending the book toward her.

"Okay, but I'm going to read it, then either bring it back or pay you for it."

"You'd better or I'll call a cop."

Alex laughed. "Thanks for the java and the book. Get this place cleaned up, okay?"

"I'll get right on it."

As Alex left, she noticed that shops were opening and a fair amount of traffic now flowed in the street. She thought of a new friend and at the contrast between Louis and the men in her life, none of them happy and not shy about letting her know it. Every day was a balancing act, like walking an emotional high wire. She looked back over her shoulder and saw that Louis had come out onto the sidewalk to watch her leave. He waved and Alex waved back, already looking forward to her next chance to step down off the wire and get away.

THREE

H arlan jumped with ease from the rear of the pickup and pulled his backpack higher on his shoulder. He banged his open hand against the sidewall and called out to the driver, "Obliged for the lift."

The truck sped out, leaving Harlan in a parking lot full of Ford trucks, Buick and Chevy muscle cars, and a half-dozen Harley motorcycles. There wasn't an import in sight. *I'll be damned,* he thought. *The whole lot is American made.*

The Wisconsin evening remained stubbornly cold, and the fifty-mile ride in the open air left him with a shiver he worked hard to control. Harlan wore a heavy dark blue corduroy top that was really no more than a thick shirt, but he was glad to have it. A wool beanie was pulled down low to just above his eyebrows. The jeans and army boots were broken in and fit well. His trip to Goodwill represented a major portion of the $227 he had in his pocket when he walked out the front gate of Red Cliff State Penitentiary. Between the clothes, food, and a few incidentals, he was down to around a hundred bucks. That, after seventeen years of on-again, off-again prison work at twenty-seven cents an hour. But the used clothing was money well spent, and Harlan was glad to shed himself of the thin black slacks, plastic windbreaker, and hard-sole shoes that were his last physical reminder of prison.

Country music poured out from inside the split-level structure located along a lonely stretch of the two-lane state highway. The building had been converted into a nightclub of sorts and was said to be the only watering hole for twenty miles in any direction. Neon signs of a half-dozen beers flashed from the windows, along with the name of the bar: Chicken Lips Saloon. Harlan walked toward the building, where a cluster of men and women stood under the lamplight, each with cigarette in hand. They looked up to watch as Harlan, a compact but muscular man with a bone-white complexion, approached. Harlan took note that as he drew close, the conversations faded away. One man in the group held a bottle down by his waist, with two fingers around the long neck and the rest of his hand buried in his pocket. The bottle dangled there, and Harlan realized at any second it could be called on as a weapon. The man's chest and arms were swollen under a flannel shirt, and his eyes stared out from a chiseled face as if he was ready to challenge Harlan's entry. Harlan slowed his step and met the man's gaze with a well-practiced hard look of his own. He kept staring even after the man looked away and raised his bottle for a nervous swallow of beer. The group retreated in unison and gave Harlan a clear path to the door. Harlan passed by without a word and stepped inside.

With all the interior walls removed, what once served as a family home was now a beer hall in every respect. Harlan saw the source of the music was a live band set off in one corner. They played a popular slow tune well enough that a crowd of men and women swayed in each other's arms on the parquet dance floor under a spinning ball of mirrors and glass. Harlan stood in the doorway to give his eyes a minute to adjust to the low light. The heavy aroma of grilling sausage served as a reminder he hadn't eaten in twelve hours.

A hundred droning voices filled his head with snippets of conversations, causing Harlan to feel unsettled and on the verge of aggravation. He set out to find the office he was told would be toward the back and marked PRIVATE.

Harlan weaved through the crowded tables surrounded by working-class folks, many wearing uniform shirts from a tool-and-die plant in nearby Chippewa Falls. Most of the patrons were men, but Harlan did notice a few scantily dressed women hustling drinks and carrying plates heaped with bar food from the kitchen to the tables. Harlan made his way to the farthest isolated corner. He stood in front of the solid steel-framed door and gave three sharp knocks. As he had been instructed, he looked up and to the right. The camera turned his way, and he heard the sound of a sliding dead bolt on the other side. The door opened, and the familiar face of the slightly built man beamed at the sight of him. Harlan stepped inside the office, and the heavy spring-loaded door closed behind him. There was a leather couch to his right that struck him as new and expensive; a coffee table was covered with business papers and financial magazines. The flat-screen television that hung from the wall was tuned to a cable news show. The volume was low and the day's closing stock prices ran across the bottom of the screen. The music faded to almost nothing, and it felt good to be out of the crowd.

"I'll be damned to hell. Harlan Lee. Out in the world." He stood, shaking his head. "Seventeen years for killing a man? I swear, it's like nobody does real time anymore."

Harlan thought that an odd thing coming from someone who served three years of a seven-year sentence. Harlan, never prone to engage in good-natured ribbing or idle conversation, ignored the comment. But the satisfaction of seeing the familiar face was undeniable.

"How goes it, Virgil?"

Virgil Anderson had entered Red Cliff just as Harlan began his twelfth year behind bars. A first-rate outlaw and con man by trade, Virgil was a computer hacker extraordinaire and one of the most prolific identity thieves the Midwest had ever produced. Over a period of several years, Virgil managed to access the computer records of over a thousand people in a dozen different countries. He had methodically bilked them for over a million dollars without anyone batting an eye and all from the comfort of his own living room. Virgil might have kept the con going for years longer if he hadn't inadvertently tapped into the credit line of a sitting congressman. The man's wife watched the family credit statements like a hawk to be sure her husband wasn't enjoying himself a bit too much on his trips back and forth to the nation's capital, and her vigilance marked the end of Virgil's long run of financial success.

"I can't complain," Virgil said as he pulled a chair up for Harlan and then took a seat behind the desk that filled a good portion of the room. The man had never had the look of a hard-core crook. Small in stature, with a handsome face and white-blond hair, Virgil had a natural ability to win the confidence of most any everyday citizen. Of course, what served him well on the outside had been a serious liability in Red Cliff. More than once, it almost proved deadly.

"Two years out now. No reason to think I won't make three. If my luck holds, maybe a bit longer." The man looked Harlan over. "How 'bout you? You settling in okay? How's your newfound freedom?"

Harlan took a seat in the chair but ignored the inquiry. He pointed toward a half-full bottle of Johnnie Walker that sat on the desktop.

"You mind? It was a cold ride."

"Help yourself."

Harlan did, pouring three fingers of the dark amber liquid into a glass. Harlan ignored the ice bucket and tossed it back neat. A warmth spread through his body and rigid muscles as he took a look around, enjoying the privacy of the office. "Big crowd out there. Seems like you're doing okay for yourself."

"This?" Virgil looked around. "It's profitable, but it's got nothing to do with Virgil Anderson. Check the records. You'll see this establishment is owned and operated by Mr. Steven Miller. Married. Two kids. A law-abiding citizen who pays his taxes on time and bears a disturbingly similar appearance to a trashy white convict who lives in the next town over."

Harlan's eyes went to the cherrywood desktop covered with credit card and bank statements. There was a pile of receipts from different stores and restaurants. Most of the papers were crumpled and dirt stained. On a legal pad there was a long list of social security numbers scrawled in pencil. Virgil pushed the papers off to the side.

"Never ceases to amaze me," Virgil said. "The stuff folks just throw in the trash."

"Still running those same identity scams?"

Virgil shrugged. "Just doing what comes natural, Harlan. Feels like what was intended for me. I could hook you up if you want. Get you out from under all that convict baggage."

"Nah. I'm good with who I am," Harlan said, then went on to a new subject. "That thing we talked about. We ready to go?"

Virgil answered with an even tone of assurance. "I did what you asked. Everything is set."

Harlan stared back at his old cell mate and gave an approving nod. When Harlan had learned of his impending release, he had managed to get a visitation with Virgil. Convicts weren't typically allowed to meet with men who were paroled, but Virgil was able to grease the right palm, and the two men had an hour of private conversation that got logged in as a legal consult. It was there Harlan called on Virgil for the use of his unique skills.

Virgil refilled Harlan's glass with another double shot of scotch, then made a drink for himself, but a single on the rocks with an equal portion of bottled water. Harlan emptied his glass in a single swallow. He watched as Virgil sipped his drink like a man who had the whole night to enjoy it.

"If everything is ready, then let's make it happen," Harlan said. "You need something from me?"

"Just say 'go.' Then all you need to do is sit back and watch."

Harlan shook his head. "I don't follow ya."

Virgil put his small girl-like feet up on the desk and explained. "The old man usually goes online from his office down at the car dealership somewhere around seven o'clock every morning. Hits a few sports sites, usually some porn shit but all legit adult skin. What he don't know is that for the last three weeks, every time he logs on, he's been sending out an e-mail blast with thumbnail attachments to a hundred and fifty IP addresses in sixteen different countries. All of 'em black market kiddie-porn exchange sites. We're talking about the real degenerate stuff. Nasty shit." Virgil shook his body in disgust. "Hard to imagine there's a market for that sort of filth, but as you and I know all too well, there're some twisted bastards out there walking around in the world."

Virgil stopped and sipped his scotch until Harlan urged him on. "Keep talking."

"The sites he's currently hooked into are pretty damn sophisticated. All of 'em well hidden and none monitored by the cops or any of those watchdog groups." Virgil raised his eyebrows and went on. "The sorts of places only a real pro would know about. Trust me, they weren't easy to find or get into. But when you give the word, I'll add one particular recipient. A shell account owned, operated, and closely monitored by our European friends."

Harlan sat in silence and shrugged his shoulders in confusion.

"Interpol." Virgil paused in what struck Harlan as a moment of admiration, then went on. "Those crafty sons of bitches . . . They really go after kiddie-porn freaks. Draw them in with an offer to trade pics, then they snatch the transmission right out of thin air. From there they follow it all the way back to the source. Don't ever let anybody talk to you about cybersecurity. There ain't no such thing."

"So then what?"

"It might take a day or so, but before too long he'll have agents from the FBI field office over in Minneapolis assigned to his case. Even if he gets a couple of clowns right out of the academy, his trail will be impossible to miss."

"What's to keep him from getting spooked? Start shutting everything down?"

"Brother, he ain't got a clue. It's all buried a couple layers down, but he's probably got over a thousand illegal images embedded in his hard drive right now. He's mailed out somewhere in the neighborhood of ten times that many. Add in a few hundred e-mails with all his personal info and a dozen or so suspicious international purchases with his credit card. The kind of stuff cops call 'dominion and control.' He'll be bagged and tagged an hour after the Feds power up that computer and crack it open."

"What kind of time is he looking at?"

"Time? You know better than that, Harlan. Officially it'll be something in the neighborhood of forty years, but it'll work out to a lot less than that."

Harlan understood the reference. As a former cop coming in with papers that say he trades kiddie porn, a man would be lucky to survive six months. Maybe a year.

"They can put him in whatever isolation cell they want, but the fellas will make sport out of who gets to put a shank in his fat ass. Course that won't come till he's been properly cornholed and wore out." Virgil's voice turned quiet. "Believe me, he won't be sorry to see the end come."

Virgil paused for a moment, then went on. "Is that pretty much what you had in mind for the good sheriff of Florence County?"

"Former sheriff and yeah, Virgil. That was the idea."

"So I guess you're really going through with it? I take it that was your work up in Hayward. That was some drastic shit you pulled."

Harlan's voice carried an edge. "You know better than that, Virgil. Let's restrict ourselves to the business at hand."

"Suit yourself, but you've chosen a dangerous course, my friend. You're a convicted killer who busted parole. They're gonna come looking for you. The state tends to keep your type on a short leash."

"The only leash they had on me was on the inside."

"No doubt about that. Harlan Lee is not known to be a man to put up with a lot of meddling by the state."

Virgil opened a desk drawer and pulled out a thick envelope.

"Take this. I'd give you some good plastic, but with all the goddamn cameras these days, everything gets filmed." Virgil winked. "It's like nobody trusts anybody anymore."

"I ain't gonna take your money, Virgil. If a man can't figure out a way to make his own stake, he oughta just stay locked up."

"I wish there was something more I could do," Virgil said. "Hell, Harlan, I'd have never made it out of Red Cliff if it weren't for you. There were a couple of times . . . Anyway. I'm grateful. I just want you to know that."

Harlan hesitated and thought back to their years in prison. On more than one occasion, Harlan had protected the man from the primitive reality of life on the inside. Never once had Harlan asked for a favor of any sort in return.

Harlan pulled his own thin wad of cash from the pocket of his shirt. "I could use some new iron. I'll be sure it never comes back on ya. I'd prefer a revolver. Less to go wrong."

"Put your goddamn money away."

Virgil bent down to a floor safe behind the desk. He spun the dial while he spoke. "It's probably too late for you to just go back up to Florence and live the life of the landed gentry, huh? I mean, I know your old man left you the homestead, didn't he?"

Harlan's tone was matter-of-fact. "What the government didn't steal away from him. Few acres. Farmhouse. Ain't nothing up there for me anymore."

Virgil opened the safe. He took out a patch of green felt and laid it across his desk. Harlan watched as Virgil's delicate hands went back and forth inside the safe until he had removed a half-dozen revolvers and set them out in a display. The guns ranged from a single-shot twenty-two derringer to a forty-four-caliber hand cannon. Each gun looked brand-new with a light coating of oil and a custom grip.

"Take your pick, although I must say I'm partial to the Ruger."

Harlan eyed them all but, yeah. He picked up the stainless snub-nosed three-eighty five-shot revolver and balanced it in his hand. It had a good feel. Nice heft to it. Substantial grip for his large hand. He dry-fired toward the wall to test the trigger pull while Virgil went on, sounding every bit like a nagging wife.

"Then get out of Wisconsin. Find someplace you want to settle. Anywhere you want. Just let me know where you land. I'll work you up a clean bill of health. Get you a stake in a place like this."

Harlan ignored Virgil's comments and held up the Ruger to signify his choice. Virgil went back to the safe and pulled out a box of ammo and a black nylon holster, pushing the hardware across the desk. Harlan picked up the box and broke out five rounds, loading each cylinder. He shoved it all in his pack and stood to leave.

"Good seeing you, Virgil. I'm glad things are working out for you." Harlan held out his pack containing the new gun. "I owe ya."

"No you don't." Virgil stood from the desk. "It's gratis. And the offer stands. I'd hook you up to a life that might not be entirely legit, but I'll be damned if you wouldn't be able to see legit from your front porch. Give it some thought, Harlan. The life of a con on the run? Never tried it myself. Can't say as I'm interested."

"I don't plan on runnin' from nobody. If there's a cop out there who figures this shit out, I won't be hard to find." Harlan paused, aware this exchange could be their last. His voice was solemn. "I'm in your debt, Virgil. I'm glad to have known you."

"Likewise, Harlan," Virgil said. "So then. Are we a 'go'?"

Harlan thought back, and in his mind he saw an image of Sheriff Henry Lipinski from seventeen years ago. "Damn right. Burn that son of a bitch to the ground."

Minutes later Harlan was back on the road, the new weight in the pack pulling on his shoulder. It brought some comfort to know he once again had a gun within reach, but he wondered, *Should I have taken the cash?* And what about Virgil's other offer? A chance to walk away clean. Start a new life. The idea hung in his mind as he walked on in the darkness, but he was quick to dismiss it. Harlan Lee lived by an outlaw code. Part of that code required pride and self-reliance. Adopting a bogus name and making a living as a con man wasn't the Lee way. That same code also allowed for avenging wrongs committed against family.

A vehicle approached from behind, and Harlan turned to face it. He jammed out this thumb and squinted his eyes, doused in bright light as the driver slowed. It came as no surprise when the engine revved and the truck sped by. Undeterred, Harlan turned back and continued his walk. No reason to hurry, he told himself. Someone would be along eventually. In the meantime he took solace in the Midwestern night sounds and the crisp air against his skin. Content, he occupied his mind with the names and faces of all those folks who were once again an important part of his life.

FOUR

Tia Suarez made her way through the parking lot of the Newberg PD in four-inch stiletto heels, pausing for a moment to pull down the hem of her short, form-fitting skirt. It had a tendency to ride up pretty high, but in her line of work that wasn't necessarily a bad thing. The cheap waist-length jacket with the faux fur collar that she'd picked up at Goodwill turned out to be worth the ten bucks she'd spent. It helped keep the chill off her slender body but still let her show off the wares. The weather was a little on the cool side for this get-up, she thought, but that's how you reel them in. *Come summertime, I'll be unstoppable.*

Four hours on a street corner in Milwaukee had been productive, but her feet were killing her and she couldn't wait to get out of the damn heels. A black-and-white slowed alongside her, and she recognized the officer behind the wheel. He tapped the air horn and called out the window, "Right on, Tia. How much for a taste of that?"

Tia flipped the cop off good-naturedly and called back, "You couldn't afford it on your paycheck, but you can take a picture."

She struck a seductive pose as the car rolled by, then continued across the open parking lot, drawing curious stares from cops and citizens. *I could probably do a little more business right here,* she thought, *but I've had enough for the day.*

When she walked into the lobby of the police department, crowded with people attending to the mundane business of bike registrations and parking tickets, every head turned to stare. Tia made eye contact with the clerk behind the desk; they exchanged smiles and Tia heard the nearby door marked POLICE PERSONNEL ONLY click open. She pulled on the chain around her neck, dragging her police badge into view as she passed through the door. The heavy gold shield was out of place with her outfit, but she was glad to be returning to her real world.

"Screw these things," Tia said to herself, stepping out of her ridiculous shoes. The act was over. Going barefoot through the PD might be frowned on by the brass, but they'd just have to understand. Tia pictured the new chief, that fat ass Jorgensen, trying to look sexy on a street corner in a miniskirt and high-heel, open-toed shoes. When her bare feet touched flat against the cool tile, every inch of her body tingled in relief.

"Oh, God . . . now that feels good," Tia practically moaned.

"No getting off in the hallway, Suarez." Another smart-ass comment from a passing cop, but Tia laughed.

Tia needed to check in with the boss and let him know the undercover vice detail had wrapped up. The four hours in Milwaukee had resulted in the arrest of eight johns. Three holding dope, and one a prior for sexual assault. *That guy was bent,* she thought. Tia figured she had probably saved a real hooker an ass beating by making the arrest. The thought of that guy being off the street and in a jail cell energized her. She took the stairs, barefoot, two at a time. Between the stairs and the detective sergeant's office, she fielded no fewer than half a dozen offers involving broom closets and the backseats of patrol cars. Tia took it all in stride, then struck a pose in her supervisor's doorway.

"Hey, baby, got any lunch plans?"

Ben Sawyer looked up from his desk with no sign of recognition. Tia laughed at the look on his face. Then the penny dropped and he smiled.

"Hey, Tia, welcome back. How was vice detail?"

"Are you kidding?" Tia said. "I rocked it. Caught my limit. Milwaukee PD says anytime you want to loan out the little Mexican girl to play hooker, they're down for it."

"I'm sure they loved having you," Ben said. "And it's a nice break from patrol, right?"

"Absolutely. One of these days you might even come to your senses and make me a full-time detective." Tia was only half kidding. She'd led the Patrol Bureau in arrests and convictions for the past six months straight. Tia made it clear to all the department bosses that she believed she had long since earned a detective's shield.

"Patience there, Suarez. Patience."

Tia had met Ben soon after his father-in-law had hired him on as a sergeant. Both Tia and Ben were often treated like outsiders by Newbergers, civilians and cops alike. Ben because he had deserted his hometown and returned dishonored to take an undeserved handout. Tia because there was no such thing as a Mexican-Newberger even if she had lived in the town for more than twenty years and served a four-year hitch in the Marines.

Tia had been born in Brownsville, Texas, in the daughter of migrant workers. She was just five years old when her family arrived in Newberg, where they were the sole nonwhite residents other than a few scattered Native Americans. Most Newbergers grudgingly conceded the Native Americans had a right to call Wisconsin home, but by Newberg standards, any third-world brown types would always be foreigners. It hadn't helped that Tia's dad had performed general labor at the dairy farms while her mom cleaned houses.

Her parents had long since returned to their native Jalisco, but not Tia. After two tours in Afghanistan, she'd been hired on with Newberg PD. To her, Newberg was home. Anybody who disagreed could kiss her brown ass.

"How about we step out and grab some coffee," Tia said. "See how long it takes for our local rag to report that Sergeant Benjamin Sawyer was seen in the company of a scantily dressed, darkskinned female companion?"

Ben gestured to the case files covering the top of his desk. "Sounds fun, but I need to get through these cases. Come on in. I got half a thermos. We'll split it."

Tia slid easily into the only chair available in the cramped office. She pushed a bare foot against the edge of her boss's desk and eased the chair back, leaving her hard brown legs much more visible than usual. When Ben's eyes widened, Tia remembered what she was wearing and let the chair fall back flat against the floor. Tia picked up on Ben's look of embarrassment and laughed at his predicament.

"I guess I should probably go change out of my work clothes."

Ben winked. "Hey, don't worry about it. You look good. Really."

Tia changed the subject from the implication that she'd make a great hooker. She gestured at the case files. "What gives? You closing in on some of Newberg's notorious criminal element?"

Ben filled two Styrofoam cups, and Tia picked up on his irritation. "I wish I had the time. It seems like I stay busy just trying to keep track of wayward detectives. You wouldn't happen to know McKenzie's favorite hiding spots, would you? He disappears first thing in the morning when he bothers showing up at all. I never see the guy."

Tia sipped the coffee and grimaced at the flavor as much as at the mention of Detective Doyle McKenzie. She swallowed hard before answering.

"Wherever he's at, I don't want to know. Careful of him, Sarge. Backbiting son of a bitch that one is. And he doesn't take little nibbles. More like chunks. Usually leaves a mark."

"Thanks, but you aren't telling me anything I don't already know. McKenzie was a few years ahead of me in school. He was already a cop here when my wife and I moved out west. From what I knew he was an unscrupulous bastard even then. But I tell you what, he keeps this shit up, he'll be assigned to crossing guard detail come this fall."

"Not likely. He's pretty insulated. Seems he's got friends in high places."

Tia thought about what she had just said and spoke up to correct any misunderstanding. "I mean, now he does. Not before. Chief Norgaard ran a tight ship. Aw, hell, you know what I mean. Anyway, ignore McKenzie. Spend your energy on something more worthwhile."

"That's pretty disappointing coming from a hard-nosed cop like you. I thought we agreed to root out evil and fight for justice, apple pie, and all that good stuff?"

Tia laughed. "Damn right, Superman. But you need to watch out for the guys with kryptonite."

Tia looked over her shoulder, then back at Ben. "Seriously. McKenzie is bad news. That asshole doesn't even deserve to be called a cop. But he's Jorgensen's boy now. Just wait it out. Let McKenzie hang himself. Guys like him eventually screw up. Otherwise, it might be you that gets run out of here."

"So what are you saying? I go through the rest of my career with my eyes closed? Let McKenzie run all over me?"

"No, Sarge. Just be careful of the guy. That's all I meant."

Tia wanted Ben to know her concern was real, but she could see his stubborn streak coming out and she heard the resistance in his voice.

"This is one screwed-up coffee break."

"Sorry. You're right." Her voice turned lighthearted. "Course this coffee is from yesterday and even then it probably tasted like tar." She took another sip and changed the subject.

"How's the family? You got the one kid, Jake, right?"

Tia noticed the change in demeanor and remembered Ben always shied away from the personal talk. He recovered quickly and seemed to try and come off as the average dad. "Yeah. That's right. He's doing great. He misses California sometimes, and he's coming up on the teenage years. You know how that goes. But he's playing Little League this year. Kid's got promise."

Tia decided to push a little.

"And your wife? Alexandra?"

"She's great." An uncomfortable silence lasted until Ben changed the subject. "I hear you made top cop this quarter. It's about time."

Tia rolled her eyes, embarrassed. "Yeah. It's cool. I was surprised, though. Usually it takes perfect attendance at the chaplain's Bible study to pull that off. I haven't made a meeting yet."

The intercom interrupted their chat. "Officer Suarez, report to the patrol sergeant's office immediately."

The voice belonged to Sergeant Billy "Plate" Boyd, and he sounded irritated. Tia looked at the clock on the wall, then rolled her head back and closed her eyes.

"Shit. I've got to do a ten-hour patrol shift," she said. "The overtime pay for these details is nice, but it's going to turn into an eighteen-hour day. You think you could tell your compadre to cut me a little slack? I'm pretty sure Plate thinks I had something to do with his getting shitcanned back to patrol. I swear the guy is going to ride my ass out the front door if he can."

Tia had been working for Boyd for the past three months, and it was obvious the old guy was not happy with his new assignment. Before Norgaard went down, Ben had inherited the Detective Squad from Sergeant Boyd. At thirty-four years of service and counting, Boyd was the current longevity champion of Newberg PD. The nature of Plate Boyd's notoriously long absences had earned him his nickname. On any given workday you couldn't find Boyd with a compass, but if you did stumble across him, he was usually tucked in behind a heaping plate of food. The size of the meal was a good indicator of the length of his subsequent nap. Just before going down with his stroke, Chief Norgaard had put Ben in the detective sergeant position. Tia knew it hadn't gone over well with everyone, especially Boyd.

"Don't worry about Plate," Ben said. "He's harmless. Not to mention a little intimidated by cops like you."

"Like me?"

"Yeah. Cops who know how to push the envelope. Here you are, five years into your career, pulling undercover details and making felony arrests almost every night. Believe me, Boyd never did the job the way you do. For most cops from his generation, it was all about crossing guard duty and cats in trees. His bluster is just his way of maintaining some dignity. Go easy on him."

"Like you go easy on McKenzie?"

Ben's voice took on a serious tone. "Different story. There's something devious about that prick. But Plate, he'll be gone in a couple of years. Until then, take care of him. We owe him that much."

"Makes sense." Tia stood to leave, once again trying to get her skirt to cover the important parts. "Fight the good fight. Isn't that what you told us in Patrol?"

"Exactly. Nice to know somebody was listening."

"Hey, don't kid yourself. We were all listening. You can come back to Patrol anytime. See you around." Tia couldn't help but leave with one last seductive leer, dangling her high heels over her shoulder and tossing Ben a wink. She walked down the hallway and headed for the locker room. She'd get suited up and do her ten-hour patrol shift. Tired as she was, Tia found herself looking forward to it. She walked past a group of patrol officers and the catcalls started up again. She joined in with the exchange, making sure the loudest and most vulgar comments were her own.

FIVE

Newberg Narcotics Detective Doyle McKenzie leaned back against the hood of the vintage Trans Am and enjoyed the low rumble of the five-liter engine idling beneath him. He ran his hand across the smooth black paint and thought how he'd waited his entire career for a car like this. *Hell, more like my whole life.* The car had come to him a month ago by way of a drug seizure. Some stupid-ass dope slinger out of Beloit who, McKenzie had learned, not only paid cash and owned the car outright, but hadn't even had the good sense to register the vehicle in his baby mama's name. McKenzie had seen to it that the dealer made his way to Newberg while holding major quantity in the trunk. Once the beat cops pulled the crook over and found the dope, McKenzie wasted no time in swooping in and claiming the car as a seized asset.

There'd been some talk of selling the car at public auction and using the proceeds for patrol equipment, but McKenzie had run to Chief Jorgensen and squashed that idea right quick. Before the previous owner even made it to lockup, McKenzie had turned in the keys to his pile-of-shit Crown Vic and assigned himself the new undercover ride. He wasn't about to give it up so some flatfoots in uniform could have a whizbang flashlight. Fuck those guys. Being a senior detective had its perks.

At the moment, the new muscle car and all the joy that came with it was a sorry consolation. McKenzie could only shake his head in frustration at the fact that he'd been standing around for damn near half an hour with his thumb up his ass. The son of a bitch was late and McKenzie's patience was wearing thin.

To make matters worse, it had been one hell of a rough night. He hadn't bothered shaving in two days and even in the bright sunlight his blotchy, spider-veined skin had a grayish tint that nearly matched the thick head of hair that he greased straight back. A sizable paunch rode high over his belt, and the audible growls from his stomach weren't due to hunger but to the aftereffects of all-you-can-eat barbequed spareribs at the Ho-Chunk Indian Casino and God knows how many whiskey shots chased with PBR.

McKenzie pushed hard against his eyes with both thumbs in an attempt to quiet the pounding in his head. He knew what he needed to do—knock off the greasy slabs of pork and buck up for a fillet once in a while. And no more happy-hour boilermakers with that shit-ass Indian firewater they sold as whiskey. From now on it's Grey Goose with a twist of lemon. Or are you supposed to drink it with lime? He laughed as he pictured himself in a joint where they kept that sort of booze on hand.

Hell, it ain't like I can't afford it.

McKenzie blew out a long breath and thought back to his glory days. Back when even after raising hell all night he'd need nothing more than a twenty-minute nap and quick line of crystal meth to get right back on the beam. McKenzie still liked his booze, but the drugs had become too risky. Even he could see the dangers of getting hooked on crank. Nowadays he sucked it up until noon or so, when he could sneak off for a little hair of the dog.

His cell phone buzzed in his pocket. Blocked number. He figured his new assbag of a sergeant was on the prowl again. Jesus, that guy. Damn supercop or some shit, him and his invalid father-in-law. But now, with Norgaard stroked out and Jorgensen at the helm, business was good. McKenzie had no plans to slow down. He punched Ignore even as he instinctively scanned the vicinity. As planned, the county park was deserted and he had a wide-open view of a half mile in all directions. Even though he knew he was covered from the top, McKenzie didn't take chances. As long as Sawyer was around, McKenzie needed to be extra cautious when conducting his special assignments.

He lit his tenth cigarette of the morning and looked on with disbelief as the vehicle he was waiting for finally pulled into the secluded parking lot.

"What the fuck, convict?" he said to himself.

The pounding bass of rap music could be heard through the closed windows of the tricked-out lowrider. McKenzie could make out two silhouettes through the smoked tint, with the driver in a serious gangster lean behind the wheel.

The long wait had left McKenzie irritable, but the arrival of two players when he expected one took him all the way to righteously pissed off. He fisted the gun in his pocket as his heart double-tapped in his chest. He mumbled a string of epithets that would have left a Klansman red with embarrassment.

Two men, dressed in warmups and heavy on ghetto bling, stepped from the car and jive-shucked it up pretty good as they approached.

"What up, McKenzie? What's happenin' in the big-time land of Newberg Five-O?" The driver attempted levity and the second man over did it on the laughter. McKenzie was glad to see them both look uneasy when they picked up on the bulge in the pocket of his ill-fitting overcoat.

The first man said, "This here is my partner . . ."

McKenzie kept one hand in his pocket and raised the other. "Shut your piehole, boy."

With near twenty years of police work, most of it working dope and working dirty, McKenzie knew that when dealing with big-city trash-talkers like these fools, it was best to keep all communications plain, simple, and in a language they understood. McKenzie maintained his posture against the hood of his prized possession and spoke directly to his contact's unknown companion. He made sure to lay the sarcasm on thick.

"Yo, Snoop Dogg. Go on and get your black ass back in that car and stay there. You ain't gonna be participating in this conversation."

The two men exchanged looks and waited for McKenzie to say more. When nothing followed, the driver smiled, flashing gold teeth. His brown eyes danced under his sideways Milwaukee Bucks ball cap. He tried to sound smooth, but McKenzie picked up on the noticeable tremor.

"Damn, McKenzie, what up with you? You ain't got no call to be goin' all badass cop or some shit. This here . . ."

Doyle stood up, one hand still concealed, and looked at his man.

"Boy, I won't tell you again. Shut the fuck up until I tell you to speak." Then, to the stranger, "I don't know and rightly don't care who you are, my *brother*. But like I said"—McKenzie pointed to the car the men had arrived in and spoke in short clips—"You. Car. Go. Listen to that hip-hop bullshit or whack yourself off with some spit and goddamn Afro Sheen for all I care, but get yourself outta earshot of me."

"Dude, you don't need—"

That was as far as the man got. McKenzie was a firm believer that when confronted with superior numbers, there was something to be said for bravado. He took one step toward both men, showing the fluid athleticism of a much fitter man. One hand grabbed the nearest man's crotch, the other emerged from his coat, wrapped around the grip of a .40-caliber semiauto. The sound of the hammer pulling back rang through the air, and McKenzie trained the barrel on the center of the stranger's head.

McKenzie bit down on the cigarette that still hung from his mouth and spoke through clenched teeth. "Listen up, Tyrone. You and me, we're going to start over. But before any of that, your boyfriend here is going to take a seat in that car. Otherwise, in about two seconds and two pounds of trigger pull, his ass is gonna be damn near headless, and I'll see to it that you do twenty-five to life for killin' him. Am I making myself clear?"

McKenzie closed his fist and squeezed, pulling down hard on whatever it was he had hold of. He got only a nod in response, but it was a nod of conviction. The stranger looked bug-eyed at the gun in a way that told McKenzie he was dealing with a couple of mopes after all. The situation was under control.

The passenger backed slowly to the car and climbed in. McKenzie had to laugh when he heard the door locks engage. His gun went back into his coat pocket while with his other hand he adjusted his grip until he was certain the pain left the strongest possible impression.

"Tell me something, Tyrone. Should I have spoken Swahili or some such shit when I said 'meet me alone'? Did my instructions somehow confuse the simple mind of a stupid-ass dope slinger like you?"

McKenzie wheeled around, putting Tyrone against the hood of the car. He loosened his grip, balled his fist, and delivered a quick punch to the same vicinity. The dealer dropped to his knees, breathing hard.

"Next time you're confused, you be sure to let me know. We can avoid all these unpleasantries. Now get up, boy, and listen to how it's gonna be."

Tyrone rose to his feet and McKenzie immediately got down to business.

"I've got half a kilo in the trunk," he said. "It's rocked up real nice and packaged to go out as eight balls. If you want, break it down to something a little more affordable for your broke-dick homies. If you go quarter grams you can stomp the hell out of it and turn it to powder. Step on it with talc, lace it with Comet, or get all generous and fire it up with a little H for all I give a shit. You sling it how you see fit, you being an independent business-man and all."

McKenzie went on in a more threatening tone. "But hear me on this, boy. You do all your dealin' with those cracked-out bros and hos one on one. Don't be tryin' to build some damn entourage. And this park is the closest you ever come to me. Don't even think about bringing any of your lowlife ghetto bullshit inside my city limits. You don't be dealing with any of the yuppies or kids in Newberg. They're taken care of, you hear me?"

Tyrone, still rubbing his crotch, took the insult in stride. "Yeah, all right."

"You got my ten grand?"

"It's in the trunk," Tyrone answered, nodding toward his car.

"Get it."

Tyrone turned and signaled to his still-unnamed partner. McKenzie shook his head in disbelief and delivered a solid kick with his booted foot. Tyrone came back around and his face flashed the anger any grown man would show over a public kick in the ass.

"Are you just ignorant, Tyrone?" McKenzie almost shouted in disbelief. "I said I don't work with third parties. Get it your damn self."

McKenzie watched the man limp to the car and pull a brown grocery sack from the trunk. Tyrone walked back, his face set to a slow burn. McKenzie drew on his cigarette, and let his hand drift back inside his coat. Tyrone was young, fit, and hard as nails. McKenzie knew if the boy put his mind to it, he could put up a hell of a fight. But there he stood with aching balls and a sore ass and no intentions of doing a damn thing about it. McKenzie under-

stood the boy's fear of the law and all that came with it. He found
it a common trait among the Tyrones of the world. Exploiting that
fear was McKenzie's greatest pleasure.

"I thought we had come to an understanding, Tyrone, that if I
let you stay out here on the street, you'd be ready to play ball. You'd
step up and start earning. I'm beginning to think I was wrong.
Seems like you're all bound and determined to reestablish yourself
as some kinda shot caller. Maybe I oughta see about canceling our
arrangement. Ship your ass off to the penitentiary."

Tyrone couldn't let it go. "Motherfucker, before you came along,
I dropped four or five keys of this shit every week all over Milwaukee, Racine, Mad-City; my name rang out all over the damn state. I
had two dozen homeboys workin' for me, doin' whatever I say.
Pretty white college girls standin' in line to get with me. And I never
needed no cracker cop kickin' me in my ass tellin' me how to do a
damn thing. And I sure as hell wasn't layin' out no ten grand for
half a key. How am I gonna make any scratch if I gotta be puttin'
up with that kind of inflated bullshit?"

McKenzie nodded his head, approving of the frank discussion.
"No shit? Five keys a week? Better price than mine, huh? How
about that last five-key deal? How'd that work out? You know, the
one where you and I got together?"

Tyrone made a click with his tongue and looked off into the
distance.

"Tell me something, Tyrone. Do you have any idea the ramifi-
cations of getting caught holding that kind of weight?"

Still looking away, the dealer's response was mumbled anger.
"I know how to jail, motherfucker."

"Oh, yeah?" McKenzie took a step forward. "Tell me this, do
you know how to jail for fifteen to twenty? Or if I take it federal,
you'd be jailin' for life, bitch. How's that sound?"

"Man, I've paid my way outta that shit and then some," Tyrone
argued back. "None of you crooked-ass pigs has cut me a damn

bit of slack." The man held McKenzie's eye, making it clear he was reaching his limit.

"That's the truth, Tyrone. I've made a pretty penny exploitin' your ass. But now tell me something. How long you figure you'd stay out here, rollin' around in that pimped-out ride of yours, blastin' that ghetto bullshit, if you didn't have me watchin' out for you? I mean, let's face it, it ain't exactly Chocolate City in this neck of the woods, and you ain't all that good when it comes to blendin' in. So tell me, what's gonna happen when you get your ass in a jam with Johnny Law and I ain't there to smooth things out?"

"Listen, McKenzie," Tyrone answered, "I know the score, all right? But you ain't gotta go all slave master on my ass, tryin' to turn me into your own Kunta-fuckin-Kinte or some bullshit, humiliatin' me in front of my boys. You gotta show me some respect, dog."

"Slave master? Kunta Kinte?" It was McKenzie's turn to yuck it up. "Now I hadn't thought about it like that till you said something, but I kind of like the sound of that. My own Kunta Kinte." McKenzie pulled hard on his cigarette and kicked his head back to exhale, enjoying the moment.

McKenzie flicked his lit cigarette and bounced it off Tyrone's nylon warmup in a quick burst of orange sparks. Tyrone jumped back in a moment of panic, banging his hands against his jacket. McKenzie closed in and Tyrone flinched. McKenzie thrust two fingers against the man's chest.

"Fact is, I *do* own your ass. You're bought and paid for. Without me looking out for your black ass, you'd be doing one hell of a hard stretch. You're out here because it works for me. No other reason. And truth be told, Tyrone, I find a little humiliation good for the soul. Helps a man like you remember your place in this world. Your place in *my world*. You're nothing more than a walking convict, boy. Your kingpin days are over. You live under my thumb, and you need to get your big old melon head around that. You hearin' me?"

McKenzie took the silence as a confirmation, but he went on to strengthen his point.

"And know this, *brother*. One more improvisation on your part, and I will personally ship your ass off to some shit hole of a prison in the middle of nowhere that specializes in attitude adjustments for smart-ass black folk. I know you're a man who loves his pussy, but you won't be seein' none of that. Shit, by the time you walk out, it won't be women who make your dick hard; you'll be all about that prison shit. You hear what I'm sayin', homeboy?"

Still nothing but a hard look. McKenzie laughed as he spoke. "So, whaddya say, Kunta? You gonna play ball?"

There was a long pause, and Tyrone's voice was filled with resignation when he eventually answered. "It's cool, McKenzie. Just fuckin' ease up on me, all right? You gotta let me build a rep if you want me to deal your shit."

McKenzie swiped the bag from his hand, aroused by the weight of it. He looked inside. "Whaddya know? Used twenties and tens. Least you got that right. It better add up."

"It's all there."

McKenzie clicked his remote and popped the trunk. "The green bag is yours. Get it."

Tyrone did as told, then stood before McKenzie, bag in hand, awaiting further instruction.

"Now I gotta unfuck one more thing because of your dumb ass." McKenzie pushed past with a look of irritation etched on his face and signaled for Tyrone to follow along. He walked the short distance to where the silent associate sat stone still. McKenzie stood outside the passenger door, and signaled for the man to put the window down. Reluctantly, he obliged.

"Never caught your name, son?" McKenzie thought he came off sounding damn near fatherly.

"Eldon."

"I have to say, Eldon, Tyrone here didn't do you any favors by bringing you to this meet, but you probably figured that out for yourself, didn't ya, boy?"

"It ain't nothin', man." Eldon's voice shook. "We were just kickin' it, so I came along. That's all. Whatever you guys got goin' ain't nothin' to me."

"That's a real nice attitude for you take, but in this business it's all about risk and reward. You know what I'm sayin'?"

The man shook his head back and forth. He used his thick tongue to wet his lips; a layer of sweat had formed along the edge of his red do-rag. McKenzie looked on and estimated he might be nineteen or twenty. Too bad.

"You see that car, Eldon?" McKenzie jerked a thumb over his shoulder. "That's the reward of this life. You, on the other hand, you're the risk."

McKenzie had been bent at the waist to speak through the window. He stood up, pulled his weapon, and fired two quick shots dead center into Eldon's chest. The man was dead before the echoing sound of gunfire even cleared the air.

McKenzie finished his conversation with Tyrone's now silent partner. "You gotta eliminate the risks, Eldon."

McKenzie turned and saw Tyrone standing statue still, mouth hanging open, arms stiff at his sides. The bag slipped from his fingers and fell with a soft thud onto the asphalt.

McKenzie laughed. "Shit, Tyrone. You're damn near white."

McKenzie's gun went back to his jacket but with his hand still around it. He wanted Tyrone to know he wasn't planning to kill him, but it was a possibility.

"That shit is on you," he said. "Now maybe you'll be a bit more mindful about the serious nature of our arrangement."

McKenzie closed in on Tyrone, who still stood like a stone.

"Listen up, homes. From now on your name is 'Alone-Tyrone,' you hear me? You don't need to be reestablishing your old lifestyle. I got enough to worry about without you adding to the mix." He picked up the bag and jammed it hard into Tyrone's chest. "Now get your ass down to Beloit and sling that shit. I've taken care of the competition. The market is wide-open. You should be able to move it pretty quick."

Tyrone stared at the dead man in his car. McKenzie reached out and gave the drug dealer an openhanded cuff to the face.

"Answer me, Tyrone. I need to know you hear me on this shit, boy."

"I . . . Jesus Christ . . . it's cool, McKenzie." Tyrone looked as if he might pass out on the spot, but he held it together. "Shit . . . I get it, dog. You ain't got nothin' to worry about."

McKenzie sauntered to his car and revved the Trannie's engine to full strength. His cell phone buzzed, and like before he looked at the blocked number and punched Ignore. With the window lowered, he called out to Tyrone, who was still hugging the bag with both arms as if it were a security blanket, staring at the corpse in his car.

"There's a rest stop on the Fifty-one just before you get to Beloit. Dump your boy there. I'll see that state patrol picks him up and that the investigation ain't all that inquisitive. Now get your ass outta here and stay off the radar. I've got another half a kilo ready to go out, so get on it."

McKenzie punched the accelerator, kicking up rock and sand and fishtailing away without waiting for an answer. He still had three more stops to make, and dealing with Tyrone had put him behind schedule. The voice mail alert went off on his cell. McKenzie didn't bother to listen.

"Fuck you, Sawyer. You ain't the only one with a crew to run."

SIX

The woman took a deep drag from his Pall Mall and passed it back, stained red with caked lipstick. Harlan made no effort to conceal his irritation. Thick smoke floated above the bed and mixed with the stale odors of a room that he figured, like the hooker, was most profitable when rented by the hour. She raised her arms above her head to stretch, and Harlan took in the sight as she arched her back so all that touched the dingy cotton sheets were the bottoms of her tiny feet, the smooth blades of her shoulders, and the cheeks of her round perfection. In terms of her vocation, Harlan believed she had chosen wisely.

"Give me another drag." She reached out, but Harlan snatched the cigarette away, his elbow striking hard against her bare breast.

"Back off, bitch. For what I'm payin', you can buy your own damn smokes."

"Jeez. You got a mean streak."

She clutched her chest in pain, and Harlan surmised she was unaccustomed to such rough treatment. A genuine and verifiable redhead, she'd earned her wages and then some, although probably not under the cordial relations she preferred. Harlan sensed her intent to wrap things up and be on her way. He had other plans, and he spoke to correct her thinking.

"I'm gonna finish *my* smoke in peace. Then we'll get back it at. Go clean up some. I want it fresh."

"This ain't no all-you-can-eat buffet. You want another helping, it'll cost you." Harlan saw her calculating the dollars against what she must know would be another rough ride. He could almost see the price going up.

"Don't worry about the money. You'll get what you earn, but right now you carry the stink of used whore. I said, clean up."

"You're an asshole," she mumbled as she strolled naked to the bathroom, massaging her still-aching breast. "Why don't you watch some TV or something? You need to relax."

Harlan took her advice and flipped through the channels, stopping when he came to a news broadcaster talking about the arrest of a local businessman. Sitting up in bed, he listened closely as the reporter spoke of a federal investigation that led to the arrest of Henry Lipinski, owner and operator of Big Henry Used Auto Sales. The reporter mentioned that Lipinski was a former law enforcement officer; his arrest was sending shock waves throughout the community of Chippewa Falls. The twenty-two-year-old prostitute stepped out of the bathroom, dripping wet from the shower and wrapped in a towel. She looked on as a disheveled, irate man was roughly shoved into a police car by several uniformed officers.

"Hey, I know him. That's Big Henry. He's one of my regulars." She sat on the edge of the bed, and her towel dropped to her waist.

The reporter continued, "Hundreds of pornographic images have been retrieved from the computers of Lipinski's auto dealership, and according to authorities, there is ample evidence that Lipinski is associated with a child pornography operation that may have spanned the country and beyond."

"Aw, Jeez. I just can't believe that. Wow. He didn't seem like that kind of a guy to me." The sympathy in her voice touched a nerve, and Harlan felt his anger start to build.

"Yeah? Well, last last I checked, dick-smokin' hookers don't get picked for jury duty. Maybe you could be like a character witness or something."

She pulled up her towel and spoke with what Harlan figured was her attempt to change the tone. "I guess you just never know about people, huh? He sure fooled me."

"I guess you don't." His attention was drawn away from her and back to the screen. "He don't look all that smug now, does he? Ask me, he looks scared shitless."

She slid up close, smelling of soap, and began to work him with her hands. Harlan went on, "Yeah. He's a son of a bitch, all right. Former sheriff Henry Lipinski of Florence County, Wisconsin. He and few of his associates locked my ass up for life. At least that's how they had it figured."

"Wow. Prison, huh? That explains a lot." There was admiration in her voice. She teased him with her tongue. "It don't seem to have hurt you any."

"I did seventeen years in their bullshit joint and I coulda done another seventeen. They ain't gonna take nothin' out of me I don't wanna give 'em." He gestured to the television. "But this jerk-off? He's going to the joint as a cop and a kiddie-porn dealer. They're gonna have fun with him. I give 'im a year tops."

She looked at the screen, her expression and tone of voice betraying her sympathy for the arrested man. "I don't know. Times I was with him, he seemed like a real gentleman."

"He ain't gonna be nobody's gentleman now. Give 'im a couple months, and I wager he'll be downright giddy to suck a cock just to avoid the alternative."

She scrunched her face at the crude image, then looked up from her kneeling position with doubt in her eyes. "How come you know so much?"

"'Cause I set his ass up. That prick is going down because of me." He glared. "Sorry if that's gonna fuck up your weekly earning capability."

She slowed her work, and Harlan, already regretting his own loose tongue, knew she was considering the exchange. A john who spoke so loose was trouble, especially one careless enough to boast about his misdeeds. She looked at him, and he gave her a hard stare.

"You've got a pryin' nature considerin' your line of work." He pushed down hard on the back of her head. "Just shut up and get at it. I gotta get on the road."

Her hands shook with nervousness, and he knew she sensed danger closing in. She backed off and her voice cracked with fear.

"You can have whatever you want. I won't charge you. It's okay. I don't even know your name."

Harlan said nothing, knowing he had already run his mouth plenty. He'd fucked up and he knew it. No question what had to be done, but no reason to interrupt the girl's work. She practically read his thoughts, and tears welled in her eyes before she finished him off with her mouth.

He lay back for a moment, spent, eyes shut. He felt her slide from the bed and knew she was trying for her clothes. She didn't get three feet before he grabbed her by the hair and threw her onto the bed. Her skull banged sharply on the wooden headboard. Before she could scream, Harlan brought a pillow down hard over her face. A ruthlessness overtook him and the menace in his voice surprised him.

"So he's a little gentleman friend of yours, huh? What are the odds of that? I pick up a streetwalkin' whore who'd stoop so low as to fuck that fat piece of shit."

Her screams were stifled, but it took his full weight to keep her on the bed. For a small gal she demonstrated a good bit of scrap. She flailed at the air for a moment as if to get her bearings, then balled up her fist and delivered a blow flush on his chin.

Harlan laughed, unhurt but impressed by her effort. He put his full weight on the hand holding the pillow and reached for his backpack with the other. She must have heard the rip of the holster's Velcro, and that brought on a whole new reaction. Her muffled screams grew more intense, and Harlan felt the violence of her kicks that were strong enough to elevate her entire body off the bed. He held firm.

Harlan kept up the smothering weight and then added a tight circle of pressure just about where he figured the bridge of her nose would be. She stopped thrashing and raised her arms. Her muffled screams turned to desperate sobs. Harlan picked up on her attempts to beg but couldn't take a chance on anything more merciful than a quick end. When he pulled the trigger, Harlan figured at worst she heard the muffled crack, but more than likely she didn't feel a thing.

SEVEN

It took several seconds for the tension to ease from his arms, and his breath was labored. After a moment's pause, Harlan pulled back the pillow and looked at the dead woman's shattered face. The bullet had caved in her forehead around a star-shaped hole big enough to stick his finger in, and he resisted a perverse desire to do just that. The body convulsed more than he thought it would, but he told himself the whore was dead. No one could live through an injury as traumatic as that. Sure enough, her legs and arms went still and her wide-open eyes were fast going dull.

The rashness of his action concerned him. This was an unplanned kill brought on by the woman's comments about Lipinski and, to a lesser degree, her overall irritating disposition. He gazed up at the mirrored ceiling and spoke to himself in a placid tone. "Keep this shit up and you'll be locked up by the end of the week."

Giving no thought to panic, Harlan sat on the bed next to the dead prostitute and planned his exit. The gun had been effectively silenced, muffled by the pillow. He took a fistful of hair and lifted her head. The exit wound in the back of her skull meant the bullet was likely buried somewhere deep in the mattress. It'd take some effort and luck to find it. "Fuck all that diggin' around."

She had picked the hotel and was probably a regular. No one would come looking for the room for a few more hours. He hadn't been seen at check-in. The car in the parking lot was stolen from the next town over but clean of prints. He dug through her purse and smiled. Not only did he recover his own money but three hundred on top of it.

"No surprise there, sister. You were a talent." He gave her a hard swat on her bare ass and stood.

Harlan spent ten minutes wiping down anything he might have touched, all the while carrying on a one-way conversation with the silent girl in bed, explaining how it was he'd come to be so ill-tempered. He stuck the bottle of Wild Turkey into his backpack and dropped the drinking glass onto the hard floor, shattering it into thousands of unprintable shards. He stopped to consider the body and thought for a moment, hands on his hips.

"Bottle of whiskey is one thing, but I sure can't be takin' you along with me."

An idea came to him, and he carried the nude, lifeless prostitute to the bathroom. She dripped blood heavily along the way, but Harlan was cautious where he stepped. Small, she slid into the damp tub with room to spare. Harlan took hold by the scruff of her neck and pulled down on the jaw, opening her mouth to its full extension. The head lolled back and forth, making him lose his grip.

"Hold still, bitch." His voice was low and lightly laced with affection.

Harlan turned the tap on full force, shooting water down her throat. Membrane and tissue bubbled out past her lips and cheeks; some pieces got caught in her open eyes and long hair. Harlan canted the head back and forth to clear away the more sizable chunks. Much of the water followed a path to the large exit wound, where it ran out red, then rose, and finally clear. For the mirth value he shot some water through the bullet hole before returning to her mouth and counting off another thirty seconds. He was amused to discover that he actually filled her. Her stomach bloated out and water gushed from the gaping mouth like a sheared-open fire hydrant.

"That oughta rid ya of anything I left swimmin' around." He looked the corpse up and down. "Glad I didn't go pokin' around the rest of ya unsheathed. That'd been a mite more difficult situation to deal with."

He dropped her head against the porcelain bottom of the tub, where it landed with a strange *tonk*. She lay there, still warm and, from the neck down at least, not at all hard on the eyes.

Harlan let the water run for another minute, using the showerhead to spray her down thoroughly. When he figured she was washed clean of him, he closed the drain and cranked the water to scalding hot. While the tub filled, he sat on the closed toilet and breezed through the copy of *Hustler* he'd brought along to help set the mood. Once she floated an inch off the bottom, he turned off the spigot. The hole in her forehead bubbled and her long hair turned a darker auburn and looped about her in the water. Her mouth, erotic earlier in the day, hung slack jawed, the still-tender tongue sticking out like a fat red worm. Her wide-open eyes stared at him from under the steaming water as if to ask what in the world had become of her.

"Ya look like a frickin' retard." He spoke as if to admonish. "If you're a whore again in your next life, keep to your work and don't talk so damn much."

Harlan went to the door, looked out the peephole, and saw no one. He walked out and pulled the door shut behind him. The stolen car he'd arrived in still sat in the lot, clean of prints, and that's where it'll stay, he thought. Harlan figured this was as good a time as any to get reacquainted with walking.

Five minutes later he strolled into the Greyhound station. He pulled the dead girl's hard-earned cash from his pocket and slapped down $42 for a one-way ticket. He checked the electronic board that listed departure and arrival times and saw that his trip would take a little over four hours. He'd get there and grab a room. Order in. Lay low. *Alone,* he told himself, now aware that his trip to Chippewa Falls had involved a foolish indiscretion. Years of planning nearly wasted for an afternoon hummer from a local hooker.

Harlan boarded the bus and found an empty seat toward the back. By the time the Greyhound reached cruising speed, his eyes were closed. The past several days had been intense, and he welcomed the opportunity to drift. His mind wandered back to the endless forest of his boyhood, to years of lean but purposeful living followed by law trouble, arrest, and finally prison. His thought of his father, dead for nearly a decade.

Pa.

Jedidiah Lee had been a cantankerous sixty-year-old recluse the day a half-breed Chippewa temptress barely of legal age wandered into his shack in the deepest woods of Florence County. Near ruined but well trained by all the substantial forms of reservation abuse, the girl sought only safety and shelter in exchange for an enthusiastic brand of companionship she willingly demonstrated within moments of their initial meeting. Jedidiah always referred fondly to those early romps and said though the couple rarely spoke, their nightly coupling left both spent but agreeable to one more day of their shared but separate existence.

The first indication of her pregnancy marked the end of their relationship, and two weeks after giving birth she was gone, leaving father and newborn son behind. Jedidiah claimed he never harbored a shred of ill will against Harlan's mother; far from it. He was thankful to her for the establishment of his legacy. From his first day of parenthood, Jedidiah devoted his life to his only child.

Harlan stared out the window at the passing signposts, barns, and cornfields, and thought about how he came to live the outlaw life. His father had always boasted that the Lee gene for emotional indifference and legal irreverence had been passed on to his son. Jedidiah and Harlan were as much notorious partners in crime as they were father and son. With Harlan's youth and Jedidiah's guile, they turned the hundred-and-sixty-acre family homestead into the most sophisticated and profitable marijuana grow east of the Mississippi. The Lees were just hitting their stride when it all came to a sudden end.

A rival dope dealer found dead. Arrested, jailed and with a sham of a trial looming, Harlan pled guilty. He got twenty-five to life. Game over.

The old man grew feeble while the state kept Harlan penned up like dairy stock. At the last visit Jedidiah managed to make, they spoke of years past, of old scores and outlaw associates.

As he left, the old man had struggled to speak.

"I'm gonna die soon, boy, and you still ain't free. I can't be here to help ya, but there will come a time that the Lee name must be avenged. It falls to you, son. It falls to you."

Harlan pushed back farther in the worn seat and shook his head with a vigor intended to clear away his pointless reminiscing. His next act of retribution was going to bring a particularly strong sense of satisfaction.

The speaker above his head crackled, and Harlan realized he had dozed off. He looked out and saw the town had barely changed, as though it were stuck in time. The driver's voice came clearly over the loudspeaker. "Good afternoon, Greyhound passengers. Now announcing arrival at Greyhound stop eleven twenty-one. If this is your destination, prepare to disembark. Welcome to Newberg."

EIGHT

B en stared at himself in the bathroom mirror, rubbing at his crow's feet, which were becoming more pronounced by the day, especially first thing in the morning. He ran a hand over his rough chin and figured he'd shave at the department. Less noise. He squeezed toothpaste onto his finger and rubbed it over his teeth, then pulled a brush through his thick, close-cropped hair. He blew out hard, looking at the half-dozen more gray hairs that seemed to have sprung up overnight at his temples. The early-morning light was enough for him to dress by. Gym bag in hand, he was heading for the door when Alex stirred and said, "Do you really need to go in this early?"

Ben stopped, angry with himself that he hadn't gotten up an hour earlier, when he could have slipped out unnoticed.

"I want to hit the gym before work. I'll give you a call later this morning."

Alex was in no mood to play nice. She rolled over in bed, turning her back to her husband. "No, you won't, but if you're going to be late for dinner, at least let me know. Jake and I will just go ahead and eat."

Ben stood in the doorway and looked at his wife. He'd known her for his entire life. They grew up together, were high school sweethearts. Hell, they practically ran away together. The return to New-berg had been hard on both of them, and he didn't deny he'd become a real prick to live with. He set the gym bag on the floor and gave a thought to crawling back into bed. Maybe form up next to her, eliminate every bit of at least the physical distance between them. She'd be a little put off, but he knew she'd take some comfort from the gesture. The best he could bring himself to do was sit at the foot of the bed, making sure not to get too close.

"What are you saying, Alex? You don't think I'm at work? Where else am I going to go? Hit the Newberg hot spots? Drink a few beers with all my buddies from the PD?"

She seized the moment as if she'd been lying in wait, her voice laced with sarcasm. "Oh, poor Ben. Are the other boys being mean to you?"

Ben narrowed his eyes and stared, ready to tell Alex where to stick her smart-ass comments, but she didn't give him the chance.

"Ben, do you hear yourself? You sound like a damn child."

She threw the covers back, got out of bed, and headed for the closet. She pulled on a Santa Clara sweatshirt, punching her arms through the sleeves, then yanking it down over her head and flat belly. Her blue eyes shone clear, and Ben had no doubt he'd been set up. Alex had been awake for a while, itching for a fight. She lobbed the first salvo like a stun grenade.

"You're not a child, Ben, and I shouldn't have to act like your mother. I'm just saying I'd appreciate some common courtesy. If you don't want to come home for dinner with your family, fine. Just let me know. We'll make do on our own."

Ben started to respond, but she cut him off. Salvo number two.

"And by the way, this pity trip bullshit has got to end. Stop feeling sorry for yourself and deal with reality. We're here, Ben. Get used to it."

Right to the gut, both times. Alex never had gone for the soft-sell approach, but that didn't mean Ben couldn't hit back.

"So, what then? I'll be a bumpkin cop while you play wet nurse to your dad?"

Ben saw her shoulders tighten and knew he had struck a nerve.

"He's not getting any better, Alex, and we can't keep paying for that country club he's living in. How much longer do you think Newberg PD is going to keep me around? Believe me, every day Jorgensen looks for a new reason to dump my ass. Hell, even if he can't find some way to fire me, between him and McKenzie and the rest of that crew, they'll make me miserable enough I'll have to quit. Shit, it's already started. If this is it—if Newberg is all we got—you might want to think about figuring out how to be the breadwinner. That should be interesting."

It was full-on now. Ben watched as Alex closed the distance, stepping from the shadows into the early-morning light. Like Ben, she had just turned thirty-five, but physically, the woman could still stop a clock. A collegiate volleyball player, she had managed to keep a trim, athletic figure. Her tan wasn't as deep as when they lived in California but enough that her skin had a healthy outdoor tone. Ben had always taken pride in her beauty. Even now, he wanted to pull her to the bed, but her next line reminded him they were in the middle of a fight.

"Hey, pal, if it weren't for my dad, we'd be on the streets, thanks to you and that hot-ass temper of yours." Alex stopped abruptly, knowing she had gone too far. "Ben, I didn't mean . . . look, let's just calm down. I don't want to fight—"

He was heading for the door, any lingering affection gone. Anger filled his voice when he said, "You're right, Alex. All this is on me. Your dad is the hero here. Hell, why did we ever go to California to begin with? Maybe I should've followed in your daddy's footsteps all along. I coulda spent my whole career being his boy, huh? What was I thinking?"

That had been the plan, as far as Lars Norgaard was concerned. He'd intended Ben to marry his daughter in a proper, traditional Newberg wedding, not some ten-minute gig in a Las Vegas chapel. At some later date Lars would have handed Ben the keys to the kingdom. Alex and Ben had had different plans, but in the end, all these years later, here they were. The only problem was, there hadn't been any kingdom to hand off.

"Ben, please. Don't leave angry." Alex took two steps closer. "I'm sorry. I was out of line, but Ben, we never talk. All of this, my dad, work, everything . . . We've got to talk. Stay home for a while, maybe take the day off. It doesn't have to be like this."

"Doesn't have to be like what? Honest? I think we could use a dose of honesty." He picked up his bag, opened the door, and lowered his voice to a normal level. "And as long as we're being *honest*, you should know. I put a call into an old commander of mine. He left Oakland a few years back to be an assistant chief in Fresno. He thinks enough time has gone by that he can get me a job as a mid-level patrol officer. If he can come through, we're outta here. You're welcome to join us."

"Us?"

"Jake will come with me. You know he'd pick home over this place any day."

"Ben, how can you even think like that?" Finally, her voice broke. "My dad needs me. I can't leave him. We belong here. This is home now."

"It's your call, Alex." Ben tried to sound resolute but failed and found himself regretting that he had even brought it up. "Anyway, nothing's happened yet. I just thought you should know."

"Know what?" The voice came from the hallway, and both Alex and Ben turned to see Jake standing in the doorway. Jake was wearing his typical sleepwear: sweatpants and a worn-out Oakland A's T-shirt. Ben could never look at that shirt without thinking he bought if for Jake at a ball game a week before all hell broke loose. "What about California? Are we moving back home?"

Ben looked at his wife and saw she was still reeling from his low-blow comment. Now his son was standing in front of him, and Ben could see by the look on the boy's face that he was wide awake and expecting an answer to his questions.

"Mom and I are just talking, Jake," Ben said to his son. "Go back to bed. It's really early."

"I'm not stupid, Dad," Jake said, and Ben picked up on the usual disrespect in his tone. "You weren't talking, you were fighting, but whatever. I just want to know if we're moving back home?" Jake's gaze flicked back and forth between his mom and dad. "Cuz if we are, it's great with me. Let's go."

Ben heard an audible sigh from his wife before she spoke. "Jake, this is our home now. Dad works here and Grandpa needs us."

Jake took a step closer to his parents. "Yeah, but—"

Ben cut him off. "We're not fighting and we're not going anywhere. Now go back to bed."

Not going anywhere. Ain't that the damn truth, Ben thought.

Jake spun around and headed back to his room. He was physically big for his age, but it seemed to Ben that in the last year emotionally the boy had regressed. "Nobody ever asks me what I want. I didn't even want to come here in the first place."

Ben waited for the inevitable slam of the door and he was not disappointed. He stared down the hallway at where his son had disappeared. Jake still resented the move, and Ben knew the boy blamed him. Ben also knew he was right.

Alex took a step forward and touched Ben on the arm. Her expression had softened, and a wave of affection washed over him. If he reached out now, right now, it might really matter. It would matter to Alex. To Jake. It could put them on the path to recovery.

Just a touch, a phone call to work that said, "I'm not coming in today." Ben knew that was all it would take.

Alex looked directly into his eyes, and her voice broke. "I love you, Ben. I don't want it to be like this. We can be happy here. We need to pull together."

Ben considered her words, holding her gaze all the while, then stepped around her.

He walked out without another word to his wife, even though his heart was filled with so much love, pain, and sorrow that he could only wonder how it was that he survived such extremes.

NINE

From his desk, Ben caught the odor of beer-laced perspiration mixed with cheap cologne. Seemed like his poke at the bear had worked; judging by the smell, McKenzie was close. Ben glanced at the clock and saw it was after eleven. He banged out a quick text canceling his coffee plans with Alex. It had been two days since their fight, and the ice around the house had just begun to melt.

Alex had reached out that morning, inviting Ben to meet her for coffee at some new place she wanted to show him. He knew she would give it to him about his last-minute cancellation, but too bad. He was closing in on his target, and one way or another he was determined to corner his most elusive detective. McKenzie loomed in the doorway, then collapsed into the visitor's chair. On the desk, Ben's cell phone buzzed and Alex's number appeared. He sent the call straight to voice mail.

McKenzie spoke, the gravel in his voice screaming of a rough night. "What's with the bullshit burglary cases on my desk? I work strictly dope, Sawyer. That's the way Jorgensen wants it. You know that."

"Hello to you too, Doyle. Nice of you to stop by." Ben made a point of looking at his watch but kept his voice cordial. "Don't worry. You're still working Narcotics, but we've been getting hit hard with burglaries lately, and you don't seem that busy. I didn't figure you'd mind helping out."

McKenzie put a hand up to block the sun streaming through the window, which Ben knew at this time of day had the intensity of an interrogation spotlight. As senior detective of Newberg PD and the holder of the prestigious title of Department Narc, McKenzie insisted he be provided free rein to develop his own cases. Property crimes such as burglary were beneath him.

"Anyway, where you been?" Ben asked. "The day's half over."

Ben watched as McKenzie worked to muster a response. He figured the old but still-cagey detective would launch into a series of bold-faced lies that would be hard for anyone to challenge. McKenzie came through.

"What the hell, Sawyer? Now you're gonna get all black assed about the schedule I keep?" McKenzie sounded offended by the idea of having to account for himself. "I worked UC last night. One of my snitches had a line on a college kid who wanted to buy a pound of weed. Guy was a no-show. The deal never went down. I figured I'd just come in late and save the overtime you're always busting my balls about."

"Is that right?" Ben made no effort to disguise the skepticism in his voice. "Then document the contact in the informant's file and write up an after-action report on the stakeout. And in the future, let me know before you work an undercover op. If something goes down, you're going to need backup."

"Jesus. Informant file? After-action report? What are you talkin' about?" "It's like you wanna be my nanny or some shit. You know, your old man and I had a good arrangement. Narcotics dicks ain't like regular police. He knew how to stay out of the way. Never went around sweatin' all this petty bullshit."

Ben was accustomed to both the confusion and the comparison. "You're talking about my father-in-law and you're right. Chief Norgaard wasn't one to sweat the small stuff; that's the sergeant's job. I'm sure Chief Jorgensen would agree."

"How is old Red, anyway? I heard he still ain't talking. Just lying around like a vegetable or something. Lars Norgaard? An invalid?"

Doyle McKenzie inquiring about his family's personal affairs felt like an invasion of privacy. Ben answered with cold detachment.

"He's getting stronger every day, Doyle. I'll be sure to tell him you asked about him."

"It's a damn shame. No doubt about it, that guy's a legend around here. Big old redheaded Norseman, forearms like ham hocks. When he was coming up through the ranks, all the crooks knew if Lars Norgaard couldn't arrest you, he'd at least put a serious hurt on your ass. He sure enough ended some criminal careers.

"Damn, Ben," Doyle went on in a judgmental tone, "it must be kind of strange for you with old Lars gone. I mean, you're his boy. He's the one that brought you on and handed you those sergeant stripes, huh?"

Ben felt his pulse pick up but didn't let it show. The day Lars Norgaard went down, everything changed. Within three weeks, Assistant Chief Walter Jorgensen had arranged for Norgaard's permanent retirement and his own installation as chief of police. A new day had dawned at Newberg PD, and storm clouds began to gather for Ben. It was pretty much accepted departmentwide that Sawyer would be gone soon, and there wasn't exactly a line of folks coming to his defense. It had reached a point that McKenzie just pretended Ben was already gone. It was obvious to Ben that a deal of some sort had been worked out between McKenzie and Jorgensen, but they struck Ben as odd pair. One was known for being politically astute; the other was nothing more than an armed snake in the grass.

Responding, Ben's tone was harsh. "I'm not anybody's 'boy,' McKenzie, and nobody gave me anything. I ran a few teams in Oakland. I think I can handle whatever might come up in Newberg."

"Oh, yeah, I know, Ben. We all heard about your time runnin' with the big dogs out in California. Actually, I got a copy of that picture where you're doing some dental work on that beaner piece of shit. I was hoping you might autograph it for me sometime."

Ben stared at him, but McKenzie went on. "Don't get me wrong, I totally approve. I'm on your side. Fact is, I was just saying to Chief Jorgensen we should let you work a beat. Our guys could learn a few things from a badass like yourself. Course, you probably prefer to keep those sergeant stripes."

"We? Who is 'we,' Doyle?"

McKenzie stood to leave, swaying on his feet. He half suppressed a gaseous belch that filled the office with the noxious stench of digesting meat and fermenting beer, then smiled when he saw Ben's expression of disgust.

"Unless you've got some objection, *boss,* I'm going to step out and grab a bite. Do I need to sign a check-out log or something? I mean, since you like keeping such a close tab on me."

Ben ignored the comment, trying to control his building anger. "When you get back we should talk about those burglary cases. I want to hear your plans for working them. It's almost noon. Let's make it twelve thirty."

"Yeah, sure. I'll hit a drive-thru and be right back."

McKenzie turned to leave, then stopped, as if a thought just came to mind. "By the way, I was wondering. You and your wife. You planning on going into the coffee business or something?"

"No. What makes you ask that?"

McKenzie's voice took on a snide quality. "Just your wife is spending a lot of time down at that new coffee joint. Heard some of the patrol dogs talking about it in the locker room. Word is she camps out there for a couple of hours at a time, talking with the stud that owns the place. I just thought maybe she was learning the ropes. Probably just killing time while you're at work, huh?"

Ben held his tongue but not his eye. McKenzie rested against the doorjamb. "Don't sweat it, Ben. I'm sure the guys were just . . . well, you know cops. They ain't happy unless they're breakin' balls."

Ben felt the blood rise to his face and his pulse bang against the collar of his shirt. McKenzie took two steps back into the office.

"Here's the thing, *Sarge*. After going and getting all famous in California, seems like you might want to ease up a bit. Hell, maybe you should think about spending a little more time at home." McKenzie winked. "Gotta keep that love light burning, right, boss?"

McKenzie turned to leave, and Ben stood from his desk.

"Hang on, McKenzie, get your—"

McKenzie spun back around. "No. You hang on, Sawyer. You got a problem with the way I do my job, go see Jorgensen. Maybe he can explain it better than I can. In the meantime, I'll give those burglary cases you're so damn worried about to the boys over in property crime. Now I got dope work to do. If you need to see me, I'll be back in around five."

Ben came around the desk, his fist balled up and his intentions clear. McKenzie stood firm but didn't raise a hand. Ben closed to within inches of McKenzie's face but he detected no fear. McKenzie smiled, exposing his yellow-stained teeth.

"Go on, Ben. Take a poke. That would solve everything."

Ben worked to keep his voice low. "Get out of my office, McKenzie. We'll finish this later."

McKenzie turned and walked away, delivering one final jab as he left.

"I'll see you around, Ben. Be sure to tell old Lars it ain't the same without him. It's a whole lot better."

TEN

Ben stood in the doorway for nearly a minute, his chest rising and falling with heavy breaths. The cell phone buzzed and vibrated across the top of his desk. He walked over, snatched it up, and saw his wife's number. Ben slammed the phone against the desk. The buzzing stopped. He wheeled around in a fit of anger and raked his hand across the venetian blinds, and the strips of thin metal crumpled noisily. He dropped into his chair.

"Fucking prick—"

McKenzie had his number, no doubt about it, but Ben knew he couldn't let people get to him like that. Alex was right. If it weren't for his temper, they wouldn't be dealing with any of this. Once again the memories burned to the surface.

"He's got my gun. He's got my gun."

Ben spun his desk chair and shook his head, trying to clear his thoughts. It didn't work.

He took an officer's gun. He was going to kill a cop. What was I supposed to do?

The air in the office grew stifling hot just like that day on the street in Oakland. Ben forced himself to stay grounded in reality. No more excuses, he told himself. Be honest about it for once. Ben sat at his desk and buried his head in his hands, but the images and the memories remained.

The second Hector Espudo's hands had gone up, the rookie cop grabbed his gun and scurried free. The officer was already back on his feet, once again screaming in the radio. Other cops had begun to roll up on the scene. The situation was under control.

That's the problem, Sawyer. The moment passed. Why couldn't you see that?

Hector kept running his mouth, but he knelt passively on the sidewalk, his hands high over his head. Everyone watching would later say Hector's actions amounted to unconditional surrender. With his gun still against the side of Hector's head, Ben knew what he had to do.

Just reholster and take him into custody. Arrest him. You're done.

But when Ben looked into his eyes, he saw something hidden behind Hector's outward display of submission. Ben knew what it was. It was hope.

Hope still survived in Hector. After all those years of drills and dry runs on the prison yard, just *hoping* for a chance to kill a cop, he had come up short. Now the son of a bitch was biding his time, hoping for another chance on another day. Ben knew one way to kill that hope once and for all. That's when all sense of reason left him. It came back clear and Ben didn't allow himself to filter the memory. Even now, he could still see the flag-draped coffin. The widow dressed in black. And three fatherless children, their eyes filled with confused innocence.

Ben pulled his gun away from Hector's temple and tucked it in close to his own body. In his peripheral view, Ben saw an officer standing by, handcuffs out and at the ready. In that last moment of clarity, Ben locked eyes with Hector and knew the man wouldn't be getting arrested.

Standing over his prisoner with a fist full of hair, Ben reared back, then came forward and rammed the blue steel barrel of his gun into Hector's still-running mouth. The torrid cursing stopped, replaced by a sound like shattering glass as the gun smashed against Hector's teeth. Ben's hand tingled with the memory of the sensation of the gun's front sight raking through Hector's lips and across the roof of his mouth, ripping away layers of tissue and skin.

He shoved the barrel three inches down Hector's throat; Hector's mouth filled with blood and his choking, gagging cough sounded almost life-threatening. Ben squeezed his finger, taking up every bit of slack, then stopped. He got down close, his lips to the man's ear and the moist roughness of Hector's unshaved face against his cheek. His words, uttered in a soft but guttural voice, flooded his memory and even now caused him to grit his teeth and tightened his jaw.

"So you wanna be a cop killer, huh, esse?"

With all the force he could muster, Ben pulled hard on Hector's ponytail, and the man went from his knees to lying flat on his back on the asphalt. Ben straddled Hector's chest and pushed his weapon deeper into his gullet. Hector's fists and boot heels scuffed desperately against the hard ground as if he was trying to run away from the gun that filled his throat. Ben imagined the trajectory of the bullet and the damage it would do. He spoke his thoughts out loud.

"Straight out the back of your neck and into the concrete. I've never seen one like that, Hector. Hell, it might not even kill a bad-ass like you, but I don't imagine your dick would ever get hard again and you can damn sure forget your aspirations of bein' a cop killer. You okay with that, big man?"

Hector's screams, muffled by the weapon, came off more animal than human. His eyes watered. The shards of his front teeth made a hideous clicking noise against the metal barrel of the gun. His bowels and bladder let loose, and the air, already oppressive with heat, took on the sour stench of urine and waste. Officers standing nearby called out.

"Ease off him, Ben. Jesus, ease off."

Ben's finger pulsed against the trigger of the gun as the hammer reached full extension. *A flag-draped coffin, a widow, and three children.*

From a thousand miles away, a familiar voice cut through the insane clutter that filled his head.

"Benjamin?"

He shook his head, dazed by his surroundings.

"Benjamin Sawyer? Did you hear what I said?"

Ben looked to the doorway and saw the familiar face of Bernice Erickson. He sat up and began to shuffle the case files on his desk.

"Hey, Bernie. How's it going?"

No one else ever called him Benjamin, and Ben was the one person on the department who could call the chief's secretary anything other than Mrs. Erickson. Ben had known Bernice Erickson since he was a boy hanging around the Norgaard household. Like Lars, Bernice had lost her spouse to cancer and was raising children alone. She and Lars had formed an early alliance in life and the police department. As Lars rose through the department ranks, Bernice worked as a civilian, filling a number of different administrative roles. When Lars was appointed chief of police, he selected Bernice Erickson as his private secretary. For now, Jorgensen had kept her on, even though she made it clear her loyalties were to Lars Norgaard. Ben figured he wasn't the only one the new chief would love to get rid of. Ben was pretty sure Bernice's days at the department were numbered.

"I said, aren't you supposed to be having coffee with Alex?"

When Ben only stared back, Bernice gave him the slightest roll of her eyes and said, "I spoke with Alex on the phone this morning. She said you two were getting together for coffee. She sounded like she was looking forward to it."

"Yes, ma'am. We were going to, but something came up."

Bernice was like a mother to Alex. They talked on the phone every day. Usually about Lars's progress, about Jake and school. Ben was pretty sure Alex also confided in Bernice about the ongoing issues in her marriage. He didn't blame her. Alex needed someone to talk to and he sure wasn't helping.

"That's too bad." The voice was more schoolmarm than motherly. "Perhaps you need to give some thought to your priorities, Benjamin. Remember, family comes first."

"You're right, Bernie." Ben knew better than to ever argue with the woman. "Family does come first."

Bernice gave him a concerned look. "Are you doing okay? How are things between you and the acting chief?"

Ben corrected her. "He's not the 'acting chief' anymore, Bernie. He's the new chief of police. We need to get used to that. And don't worry about me. I'm fine."

Bernice, a slender and graceful woman, was wearing a maroon dress that fell just below her knees. Her smooth, unblemished skin gave the impression of a woman ten years younger than her actual age of fifty-eight. Her gray hair was worn in a tight bun that might have looked severe on someone else, but on Bernice it fit the image of a dignified professional woman.

"Call him what you want, but if he makes things difficult for you, I want to know. He and I will have a talk."

"Thank you, Bernie, but I can handle Chief Jorgensen."

Bernice straightened her shoulders and turned to leave but not without a parting comment. "Call your wife, Benjamin. And make sure you get home on time for dinner."

Bernice walked away, and Ben stared at the empty doorway. He picked up the cell phone and saw that Alex had not left a message. He gave some thought to driving over to the coffeehouse. He could be there in five minutes. He'd be late, but maybe she was still there. It would mean a lot to her.

Or would it? Ben recalled McKenzie's comments about Alex hanging out with the guy who ran the place. *Have your little fun,* he thought. Ben rummaged through the pile and picked up a robbery case from his desk. As he read about the details of the crime, he did his best to block out any thoughts of dead cops and a lost career, a smart-ass detective, and a wife he loved but knew he was losing.

ELEVEN

A block from the coffeehouse, Alex's phone chimed: a text. She wasn't surprised to see that Ben was canceling on her again. Her husband wasn't the forgiving type. The aftereffects of their throw down still lingered, and most of the blame, she realized, fell on her. She'd said some pretty harsh things. She called him, thinking they could reschedule, but the call went straight to voice mail. She thought about leaving a message, but snapped the phone shut instead and once again settled for talking to herself.

"Shit, Ben. You have to at least try."

No matter, she thought. She'd go anyway. Approaching the store, she noticed a new sign over the door, an old-fashioned wooden shingle that read BOOKS AND JAVA. The scripted lettering was pleasing, as was seeing the name she'd suggested in the first place. Louis had given Alex credit for that almost every time she visited, and each time she stopped, he had made some sort of improvement.

Today was no exception, she found as she walked into the store. Shelving had been installed on all the walls—heavy black iron brackets that supported thick shelves cut from rough wood left unfin-ished. Unlike a traditional bookstore display that concentrated on economy of space, each shelf held just a few hardbound works. An interesting assortment of found objects were used as bookends, like the old steel fishing reel, nearly the size of the book itself, that held a leather-bound copy of *Moby-Dick* upright.

The plaster walls had been textured and painted a deep shade of khaki. The linoleum had been stripped from the floor, and the rough, unfinished cement felt good and solid under her feet. Where there were no shelves, the walls displayed artwork—Americana in style; Alex recognized pieces by several local artists. The recessed track lighting was subtle, and the rich aromas of coffee and tea filled the air. The positioning of the half-dozen tables conveyed a sense of privacy and invited people to linger over coffee and a good read. Several patrons were doing just that, each one drinking coffee and perusing a book.

"Hey, Alex." She turned at the greeting and saw Louis Carson step out of his small office.

"Hey, Louis. The place looks really great."

Louis was clearly pleased with her response but didn't say so di-rectly. "I live right upstairs. The easy commute lets me stay late. Yesterday, I pretty much worked the whole day." Louis looked around as he spoke and shrugged as if to say people could take it or leave it.

"It's amazing," Alex said. "I mean, I've been in some great coffee-houses in San Francisco and San Jose. I don't know that I've been anywhere with a better feel than this. I'm really impressed."

"You've been a big help. Lots of good suggestions. Seems like you've got a head for the business. Thanks again for the name idea. People seem to like it."

"No sweat. What's my cut of the take?"

"First there has to be a take, then I'll let you know what you're in for. Settle for a cup of coffee for now?"

"Sounds like you're going to give it to me again, Louis. Knock it off. You need to take people's money."

"You're such a purist. Darkest blend black?"

Alex looked at the dozen large jars of coffee beans arranged neatly on the counter. "Yeah, I really liked that last time. What do you call it again?"

"Heart of Darkness. I'll get it."

Alex took a seat near the window. Cool morning air mixed with the aromas of coffee, wood, and old books. Alex relaxed and felt at ease. Maybe Ben's not making it wouldn't be all that bad. *We all need our own space,* she thought.

Louis arrived with two steaming ceramic mugs. "If I ever get successful enough that I start running people in and out of here with Styrofoam cups, just kill me."

"Yeah. In a place like this that would be a disappointment. My husband was going to join me, but he's stuck at work."

"Then I guess you're stuck with me."

"Careful. I might just talk your ear off again."

"How's your dad?" Louis asked. "Did you see him yesterday like you planned?"

"Yeah, I got to spend an hour with him. He's doing all right. Still struggling with motor skills, speech, that sort of thing."

Alex paused to sip the hot coffee and tried to remember the last time Ben even asked about her father. "I'm enjoying the book. I've been reading it to him. He loved . . . I mean he *loves* Cather. He actually named me after Alexandra Bergson in *O Pioneers!* I think it's good therapy for him."

"The power of great literature, I guess," Louis said.

They talked for an hour, only occasionally interrupted by a customer coming in for coffee.

"I wish Ben could have made it today," Louis said at one point. "I was hoping that might get some of the local cops to start coming in. Maybe he could put in a good word for me? It'd be good for business to see cop cars out front."

"Yeah, that could work, I guess." Alex found herself saying more than she'd intended. "Then again, the picture at the PD isn't all that rosy right now. If you're thinking it's like one big happy family of heroic cops, that ain't happening."

"You mean it's not like TV?"

Alex smiled. "Not quite. A lot of cops were very loyal to my dad, but since his sudden retirement, there's been a real power shift. Now there's a new guy in charge, and from what Ben has told me, the new chief is not all that thrilled about the old boss's son-in-law hanging around watching his every move. Apparently nobody is. It's a pretty lousy work environment right now."

"How are you and Ben holding up?"

This wasn't the first time Louis had impressed Alex with his intuition. More than once he had keyed right in on the real issue, no matter what her words said on the surface.

"It's been tough, but we're hanging in there."

She was about to say more when a woman called out, "Excuse me. Does one of you work here or what?"

Several women in leotards and sweatshirts were standing at the counter. Alex blinked, wondering how she had missed their entrance. Looking at the group, she was suddenly self-conscious of her jeans, hoodie, and ball cap. Alex noticed they all had perfect makeup and manicures. *Forget the outfits—these chicks have no plans to work out.*

Louis looked at Alex with an apology in his eyes and touched her lightly on the shoulder. "Back in a minute, okay?"

He strode to the counter and quickly engaged the group, who all seemed to be around twenty-five. Alex listened as each woman ordered some foamy, sugar-laden concoction, clearly flirting with Louis the whole time. One of the group, Alex guessed she was somewhere around legal age, ordered a caramel triple-shot skinny something or other and practically undressed Louis with her eyes. Louis glanced at Alex and tried to smile an apology, but Alex couldn't deny she was put off by the noisy intrusion and equally pissed that he was obviously enjoying the women's attention.

When he turned away, Alex took the opportunity to leave. On the sidewalk she quickened her pace, fumbling for her keys. Unlocking the door of the eight-year-old family minivan, she tossed her purse inside, slid into the driver's seat, and slammed the door. She caught a look at herself in the rearview mirror, her face flushed, and abruptly realized that she was experiencing the sudden flood of an emotion she hadn't felt in a long time.

There was no denying what it was.

Jealousy.

TWELVE

Alex sat in the sunroom of Newberg Convalescent and read silently while her father dozed in his wheelchair nearby. The episode at the coffeehouse had thrown her off a bit until she reminded herself that when she and Ben were good, they were very good. *We'll get it back*, she thought. One way or another. She remembered Ben's comments about moving to Fresno. How maybe he would even go without her. She pushed the thoughts out of her head. *Ben would never leave me*, she told herself.

She rocked the porch swing back and forth with her stocking foot, comforted by the warmth of the sun and her father's long, steady breaths. She watched a pair of tundra swans break the glassy surface of the nearby pond as they glided in for a spectacular landing. Any sound made by the graceful couple was covered by the wind passing through the blooming branches of the hemlock and maple trees. *Welcome home*, she thought to herself. It looked as though spring had arrived in earnest, and in Wisconsin, that was everyone's favorite time of the year.

Newberg Convalescent was a first-rate medical rehabilitation center, and she and Ben had the debt to prove it. The family had adjusted to make the necessary sacrifices, but how much longer could they keep it up?

Alex looked at the man sleeping peacefully beside her. She knew Ben was right that substantial recovery seemed unlikely. In four months' time her father had gone from larger-than-life local hero to slobbering invalid tucked away and forgotten in an old folks' home.

"Wake up, Papa."

The old man stirred, and before he was fully awake, grunted in an attempt to speak. Alex knew her father was in there—his soul, his warrior spirit trapped inside a worn shell of thin skin and brittle bones. If he could speak, he would not hesitate to let Alex know her place was by his side.

"I have to go, Papa. Ben and Jake will be home soon."

The old man managed a scoff at the mention of her husband's name.

"Stop it, Papa. Ben is a good man and you know it. You need to remember he is my husband and Jake's father."

Alex knew the pain she saw in his eyes had begun with her sudden departure for California and extended absence. A pain that had deepened with a return that came only after public humiliation. To Lars, it was all Ben's fault, and when the old man assigned blame it wasn't something he was quick to take away. Especially when he felt the family had been dishonored.

"Ben loves me, Papa. And I love him. You need to understand how much he means to me and to Jake."

Another, less intense grunt and Lars looked away. His wordless method of saying he wanted to change the subject.

Lars Norgaard had always been a strong, prideful man. Robbed of his commanding voice, these days he rarely attempted to say anything. Alex assumed his grunting and slobbering humiliated him and that he preferred to suffer in silence. Sometimes she found him too proud for his own good.

"You stay out here. The sun is beautiful today. Enjoy the early spring. Shall I leave the book? Maybe one of the nurses can read to you later."

He shook his head vigorously, and Alex got his meaning. The newspaper was one thing, but books like these were family.

"Okay. I'll bring it tomorrow." Alex bent down close. "Say good-bye now, Papa."

He looked at her, his milky eyes filled with love, but made no effort to speak.

"Papa, I know you can do it. Promise me you'll do your exercises today. Practice your sounds, okay?" Still nothing but a determined expression Alex knew meant there were parts of his life he would still control.

"I love you and I know how much you love me. This weekend I want you to come to the house, okay? See Ben and Jake. We'd all like that."

Lars looked away. His visits outside the care home were rare and had to be carefully orchestrated. Alex knew her father resented the complexity of the arrangements. Wheelchairs, ramps, special foods. It was an endless list of indignities, and Alex was certain if Lars had the ability, he would end his life tonight and be done with it. In that way she was thankful for his physical limitations.

Alex kissed her father wistfully on the cheek, thinking again of the strength he once possessed. She lingered another moment before leaving him alone in the afternoon sunlight, trapped in the prison of a broken body and a mind cursed with memories of the man he used to be.

THIRTEEN

The muscle car caught six inches of air as it hauled into the lot crowded with black-and-whites. Half a dozen cops looked up at the sound of the downshifting engine, but their faces registered only mild annoyance. Everyone had grown familiar with the car and its driver's antics. McKenzie swung hard into an open spot, almost clipping a motorcycle cop, who made an abrupt fishtail stop to avoid the collision. The helmet head gave a blast of his siren and extended the middle finger of a leather-gloved hand.

McKenzie gave a dismissive wave. What some traffic cop might think of him didn't matter a damn bit. McKenzie tapped his jacket pocket. It was time for his regular meeting with the boss.

McKenzie strutted through the building and headed straight to the chief's office, a swagger in his step. He entered the executive suites and passed the desk of Bernice Erickson. When she picked up the phone as if she intended to inform the chief of his arrival, McKenzie waved her off.

"Don't bother, sweetie, he's expecting me."

Bernice scowled at the term but put the phone down and returned to her work. McKenzie smiled with the knowledge that only certain individuals enjoyed unfettered access to the standoffish new chief, and he was one of them. As was customary with the man, the door to Jorgensen's office was closed. McKenzie gave a light knock then went in, reclosing the door behind him.

Jorgensen was enjoying his rise to power with a fat Cuban Punch Corona. The chief motioned to a box of twenty-five on his desk. McKenzie made his selection, then rolled the cigar under his nose for a moment before leaning in and allowing Jorgensen to blaze him up. Lars Norgaard's long-standing enforcement of a smoke-free environment was gone; the two men sat in silence, enjoying the elite cigars.

Walter Jorgensen had been with Newberg PD as long as old man Norgaard himself. The two crusty old vets had come up through the ranks together, rivals of a sort. Where Lars Norgaard might bend a rule or two in order to catch a crook, McKenzie knew that Jorgensen was more about looking out for his own self-interest. That was why McKenzie had fallen in with Jorgensen at the start of his own career, recognizing it was Jorgensen that would get him what he wanted.

Over the years, there had even been rumor of some major confiscated dealer swag that had somehow disappeared off the department evidence logs. Jorgensen had never been in the middle of any inquiries, but you could always find him on the edges.

When Norgaard and Jorgensen competed for the job of chief of police and Norgaard won, it was assumed Jorgensen would follow the law enforcement tradition that ensured smooth operations and retire. Instead, Jorgensen not only remained, but Norgaard surprised everyone by naming Jorgensen his number two in a public gesture of conciliation.

Over time, an uneasy tension had developed between the two men. The day Norgaard stroked out, Jorgensen wasted no time in taking over department operations. Now, with his hands firmly on the department controls, Jorgensen and McKenzie had established what Jorgensen liked to call a "mutually beneficial arrangement." When Jorgensen finally spoke, the office was blue with smoke.

"Sawyer dropped by this morning. Gotta give him credit, the boy's got a sac. Struts right into *my* office with no more than a by-your-leave. Had some wild-ass idea about moving all you dicks around to new assignments. Your name came up. He's thinking you've been in the dope game long enough. He also tells me you pretty much went off on his ass in his office. Says you were insubordinate as hell. He figures on doing something about it. He seemed pretty fired up."

McKenzie felt gut punched. This was not what he had expected and he jumped to defend himself.

"Look, Chief, there's no need to—"

"Take it easy, Detective." Jorgensen raised his hand, then gave McKenzie a long, assessing look through the clouds. The chief took a hard pull on his Cuban, then went on. "I gave it some thought, but it seems to me you got a good handle on things. I told Sawyer to make whatever other changes he wanted, but I didn't see any reason to pull you off the narc detail. You're safe. For now. Far as any issues of improper conduct, consider yourself admonished."

Jorgensen paused to work the cigar, leaving the scent of wet leather in the air. McKenzie waited for the other shoe to drop. At some point it always did. Sure enough, Jorgensen wasn't done.

"Of course, you know I worked a bit of narcotics in my day. I've got a pretty good understanding of how a narc needs to be given a great deal of independence. Can't be tied down with a bunch of rules and regulations. You need to be able to motivate all those fine citizens who want to be sure that Newberg's contribution to the war on drugs is effectively waged . . . properly financed, if you know what I mean. How are things going in that area, Detective?"

McKenzie stared back, not surprised. Jorgensen never just came out with it. He always watched every word, but McKenzie understood. He pulled a thick envelope from his inside jacket pocket and tossed it onto the chief's desk.

"Just so happens some business-minded folks approached me today. Told me they wanted to make a contribution to the department's scholarship fund. You're still handling that program, right, Chief?"

Jorgensen didn't flinch, just stared back. He shifted in his Italian leather chair and propped his Bruno Magli shoes on the mahogany desk he had bought a month after taking over from Norgaard. For a large man—McKenzie figured him to be all of two eighty—Jorgensen carried himself with ease. He never wore the official blue uniform that Norgaard had been famous for, preferring conservative designer suits tailored for his large frame. Today he wore a starched white button-down shirt and a pin-striped charcoal gray vest; a SIG Sauer 9mm was neatly tucked against his body in a custom-made leather shoulder rig. His deep burgundy tie was finished with a perfect Windsor. Jorgensen picked up the envelope and took a look inside, nodding his massive bald head as he fingered through the cash. The envelope disappeared into a desk drawer.

"I'll see to it, Doyle. You be sure to extend the thanks of the department." Jorgensen gave McKenzie a sharp stare. "But this seems a little thin. You might want to shake that tree a little harder next time around."

McKenzie nodded in acknowledgment. Jorgensen had a real impact on the bottom line, but McKenzie told himself it was worth it. Now that he was finally out from under Norgaard's microscope, he could get down to some serious earning. Better yet, he could tell Sawyer to go fuck himself. Yep. Under the new administration, business was good.

Jorgensen sat up, his body language making it clear he was changing the subject. "We need to talk."

McKenzie picked up on the serious tone and immediately thought of the incident with Tyrone. Jorgensen couldn't know about that, could he? The guy had his finger on the pulse, for sure, but there was no way he could be up on that.

"Bill Petite's been hooked for murder up in Hayward. You know about the case?"

"Bill Petite? Name rings a bell, Chief, but I can't say as I can place it right offhand. Who is he?"

Jorgensen sounded less than pleased. "So you're telling me you haven't heard anything about it? I would think that as the department narcotics detective, you would stay up on major cases."

"Damn, Chief," McKenzie said, hating that he was already on the defensive, "Hayward is three hundred miles from here. Why would I know about the local stuff up there? I got plenty to work on right here in Newberg, you know what I mean?" He shot a look to the desk drawer, trying to remind Jorgensen of his primary concerns.

Jorgensen ignored him and began to lay things out. "Bill Petite served three terms as the district attorney of Florence County. He left the DA's office quite a few years back, relocated to Hayward, and went into private practice. Specialized in personal injury and medical malpractice. A real ambulance chaser. It's been seven or eight years. He made himself a fortune torturing doctors, cops, anyone with deep pockets."

At McKenzie's blank look of ignorance, Jorgensen appeared frustrated but went on. "Petite had a lady friend on the side. Couple of months ago, it got ugly. Seems he shot her in her own kitchen. Shot her dead." Jorgensen's tone changed as he looked hard at McKenzie. "At least that's how it would appear to the uninformed populace."

"You never know about a man, Chief. I don't suppose he did us all a favor and killed another lawyer, did he?" McKenzie tried to humor the man. "You know what it's called when one lawyer kills another lawyer?"

Jorgensen said nothing, just looked at McKenzie and waited.

"A good start." McKenzie laughed, pleased at his own stale joke. Jorgensen didn't even twitch a lip in laughter.

"You probably don't know about Lipinski either, is that right?"

McKenzie cocked his head. "Henry Lipinski? What about him?"

Oh, yeah. McKenzie knew Lipinski. The man was a law enforcement legend. Lipinski had spent more than thirty years as the elected sheriff of Florence County, along the Wisconsin-Michigan border, well known as an outdoorsman's paradise. The Nicolet National Forest covered over a million acres of unspoiled beauty, attracting tens of thousands of hunters, campers, and other visitors every year. Less famously but more important in the law enforcement world, the Nicolet Forest was also home to the most expansive and profitable marijuana crops in the entire Midwest. With fewer than five thousand permanent souls in the entire county, a grow could cover hundreds of acres and go undetected for a generation.

But nothing got past Sheriff Henry Lipinski. Rumor was no plant ever grew to be more than six inches tall without Lipinski's consent. Lipinski was said to have ruled over one of the largest marijuana empires in all of rural America. College students throughout Wisconsin, Minnesota, Michigan, and beyond had a greatly enhanced scholastic experience because of his organization and distribution skills. Lipinski eventually retired and laundered all his ill-gotten earnings through a used car dealership with outlets in sixteen counties. Word was he had walked away from all the shady stuff and gone legit. To McKenzie, Lipinski was a real law enforcement success story.

"He's sitting in Chippewa County lockup," Jorgensen said. "Got hooked up over the weekend for distribution of kiddie porn. Word has it the Feds are on the case. They'll be picking him up next week. He's looking at twenty-five years minimum."

"Shit," McKenzie said. "That'll be a hard row for a career cop. I sure as hell wouldn't want to carry that water. But I gotta tell ya, that guy always struck me as a bit of a pervert."

Jorgensen disagreed. "I don't see it. He's about as dense as a block of wood, but I can't figure Henry getting off on kids."

McKenzie shifted in his seat, his mind now turning. "Okay, boss. Two players from Florence hit the pit. You got my attention. What are you worried about?"

The look from Jorgensen was less than complimentary. "Jesus, Detective. Allow me to spell it out for you."

Jorgensen tossed a yellowed folder across the desk, a Newberg PD arrest report with a date that went back seventeen years. McKenzie recognized the neat block handwriting as that of his former chief, and sure enough Lars Norgaard's name appeared as the arresting officer. McKenzie looked at the subject block of the report. In bold, black ink the name jumped out: Harlan Lee.

Jorgensen offered an explanation.

"Harlan Lee killed a man back seventeen, eighteen years ago, some beef he had with a rival dope dealer. Lee had a big grow up in Florence. Cultivated a good bit of the ganja with his old man. I gotta admit the Lees grew some high-quality shit. But then again, the Lees had a habit of being a bit standoffish. Never did come under the protection of any sort of collective."

Jorgensen seemed lost in thought for a moment, then went on. "Anyway, the murder case was out of Florence, but Lee got arrested right here in Newberg. It was Norgaard who caught him with a stolen gun on a traffic stop. Turned out to be the murder weapon. Course, that led to a search warrant of the old homestead up in Florence. Everything fell into place after that. Lars was just a young buck at the time, but I gotta tell ya, he put together a hell of case. Lee was screwed and he knew it. He plead out and Petite hammered him with twenty-five to life."

McKenzie still couldn't put it together. He shrugged sheepishly, inviting Jorgensen to continue. The big man stood up and paced the office as he continued.

"Lee was released three months ago. I put in a call to my contact up in Florence County, Scott Jamison. He stepped in as sheriff when Lipinski went off to be a used car rock star. Jamison tells me Lee never reported for parole. He's not at the old homestead. It's still sitting empty like it has been since his old man kicked off about ten or twelve years ago."

"So what are you thinking?" McKenzie regretted the words as soon as they left his mouth, and the chief's booming voice rained down.

"I'll be goddamned, McKenzie. I thought you were a pretty sharp fella, but I'm starting to think you're just some special kind of stupid. One of them there idiot savants or some shit."

Jorgensen waited, allowing McKenzie to respond. When the detective sat quietly, the chief went on.

"Seems like the Lee boy might have gotten some wild hair up his ass. Didn't think much of having to pay for his crime. Seeing that there is a local connection, I want to be sure none of his bullshit rains down on Newberg. That sort of thing has a tendency to draw a lot of attention. No good for business. You hear what I'm saying?"

"I hear ya, boss."

"Get up to Chippewa. Have a talk with Lipinski before anyone else puts this together. See if he's been in contact with Lee. Remind his dumb bumpkin ass this is why you don't just get to walk away."

"You got it, Chief." McKenzie did his best to portray confidence. "Anything Henry knows about this Harlan Lee fella, I'll get it."

"Forget that." Jorgensen nearly shouted. He emphasized his words with the point of his cigar. "Don't be turning this into some kind of history lesson. Just find out if Henry has any *current* intel on Lee. If he has any reason to think Lee might be behind this shit. That's as far as you need to take it. Once you got what you can out of him, it would probably be best if Henry didn't talk to anyone else."

Jorgensen hesitated, then clarified his point.

"Ever."

The room went quiet.

"You get my meaning?" Jorgensen said after a long moment.

McKenzie thought over the exchange. His heart picked up its pace in his chest.

"Boss are you—?"

Jorgensen cut him off and returned to the protective curtain of his desk.

"I'm saying I don't want to worry about Henry Lipinski running his mouth. I don't want Henry getting some idea that he needs to go providing any details about this Harlan Lee situation to any swinging dick who comes calling. Especially some federal prick." Jorgensen held up the case file. "The Lee file is not to see the light of day, and it sure as hell ain't going to be a matter of discussion in a federal courtroom."

Jorgensen took another strong puff, then stared down his detective.

"You follow me?"

Yep, there was definitely a new chief in town. This was it. In or out. Jump in with both feet or get the hell off the ride. Easy call. The big time had come knocking.

"Like I said, Chief, I'm on it." McKenzie tried his best to sound matter-of-fact. Standard procedures. "I'll let you know how it goes."

Jorgensen narrowed his eyes. "No, you won't. I can read a newspaper."

McKenzie recognized the chief's habit of keeping his distance.

"Use those instincts of yours, Doyle. Take care of this shit and keep it out of Newberg. Keep it away from me. Now, if you'll excuse me, I got other things to attend to."

McKenzie stood to leave, realizing he'd been dismissed. He also realized he had underestimated Jorgensen, but that would not happen again. For the first time in their dealings he felt a trace of fear.

It was as though Jorgensen sensed it and decided to show McKenzie that his newfound respect was well placed.

"By the way," Jorgensen said, settling back into his overstuffed chair, "I got a call from an old colleague from the State Police. He mentioned your name. Said you two worked a few special details over the years."

McKenzie waited.

"Anyway, he called to tell me about a local boy they found dumped outside Beloit. Eldon something or other. Two forty-cal slugs in his chest. Wasn't no ghetto ammo either. Some of that really high-performing shit that can turn a man's insides to Jell-O. An alarming situation, no doubt. Probably dope related. I told my contact to keep me up on any developments in the case. Being that you are the department narc, I thought you'd want to know."

McKenzie knew if he'd ever had the upper hand when it came to Jorgensen—and right now, he wasn't sure he had—he had definitely lost it.

"Sure thing, Chief. Thanks for the heads-up."

"Oh, and one last thing, Doyle. I'd like to expand the kids' soccer league this year but fees are way up. See if you can get a few donations put together for me. I think twenty grand oughta get us off the ground."

McKenzie quailed at the thought. This was going to cut into his own take. "Twenty grand, huh? That's a hell of soccer program, Chief."

Jorgensen sat back, wrapped his thick lips around his glowing cigar, and puffed out a long string of perfect blue rings. "Only the best for the people of Newberg, Doyle. Only the best."

FOURTEEN

Harlan rested a solid arm against the aged oak growing along the boulevard and took in the scene just a few houses down the street. *Yep. This is it.*

The first address he'd come up with had been an empty house. A few questions to neighbors—posed as if he was an old family friend—had led him to a live-in hospital for old folks with all sorts of ailments. It had the look of a top-shelf sort of facility although security was nonexistent. Finding the exact room had been as simple as walking in and reading the directory posted in the lobby. Once he had the old man pegged, he spent a few days in surveillance mode. Harlan had watched the blond dish sit for hours reading aloud and talking to the old guy, though it didn't appear to Harlan she ever got much of an answer back.

Today Harlan had watched as the woman and a couple of orderlies bundled the old man into her minivan. Harlan followed them across town to a Victorian house on a manicured street of stylish homes. A man and a boy threw the football across the lawn; the same pretty little thing he'd seen all week hung back and watched, her arms draped over the old man's shoulders. The years had left a hard mark on the man, but the resemblance was still clear. "So what the hell happened to you?" Harlan spoke in a low voice. "Stuck in a wheelchair. Drooling all over your damn self?"

The woman continued to dote on the old man just as she had at the care joint. At first Harlan thought maybe she was one of those kindhearted volunteer types, but no. That wasn't it. Even from this distance Harlan could see the affection in the old man's eyes. Those two were flesh and blood.

"Officer Lars Norgaard, in the flesh," Harlan mused out loud, "looks like you went and got yourself all fucked up and crippled somehow, didn't ya? Little justice came early."

His initial disappointment at the old man's condition was short-lived. Harlan thought back to the last bitter years endured by his own father. Alone and abandoned, in failing health, with his only kin locked away. Standing under the tree watching the family scene, Harlan wondered why he hadn't seen it before. Course he hadn't known the details, but now it all came clear. With a few minor deviations, with some careful planning, he would strike a most meaningful blow.

"Looks like we got us a chance for some true symmetry."

As he stood there with his new plan beginning to fall into place, Harlan noticed the stalwart figure giving him the once-over from his place on the lawn. With the ball in one hand, Norgaard's son-in-law began a slow walk to the curb that drew Harlan's attention. *Time to get gone.*

Fifty yards down the road, Harlan allowed himself a last look over his shoulder and saw the man was still watching. Harlan turned away and kept walking, deciding to himself that he'd be sure to give this guy a wide berth.

FIFTEEN

Standing behind her dad, Alex thought it was shaping up to be a good afternoon. With Lars visiting for the day, Alex and Ben had done their best to bury the hatchet and put on the happy family act. Jake could never resist an offer to throw the ball around. Alex hoped she and Ben could use the time together as a chance to sort of regroup.

"Throw the ball, Dad." Alex watched as Jake took off and ran another down-and-out pattern. The boy turned for the pass, but his father paid him no mind. Ben was staring down the road.

Alex walked up and playfully swatted the ball from Ben's hand. He ignored her, continuing his long stare. Alex followed Ben's gaze into the distance where a man walked away from them along the sidewalk.

"What's up? You playing or not?"

"Did you see that guy? Looked like he was watching us or something."

Alex was used to Ben's hypervigilant cop instincts. After all those years in Oakland, Ben could see a bogeyman around every corner. It didn't matter if they were in a restaurant, a movie theater, or even church. Ben was always suspicious of what to anyone else seemed like a part of everyday life. It made sense in the big-city world of Oakland, but this was Newberg.

"He's gone now. Come on back and play." She pulled on his arm, but Ben stayed put. The stranger, far off now, turned and gave a last look.

"I'm telling you, that guy was checking us out. I got half a mind to go ask him what the hell he wants."

Jake tried again to get his father's attention. "*Dad*. Throw me the ball."

Alex hooked one leg around her husband's and hugged his waist from behind. "Tell you what. Let's write this one off as a nothin' burger. If we see him around again, we'll get all of Newberg PD on him. Run his ass out of town." She kissed him lightly on the cheek. "Forget about him, Benny. This is nice. Jake and Dad are having a great time. Let's just enjoy it."

Ben couldn't let it go. Alex could only watch as Ben continued to stare and took another three steps toward curb.

Jake finally lost his patience. "Dad, would you just throw the damn ball?"

Ben and Alex stared at each other, then swiveled their heads to look at Jake.

"Uh . . . sorry?" The boy went scarlet and waited for the punishment he knew must be coming.

Ben was about to speak, when coarse laughter came from nearby. Alex, Ben, and Jake turned to Lars, who had a broad grin on his face. The old man's eyes were sparkling. After a beat, Ben dropped back and signaled to his son to go deep.

"Okay, Jake. Go down fifteen yards, then cut right, and I'll throw you the *damn ball*."

Ben looked at Alex and smiled. She thought she saw a spark in his eye that took her back to younger days, less complicated times. She watched as her husband reared back and threw a perfect spiral that Jake caught in stride. Within a few minutes any ill wind that had been stirring melted away and was forgotten.

SIXTEEN

B en sat in a stiff-backed chair outside the office of the Newberg PD chief, determined to gut it out. It had been thirty minutes since he had asked to see Chief Jorgensen and, if need be, he'd wait all afternoon. His new place in the department pecking order was right around the level of whale shit, but he told himself that just meant he could sit right there and put out a serious stench.

It had been right in this room that Lars Norgaard had been recognized as Newberg's Officer of the Year almost twenty years ago. Ben remembered standing beside Alex during the ceremony. It was their sophomore year at Newberg High. They were crazy in love and already dreaming of a future with each other. Lars had introduced Ben to the mayor and chief of police, bragging that someday Ben would join the ranks of Newberg PD. Well, Ben thought, the old man was right. Just took a few years longer than expected.

"This is just ridiculous." Bernice was on her feet in a huff and headed for the chief's closed office door.

"Hang on, Bernie. I can handle this," Ben said with a wave that stopped her at her desk. "I'll announce myself."

"I must say, Benjamin. You need to stand up for yourself."

She's right, Ben thought. You've got an out-of-control detective and a chief holed away in his office. Get on top of it, Sawyer.

He stood and gave a light knock on the chief's door, then pushed it open.

"Excuse me, Chief, I've been out here for a while. I just need a couple of minutes."

Thirty seconds and Jorgensen didn't bother to look up. Ben rested his shoulder against the office doorjamb, projecting an air of *I can wait all day.* When it became clear that Ben wouldn't leave, Jorgensen exhaled in exasperation and spoke.

"What do you want, Sawyer?"

Ben walked into the office, still uninvited, and took a seat in front of the chief's massive desk. "I want to revisit the idea of a transfer for Detective McKenzie. I think we'd be better off with some new blood in Narcotics."

Jorgensen reached forward and opened the glass-topped humidor on the corner of his desk. He pulled out a fat one out and snapped the lid shut, making it clear that he wasn't in the mood to share. The big man took a V-cutter from his vest pocket and, with a quick flick of his wrist, expertly removed the end of the cigar. A silver lighter came from another pocket and he lit up. After several puffs, he had the cigar stoked to a full smoke. He took it from his mouth and spit a flake of tobacco off his tongue.

"We've been over this, Sawyer. McKenzie has the contacts, he has the experience. He is the department expert. I don't know what you and Lars had cooked up, but under my administration McKenzie will be the narc for NPD. Now if that's all you wanted, we're done. Get out."

"I'm surprised you want to involve yourself in the day-to-day operations, Chief. I thought that's what I was brought on to do."

"I had nothing to do with bringing you on, Sawyer. I think it's been pretty much established how you got here."

Ben ignored the jab and returned to the subject of McKenzie.

"I know McKenzie's type, Chief. He talks a good game, he may even put together a major case once in a while. But he's cutting corners, and from what I can tell he might be even be cookin' the books a bit. He needs to be given an assignment where he can be more closely supervised."

"That's a powerful accusation," Jorgensen said. "Particularly coming from you. You really think you're in a position to accuse another cop of misbehaving?"

"Chief, if you've got something to say, then fire away. Let's get it out in the open."

Jorgensen got up and walked around his desk, and his large frame towered over Ben. "I've got a lot to say, Sawyer. I've got a sergeant in my department who was shitcanned for abusive force and then has the balls to waltz in here and attack the character of a veteran detective. The only reason you're here is that your father-in-law felt sorry for your dumb ass. Believe me, Lars and I had that argument more than once. I lost."

Jorgensen paused, but when Ben offered no comeback, he went on. "If I had my way, you'd be gone already, but it's out of my hands. You might not be the chief's boy anymore, but you're still a union-protected cop. But know this. You're damn right I'll be ass-deep in day-to-day ops, and if you don't like it, you can walk. And if you can't work with McKenzie in Narcotics, then you can go back to graveyard patrol. Is all that clear to you, Sergeant?"

Ben reached into his inside jacket pocket. He pulled out a tri-folded piece of paper and laid it on the corner of Jorgensen's desk.

"This is my official recommendation that McKenzie be transferred out of his current assignment. I've provided ample written documentation as to why. You're free to ignore it, but there may come a time you regret that decision."

Without ever breaking eye contact, Jorgensen picked up the paper, crumpled it into a ball, and tossed it into the nearby trash can. Ben smiled.

"I kept a copy, Chief. I'll note the time and date of delivery."

At the door, Ben stopped and looked back at the chief of police.

"By the way. McKenzie didn't show up today and he's not answering his department cell. You wouldn't happen to know where he is, would you?"

"How would I know? You expect me to keep tabs on him?"

Ben sauntered toward the door, talking over his shoulder as he left. "I heard there was an opening for Chief's Boy. Word has it McKenzie got the job."

SEVENTEEN

McKenzie sat in the jailhouse hallway and tapped his open hand against the slender flask that hung heavy inside his coat pocket. He resisted the temptation to pull it out for a quick fix of bourbon, a little something to steady his nerves. It wasn't fear. Hell, no. More like anticipation. The energy of the assignment. If anything, he needed to quell the rush he was feeling from the opportunity Jorgensen had laid out.

The two-hundred-sixty-mile drive to the Chippewa County Jail had given McKenzie plenty of time to think things over. A few months back he had been taxing petty dope dealers for chump change. Then old man Norgaard went down and Jorgensen stepped in. All restrictions had been lifted. McKenzie could do the math. Pretty soon he'd be closing in on six figures a month. And there's no doubt, he told himself, Jorgensen's got interests way beyond Newberg. Big interests. Profitable interests. If McKenzie could navigate this shit storm, whatever it entailed, and bring Jorgensen out unscathed on the other end, the chief might start to see him as partner material.

One thing was clear: Something about this Harlan Lee worried the new chief. Left him exposed. That knowledge could give Mc-Kenzie an advantage. Not now, but someday. The task at hand was to get as much out of Lipinski as possible. Find out what had Jorgensen concerned about Harlan Lee. Then make sure no one else got a damn thing out of Henry Lipinski.

"Yo, Doyle." The deputy poked his head out of an open doorway. "Down here, man."

McKenzie rose from the bench and looked up and down the long corridor. His boot heels echoed on the hard floor as he strode along. He shook the deputy's extended hand and spoke in a low tone.

"We good, Billy? This shit has got to happen today." McKenzie put the thick wad of hundred-dollar bills into the deputy's outstretched hand. "There's half now. The other half after the job is done."

The deputy looked at the money. McKenzie picked up on the man's hesitation.

"Believe me, Billy," Doyle said, "this is gonna be good for both of us. I'm talking long-term good, brother."

The money disappeared into a pants pocket and the deputy in the tan and green looked down the hallway one last time before shutting the door to the anteroom where he and McKenzie stood.

"Listen, Doyle. I don't give two shits about some ex-cop who's got a thing for kiddie porn, but this is going to raise a lot of eyebrows. They got this guy hooked up on a dozen federal charges. The FBI is coming in on Monday and probably transferring him to federal lockup in Saint Paul. Not to mention he's got one prick of a lawyer. You sure you can handle the fallout on this?"

Doyle tapped the man, who appeared to be about ten years his junior, lightly on the chest with an open hand.

"We'll be all right, you'll see. I just need a few minutes with him. Then it's on you."

McKenzie paused for effect and was pleased to see the man swallow hard. McKenzie knew he had his attention.

"I told you when you came on that we'd be getting into some high-stakes poker. Don't go folding on me now, you hear?"

"We got forty-five minutes before the next shift shows up," the deputy said. "If you want to be sure this gets done right, you can have five of it. The lieutenant could stroll through here anytime, so get at it."

The officer opened another door and motioned McKenzie through. In the next room, Henry Lipinski sat at a table, dressed in orange, his hands cuffed to the front. A guard hovered nearby.

McKenzie hadn't seen Lipinski in a while. When he'd first hired on at Newberg, Lipinski had been in his second term as Florence County sheriff. Now he was just a frumpy old man, white hair going in a hundred directions and three days of gray stubble on his bloated chin. His lips were too red and his skin too pale. Guilty or not, McKenzie thought, the son of a bitch sure looks the part of a child molester.

Lipinski's eyes fell on McKenzie, and he half stood in shock. The guard pushed on his shoulder, keeping him in the chair.

"Hey, Henry," McKenzie said, enjoying the moment of surprise and superiority. "It's been a lot of years."

"Doyle McKenzie? What the hell are you doing here? You got something to do with this bullshit?" The old man's voice rose. "You running a con on my ass? Because if you are, you better know I can still reach out and make bad things happen. Very bad things, Doyle."

McKenzie ignored the threat and look toward the guard. "Give us a few minutes in private, will ya, deputy?"

When the man hesitated, McKenzie went on. "Don't worry. Henry and I go way back. We'll be fine. Ain't that right, Henry?"

Lipinski remained silent. McKenzie winked at the guard. "We'll be fine. Really."

The guard left the room, and when they were alone, McKenzie turned his attention to Lipinski.

"Damn, Henry." McKenzie kept his voice low. "You need to calm down. I'm here to help. Walter Jorgensen sends his regards."

At the mention of the chief's name, Lipinski's attitude abruptly changed.

"Jorgensen? Walter sent you? Look, whatever he thinks, I'm telling you, I'm out of the game. I sell junk-ass cars to shit-kicker farmers. I got nothing going on that would concern Walter Jorgensen."

McKenzie sat in the chair on his side of the table, the disheveled heap before him.

"Henry, Walter wants to help. He sent me to try to get to the bottom of this. Hell, man. He knows you ain't no pedophile."

Lipinski's chin quivered and his eyes began to swim.

"You gotta believe me, Doyle, I got no clue how any of that shit got on my computer. Jesus. They say they got pictures of kids doing all kinds of nasty stuff; they got records of files going all over the country. Hell, man. I can't hardly send a damn e-mail. I got an entire geek squad that handles all that shit."

McKenzie looked at his watch. Time was running out. He didn't need Lipinski carrying on about his innocence.

"Listen, Henry, Walter wanted me to tell you something. An old associate of yours, Harlan Lee, was released a few weeks back. He got out and fell right off the planet. No one's seen hide nor hair of him."

Lipinski's face went from pale to ghost white. McKenzie thought the man was going to throw up.

After several seconds, he spoke, the words coming slow. "Jesus. Lee is out? Why didn't I get a call, for Christ sake? Seems to me that one of you active-duty sons of bitches oughta have been on top of this."

McKenzie lit a cigarette and offered one to Lipinski, who took it eagerly with a shaking hand. McKenzie pulled on the flask but kept it to himself even when Lipinski's mouth seemed to water at the sight. The old man settled for a deep drag off a non-filtered smoke, while McKenzie answered the hanging question.

"You didn't get a call, Henry, because, what did you just say? You're 'out of the game'? You walked off and no one minded the store," McKenzie said. "Now he's out."

Lipinski's voice took on a tone of desperation. "It's him, Doyle. This is Lee."

"That's what Walter sent me to find out," McKenzie lied. He wanted to see what he could get out of Lipinski that might be of use to him.

"All I know is that hayseed little bastard pled guilty. He got twenty-five to life. Shit, they could've kept him another ten years." Lipinski said. "I swear, the pussy liberals are ruining this state."

"You have any contact with him after he got locked up?" McKenzie asked.

"Not with him, but I kept his old man under my thumb. Old Jed never made another dime after that day that I know of. Lived like a goddamn pauper in that old shack of his until he died, ten or twelve years ago. That was the whole idea. Take him out of the game."

"So you're telling me . . ." McKenzie stopped and corrected himself. "Or more important, you're telling Walter Jorgensen you're straight-up innocent of all this kiddie-porn shit? You're saying someone put the hex on your ass?"

"Hell, yeah. I told you. I got no interest in any of that perverted shit, financial or otherwise. I'm a car salesman. That's it. This shit has got Harlan Lee written all over it."

"Tell me this, Henry." McKenzie spoke slowly. "How much did Lee figure out about the Newberg connections? I mean, you handled the case and all that shit up in Florence. How much came out at trial?"

"There wasn't a trial. Just the preliminary hearing, and it went right by the numbers. Not even a ripple in the water. That pencil-neck district attorney . . . uh . . . Petite, that was it. With the gun arrest coming out of Newberg, the case was rock solid and he didn't bat an eye. Just like we thought. Walter put that straitlaced Boy Scout on it. You know? What was his name?"

McKenzie remembered the arrest report. "Norgaard."

"Yeah. That was it. Petite put Norgaard on the stand at the pre-lim, and he stuck it to Harlan. Kid had no choice but to plead. After that we all moved on."

McKenzie didn't care about Petite and Norgaard.

"So what about Jorgensen? Is he gonna be on Harlan's hit list?"

"Shit, Doyle. Haven't you learned anything? Jorgy knew better than to put his name on any shit like this." Lipinski's voice took on a tone of stubborn admiration. "Jorgy always was good at keeping his hands clean."

McKenzie saw no reason to give Henry any more background. Shit, the old sheriff might have a coronary right on the spot if he found out Petite was locked up three counties to the north.

Lipinski suddenly grabbed McKenzie by the hand. His cuffed wrists scraped across the wooden table. The lit cigarette spilled ash.

"Doyle, this is Lee. It's gotta be. You guys need to get me outta here. We can hunt his ass down. I still got plenty of muscle on the street. Hell, tell Walter if he'll get me clear of this shit, I'll take care of Lee myself. I know the boy. Eventually he's going back to the homestead. Nobody knows that forest like I do."

McKenzie had what he needed, and Lipinski's desperation told him it was time to play the hole card. High-stakes poker. Time to step up.

"I got no issues with that, Henry. Really, I don't." The hesitation in his voice came through just as intended. "But it's really not up to me. You know that."

Lipinski's face lit up with hope, his fish lips going strong.

"Listen, Doyle. I got over a million in inventory on my lots right now. One phone call and I can have a hundred grand. You want cash? Gold? You tell me. It's done. I just gotta know you got my back on this. That you'll get to Walter and tell him I'm good. Help figure a way to work me out of this shit, eh, Doyle?"

"Make a phone call, Henry?" McKenzie took a quick look over his shoulder to make sure they were still alone. He pulled his cell phone from his jacket. "That's all you need to do?"

Lipinski tossed the smoke on the cement floor and snatched McKenzie's phone with both hands. The cuffs made him clumsy, but he pushed the buttons with shaking fingers. The conversation took less than two minutes and sounded to McKenzie like a load of money was definitely getting moved around. When Lipinski got off the phone, he was direct and to the point.

"There'll be a hundred large, cash, in room eight at the Chippewa Falls Motor Inn in an hour. A black case in the back of the closet. The key will be under the mat. Don't take too long getting there. We good? You'll talk to Walter for me?"

"Yeah, Henry. I'll be sure to give Chief Jorgensen a full report."

McKenzie stood and gave a sharp rap on the locked door. A moment later the door opened and the two guards came in, looking grim. McKenzie nodded his head at the deputy from the earlier hallway conversation.

"These fellas are going to take you back to your cell now, Henry."

Lipinski looked at the guards leering back at him. He seemed to clue in on what had been finality in McKenzie's voice.

"Son of a bitch. Come on, McKenzie," Lipinski pleaded. "I ain't going to talk to nobody. Hell, what would I say that wouldn't make me sound like a crazy-ass cop trying to beat a porn rap?"

"It ain't nothing personal, Henry. I always enjoyed our dealings."

Lipinski stood up, his large frame quaking like a three-hundred-pound bowl of orange Jell-O. "Let me call my family. My kids. Just give me a few minutes on the phone."

McKenzie thought about the money that was probably already on its way to the motel room. His money. He wasn't going to risk Lipinski making any more phone calls.

McKenzie looked at the guard. "No calls, Billy. Straight back to his cell."

Lipinski walked toward the guards, then turned back to McKenzie. When he spoke, it was without fear or submission.

"You should know, McKenzie, you've always been seen as nothing more than a kiss-ass punk. Hell, when you first came on and were trying to get in with Jorgy, man, he used to love to talk about you. He said he could probably whore you out on a street corner to the boys in Milwaukee and you'd take a dick right up the ass if it meant a buck in your pocket and an 'atta boy' thrown your way."

McKenzie puffed on his cigarette and was ashamed to see that his hand trembled. He knew that everyone in the room picked up on it. Lipinski, a man who knew he was down to his last minutes on earth, managed a smile.

"Enjoy your time in the sun, Doyle. Something tells me it's gonna be a short run."

An hour later McKenzie was on the road to Newberg, a hundred thousand to the good. He enjoyed a long taste off his flask, Merle Haggard blaring. In the dying light of the day, he cruised along at eighty-five miles per hour, putting distance between himself and the words of Henry Lipinski. A jerk-off has-been who even now probably dangled from the end of a bedsheet.

McKenzie knew it was true. Men like Walter Jorgensen had never taken him seriously. Kept him begging for what amounted to table scraps. The legit types like Norgaard and Sawyer looked down their nose at him as if he were some small-time chump crook. No trust or respect from either side.

McKenzie ran his hand over the black briefcase in the passenger seat. His play on Lipinski had taken some brass balls, and now things were really looking up. Jorgensen couldn't possibly get wind of this take. There'd be no split.

McKenzie shouted out in the car. "Who's the punk now, Henry?"

This was McKenzie's chance. He'd get ahead of this Lee character. He'd get an edge on Jorgensen and rewrite their business arrangement. And the Norgaards and Sawyers of the world?

McKenzie mashed the accelerator, and the needle jumped to ninety-five. Fuck 'em. They could think what they want. They didn't have anything he needed anyway.

EIGHTEEN

Right on time, Harlan thought. *Bitch, you're gonna make this too easy.*

Harlan sat on the bus bench and watched the Sawyer woman arrive at the coffeehouse. Every morning this week she had shown up around this same time and stayed at least an hour. Sometimes longer. Yesterday she had even gone upstairs to what Harlan figured must be the man's apartment. It had been twenty minutes before the two of them came back down and the woman hurried off to her car.

Got yourself a little fuck buddy, hey, boy? Not sure how much her old man would approve. Either one of 'em.

He had to give the fella credit. The woman—now he knew her name was Alex—was worth the risk. Blond, Nordic, and built for pleasure the way Harlan saw it. She was the Midwestern dream girl. He'd love to have at it himself, but Harlan knew that wasn't in the cards. This was all business. He sat on the bench and lit a Pall Mall and gave some thought to recent events. The Sawyer woman brought a whole different opportunity for a particular flavor of revenge.

Harlan could see why people would assume such an occurrence must somehow be borne of divine providence. It was nearly too good to be consider coincidence.

He watched through the glass as Alex and Louis sat and talked together near the window. Louis was big in the shoulders and had some guns for biceps. Harlan didn't doubt for a second he could kick the boy's ass in a no-rules knife fight, but they'd definitely make a ruckus and that wouldn't do. Harlan began to lay plans for the coming confrontation.

Before too long another familiar figure came into view.

Harlan thought back on the family scene in the front yard and spoke out loud. "If it ain't Mr. Neighborhood Watch."

NINETEEN

H ey, Louis, how's it going?" Alex walked into the store with comfortable familiarity and was immediately pleased with what she found. She had come by Books and Java every morning for a week, and today was the first time the store had been free of customers. Most days Louis stayed busy making specialty drinks or talking books with patrons. Business was definitely picking up. Part of her was happy for Louis, most of her, even, but she couldn't deny there was some sense of reward that today she would get a few minutes of having Louis all to herself. The fact Ben still hadn't come down to meet her for a cup of coffee and a little small talk was becoming less of an issue. He was supposed to drop by today, but Alex fully expected him to call and cancel or just not show up at all.

"Morning." Louis's face lit up. "Thanks for the help yesterday. I don't think I was meant to live in the computer age. Believe it or not, in my previous life I had people who took care of that sort of thing for me."

"You're right. Between this passion you have for old books and your lack of computer skills, it's like you weren't meant for this century. You're more of a nineteenth-century man, I think." Alex walked up close enough to playfully pat Louis on the arm. "It's called a defrag. Pretty simple, really. But now that I've seen your place, I'm going to insist you come over to the house and get some home cooking. What you call a kitchen is kind of scary."

"I wouldn't argue with you about that." Louis walked away and disappeared into the office, then came out holding a small package. "Here. This is for you."

Her heartbeat jumped with genuine surprise. "What's this?"

Louis sounded both pleased and anxious. "Open it and you'll see."

Curious, Alex pulled at the edges of the deep red paper, exposing the dust jacket of a hardcover book. The scent of aged paper and print wafted up, and Alex inhaled deeply, savoring the smell. The cover image was of a woman standing on a grassy prairie, one hand to her brow and the other on her hip. The title *O Pioneers!* was bold across the top and the name Willa Cather ran along the bottom. Alex's fingers trembled as she opened the book. She looked closely at the print on the opening page, stunned.

"Oh, my God. An original printing? Where did you find it?"

"Boxed up at an estate sale." Louis's voice was charged with excitement. "Along with about three hundred other books that I don't think anyone has touched in fifty years."

Alex opened the book and stared in silence at the clear black print. She remembered the old family reading room. Thoughts of sitting in her father's lap. The fireplace snapping and popping, the smell of burning hickory in the air. A woman seated nearby knitting quietly and smiling. Classical music playing softly on an old-style record player. Her father's rich voice reading the words; her mother looking on. Unconsciously, Alex began to speak out loud, "Mom was still alive the first time I heard this story. I couldn't have been more than three years old . . ."

Alex pulled away from the memory and looked up at Louis, who was now looking down over her shoulder. He was close enough that she could feel his breath on her cheek. Flustered, she turned to him and took one step back. She studied his face. "You're telling me you found a 1913 first-edition Willa Cather at a garage sale?"

Louis laughed. "Not a garage sale, an estate sale. I bought a bunch of boxes, sight unseen, for a hundred bucks. Last night I started going through them. When I saw this . . . it was an amazing feeling. Like those people you hear about who discover a lost Rembrandt under a painting of dogs playing poker. Can you believe it?"

Alex didn't understand. How could *Louis* make her feel this way? It was just a simple, thoughtful gift. How could it be that she suddenly felt this connected to someone? *Why,* she wondered, *do I feel this with him? Why him?*

Alex closed the book and held it out to Louis. Her voice was matter-of-fact. "Thank you, but I can't accept this."

Louis looked dumbfounded. "What are you talking about? You have to take it." He paused, then went on speaking more earnestly. "I was meant to find this book for you, Alex. You told me your father took your name from this book. There's no coincidence here."

Alex knew Louis was missing the point, but she wasn't about to try and explain it to him. It wasn't the book or even its value that concerned her. Not at all. Her fear was knowing that every time she held the book, every time she opened the pages, she would remember this moment. This moment when he got close enough it was like he had stepped inside her skin. Alex knew that the feeling inside her needed to be tucked away and forgotten. She couldn't go through life reliving it over and over.

"Louis, you can't just give away something like this," Alex tried to laugh but came closer to crying. "You're supposed to be *selling* books."

Louis took hold of Alex by her wrists and pushed the book until his hands were inches from her breasts. Her breath got caught in her throat and she wondered, *Is he going to come closer? Is he going to kiss me? Please don't. Please.*

The look in his eyes reassured her that he would never do that to her. He would never make her choose. The tone of his voice conveyed a sense of trust she had rarely experienced. "Either you take it or I'll return it. I won't keep it and I am certainly not going to sell it. This book was meant for you."

Alex's eyes brimmed with tears. In an instant her heart turned and the closeness she felt to Louis was no longer a threat. It *was* a gift. That was all he wanted to offer her. He was her friend and he always would be. "I don't know what to say. This is an amazing gift."

His hands went to her shoulders for just a moment, then dropped away and he smiled, taking a step back. He jammed both of his hands in the pockets of his jeans and shrugged his shoulders. "Exactly. It's a gift. Now just take it and be happy, for goodness sake."

"I guess I'm a little early, huh?"

At first Alex remained stuck in the moment, then she turned to see Ben standing in the doorway, his face drawn into a scowl. Not directed at her. Alex's feet felt stuck to the floor, and it seemed like it took forever before she went to greet her husband. She kissed him on the cheek and felt his body go stiff.

"Hey," she said uneasily, responding to his tension. "Wow. You made it."

"Sure did." Ben's eyes stayed on Louis.

Alex began to recover. "Good. Come in. I want you to meet Louis."

Louis stepped forward. "Hey, Ben. Nice to finally meet you." He stuck his hand out and Ben just looked at it for several seconds before grasping it. Their handshake was brusque and awkward. Alex thought she saw Louis flinch and wondered how hard Ben was gripping his hand.

She intervened. "Look at this, Ben. Louis found it at a garage—I mean an estate sale. This is the book I've told you about. The one my dad loved. Remember?"

Ben, still staring at Louis, said, "Not really."

Alex looked at her husband and wordlessly communicated in a way reserved for long-married couples. *Knock it off and I'll explain everything later.*

An uncomfortable silence fell. Louis broke it, speaking in a voice slightly higher pitched than usual.

"Let me get you guys some coffee. The usual for you, Alex, and what can I get for you, Ben?"

"My *usual* would be black coffee."

Louis headed for the counter and the coffee machines. Alex pulled Ben to a table and tried to smooth over their rough start. "Isn't this place great? I'm glad you could finally get here."

"You sure? Because it felt like I walked in on something." Ben's tone was challenging and Alex was thrown off.

"What are you talking about?"

Ben ignored her question and came at her from another direction. "How much do you have to hang around here to have a usual?"

"Ben, stop." She reached out to him. "He gave me a gift because I fixed his computer yesterday. That's all."

"What computer?" Ben glanced around the small store, clearly looking for a computer and not seeing one.

"In his apartment upstairs," Alex said, without thinking of how her husband might react. She was startled when color rose in his cheeks.

"What the hell," he said angrily. "You've been to his—"

Louis returned, excited to be showing his business off to a new customer. "Here you go. Ben, I brought you a biscotto. It's made with organic almonds. Let me know what you think."

Alex laughed. "I can tell you already. Ben thinks biscotto is Italian for dog biscuit."

"In that case, don't tell me."

Ben spoke flatly, looking at his wife. "Make mine to go. I need to get back to the office."

"Uh, sure," Louis said in an uncertain tone; Alex realized he had clued in on the tension between her and Ben. "Just give me a second."

Alex waited until Louis was out of earshot before pleading with Ben. "What are you doing? Sit with me for five minutes. Please."

"Not now." Ben's voice was tense. "You stay, though. This is your thing, not mine. By the way, I might be late for dinner. You and Jake should plan on eating without me."

She reached across the table, trying to touch his hand, but Ben stood up as Louis returned. Alex pulled her hand back into her lap.

"Here you go, Ben. It was nice to meet you," Louis said, trying to save the moment. "Come back when you can stay a while."

Ben looked hard at the other man and said nothing. As angry as he might be, Alex knew her husband was dying inside. She was ready to forget having a friendship with Louis. At that moment, she'd do anything to feel her husband's affection.

Alex started to stand, saying to Ben, "I'll walk out with you."

"No. Don't get up." He looked at her in a way that made Alex feel like a stranger to him. "Like I said, I'll be late tonight. Don't wait up."

Louis said, placating, "Look, Ben. I think you somehow got the wrong idea about Alex and me. It's my fault; I'm sorry. But you need to know that—"

Ben locked eyes with Louis and cut him off. "Anything I need to know, I'll figure out for myself. Okay by you?"

Alex saw the pain in Ben's eyes. Ignoring his order, she followed him out the door. On the deserted sidewalk, she laid a hand on his arm, stopping him, then hugged him close and whispered in his ear.

"I'm sorry. There's nothing going on between Louis and me, I swear. And I don't care how late you are, I'm waiting up."

She kissed him on the neck and wished he would relax into her embrace, but after a moment Ben pulled away and left without looking back. Alex stood and watched him go.

TWENTY

Tia Suarez stopped her '64 GTO convertible in front of the Sawyers' house, where Ben and a younger version of the man were
exchanging pop flies on the lawn. She waved and called out a friendly
hello. The boy's gaze locked on the car as he walked to the curb.

"I like your car."

"Then you've got good taste," Tia said. "It's a GTO, but some
people call 'em Goats. This one's almost fifty years old. Cars were
built to get up and go back then."

The boy stared intently. "Cool."

Ben glanced over his shoulder at the house as he walked up,
and Tia thought he seemed a bit nervous. "Hey, Tia. What's
going on?"

"Hey, Sarge. Sorry for just dropping in, but I was in the neighborhood and thought I'd say hi."

A screen door screeched, and Tia looked up to see a woman coming out onto the porch of the Sawyer home. She assumed this was
Ben's wife, Alex. The woman's light blond hair was pulled back,

and she was dressed casually in jeans and a man's button-down white cotton shirt tied off in a knot just above her waist. The woman eyed Tia with a mix of friendly curiosity and what struck Tia as mild surprise. Tia had heard talk that Ben's wife was a looker, and this woman was certainly that. Her skin nearly glowed; her cobalt eyes were piercing even at this distance. As Alex approached the group at the curb, her face warmed with an inviting smile. Barefoot, with her ponytail bouncing slightly and her hands in the back pockets of her jeans, she looked like she had walked out of a photo shoot for Liz Claiborne.

"Hello, ma'am, I'm Tia Suarez. I work with your husband. I mean, Sergeant Sawyer."

"Wow. Tia Suarez?" Alex put out a hand and shot a glance at her husband. "I'm Alex. It's great to meet you. Ben's told me all about you, says you're a great cop. And believe me, he doesn't just throw that kind of stuff around."

Eager to change the subject to anything but herself, she said to the boy, "So you're Jake?"

"Yep."

"Nice to meet you," Tia said, extending her hand. "Your dad tells me you're a pretty good ball player. You like the Brewers?"

Jake reached out and awkwardly shook Tia's offered hand. He shot his dad a look before answering. "Nah. Dad is the Brewers fan. I'm a West Coast guy. I go with the A's. They're playing in Milwaukee in a week or so. I hope the A's sweep 'em."

"That's kind of why I came by." Tia looked at Ben. "I've got two box seats for one of the games, Sarge, but it doesn't look like I'm going to be able to make it. I wanted to see if maybe you and Jake might want to go?"

Jake didn't wait for his dad to answer. "Box seats? Like the ones down by the field? Oh, man, you bet we can go." Jake turned to his mother. "You don't mind, right, Mom?"

Tia realized her mistake in an instant. "Uh . . . I can probably get a third seat, Alex. I mean . . . I can check on it."

Hell, she'd call the stadium, get the name of the ticket holder, and make an irresistible offer.

Alex didn't miss a beat. "Don't even think about it. These two are the baseball nuts. The game is too slow for me and I'm usually scanning the crowd with my binos by the third inning. Now if you get a line on some Packers tickets, you'd better count me in."

"Those are a little harder to come by, but I'll keep it in mind." She drew the tickets out of her pocket and offered them to Ben. "Sound good, Sarge?"

"Sounds great, but you gotta let me pay you for them. What are those, like a hundred bucks apiece?"

"I got 'em from a friend. Spent about fifty dollars."

Alex spoke up. "Smokin' deal, Ben. You should go for it."

"All right, Tia," he said. "Fifty bucks sounds great."

Jake pumped his fist. "Hey, Dad, Officer Suarez's car is way cooler than ours. Why don't you get something like that? Something that'll get up and go."

Ben gave Tia a look that clearly meant—sarcastically—*thanks a lot.* Alex said, "I'm throwing some steaks on the grill. Will you stay?"

"Thanks, but I don't want to put you out."

"Stay," Ben stage-whispered. "If you don't, it'll be hot dogs she throws on the grill."

Tia looked at Alex and shrugged. "If it's not too much trouble, I'd love to."

"Great. Okay, Ben, fire it up. You're cooking. Come on in, Tia. How about a beer?"

Tia joined the family walking toward the house, and Jake fell in alongside her.

"So my dad said you used to be a Marine. It that true?" Jake asked.

Tia turned to the boy as they kept walking. "Yeah. Four years."

Jake's voice picked up a level of excitement. "That's what I'm gonna do. As soon as I turn eighteen I'm gonna join up. Where did you go? Did you like it?"

Tia noticed that Ben's expression took on a bit of a sad smile. She wondered about the backstory but answered the boy's question honestly. "I was mostly overseas. Afghanistan. Yeah, I liked it, but the best thing about it was it got me ready to be a cop. You could do that too, you know."

"No way. I just want to be in the Marines and travel all over the world."

Jake ran ahead and Tia walked along with Ben and Alex in a moment of uncomfortable silence. She saw Alex reach out and squeeze Ben's hand as they headed into the backyard.

After dinner and several beers from a local brewery, the adults sat outside and enjoyed the perfect spring evening. Jake had hung around for a while but eventually retreated to his room. The boy struck Tia as a nice kid who had been through some tough times. Though Tia liked and respected Ben as Sergeant Sawyer, they'd had little personal interaction. Now, sitting with the Sawyers in their backyard, she felt a pang of envy for the closeness of family.

"So how's your dad doing, Alex?" Tia asked. "We miss having him around down at the station house."

"He's come a long way, but it's been tough. He's hanging in there, though. Thanks for asking."

"Let him know I said hello. He hired me, you know. I think he took a lot of heat for it. There were some other top candidates."

"I'll tell him, Tia." Alex got up easily from her low-slung Adirondack chair and lightly patted Ben on the head. Tia noticed that Ben turned his head up at her touch, much like a happy dog. "I'm going to tackle the kitchen. You guys keep talking."

"No way, Alex. I'm helping." Tia started to stand.

"I got it, Tia. Ben loves shop talk that he doesn't have to filter for me." She tousled his hair again. "Cause you know, growing up a cop's daughter and all, I just can't take it . . ." She paused and looked straight at Tia. "By the way, Tia, it's been a long time since I've seen Jake smile like he did today. The whole adjusting to a new town, changing schools, trying to make new friends, all that. It's been tough on him. When you pulled out those baseball tickets, you made his day and mine. Actually, you made my month. Thanks for that."

"Thanks, Alex, that's really cool to know."

Tia watched her boss as Alex walked away; emotions flickered over his face, too fast for her to identify. She wouldn't think of prying, but she hoped the Sawyers were as happy as they should be.

With their fill of beef and brew, the two cops opened up a little more than the separation of rank and a dozen years would normally allow.

"Alex and I, neither of us was quite twenty-one yet when we just blew out of town. Drove all the way to California. We stopped in Vegas and got married." Ben laughed. "Jesus, her old man hit the roof. If he could have put his hands on me, I would've been swinging from a tree branch."

"So you got on with Oakland?" Tia asked.

"Not right away. I applied for LAPD first. I was all set to be a big-city cop only to find out my eyes weren't good enough. Doc told me I didn't meet the vision requirements and that was that. DQ'ed me on the spot."

"So what? Oakland didn't have the same requirement?"

"Yeah, actually they did." Ben took a swig of beer. "But I memorized the eye chart before I took the test."

"Bullshit." She wasn't buying it.

"No. It's the truth. Haven't you noticed that all doctors use the same eye chart? The twenty/twenty line is D-E-F-P-O-T-E-C." Ben took another, larger gulp. "I know it backward, too."

"Are you serious? You memorized it?"

"I like to think of it as studying."

"Yeah. More like you copied off another kid's paper."

"What would you expect? I plan on being a cop all my life and then I'm going to let some geek with a stethoscope turn me away? Bullshit."

"Oakland PD." Tia's voice filled with admiration. "Bet you got some fish stories out of that."

"One or two." Ben drained the longneck, dropped the empty bottle onto the grass. "I'll bet you've even heard a few of them."

"Just the one."

"Which is . . . ?"

"Story is you invoked a little street justice on some sack of shit, something about stoving in his teeth with a forty-cal? Word has it you got tossed out of OPD."

"That's pretty close."

Tia laughed and took a long pull of beer. Ben found he was enjoying their candor. He opened another beer and turned a bit more serious.

"Actually, your version gives me too much credit. It had nothing to do with justice. I snapped and nearly killed a guy. Lucky I didn't end up in my own jail."

Tia spoke with genuine understanding. "I went online and read the case file, Sarge. You should know, most of the cops at the PD have read it. Public record, ya know. And all the press shit too. The guy was right out of the joint and wanted for murder. From what I read, he was pretty close to killing a cop when you showed up. That means all bets are off. You could have shot the son of a bitch on the spot, but you took him into custody alive."

When Ben sat quietly, staring across the yard, she went on.

"So you probably save a cop's life *and* you avoid killing the crook, and they railroad your ass out the door? Hell, if you hadn't intervened—"

"None of that matters." Ben looked at Tia, respecting the honest nature of her inquiry. There was no denying it felt good to have a cop come to his defense, especially a cop of her quality. But it didn't change the facts and he knew it.

"There's no 'use-of-force' expert in the country willing to testify that deep-throating a guy with the barrel of a gun is an acceptable way to make an arrest. No way, nohow. Believe me, I checked. It was a jacked-up situation, no doubt, but I had other options. I knew better, and in the end I got what I deserved."

"That's bullshit and you know it. You made an on-the-spot life-or-death call. Then some jerk-offs in a courtroom come along and start taking it apart frame by frame. Didn't you want to fight? Push back on those sons of bitches?"

"It doesn't work that way, Tia. Hell, I guess if just one person had offered me the slightest support, maybe I would have pushed back. If someone had shown the slightest benefit of the doubt instead of filling in the blanks before we even got started, yeah, maybe I would have tried to tell my side."

"So then," she asked quietly, "what was your side?"

Ben only stared ahead and Tia tried to prompt him. "I read about the Oakland cop that was killed a couple of weeks before all this shit went down. Shot to death. You were on that call too, weren't you?"

Ben looked at Tia with what struck her as mild surprise. "Damn, Suarez. Maybe I should make you a detective."

They went quiet for almost a minute, then Ben started back up. "That was a tough time to be a cop in Oakland. We lost four in eight months. This jerk-off Espudo had it in his head he'd do number five." Ben took a hit off his beer. "Fuck him. I should have just blown his head off before he could get his hands up. Then everything would've been fine."

"So what happened? I mean after the actual . . ." Tia didn't know what to call it. "I mean, what happened after the event?"

"The event, huh? I like that. Kind of like something where you'd charge admission."

He paused as if thinking, then went on. "What happened? The world spun off its goddamn axis is what happened. The press went absolutely bat shit. They practically penned the stories in blood. Course there was that damn picture. Seemed like it was on the front page of every newspaper in California."

Tia had seen the photograph, and it was something to behold. The sharply focused photo depicted Ben Sawyer as an Oakland PD officer, his eyes hidden behind dark mirrored glasses, mouth open as if in midshout, the veins in his neck bulged and pronounced. Clad in a black, militaristic uniform complete with load-bearing vest and leather gloves, he straddled a prone and terrified Hector Espudo. In his hand, Ben held the gun that practically raped the man's throat. Tia knew it didn't help that the picture perfectly captured the whole white-on-brown thing.

"Yeah. I've seen it. Nice Ray-Bans. And the gloves were a great touch."

"Very funny." Ben laughed, flipping her his middle finger, then went on.

"It started the first morning. The media found our house, and they went into some kind of feeding frenzy like they hadn't eaten a cop alive in years. We could hardly get out of the driveway. Things got rough for Jake. We had to pull him out of school. All the teasing, name-calling. Even a few threats. Crazy stuff." Ben's voice turned serious. "Used to be that boy couldn't wait to be a cop. It was all he ever talked about. Now . . . well, you heard him. All he wants is to get away from me."

Ben sat silent, and Tia couldn't think of anything to say. She hadn't expected this kind of revelation. Of course she had heard the stories and read the newspaper, but it had never dawned on her how the whole mess might impact the Sawyer family. Ben seemed to want to keep talking, so she just listened.

"Then there's Alex. Man, I know she was really trying, but I think she was hating me right about then."

Another moment of apparent reflection and a long taste of beer while Tia waited patiently. Ben went on. "Just when things seemed like they might die down a little bit, one of the cable news channels would get hold of another grainy cell phone recording and it would start all over. Course I didn't do myself any favors with some of my more colorful comments. Those got plenty of air time."

Another swig. Tia hoped it felt good for him to open up.

"Yeah, old Hector ended up beating the rap for the whole trying-to-kill-a-cop thing. The district attorney wouldn't touch the case, said I poisoned the water with my over-the-top reaction. But home-boy still had the murder of the gang member to deal with. He got twenty-five to life for that."

The tone of Ben's voice finally lightened, and he looked at Tia and winked. "He's gone and made quite a name for himself. I hear he even got a couple of marriage proposals from his jail cell. But the word from the joint is the son of a bitch has one hell of nasty lisp."

Tia laughed and Ben joined in.

After a few seconds, she asked, "But they still went ahead and fired you?"

"Not fired. I resigned in lieu of termination, which I guess is pretty much the same thing. The PD bosses threw my ass under the bus, then drove over me a few times. My union reps hid under a rock. My lawyer was from the bottom of the barrel. The county DA said resign or he'd rain hell down on my ass like I couldn't imagine. And at that point, I could imagine a lot. He said it would all go away if I would go away." Ben shrugged. "So I did."

Ben drained his beer and looked with surprise at the empty bottle.

"I thought I'd be able to find another department in California willing to take me on. You know, just start over as a patrolman. But no one wanted anything to do with me. Eventually I reached out to Lars . . . Chief Norgaard."

Ben stared into space for several seconds. "Let's just say he wanted his daughter to be happy. He took a chance on me. Brought me on and let me keep my sergeant rank. You know the rest. All that effort to make it on my own, and I still end up in the shadow of the great Norseman."

"Don't kid yourself, Ben," Tia said. "Oakland's loss is our gain. You've been a great sergeant."

"Yeah? Somebody better tell Chief Jorgensen. I think McKenzie has been giving him an earful. I'm starting to think my days at NPD are numbered."

Tia thought Ben would go on, but he turned the conversation to her. "Tell me about this time you spent in the Marines. You've never really talked about it."

"Yep. Four years. Most of it good. Got a little dicey at times."

"How so?"

"I was an interrogator in Afghanistan for most of my hitch, doing what they call black-bag ops. Dark locations. Capturing and interrogating high-level targets, that sort of thing."

"You mean like speaking in Arabic kind of interrogation?" Ben sounded surprised.

"Farsi, actually. It's a Persian language that a bunch of very bad people in Afghanistan speak. It was my job to get them talking."

After four beers, Ben didn't hold back. "What the hell, Suarez? I thought you were Mexican? You speak . . . what did you call it? Farki?"

"Farsi. I have a way with languages. Apparently it comes from growing up bilingual. A few months of formal training, then an immersion program. Leave it to the Marines to exploit my impoverished upbringing."

"That's wild. What kind of stuff did you do?"

"Like I said, mostly interrogations. Intelligence collection and analysis. Developing intel to give to the spec ops guys, and believe me, you don't even want to know what they did with it." She paused smiling, now giving a wink of her own. "Let's just say it was probably a little worse than memorizing an eye chart and more along the lines of forcing a guy to suck on a pistol barrel."

Ben laughed. "So you're like that group of clowns who took the pictures of naked guys in pyramids? The dog collar thing?"

Tia feigned insult. "Oh, hell no. That juvenile shit was a bunch of army jail guards. Dumb-ass rednecks on a power trip. No, my team was a little more sophisticated than that and a whole bunch more imaginative, you might say. Most of the time we kept it civil, but if we didn't, we damn sure kept it out of the papers. But hey, the stakes were high. Lots of lives on the line." She took a long pull from her beer. "Like they say, war is hell."

There was a long silence between them, but it felt comfortable and appropriate. Tia broke it.

"So how do you do it? I mean, after working in a place like Oakland, how can you stand it around here?"

"You're asking me? Sounds like you had some adjustments to make yourself." Tia waited while Ben seemed to give more thought to the question. "Alex and I both grew up here. We know this town. Here, we're connected. In Oakland, I felt like a mercenary or something. Cops need to be invested, otherwise we're just hired guns and it's easy to lose perspective."

Tia nodded in understanding. "I hear ya, but a bunch of our guys grew up in Newberg and still don't give a rat's ass. Like McKenzie, for one, and I don't get a great feel from Jorgensen. I don't give a shit if he is the new chief."

"Screw McKenzie, and it's really not about who runs the show." Ben gave Tia a long look and spoke more seriously. "As far as the average shit-bag crook is concerned, it's not our job to go around handing out any kind of street justice. I'm not proud of what I did. Hell, it got me run out of a good department, and rightfully so. I can see how that kind of shit might fly in a combat zone but not in our line of work. Not in police work. Not Oakland, not here. Nowhere."

Tia felt her respect for the man grow. She flashed back to the desert and the times she wondered if maybe her team jumped to a few conclusions. Some interrogations lasted for hours, if not days. Frustration reached a breaking point, and the rule book was tossed aside. But unlike the city of Oakland, there was no one there to yell foul. The faces of men young and old alike began to pass through her mind until Ben's voice refocused her on the present.

"Anyway, I like the idea of being a cop where I grew up. I feel good about it. You should too."

Tia looked to her boss and saw that his eyes had turned to the house. She followed his gaze and saw Alex at the kitchen window looking back at Ben, uneasiness on her face. Tia wondered how much of a mark the whole Oakland experience had left. The story had been news even in Wisconsin; she couldn't imagine what it was like in Oakland. It probably tested the relationship, no doubt about that. Tia looked on as Ben smiled at his wife, and felt certain these two were together for the long haul.

Tia turned her attention to the darkening evening sky. The temperature felt like it had dropped ten degrees in the last hour.

"I should probably be hitting the road, Sarge."

Ben stood and extended his hand to pull Tia from her chair.

"I don't think so. You drank four of those. That means you're camping here."

"I'm fine. I'll just be careful driving home."

"Nope. There's a nice room over the garage. Key is under the mat. Bed, TV, shower, whatever you need. Pull the door shut when you leave in the morning."

"Really, I'm fine—"

Ben cut her off. "Bullshit, you're fine. At your weight, with four brews you're about a point one three, so forget it. You're not driving until tomorrow."

Humbled, Tia gave in. "Yes, sir. I appreciate the concern and hospitality."

As she reached the garage, Tia turned back one last time. She looked through the kitchen window where Alex was busy at the sink, washing dishes. Ben came into view, then stopped behind her and looped his arms around his wife's waist. Alex settled into his embrace, then wiped her eyes with the back of a soapy hand.

Tia wondered if what she saw on Alex's face was grief or joy. Feeling vaguely like a Peeping Tom, Tia turned away and let the Sawyers have their moment.

TWENTY-ONE

S he seems like a nice gal. But you forgot to mention she's a stone fox."

Ben and Alex lay side by side in bed, sharing the last beer of the day. The weather had grown cold and the wind had picked up. The forecast called for temperatures to drop thirty degrees in the next twenty-fours and the weatherman had threatened snow. Winter had returned, at least for a while, but some warmth had found its way into the Sawyer home. Alex propped herself up on one elbow, dressed only in one of Ben's sleeveless workout jerseys, and took a long taste. Ben could see from her neck clear down to her navel and thought that she still had the body of a coed athlete.

"You're right." Ben laughed. "I mean you're right, she's a nice gal and a good cop. Most of us turn into real assholes after a few years, even in little old Newberg. But not Tia."

"I know a cop who's been around a lot longer than that and he's still a pretty neat guy."

"You're biased."

"Course I am. I love the guy." Alex fell against her husband and stayed there.

They still hadn't talked about the episode in the coffee shop from the day before. At this point, they could probably get away with pretending the whole thing had never happened, but neither of them had ever been good at that.

"Benny, you know that, don't you? That I love you?" She pulled back to look at him. "All we've been through, I couldn't love anyone else."

"I know." Ben knew what his wife was getting at. "I'm sorry about what happened—the thing with Louis yesterday. I acted like an idiot. But I swear it was like that time in high school. Remember? Our senior year when we broke up for a few days?"

"That was your idea, pal. Seems like I remember you had a rep as the big jock. Thought you'd sow some wild oats or something."

Ben dismissed the comment. "Whatever. I just remember it was all over the school by lunch, and guys were falling all over themselves to step in. Couple of 'em were friends of mine."

Alex laughed at his interpretation of the memory, but Ben was serious.

"Really. I had that same feeling the other day, that I was losing you. I hated that feeling when we were in high school and I hated it even more yesterday." Ben said, looking straight into her eyes. "We've been through a lot, and I guess we're hanging in there. But I don't think I could survive losing you, I really don't."

She kissed her husband softly on the face. "The one thing you never have to worry about is losing me. Ever."

She kissed him on the mouth and he responded, kissing her hard and pulling her close. His hands explored freely over her body. Alex climbed on top of him and smiled. She sat up straight and straddled his chest. She balanced herself, resting the fingertips of one hand lightly on his skin, then tilted her head back and drained the last of the beer. She set the bottle aside and pulled off her shirt. Their gazes locked.

They were a little clumsy. It had been a while. But for the better part of the next two hours, husband and wife enjoyed an affection that they had never shared with anyone else, and that they knew with an absolute certainty they never would.

TWENTY-TWO

The black Crown Vic entered the deserted county park just as the sun disappeared below the horizon. McKenzie got out of his own car and made his approach, surveying the parking lot one last time. It was empty. The Crown Vic slowed to a stop. The limousine tint on all four windows left McKenzie feeling unsettled and determined not to show it. *He's gotta be alone.*

Better be. This was a private matter. McKenzie gripped the gun in his coat pocket and waited.

A moment later Jorgensen emerged, and McKenzie forgot all his apprehension as he took in the chief's appearance. He felt like a slob, standing there in his jeans, T-shirt, and denim jacket while the big man was dressed to the nines in a tailored suit, looking like a page from a big-and-tall mail-order catalog.

"Any sign of him yet?" Jorgensen asked, scanning McKenzie from head to toe. His gaze settled on McKenzie's hand buried in his pocket.

"All quiet, Chief. Maybe he checked things out and decided to give it a pass. Would kind of make sense, considering the circumstances. Or hell, who knows. Maybe it is all just some wild-ass coincidence."

"Seems unlikely."

Always the man of few words, McKenzie thought. Easier to defend or deny in the future. McKenzie knew no such caution.

"If Harlan Lee does come to town, Chief, it ain't going to be a problem for you. I'll take care of it, just like Chippewa Falls. And don't worry. You'll be a hundred percent off the radar."

"I'm not worried about Harlan Lee," Jorgensen said. "I'm worried about all the bullshit that can come out of the sort of ruckus he might raise. Somebody plays a game of connect the dots, that could lead to problems."

"Here's how I see it, Chief. This Petite guy? He don't have a clue. And Lipinski? He went six feet under with a toe tag that said child molester. Not a soul outside of family even took notice. But if Harlan Lee shows up here, that'll be the end of it. He'll be chum for the pikes and sturgeon in Lake Winnebago."

"That's a bold statement, Doyle. Seems to me this fella is on a mission. I'm not sure he'll be easily dissuaded."

"No worries, Chief. I got eyes on the street. A convict of his pedigree will stand out. Just a matter of paying attention and knowing what to look for. Leave it to me."

Jorgensen leaned against his car.

"If it's all the same to you, Doyle, I'd like to take a few precautions."

"What you got in mind, Chief?"

"I pulled our local case file regarding Mr. Lee. I want you to make sure there's no other paperwork out there. Computer entries, evidence files, all that stuff—I want it purged. If anybody notices what you're doing, tell them it's related to a joint task force narcotics investigation. Need to know only.

"I called up to Florence County. Scott Jamison is the sheriff up there these days. He's all over it. Says it'll be like Harlan Lee never set foot in Florence County. I'd like to think I could get the same assurance from you."

"Seems like you're going through a lot of trouble here, Chief. If you're worried about old Lars Norgaard, I can look out for him. I figure—"

"The hell with Norgaard," Jorgensen said with more emotion in his voice than McKenzie was used to hearing. "Lars can sink or swim on his own."

"Okay, then I guess I gotta ask what's the big deal? You seem to be puttin' a lot of energy into this. For what?"

Jorgensen looked off into the distance. "You let me worry about my motives. Just make sure that nobody can walk in and pull this boy's name off some old, dusty shelf in the PD. You hear me?"

"I'll take care of it, Chief."

"See to it. Don't miss anything."

"You got it, boss," McKenzie said. "Chances are Harlan's had his fill. Give him a week and I'll bet we find him tucked away in that shack of his up in Florence. He'll be easy enough to deal with."

Jorgensen opened the driver's door of his car and tucked himself into the leather upholstery.

"You know, Doyle, Sawyer warned me about you. Says you talk a good game." Jorgensen paused, sizing the man up. "But I'll be judging you and your future prospects based on results."

Doyle watched as the black sedan pulled away, leaving him alone in the parking lot. He couldn't help but think back to his days as an independent freelancer. Not as profitable but a whole lot less stress.

TWENTY-THREE

Harlan approached from behind. The old man was facing the setting sun. The daughter had left, and based on his observations during the past few days, Harlan figured it would be at least ten minutes before an orderly showed up to wheel the man back to his room.

The sunroom stood empty accept for his target, who sat with eyes closed, dozing and grunting to himself. Sure not the man he once was. Not the man he was last time they had run across each other. Harlan took one last look over his shoulder, then closed in. He pushed the wheelchair toward the most secluded part of the room. The sudden movement made the old man jerk, and his raspy breath immediately grew heavy.

"If memory serves, you were a bit spryer back in the day, weren't ya?"

The old man cocked his head, and Harlan could see Lars struggling to turn, but his body wasn't cooperating.

"You probably can't even wipe your own ass, huh? Somebody's

gotta spoon-feed ya and all that sorta bullshit. Hell, I guess you'd welcome a bullet in the head right about now, wouldn't ya? I'm here to tell ya it won't go that easy."

Harlan felt his anger surge and didn't try to stop it. Though he was a cripple, Norgaard had no doubt been pretty well cared for. Harlan figured the man had never felt mistreated or abused. That was a luxury Harlan intended to snatch away here and now. Replace it with fear. Harlan bent down close.

"I've been tucked away seventeen years because of you and a few others. Let me tell you, Lars, a couple of your boys still don't know what hit 'em."

Harlan spun the chair and stared at his victim as the old man seemed to scan his memory. With their eyes inches apart, Harlan enjoyed the moment as the gravity of his circumstances took hold and a look of terror came over the old man's face. What little color there was drained away, and his head began to bob in an aimless motion. In the otherwise silent room, Harlan heard the sound of a weak running stream in the plastic bag strapped to the side of the man's chair.

"Yeah, there you go. You remember, huh?" Harlan patted Lars on the cheek with an open hand. "You were a regular bad-ass with a badge back then. Look at you now. Nothin' but a droolin' sack a shit who can't so much as string a few words together."

Harlan got even closer, his lips almost touching the man's ear.

"Now, about the gal who just left. You two sure spend a lot of time together. Makes for a pretty picture. Seems to me she's the only one willin' to have anything to do with your cranky ass. I'm guessing she'd be your daughter. Am I right, *Officer* Norgaard?"

Harlan watched the old man's eyes dance to life at the mention of his daughter. Lars seemed to try and shape a word in response, but it came out like nothing more than a light gust of wind on a hot, dry day. Harlan nodded his head.

"I know, you have a tough time making yourself heard these days, don't ya? Don't worry about that, old man. All you need to do is listen."

Harlan whispered low into the man's ear, making it clear the words were meant for no one else.

Harlan backed away and watched the rage set in. Lars managed to ball his fists and raise up in his chair. The string of coarse grunts caused Harlan to laugh in response.

"I sure enough struck a nerve, didn't I?" Harlan said. "Imagine how that'd feel, Lars. Your daughter . . . *your child,* took from ya."

Lars tried again to speak, and Harlan raised his voice to a loud and angry whisper to talk over him. "What's a cripple like you gonna do about it? Not a damn thing you can do, is there? I know an old man who suffered a similar fate."

Harlan knocked the wheelchair to one side, dumping the old man out. Norgaard's body twisted in the air and crashed onto the hardwood. Harlan heard a deep *thunk* as the man's head hit the floor, and for a moment he worried that he had killed the former cop. Harlan looked closer and saw shallow breaths. Blood ran from a deep gash, turning Norgaard's wispy white hair red. The man's eyelids fluttered open.

"Don't you go dyin' on me now. You still got a good bit to learn about pain, about sufferin' and loss. You'd think a man in your position would be learned out in those areas, but that ain't so. You got a good ways yet to go."

Harlan stepped over the sprawled body and feigned a kick to the head. Norgaard flinched and Harlan squatted down for a few parting words.

"Someone will be along directly, Norgaard. I'm sure they'll patch you up. I want you to be around to see what I got planned for that pretty little girl of yours."

Harlan brought his face close and once again whispered in his ear. "Just know this, Norgaard. You brought all this shit on yourself."

TWENTY-FOUR

Sitting on a wooden bench in the hallway of Newberg Convalescent, Alex remembered swinging in the backyard of her childhood home, her papa pushing her higher and higher. Her bare feet reached out to touch the perfect blue sky before falling back, accompanied by gales of laughter from both father and child. Alex was almost five when her mother died after a yearlong fight with breast cancer. After that it was Alex and her dad, alone against the world. They were a family.

The double doors swung open and jerked Alex back to reality. She was on her feet in an instant. Beside her, Ben jumped up as well and spoke first.

"What the hell happened, Doctor? We got a call that Lars fell out of his chair? He can't even pull himself up. How's he going to fall?"

"Hard to say." Dr. Carl Schneider, resident physician of Newberg Convalescent, turned to Alex. He looked through his blond bangs and eyeglasses with fingerprint-smudged lenses as he spoke. "I've told you all along, Alex, much of stroke recovery is about willpower. If your dad decided to stand up, I wish he'd waited until someone was there to help him. He took a bad rap on the head. He's pretty agitated. I'd like to keep him sedated overnight. I don't want this to cause any major setbacks."

Alex wasn't convinced that the situation was that simple. "I agree with my husband, Doctor. I was with my dad most of the day. There was no indication that he could work himself out of his chair or that he even wanted to try. Are we sure he didn't have some sort of seizure? Could something else have happened to him? Do we need to talk to some of the staff? Do we need to call the police?"

Some measure of offense and wounded dignity could be heard in Dr. Schneider's response. The man always sounded a bit snobbish. Now Alex thought he just sounded like a pompous ass. "I can rule out both those possibilities immediately. Tests show no signs of a seizure or recurrence of stroke, and we have never had a suspicious injury of a patient at Newberg Convalescent. Your father took a fall."

Before Alex could respond, Ben jumped in to speak. "When can we see him?"

"Like I said, he's sedated. Alex, why don't you just come by for your normal morning visit. Even if he's still unconscious then, your voice will be good for him. When the lump on his head goes down a bit, we'll bring him around." Dr. Schneider laughed. "See if we can get your dad to show us his new trick."

Ben shot the man a look. "Careful, Doc. He's not a circus act. He was a cop for thirty years. Longer than you've been alive, I'd imagine."

"Sorry. I meant no disrespect." The man's voice was curt as he excused himself. "Mrs. Sawyer, I'll check in with you in the morning."

Alex ignored the doctor's offense and instead stared at her husband. Ben looked back at her and rolled his eyes.

"Don't make a big deal out of it. The guy was acting like a horse's ass. I don't go for that shit."

Alex hugged Ben tight. "Especially when it comes to somebody you love as much as old Lars Norgaard, huh?"

TWENTY-FIVE

T he pounding roused Ben from a dead sleep.

Alex must have forgotten her key. For the past two nights, his wife had been sleeping in her father's room at Newberg Convalescent. He shifted in the bed and found Alex asleep next to him. *Dream, I guess. Man, it got cold in here.* He snuggled in closer to Alex, seeking her warmth, but the pounding resumed.

Ben maneuvered around Alex, trying not to disturb her. He stumbled into the living room and finally came fully awake at the sight of Doyle McKenzie and Plate Boyd standing on his porch. Ben opened the door just as McKenzie raised his fist to knock again. The rudeness of it got the conversation off to a bad start.

"Jesus, guys," Ben said, stepping into the doorway, "what's going on? What time is it?"

McKenzie closed in, a cigarette hanging from his lips. He began to speak, but Plate put an arm across his chest and cut him off.

"Sorry, Ben, but something's come up. There's been a homicide. We need to talk with you."

"A homicide? No shit, you need to talk to me," Ben said. He

looked at both men and saw they were dressed in jeans and jackets as if ready for a long, cold night. Plate had a five-cell flashlight tucked under his arm and a notebook in his hand. McKenzie was holding a brown paper bag that looked unsealed but was marked with evidence tape. It was obvious to Ben both men were working and had been for a while. "How long ago did this happen? Is the body still at the scene? Doyle, how come I didn't get notified?"

Boyd jumped back in.

"That was my call, Ben. I've got a few questions."

"What do you mean, questions? Just fill me in."

"Ben, is your wife home?" Boyd asked. "We need to talk to her."

Dumbstruck, Ben stared at his fellow cop.

McKenzie sucked on his cigarette, then spoke. "How 'bout it, Ben? Is the little missus in?"

Ben looked back and forth between the men, who stood silent, waiting for an answer. "What are you guys talking about? Why do you want to know about Alex?"

McKenzie blew out a puff of smoke. "Don't worry about why. Just answer the question. Is she home or not?"

Plate stepped in front of McKenzie. "Shut up, Doyle. I told you I'd handle this." He turned to Ben and softened his tone. "We just need to have her account for her whereabouts this evening. Say over the past several hours?"

Ben was on the verge of responding until he ran the day through his mind. Alex had not been at home when he'd gone to bed. She'd been with her father. *What's going on?*

"She's home. Home and asleep in bed. Now can I ask why that's any of your business?"

"So you can vouch for her, then? She's been home all night?"

Ben felt vulnerable, standing in the doorway while the two police officers looked into his dark, quiet house. He stepped outside and pulled the door closed behind him. He noticed a light frozen rain had begun to fall. Barefoot, in flannel shorts and a T-shirt, he worked hard to ignore the cold and to sound direct in his answer. "Yes. She's asleep in bed." Ben could tell that both men picked up on his evasive response.

"What can you tell us about this?" McKenzie pulled a heart-shaped glass picture frame from the brown paper bag. In the picture, Alex was smiling, looking past the camera, her hair blowing gently in the wind. "This is your wife, isn't it?" McKenzie asked.

Ben found he had no voice. He tried, but nothing came out. Finally he mustered, "Where did you get that?"

Boyd began to speak, but McKenzie talked over him. "The guy that owns that coffee shop downtown, Java and whatever. He's dead. Stabbed in the gut in his apartment over the store. This picture was on his desk. Couple more on the bulletin board. So like I asked you before: Is this your wife?"

Ben could only stare at the photograph in McKenzie's hand. Somewhere in the far distance, McKenzie kept talking.

"We also found a couple of wineglasses, broken, on the floor. Looks like our victim was entertaining, then it must have got ugly." McKenzie paused to drag cigarette smoke into his lungs, then exhaled as he spoke, releasing a puff of smoke with each word. "By the way, the dark green minivan in the driveway—anybody been driving it tonight? Say in the past two or three hours?"

Ben couldn't tear his gaze from the photograph. "What are you guys getting at? This is insane."

Boyd chimed in, his voice sympathetic. "All the same, Ben, we'd like to have a talk with your wife. Probably best we do that tonight. Mind if we come in while you wake her up?"

Ben came to life. "I got a better idea. Let's go down to the scene. I want to walk through it myself."

"I'm afraid we can't let you do that, Ben," Boyd said. "Chief Jorgensen's orders."

"Jorgensen? Who called him? For Christ's sake, Plate, am I the detective sergeant of this department or not?"

"You ain't calling the shots here, Ben. Now go wake up your wife. Tell her we want to talk."

McKenzie stepped toward the door, and Ben blocked him. "Go to hell, McKenzie. Get a warrant—if you think you know how to write one."

Boyd tried to interject. "Ben, calm down. Listen to me for a minute. We got a call of screams coming from the apartment and a blond woman in a green minivan hightailing it out of the area. The door was wide open and we find a guy stabbed to death inside. Looks like he had some kind of relationship with your wife, who happens be a blonde and drives a green van, right? Of course we need to talk to her. You can see that, can't you?"

Ben's head was reeling as he processed the information. "Got a call from who? When did all this happen?"

Before Boyd could answer, the front door opened and Alex stepped outside, wearing Ben's robe. She saw the two strangers on her porch and pulled the robe tighter. Her voice was sleepy. "Ben? What's going on? Who are these guys?"

Ben turned to her. "Alex, don't say anything. Go back—"

McKenzie butted in. "Detective Doyle McKenzie, Mrs. Sawyer. We're investigating the murder of Louis Carson."

In that instant, Alex came fully awake. She grabbed Ben's arm but looked straight at the detectives. "Louis? Killed? Oh, my God. What are you talking about? How—"

"Alex, go inside. Right now." Ben held Alex by her shoulders and began to push her back across the threshold, but she pulled away from him and stepped farther onto the porch until she stood between Ben and the detectives.

"Hey, Doyle." Ben looked up to see a uniformed officer he recognized as a perennial graveyard slug walk around from the back of the house. "Look what I found in the trash can." The cop held up a kitchen knife—a large, nondescript knife that belonged on someone's countertop, not in his garbage can. The cop went on. "Looks like it might have some blood on it."

This time Ben grabbed Alex by the waist and pulled her back toward the door. His voice was elevated and desperate. "Alex, get inside the damn house."

McKenzie reached toward Alex and grabbed for her arm. Ben pushed his wife aside and stepped in to deliver a full punch to McKenzie's jaw. The blow hit solidly, and McKenzie fell backward off the porch, landing in the half-frozen mud. Alex screamed her husband's name but Ben ignored her. He jumped from the steps and stood over the prone detective.

"You keep your goddamn hands off my wife, McKenzie."

"Damn it, Sawyer." McKenzie's voice was fierce with anger as he pulled himself up off the muddy ground.

Uniformed officers began to pour onto the lawn, coming from down the street and around the house. It seemed to Ben half of Newberg PD had descended on his home.

"Hold him," McKenzie barked. Ben spun around and tried to climb back onto the porch, but three officers were on him. Ben struggled but couldn't break free. McKenzie managed to get to his feet, breathing hard. The rain kept coming.

Plate tried to reestablish some level of control. He turned to the officers who were working hard to keep Ben off the porch.

"You guys back off," Plate said. "Let's just all calm down."

McKenzie would have none of it. "Shut up, Plate. I got this." McKenzie turned to the officers who had their hands full.

"Hold on to that bastard. Sawyer, I'll have your ass for that, but right now I got more important matters."

Alex shouted from the porch, "What's wrong with you people? My husband is one of you. He's a police officer. Why are you treating him this way?"

Ben did his best to break free, calling out to his wife, "Alex, get inside the house. Lock the door."

Alex turned to the door, but McKenzie climbed the three porch steps and stood in front of the bewildered woman. Ben could only watch. McKenzie struggled for breath but with what struck Ben as excitement, and his voice sounded labored. "Mrs. Sawyer, you are under arrest for the murder of Louis Carson."

Ben roared, "McKenzie, stop. Plate, do something." He tried to jerk free, but the men holding him kept a strong grip. Ben watched as McKenzie pulled Alex's hands behind her back and handcuffed her. McKenzie began a recitation of her Miranda rights.

Alex looked at Ben as if she was finally ready to listen to him. "Ben, what are they doing? Help me. Where are they taking me?"

McKenzie took Alex by her elbow and led her off the porch. She passed within inches of him and Ben again tried to pull away. His bare feet slipped in the mud that was growing thicker with the rain. He fell onto the cold ground and could only watch as his wife was led to a nearby patrol vehicle. As they approached the car, Alex began to resist in earnest, screaming for Ben to help. She fought and thrashed, refusing to walk. McKenzie pulled and shoved Alex toward the open door and into the backseat of the car. Ben's oversized robe fell away from her shoulder showing her bare skin. Jake shot out the front door wearing only his pajamas. He jumped from the porch and ran past his father. He reached the police car just as it pulled away with his mother inside, her face pressed against the window screaming his name.

"Mom! Mom!" Jake turned to a uniformed patrol officer who stood statue still in the rain, dazed, as if overwhelmed by the scene that had just occurred all around him. Jake shoved the officer with his hands, knocking the man back a couple of feet. He screamed out, "Where are you taking my mom? Bring her back!"

Blood rushed to Ben's head, flooding his ears. He looked toward his son's face, contorted in fear and desperation. Finally the uniformed officers released him, but Ben found he didn't have the strength to stand. His body was spent. He struggled to his knees. The rain was pouring now. The uniformed officers began to regroup. Car doors slammed and the remaining police vehicles sped away. Jake ran to the edge of the road, and once again Ben could hear the boy's screams as the last car disappeared into the night.

Then the only remaining sound was the falling rain and Jake's softer pleas. Ben and Jake were alone.

TWENTY-SIX

Harlan arched his back as the hefty woman bounced on top of him.

"Come on, bitch. You can go harder than that."

The woman stopped and draped herself over his chest, her ample breasts arriving noticeably sooner than the rest of her. "You're gonna split me in two, honey. Give me a minute to rest."

Harlan grabbed the back of her neck and rolled them both over so that he wound up on top of her. She called out in mild protest, but she'd been in the business long enough to know better than to fight back.

"If that's all you got, you picked the wrong profession." He worked it hard, ignoring her high-pitched yelps. Several minutes later, with a final thrust, he rolled off. The room was quiet except for her occasional gasps and whimpers.

After a minute the woman said, "Mister, you got a lot of anger built up in you, don't ya? I hope we aren't gonna have no trouble, okay?"

Remembering the last prostitute who talked too much, Harlan worked hard to control himself. Two killings in one night in this little town would not go unnoticed.

The first had gone smooth enough. The coffee guy, Harlan heard folks call him Louis, was incapacitated by the rat poison and drain cleaner Harlan had slipped in his coffee earlier in the day. He could offer only cursory resistance. Harlan had gotten in and out without notice. The other actors—who didn't know they were moving at Harlan's direction—had played their parts beautifully. Harlan had watched the goings-on from a safe distance. Two hours after discovering the body, detectives went to the Sawyers' home. Harlan had wondered if they would wait until morning but found it much more entertaining to know that the Sawyers' neighbors had to have been woken in the middle of the night. He'd nearly danced in the street as he watched officers pull the screaming woman into a Newberg police car.

"You got it wrong, little lady," Harlan tried to sound hospitable. "I ain't got an angry bone in my body. Just a little pent-up energy is all. Rest yourself. Go on and take a break for a minute."

Harlan stepped to the window and lit up. He drew the smoke deep into his lungs and let it settle there as he thought back over the past few hours. Quick flight was best, but he'd needed to get high and get laid. Getting high hadn't been hard, but this beefy middle-aged hooker was a far cry from his last, although less irritating.

Harlan looked at the sizable prostitute, who was lying prone on the bed, still struggling to catch her breath. Pent-up energy, sure enough. He'd come out of the joint with plenty of that. A hooker, a joint, or a bottle of booze could be arranged through a crooked guard or other member of prison staff for a price, but Harlan prided himself on the restraint he had demonstrated through his years of captivity. If a fellow inmate arranged for the trick or bag of weed,

Harlan would sure enough participate, but he stood firm in his conviction that he did not make deals with the law.

Throughout his life, Harlan's closest associates had exclusively been crooks of one sort or another. His father had been nothing more than a career moonshiner, an outlaw to the core. Their home was open to cat burglars, car thieves, and country drug dealers. Harlan shared home brew and swapped stories with a few hundred such men, and his loyalty to that lifestyle ran marrow deep.

By the time Harlan reached his seventeenth birthday, he was running a marijuana operation that supplied most of the college campuses in Wisconsin, making life a little easier for his aging father. That was what had caught the attention of the likes of Lipinski, Norgaard, and others. They just couldn't stand the idea of a kid like Harlan being that successful.

The woman spoke. She seemed afraid to look at him directly— she glanced at him from the corner of her eyes and then stared at the yellowed popcorn ceiling as she said, "If we're finished, I'd like to be on my way. My husband is gonna be waiting up."

Harlan wasn't through, and the day's success left him feeling generous. "How about we take it up to a hundred bucks' worth and I'll just lay back this time. You can go nice and easy on me for another round, all right?"

Her face lit up at this turn of events. Harlan wondered idly if anyone had ever offered her that kind of payment before and guessed not.

"A hundred bucks? Shit, for that kind of money, my old man can wait all night. Come on over here and let me show you how much a lady loves that sort of appreciation."

He returned to the bed. With closed eyes and an open mind, Harlan let the woman work a miracle. For a hefty gal she had a gentle sway, and before long she lulled him to sleep.

He didn't stir until the sun found a crack in the thick motel curtain. The woman was gone and when he quickly grabbed his wallet he found a hundred dollars missing. The rest of his diminishing funds remained. Harlan smiled, his heart stirred by the wonder of an honest whore.

TWENTY-SEVEN

In front of a five-story fortress that rose from the tundra, Ben stood with his back turned to the bitter prairie wind. Spring had been overpowered, winter had returned—in Wisconsin, cold never seemed far away.

Ben rocked on his heels outside a locked double door marked VISITOR ENTRANCE—an irritating reminder of his new place in the world. He could no longer slip around back and badge his way in, could not signal he was a friendly with a soft knock. His options for getting past locked jail doors were now like those of other mere mortals. Ben looked at his watch and saw that visiting hours should have started ten minutes ago. He had been waiting three days to see his wife, and he wasn't in the mood to wait another minute.

"Ah, the hell with this."

Ben walked briskly to the entrance of the jail, a thin layer of hard-packed ice and snow crunching under his boots. He squared himself in front of the door and with no thought toward the consequences, kicked the metal frame hard enough to shake it. He took a single step back and waited, feeling defiant.

The Waukesha County Correctional Facility for Women, located twenty miles outside Newberg, was controlled by a private security company. When the door opened, a crew-cut blond appeared, dressed in a military-style black jumpsuit with a shoulder patch that read SCREAMING EAGLE SECURITY. With a look of righteous indignation, the jailer said scornfully, "Who the hell is kicking my door?"

Ben wasted no time. "It's fifteen degrees out here, pal. How about you guys quit dickin' around in there and let us into the lobby."

The guard immediately recognized the husband of the facility's most famous inmate.

"Are you serious, Sawyer? We've already been over this with you. If you can't play by the rules, you won't be allowed visitation."

Because of his physical confrontation with the officers that came to his home, Ben had been denied the right to visit Alex. Now three days had passed, and Alex would be making her first appearance in court. After much negotiating over the phone and promises of better behavior, Ben was granted a thirty-minute "precourt" visit.

Ben started to respond, but the jailer cut him off. "And if you kick my door again, you won't have to visit your wife. You can bunk with her, *Sergeant*." The reference to rank smacked of sarcasm and disrespect.

Looking at the man's Nordic features, Ben estimated he was about twenty-two. Accent and inflection indicated that he was a native of the area. The hard face and unsympathetic voice brought out an anger in Ben that, mixed with his utter exhaustion, was nothing short of dangerous. But Ben realized he was in a no-win situation. Alex was due in court in less than six hours and this was his last chance to see her before the hearing. Ben took a deep breath and exhaled a cloud of frost.

"I'm sorry about the door, officer, but it's cold." Ben looked over his shoulder at the crowd, now aligned behind him in tepid allegiance. "Can we wait inside? Just in the lobby?"

The guard gave Ben a disdainful look, never losing eye contact. Not a moment of consideration passed before he responded.

"You can come in when I say you can come in. Kick the door again and you won't come in at all." The guard shot a look at the crowd to discourage any feelings of solidarity among the rabble. "None of you will."

The door slammed. A brief stillness ended with a murmured voice from somewhere in the group: "Trash-talkin' son of a bitch."

Another voice picked up, "Wouldn't be shit without that badge."

As he stood in silent agreement with those around him, Ben realized he was in every respect on the outside looking in. Ben spun away and fought to control the tremble caused by days of aggravation and now the frigid air.

What the hell have you gone and done, Alex? Murder, for Christ's sake?

A dozen or more men lingered nearby, some with children. The few women in the small crowd stood out, oddities. All were braving the elements for the same reason—to visit a wife, mother, sister, other relative, or friend.

In Ben's way of thinking, lining up to visit a spouse at a jailhouse belonged in the category of women's work. Real men would never find themselves in such a predicament. The way Ben saw it, if one half of a married couple is called upon to go behind bars, by God, the man better be ready to step up. Looking around, Ben saw the shame lining the faces of his newest cohort: men with jailhouse wives.

These were people Ben had always categorized as "them." He had long since lost patience with the tired excuses of how a husband or a brother, or in rare cases a wife or sister, ended up doing time. Without fail the stories involved bad breaks and hard luck and rarely ended with "because the little shit deserved to go." Ultimately the tales were all similar in one important way: They had always belonged to someone else. Now Ben had his own story to tell, and were he inclined to talk about it, he knew any listener would find it the most tantalizing of all.

Standing outside the jail, Ben looked to the upper floors and the thin openings that passed as windows, a design Ben knew was to discourage thoughts of escape or suicide among the occupants. His wife was somewhere inside. Locked in a cell. Three days since her arrest. Since officers from his own department had descended on his home and taken his wife away in handcuffs. His life had been turned completely upside down, and already Ben was questioning his ability to cope. Ben couldn't help but think back to an earlier point in his life. The feeling was familiar. *Here we go again,* he thought. *Where will it end this time?*

For the second time in his life, Ben was the subject of a media circus. Within hours of that hellish event, a half-dozen camera crews had arrived outside the Sawyer home and set up camp. White vans each emblazoned with a different media logo lined the curb. Milwaukee, Madison, Chicago, and Minneapolis were all represented. Even a national cable channel hailing out of New York City had joined the party. The portable antennas had been raised like flags claiming new territory. Each night from ten to eleven o'clock, bright lights illuminated the front yard as the latest reports were broadcast live for the evening news. Shifts of different reporters came and went, but there was always someone at the ready to pounce on anyone who emerged from the front door. Jake sat in his room like a hapless shut-in, afraid to even peek through the blinds. Ben didn't have that luxury.

The morning after Alex's arrest, he was forced to run the media gauntlet to report to the office of Chief Jorgensen. Ben, exhausted and still muddy from his wrestling match the night before, had held out hope that Jorgensen would rise to his defense, that he would refuse to allow this obvious rush to judgment. Hoping to avoid a scene, Ben entered the building through the chief's private entrance and nearly ran over three of the officers who had come to his house the night before. The group was leaving as Ben arrived, and from their looks of indignation, Ben had an idea of what would come next. Thinking back now, Ben remembered every word of the chief's sanctimonious speech.

"I'm sorry as I can be about your wife, Ben. Terrible thing to go through." The chief had been in his impeccable attire and smelling of soap and expensive cologne. "I know you want to be as supportive as you can. Speaks well of your character. But your conduct last night was inexcusable. You're lucky Detective McKenzie has decided not to press charges. But you've put a cloud over the entire department."

Ben was beyond offering arguments or comebacks. The obscenity of officers from his own department coming to his house and dragging his wife to jail went beyond any offense he had ever known. He chastised himself for not having fought harder. If offered a do-over, he'd kill McKenzie before he let that man, or anyone, put a hand on a member of his family.

"Truth be told, Ben, most of the officers and even the civilian employees have come to me. They've told me that if you continue to work here, they'll quit. All things considered, I can't say I blame them."

The chief had paused again, apparently hoping Ben would offer his resignation. But Ben just stared at him through glassy eyes, hoping that some fraction of the hatred he felt showed through. Jorgensen delivered his final blow.

"If you're going to insist on trying to keep your job, for now the only fair thing is to minimize the hostility around here. You're suspended without pay. You can leave your badge and police ID with me. Turn your firearm in at the armory. You'll be advised of the date of your disciplinary hearing by mail."

Just quit, he thought. *The whole department wants you gone.*

Now sitting idly on the bench outside the jail, Ben resigned himself to the cold wait, which he felt certain had grown longer because of his outburst. Several of the other men shot looks his way, letting Ben know they blamed him for their troubles. Another twenty minutes passed before the correctional officer returned and, without comment, unlocked the door.

The slow-moving line shuffled inside, and Ben waited his turn to be subjected to the indignities that come along with visiting an inmate. He emptied his pockets into the orange plastic dish and fell in line to be searched. After a pat-down, conducted by the officer from the doorway with more than a little personal violation, Ben collected his property and followed the crowd through the doors to a large open area about the size of a basketball court.

The linoleum floor gleamed from thirty years of daily buffing by inmates who stretched that sort of light work to take up as much time as possible. The air reeked of bleach and lime disinfectant. Ben watched as the others fanned out across the room. He looked around at the metal tables and chairs, all bolted to the floor, and saw that the available space was filling up quickly. Ben sat down to claim one of the last vacant tables only to learn that once all the tables were occupied, people just started doubling up. A large man, unshaved and with heavy body odor, joined Ben, taking a seat across the table. He nodded his head as if to say he wasn't any happier than Ben about their forced association, but it would be short-lived.

The entrance doors slammed shut, and Ben heard the steel bolts engage. A few moments of uncomfortable silence passed among the visitors, who were now practically inmates. A deep-throated buzzer cut through the air, its ominous tone causing Ben and the other first-timers to jump in alarm. Large automated steel doors on the far side of the room opened slowly, grinding across heavy iron rails. Several guards, including the doorkeeper, emerged and took up positions in different areas of the room, standing with arms folded across their chests, nonverbally establishing a sense of control.

A sharp bell chimed and women clad in navy blue jumpsuits began to enter the visitors' room through the open doors. With quick, darting eyes, they scanned the room for a familiar face and then sped toward friends or relatives with a purpose that said every second counted. Ben craned his neck, trying to catch a glimpse of his wife. In a moment he spotted her.

Unlike the women around her, Alex's jumpsuit was bright orange. She walked slowly, shuffling her feet in cotton slippers, rattling the silver chains that connected her cuffed hands to her waist and the ankle chains that restricted her steps. Her very appearance distinguished her as a high-risk prisoner.

"Oh, my God." Ben's voice was low.

He couldn't believe his eyes. In just three days his wife had aged three lifetimes. Ben looked at the woman coming toward him, her face splotched with streaks of gray and yellow. Although her jail attire was of the one-size-fits-all variety and offered no sense of the outline of her body, the gauntness of her face told Ben she had no weight left to lose. Her uncombed hair hung in clumps; her eyes had gone dull. *This after three days,* he thought.

Ben rose to his feet and every guard turned to look. Physical contact was forbidden. Alex stopped two feet in front of Ben, her eyes searching his face. The din of a hundred voices bounced off the unforgiving walls, making quiet conversation impossible. He struggled to speak and his voice cracked with emotion.

"Hey, Alex," he stammered. "I-I don't know what—"

"Today, Benny?" Her voice was desperate. "Have you come to take me home? Can I leave? Can you get me out today? How's Jakey? And Papa? You didn't tell him what happened, did you?"

After waiting all this time, Alex stood in front of him, but Ben had no idea what to say. Words of affection, comfort, or encouragement escaped him. The enormity of the circumstances and his failure to control them weighed him down, and it took all his strength not to break.

"Talk to me, Benny." Her voice was cracking too. "Please tell me what is going on. Please, Benny. Get me out of here."

Ben motioned Alex to sit at the half-occupied table.

"I'm trying. But even ten percent of two million, we just don't have it. Jake won't talk to me. I think he blames me for letting them take you. He won't eat."

Ben struggled to continue. "And your dad . . . Jesus. I think he believes you're dead. I'm going to have to tell him something. I don't know what else to do. But how do I tell him this, Alex? It might kill him."

Alex put her manacled hand on Ben's arm.

"Inmate Sawyer, no physical contact." The nearest guard closed in. Alex pulled back and acknowledged the guard with a look of compliance.

"Ben, listen to me." Her voice grew a little in strength but still wavered with emotion. "We need to be strong. We've got to figure out what is going on. Why I'm in here."

"Figure it out?" When Ben heard his own voice, louder than necessary, he realized how close he was to losing control entirely. "How? How am I supposed to figure this out? You tell me: What the hell is going on?"

In the days since the murder, a steady flow of leaked information had appeared in the press. Reports of witnesses. Evidence collected from the scene. Experts on crime scene evaluation had begun to appear within the media reports. None of it looked good for Alex, and Ben needed answers.

"Why did Louis have pictures of you? Your fingerprints are inside his apartment. An eyewitness saw your van parked outside his apartment. And nobody at the Convalescent Center saw you after seven o'clock that night."

"Ben Sawyer," Alex said with anger in her voice, "do you think for one minute I did this terrible thing? That I killed Louis? That I stabbed a man to death?"

"Alex, they pulled a knife with his blood on it from our trash. They even found blood on the screen door at our house."

"I asked you a question?" Alex sounded like she was on the verge of tears. "Do you think I killed Louis?"

"You tell me what happened, then." Ben was almost shouting now. "The newspaper interviewed someone who said he saw you running from the scene. Seems like they got people lining up to be eyewitnesses. And everybody knows how much time you were spending there."

Alex cringed in her seat. "I can't believe what I'm hearing. You think . . ."

"Just tell me what you know," Ben said, almost pleading with her. "If there's something you need to tell me, now's the time."

The other couple at the table had become mired in a heated argument as well. Ben heard mention of money for booze that should have gone to bail. The nearest guard smirked as if he were watching Jerry Springer.

Alex spoke in a low voice. "I can't believe you would for a second think I had something to do with this. I was with Dad until almost ten o'clock. I left the building through the employee entrance. That's why no one at the front desk saw me."

Ben stared at his wife. He thought back over the dozens of cases he had worked where spouses stood by their partners even when their loved one was guilty beyond any doubt. Alex picked up on his uncertainty, and looked down at her hands.

"What about Dad? What about his accident or whatever it was? Remember, I asked Dr. Schneider if someone could have pushed Dad out of his chair? Attacked him in some way?"

"So what?" Ben's voice was incredulous. "What if your dad did have it out with a nurse or an orderly or whoever? What's that got to do with what was going on between you and Louis?"

Alex stared at Ben with a stunned expression on her face. "What did you just say? What are you thinking?"

"Excuse me. Mrs. Sawyer?"

Ben looked to the sound of the voice and saw a heavyset, disheveled man with a walrus mustache stained yellow by nicotine and a mop of bushy gray hair. He tossed his brown wool overcoat on the bench and set a battered leather briefcase on the table. He fumbled with the metal latch to open it, then pulled out a folder containing a bundle of crumpled sheets of legal-size paper. He drew a pocket watch from his vest as he spoke. Surprised at the interruption, Ben fell silent.

"I'm Jean Marquette, your court-appointed attorney." The man spoke as he looked at his watch. "I'm sorry, but we only have a few minutes. I had to meet with another client who is also making an appearance this morning."

Ben stared as the man shuffled through the papers for what looked to be the first time. Ben figured the other client was of the paying variety and not court appointed. Marquette seemed to feel Ben's eyes on him and he looked up.

"Is this your husband?" Marquette looked Ben up and down as if to check him out more thoroughly. "May we speak freely in front of him, or would you rather I ask him to leave?"

Ben didn't hide the coolness in his tone that conveyed a great deal of what he thought of defense attorneys. "I'm her husband, Ben Sawyer. Don't worry about getting all that familiar with the case. I'm hiring a private attorney as soon as I can get the retainer together."

Ben noted the ill-fitting suit, sweat-stained collar, and overall comical appearance. It didn't matter what the truth was, he knew he could never place Alex's life in the hands of this man. Marquette seemed to read his mind.

"I'm sure you'll find someone." The man smiled, dismissive and curt, then looked directly toward Alex, effectively cutting Ben out of the conversation. "But in the meantime, Mrs. Sawyer, until your husband can arrange for a member of the A-team, I'm all you got. The state has appointed me to represent *your* interests."

His voice carried no offense, as if he understood why anyone might have misgivings. He elbowed his way onto the bench next to Ben and took a seat.

"I am already familiar with the circumstances of your arrest and really must advise you that the prosecution has a compelling case. We needn't discuss any details here and now, but I recommend we enter a plea of not guilty at today's hearing. After that we can start to formulate a self-defense argument, see what sort of deal the district attorney might be willing to make. By going self-defense we'll be able to offer a plausible story, something a jury can believe. If we stick with a plea of not guilty, no one is going to buy that—and the district attorney knows it. She'll take us to trial, and with all her resources . . . it would not be a good outcome for you."

"Plead?" Alex sounded shocked. "You mean say I did it?"

"I'm not terribly concerned with whether or not you *'did it,'* Mrs. Sawyer. I am only concerned with what the state can prove. In this case, they can prove a lot."

Ben turned to face the lawyer directly. He tried to speak firmly, but his voice was hollow and lacked conviction. "Forget it, Marquette. We're not interested in any deals at this point. The only plea Alex will be entering is not guilty."

"That's fine, Mr. Sawyer." Ben picked up on the faint odor of bourbon and cheap pipe tobacco. "But once again, let me remind you I represent your wife. Not you."

Marquette turned back to Alex. "Mrs. Sawyer, I've practiced law in this county for over thirty years. This is a high-profile murder case and the district attorney will be swinging for the fences. If, and I emphasize if, she offers any sort of deal, it will be one-time only and it will come after today's hearing. Beyond that, suffice it to say, there will be no more offers."

Alex's voice faltered. "So what are you saying?"

"I'm saying, Mrs. Sawyer, that if you don't seek a plea bargain, *when* you're convicted you will receive a life sentence. I'm certain of it."

The long buzzer sounded, signaling the end of visitation, and guards began to herd the women back to the cells. Alex didn't budge, looking at Ben with a dumbfounded expression.

"Ben, he can't be serious. I can't plead guilty."

Ben stared at the attorney. "Marquette, consider yourself relieved."

"Excuse me?" Marquette turned again to face Ben, clearly put out by this man who kept butting in.

"I said, you're fired. Get lost."

"Mr. Sawyer, I am the state-appointed counsel for your wife," he said smugly. "You can't fire me and neither can she. Only the judge can."

Ben shifted until his face was an inch from Marquette's. He spoke soft but clear. "Fine. Let me put it to you like this. Talk to my wife again and I'll kick your ass back to whatever horseshit law school it is you came from."

Unconcerned, Marquette responded to Ben. "University of Michigan School of Law, cum laude." The lawyer stuffed the papers away and snapped his briefcase shut. He looked at Alex.

"Consider what I've told you, Mrs. Sawyer. We'll make our appearance today, and after that, we'll have about ten days to trial. That will give me time to negotiate with the district attorney."

"Ten days?" Ben was stunned by the short length of time. "Aren't you going to make a motion for a delay? This is a murder case, Marquette. We need more time."

The lawyer picked up his overcoat and stood to leave. Ignoring

Ben, he directed his response to Alex. "I disagree. We need a quick settlement. If we go self-defense and offer to plead to manslaughter, I can probably get you ten to fifteen years. If you behave yourself, you could be out in eight." Marquette went on in a matter-of-fact tone. "You should know there are plenty of people serving longer sentences for murder on a lot less evidence than what the state has got against you."

Ben worked to control his temper. "Get away from my wife, Marquette. That's the last time I tell you without punching your lights out."

Marquette again dismissed Ben with nothing more than a sideways glance and turned to Alex. "Do not say anything during the proceedings this morning unless I direct you. I will do all the talking. I'll see you in the courtroom. Now, if you'll excuse me, I do have another client to attend to." Marquette gave Ben a last look before turning away. Ben watched the man waddle through the female prisoners until he disappeared in the crowd.

"Inmate Sawyer," a guard called out. "Proceed to the holding area now. Visiting hours are over."

Alex looked at her husband and spoke, her voice trembling. "Benny, you've got to believe me. I didn't kill Louis. You've always told me the whole system is based on scaring people into pleading out, into not fighting back. You told me that was what they did to you. Can't you see, it's happening again? It's started already."

Ben turned away, not wanting to listen to his old opinions.

"Listen to me, Ben. I didn't do this. I'm not guilty. I need you to believe me. If you don't . . ." Alex's voice trailed away, then returned. "If you don't believe me, Ben, then I've got no one."

"*Now*, Sawyer. Move your ass." Alex rose with a rattle of chains, then looked one last time at Ben before walking away.

"Hear me on this, Ben. I'm not caving. I don't blame you for what happened in Oakland. You did what you needed to do to take care of your family. But I'm not you."

The guard with the mouth took hold of Alex at the crook of her arm, spun her sharply, and pushed her toward the door leading to the cells. The chain around her ankles had little slack and Alex fell. She did her best to break the fall with cuffed hands, but it was an ugly landing. Ben tried to reach his wife but was intercepted by three additional guards, one of them the blond jerk from earlier in the day.

He sneered at Ben. "You just can't go by the rules, can you, Sawyer? If you're not out of here in thirty seconds, that'll be the last visit you ever make in this facility."

Ben's voice held no anger, only an imploring tone. "Jesus, man. Just let me help my wife. I'm a cop, for Christ's sake. What is wrong with you people?"

Two guards hauled Alex to her feet. She pulled herself free of the men, drew herself to her full height, and walked with short choppy steps to the cell block. She looked over her shoulder just before she passed through the doors and said in a resolute voice, "You can give me up on me if you want, Ben. But I never gave up on you."

TWENTY-EIGHT

McKenzie dreaded the unavoidable meeting and had no idea how it would play out. Driving across town, he kept an eye on the rearview mirror and his forty-cal at the ready in the passenger seat. Three days had passed since the Sawyer arrest, and at last Jorgensen had reached out for a confidential meet. Wanting to try and establish a tactical advantage, McKenzie pulled into the usual meeting place twenty minutes ahead of schedule. But the familiar black Crown Vic was already there, parked in the shadows.

Frustrated, McKenzie shut off his engine, tucked his gun into the back of his waistband, and approached Jorgensen's car on foot. The vehicle was idling smoothly, with the dark windows rolled up. McKenzie stood outside the car like a child waiting for a scolding. After a full minute, he bent over to peer through the window.

"So much for your eyes on the street, eh, Detective?"

The voice came from behind him. McKenzie stumbled as he turned and fell back against the car. His gun clunked heavily on the metal door. Jorgensen emerged from the shadows, the round orange glow of his cigar illuminating his head and face. The padded shoulders of the chief's black camel hair trench coat cut a very impressive figure. A matching fedora was pulled low over one eye.

"Jesus, Chief." McKenzie tried to control his anxiety, but it came through loud and clear. "Scared the shit outta me. Coming out of the woods that way."

"Sorry. Nature called. Had to piss."

McKenzie took a deep breath. In terms of gaining the upper hand, advantage Jorgensen.

The orange circle grew brighter as Jorgensen took a long draw on his cigar. "It would appear our missing man poked his head up, wouldn't you say?"

"You called it, Chief. This guy is one crafty bastard."

"Right in the middle of Newberg." Jorgensen's words were slow and measured. "You want to tell me how a con of his 'pedigree' can work freely enough in my town that he can pull off this kind of bullshit?"

"I know it looks bad, Chief," McKenzie said, "but we're going to be all right. I'm telling you, if I didn't know better, I'd swear this Sawyer woman actually did the killing."

"The problem is, you don't know better," Jorgensen said. "From the beginning you haven't known jack shit. Now we're stuck navigating a high-profile murder case against an officer's wife. Do you realize the media attention that will cause?"

"We can handle this, Chief. The case is solid. I've convicted plenty of shit bags on a lot less."

Jorgensen continued to stare, and said, "Run the case down, Detective. Tell me where we're at."

"First off, manner of death is homicide. No doubt about that. Single stab wound to the torso. The victim, Louis Carson, was standing at the time he sustained the wound. May have even been lunging forward. Bled to death on the floor. The coroner puts time of death between nine and ten o'clock at night. The Sawyer woman can't account for herself."

McKenzie's tone changed to display levity. "I'm tellin' ya, Chief, either this gal has some shit-ass bad luck, or your boy Harlan really knows how to set the hook."

"Continue." The chief did his best to sound bored, but McKenzie figured he had the man's interest.

McKenzie went on. "When it comes to an alibi, she's screwed. Her husband says she was with her father at Newberg Convalescent. We checked with the on-duty staff. No one recalls seeing her after seven P.M. No one recalls seeing her leave, and that includes the staff at the front desk. There is no surveillance equipment or security. Course there'll be no interview of Lars. He's about as talkative as a crown of broccoli."

"So where does our boy fit in?" Jorgensen asked. "What's his role?"

"I figure he made the original call." McKenzie said. "Came in on nine one one from a payphone. That was at about ten o'clock. Gave up some good stuff. Sounds of screams. Green minivan. Pretty good description matching Sawyer. Like I said, the boy really knew how to get the ball rolling right at Sawyer's wife."

"People are going to want to know who this star witness is."

"So happens he hung up before we got his name. But we've got the nine one one recording, and that'll be a big hit in court."

Jorgensen looked off into the distance as he asked his next question. "What can I tell the public about the efforts being made to ID this caller?"

"A canvas didn't find any witnesses. The patrol dogs threw some dust on the phone, they even swabbed it for DNA. Got nothing but a jumbled mess of a couple hundred samples. No way to follow up. Assuming our guy ain't planning on stepping out of the shadows, that lead ain't shit."

"This case sounds like it could use another witness or two," Jorgensen said. "A witness that actually speaks."

McKenzie jumped in. "Already taken care of, Chief. Got just the guy. Says he saw a green minivan, driven by a woman, leaving the area that night. The timing with the nine one one call would make it around the time of death."

"How convenient." McKenzie smiled until Jorgensen went on. "I don't want this case riding on the word of some dope fiend who might cave when someone puts the screws to him."

"He'll be fine. He's got plenty of skin in the game."

McKenzie pulled a miniflashlight from his coat pocket and a notebook from the pocket of his jeans. He lit up his notes to see if there was anything he had forgotten to cover.

"Good physical evidence all the way around. Pictures of the suspect in the victim's home. Fingerprints in the kitchen area, on the computer keyboard, the light switch. Hell, Chief, son of a bitch even left us the weapon and blood transfer. Pulled the knife right out of Sawyer's trash can, found a spot of blood on the rear door of the Sawyer home. I'll put up a week's pay that the blood will come back to our victim."

McKenzie shut his notebook and looked up to signal he was done. "I'd say you gotta admire the man's work. Course, Sawyer's wife is no dummy. Clammed up quick. The only statement we got was her initial alibi. I got a contact at the DA's office. Tells me the public defender assigned to the case has been trying to reach out for a deal. Talking about pleading to manslaughter. They want to go self-defense. Can you believe it? Sawyer's wife is gonna be a convicted killer?"

"What else?" Jorgensen asked.

"What else?" McKenzie replied, allowing himself a slight air of superiority. "You mean other than all the shit I just covered? You mean what more than her own frickin' attorney is already trying to plead her out? You mean what more than that?"

"I mean, how can this thing fall off the rails? Ben Sawyer's not going to just lay down for this shit if he smells a con. You've told me how great the case is. Where can Sawyer come along and punch a hole in it?"

"I don't see it, Chief." McKenzie was matter-of-fact. "This Lee guy put a lot of thought into this shit. Course, he had plenty of time to think it through, wouldn't you say?"

Jorgensen ignored the joke. "I told Sergeant Boyd that due to the sensitive nature of this case, I wanted my most senior detective as lead. That's you. Boyd wasn't too happy about it, but he'll go along. Just make sure you keep everyone else at arm's length. No backup. Nobody riding second chair on this. Don't even tell Boyd any more than necessary. You hear me?"

"I appreciate the vote of confidence, Chief."

"Don't kid yourself, McKenzie. This isn't about confidence. I need to know that I won't have some supercop digging too deep on this thing." Jorgensen opened the driver's door of his car and settled into the leather seat.

"I need my boy on this case. That's you, right, Doyle? You're my boy?"

McKenzie knew how he had to reply. "Yeah, Chief. If that's how you see it. I'm your boy."

Jorgensen clamped down on his cigar as the window went up, making him disappear behind the dark glass. He drove away and left McKenzie standing alone in the middle of the deserted parking lot.

TWENTY-NINE

Tia stood over McKenzie, who was leaning back in his chair
with his feet propped on his desk, reading Newberg's single
daily newspaper. From her vantage point, given the position of the
paper, Tia could easily scan the headlines. The Sawyer case still
dominated the front page.

Holy shit, she thought. *What's left to write about?*

The murder of Louis Carson and arrest of Alex Sawyer was the
biggest Wisconsin crime story since Jeffrey Dahmer. The case even
gained national coverage on the biggest cable news shows and dominated talk radio. For the first days after his wife was arrested, Ben
Sawyer had been accosted by cameras and microphones anytime a
part of his body broke the plane of his front door. The unwritten
media law of "don't screw with the kids" had been tossed aside, and
Jake's face had become familiar to readers of publications stocked
in grocery store checkout lines.

Everyone had an opinion as to why Alex Sawyer went crazy and
killed her secret lover. But although motive was a matter of debate,

that was where the argument ended. Everyone knew Alex Sawyer was a killer.

Sighing, Tia gave one of McKenzie's shoes a hard swat with her hand.

"Hey, Doyle, you got a minute?"

McKenzie looked over the top of his paper. As was always the case when McKenzie greeted Tia, he spoke mockingly, in a thick accent that Tia assumed was supposed to be the Frito Bandito or some such shit.

"Hola, señorrrita."

McKenzie lowered the paper and pulled himself to a sitting position, using one hand to adjust his crotch. Tia picked up the scent of Old Spice and bourbon. She had just come from the gym; her sweats clung to her trim body and she knew her face was flushed. McKenzie's gaze wandered openly, and he made no effort to conceal his thoughts. Tia, for her part, did her best to hide her disgust. She was hoping to get some cooperation.

He spoke again, this time in his natural Wisconsin twang, which had been coarsened by a forty-cigarette-a-day habit.

"Nice surprise. I'm not sure you've ever taken the time to stop by and chat. Grab a seat. Want some coffee?"

Not on your life, pal.

"No thanks," Tia answered. "I just wanted to check and see how the Carson murder case was coming along."

McKenzie looked disappointed. "It ain't 'coming along,'" he said. "That ship has sailed."

"What do you mean? You must have a bunch of leads. I wanted to let you know, I can help out. If you've got some legwork that needs doing, just let me know."

McKenzie surveyed the bottom half of her physique. "Legwork? Yeah, I'll bet you could do some amazing legwork. I just might have to take you up on that."

"Knock off it," Tia said. "I'm serious. What's left to do?"

McKenzie didn't try to hide his annoyance. If Suarez wasn't going to play along, then they had nothing to talk about. His feet went back to his desk and the paper went up.

"This is the Detective Squad. Go work your beat. Like I said, that case is a wrap and Alex Sawyer is dead-bang guilty. I hear she's thinking of pleading out early and getting the best deal she can. The DA might make an offer."

"Pleading out? Bullshit." Tia was stunned.

"Damn, girl. You oughta read the papers. This wasn't no whodunit. Sawyer was screwin' the coffeehouse guy." McKenzie looked at Tia over the top of his paper and changed his tone. "People do that, you know. Men. Women. They get together, and crazy shit happens."

"What about Sergeant Sawyer?" Tia asked. "How's he doing? I've called the house but no answer."

"You called the house?" McKenzie said sharply enough that Tia knew she had crossed the line. "No one in the department is allowed to have any contact with him. And no one better be talking to him about my murder case. That guy assaulted me. His policing days are done."

Tia ignored McKenzie's complaints in her response and tried to turn the conversation away from Ben.

"Look, I know Alex Sawyer. She didn't kill anybody. That's crazy talk. I've worked a few high-profile investigations myself, McKenzie. How about I just read the case file?" She paused. "Maybe we can compare notes."

Too late. McKenzie wasn't biting.

"Interesting as that sounds," he said, "no split-tail patrol cop is nosing around my murder case. Now, if you ever want to just step out and have a drink or something, you be sure to let me know."

Plate Boyd's voice boomed with annoyance from his adjacent office. "McKenzie, get over here. I got Nancy Grace on the line."

McKenzie jumped to his feet and headed out the door. He brushed against Tia as he passed.

"This case is the big time, Suarez. When it's over, I'll tell you all about it. Like I said, you want to step out for a drink, I'll buy the first four or five rounds and we'll see where it goes from there."

A moment later Tia could hear McKenzie on the phone in the next office, ingratiating himself with the celebrity reporter. It took McKenzie less than a minute to comment on the woman's "sexy mouth."

Tia glanced out into the hallway and saw it was clear. She studied McKenzie's desk. His discarded newspaper partially covered several case files. Most documents were marked by coffee ring stains. An overflowing ashtray cast a pall of nicotine dust over all exposed surfaces. Tia gave some thought to riffling through the desk, but that could spell trouble. Last thing she wanted was to be in a position where McKenzie had any leverage over her. Not to mention, the idea of touching anything that belonged to the guy disgusted her.

As she turned to leave, her eye was caught by a disc half buried under several pieces of paper. She glimpsed a large letter *S* on the disc, but the rest of the label was hidden. Tia made sure no one was watching, then pushed aside the documents to read the full text: "Sawyer 911." Tia had heard from patrol officers that the whole Carson murder case had started with a 911 call from a pay phone. After a final check of the door, Tia slipped the disc off McKenzie's desk and tucked it under her shirt.

She hurried down the hallway, passing Sergeant Boyd's office. She could hear McKenzie telling his new celebrity friend one of his favorite stories, about the time he nabbed a bank robber dressed like a clown. His voice boomed into the phone, marked by indignation.

"No, not me. The crook. *He* was dressed like a clown."

THIRTY

Though the old man was breathing steadily, Ben couldn't help but wonder when his last breath might come. Remembering the robust street cop of his youth, he felt certain Lars would welcome an end that allowed for some level of dignity. In the days since he'd been found lying on the floor, Lars had for the most part remained unconscious. He was being fed through a tube. During the rare times when he was awake, he fought—as best he could, given his physical condition—with the nurses and aides, or anyone else who tried to help him. Ben knew Lars wanted his daughter, but Ben couldn't bring himself to tell Lars what had happened.

What are you going to do without her, old man? What are we all going to do?

Ben had been nine years old the first time he walked Alex home from school. Before they reached her house, a police cruiser pulled up. When the cop got out, Ben stopped in his tracks. The boy gawked at the man he was sure stood ten feet tall as Alex flew into her father's arms. Ben had looked on and wondered how it would feel to have a girl like Alex love you that much.

Little Alex—also nine years old—had said, *"Daddy, this is my friend Ben. He sat with me at lunch today and now he's carrying my books, see?"*

Twenty-five years had come and gone, and Ben still remembered the first words Lars Norgaard ever directed at him. *"You must be a mighty special young man. Usually I carry her books."*

Ben looked at the old man's deeply lined face. "You knew right then, didn't you? Even then, you knew where we were headed."

As if on cue, Lars's eyes fluttered open. Ben stood at the bedside, afraid to speak, while Lars stared at the ceiling above his bed. After several seconds Ben bent in close. He tried to speak in a normal, conversational tone.

"It's me, Lars. It's Ben. I'm right here with you."

"Be-n."

It was weak but unmistakable. Lars was speaking for the first time in months.

"Beee-nnn."

"I'm right here." Ben stood where Lars was able to see him. A withered hand moved slowly across the bedsheet as if Lars was trying to reach out. Ben took the old man's trembling hand and held it gently in his own. Lars struggled to speak.

"Haarr-leeee."

"What, Lars?" Ben was stunned. "What did you say?"

"Haaar-leeee."

Ben couldn't keep the excitement from his voice. "What are you saying, Lars? Are you saying Harley? Who is Harley? What does that mean?"

"Haaaar-Leeee." The required effort caused Lars to struggle for breath. His hands shook, his eyes rolled back in his head, and his body began to convulse. Ben shouted for help and heard someone running.

A nurse entered the room and Ben moved aside. The nurse smacked the panic button on the wall above the old man's bed with the palm of her hand and Ben heard an alarm sound down the hall. Seconds later more medical personnel raced into the room, including Dr. Schneider, who immediately began calling out instructions.

The team worked in concert, quickly and smoothly. Within a minute, Lars was sedated and again unconscious, his face contorted under an oxygen mask.

"Let me see you out in the hallway." The doctor's voice was firm, and Ben followed him out of the room.

"What happened in there?" Dr. Schneider asked.

Ben was still dazed by his father-in-law speaking for the first time in almost four months. "He woke up and started talking. He was trying to tell me something. After a couple of attempts, the seizure started."

Schneider was skeptical. "He spoke? What did he say?"

"He said my name." Ben thought back. "Then he said, 'Harley.' He said that a couple of times."

"Does your father-in-law know someone named Harley?"

"I wish I knew," Ben said. "It seemed really important to him."

"I wouldn't read too much into this. Fact is, the chances are pretty good the man was hallucinating. For all we know he may want to take a ride on a motorcycle."

Ben shot back. "Knock off the glib shit, Doc. My father-in-law was trying to tell me something. With everything that has been going on, it could be important."

"I apologize, Ben," Schneider said without a hint of sincerity.

"I don't need your apologies. I just need straight answers. When can you bring him around? I know he was trying to tell me something."

Schneider spoke in a fast and officious clip. "Ben, Lars has been slipping in and out of consciousness since suffering a blow to the head. The impact may have caused neurological damage. I'm sorry to tell you this, but it is highly unlikely this episode had anything to do with an attempt to communicate. But you're right. Until he is awake and calm for some length of time, we won't know for sure. Is that straight enough for you?"

Ben didn't miss a beat. "Yeah, Doc. Your faith in the human spirit is a real inspiration."

When the man made no reply, Ben went on. "Look, I know what I heard. Lars spoke my name and then repeated the name 'Harley' two times. So yes or no. Is there a person with the first or last name of Harley on your staff?"

"No. There is not."

Ben looked through the open door, at the old man sleeping in the bed. "I want you to hold off on the drugs. I know this man. He's got something on his mind, and he isn't going to give up until he gets it out. No more sedatives, all right?"

Schneider folded his arms across his chest. "Mr. Sawyer, perhaps it would be best for you to begin seeking alternate arrangements for your father-in-law. I have been as patient as I can—"

Ben turned away. "Oh, lighten up, Doc. This isn't about your ability. I'm not insulting you. Just quit shooting Lars full of dope until he can get out whatever it is he's trying to tell us, okay? That's all I'm asking."

Schneider pursed his lips and responded. "I'll note Mr. Norgaard's file that there will be no further pain management without your consent. Good day, Ben."

Ben watched as the man turned and left, and gave some thought to how it was that doctors were almost always assholes. Stepping back into the room, Ben looked at his father-in-law, a man he had known for most of his life. The old man's gaunt face was troubled. His eyes were closed, but Ben could see rapid movement beneath the lids. His lips quivered. Ben knew Lars had said something to say, all right, but not to a doctor. Not even to his daughter. Lars wanted to talk to a cop.

THIRTY-ONE

As advertised, the wind blew hard in downtown Chicago. Harlan raised his voice and leaned toward the passenger window to make sure he was heard.

"Get in."

All things considered, the man negotiated himself into the front seat with a fair amount of grace. He was a good six feet tall, well over that with the heels, and Harlan figured him to be in pretty good shape underneath all the window dressing. The he-she hiked up his skirt and looked directly at Harlan.

"Tell me exactly what it is you're after and don't mince words." The voice was a practiced falsetto. "Cops like to be coy. Men who know what they want speak their mind."

Harlan shot back. "How do I know there ain't a cop with a wire in there somewhere?" He gestured toward the prominent forty-inch chest.

"Honey, I don't know any self-respecting officer who would go this far to nab a john," the man said, his Adam's apple jumping as he spoke. "Besides, cops won't get in the car. If they can't reel you in from the sidewalk, they're not interested. My name's Renee. Is there something you wanted to ask me?"

Harlan looked out the windshield and spoke in a casual tone. "I'm in town for the weekend. Staying at the Hilton up the road. Come on back to my room and we'll talk about it there."

Renee laughed, trying to sound effeminate. "Nothing is going to go on there that will cost you less than a hundred dollars. Pay me that now, and we'll talk specifics about what that will get you later." He reached out and squeezed Harlan's crotch.

Harlan couldn't contain his disgust as he grabbed Renee's hand and jerked hard. Renee's real voice came through. "Let go. You're hurting my wrist."

"What I'm gonna want won't involve you puttin' your hands on my prick, you queen fuck. Don't touch me again." Harlan used his "inside" voice—fearsome by any measure.

Renee reached for the door handle, ready to get out. Harlan hit the locks and regrouped. "Hang on now. Relax. I didn't mean to hurt you."

"Don't worry about it. Just unlock the door." The prostitute's voice was back to its artificial high pitch but had an audible tremor.

"Look," Harlan said, "I'm doing a favor for a friend of mine, a client, actually. He's a bit shy but I know how he goes."

After the bad start, Harlan was off his prepared script, trying to make the story work. He opened his wallet and pulled out his last hundred dollars, closing it quick before the prostitute could get a look. "Here, I'll pay you the hundred bucks now, and another two hundred when I bring you back in an hour or so."

Renee looked skeptically at the bills in Harlan's hand.

"You're going to pay me three hundred dollars for an hour's work? Must be an important client."

Harlan keyed in on the greed in the man's voice and played to it.

"It ain't my money," he said. "Comes out of an expense account that'll get charged back to the business. But he does strike me as the generous type. You do your thing, and I imagine he's gonna tip pretty well. Could work out for you."

"Sounds like I might like your client more than I like you." Renee took the money; it disappeared into his impressive cleavage. "Let's go see him."

Twenty minutes later, Renee, who said his given name was Bobby, was handcuffed to a wooden chair in an empty storage unit in west Chicago. Harlan had run the cuffs under the seat of the chair, making it impossible for a man of Bobby's height to sit up straight. From a long canvas bag, Harlan took out a thirty-six-inch Louisville Slugger and slung it casually over his shoulder. Bobby eyed the bat and sobbed into the three-inch ball gag Harlan had strapped over his mouth.

Bobby struggled to speak. He wriggled his wrists, but it was a useless effort. Tears smeared the thick paste makeup all the way to his jawline, exposing a day-old growth of beard. His wig had come off during an earlier struggle, and his thinning hair made him look at least ten years older than the twenty-four years he had claimed when he and Harlan had still been on speaking terms.

"Ya know, Bobby, I knew this fella in prison, pig farmer from Iron County," Harlan said while twirling the bat over his shoulder. "Tall like you but a good bit thicker. Strong fucker too. Son of a bitch was always trying to turn self-respecting men into cock smokers."

Harlan had always liked the sound of a Louisville Slugger moving through the air. He took a couple of healthy swings with the bat.

Whoosh. Whoosh.

"Far as I'm concerned, Bobby, a man can find his pleasure wherever and however the hell he likes as long as whoever is on the receiving end don't object none. Particularly in prison, where pickings are slim and we're all fairly accustomed to the depraved side of people. I'm damn open-minded about such things as that."

Harlan stepped into a full swing, as if he was standing at home plate, and the sound could be heard clear through the room.

Whoooosh.

Bobby yelped with fear and screwed his eyes shut tight.

"I made it clear I wanted nothin' to do with that old boy, but he came callin' on me anyways. Brought a couple of his farm boy associates to hold me down. I'll admit he got the better of me to begin with."

Whoosh.

"But after that day, he didn't ever shove that nasty hunk of flesh in anyone's mouth again."

Whoosh. Whoosh.

"You know why, Bobby?"

Bobby's chest heaved. Vomit oozed out around the edge of the red plastic ball and dribbled down his chin. He reflexively breathed in, then gagged, starting the process over. Harlan ignored the man's discomfort.

"Cuz I bit that thing clean off."

Whooooooosh.

"Took a good bit of work, and that old boy was banging on the back of my head with both fists the whole time. Damn near knocked me out."

Whoosh.

"But yeah, it came off all right. I spit that prick out right there on the cell floor. Come to find out that makes for a serious injury. His boys carted him off, smearin' a blood trail that ran all the way to the damn infirmary."

Whoosh.

"And they don't be offerin' none of that reconstructive surgery shit in a prison hospital. No, sir. Prison docs just threw out the spare parts and stapled 'im up. Hooked in a tube to piss out of and told him, 'Guess you'll just go dickless.' That's some cold shit for a doc to tell a guy, ain't it?"

Whoosh.

"And that, Bobby, is the only time I ever felt the slap of a man's balls against my chin. First, last, and only."

Harlan used his empty hand to position Bobby's head while the other held the bat poised over his shoulder. In anticipation of what might be coming, Bobby made a terrible noise that Harlan took for begging. Harlan pulled on Bobby's chin, and the man's eyes swam in deep pools of mascara-colored tears.

"I make no judgments about ya, Bobby. I want you to know that. Now just go on and hold still."

Bobby rocked his head back and forth. Even with the gag, he managed to make such a racket of guttural screams Harlan feared the noise might bring notice even at this late hour.

Harlan improved his stance and again recollected the face of the Iron County pig farmer. Gripping the bat with both hands, he lifted his front foot and stepped into the swing with every bit of strength he possessed. Wood connected with bone, and he rotated his hips like he was swinging for the fences. There was a loud pop as the man's skull broke into a half-dozen sections, a good bit of the contents spraying out against Harlan's hands, arms, and face. A sizable chunk that included one eye smacked against the wall, where it stuck for a second or two before falling to the floor, staring back from where it had come. The chair that held the now nearly headless body began to lean to one side, hung balanced for a moment, then toppled over. The man's head had the look of a giant eggshell shattered beyond any hope of repair. A moment passed, and then Harlan's hard breath and the settling cranial contents were the only sounds left in the room.

THIRTY-TWO

Tia parked in front of the Sawyer house. It was just after sunup and only one media truck was parked outside the home. The lone occupant dozed in the driver's seat, so Tia exited her car doing her best to keep the noise down. Tia slipped past the man who had the seat halfway reclined and was snoring loudly. She jogged to the front porch, thinking back on her last visit. *Could it have been just a week ago? It doesn't seem possible.*

She had tried to call Ben half a dozen times over the past three days, but an answering machine with Alex's voice was as close as she got. This morning she decided she had waited long enough. The house stood quiet, and she gave the screen door a light rap of her knuckles. A moment later a woman came to the door.

"Oh." Tia was surprised. "Hey, Mrs. Erickson. I'm here to see Ben—I mean, Sergeant Sawyer. I called ahead but there was no answer. I just thought I'd come by."

Bernice was drying her hands on a dish towel. Dressed in a blouse and casual slacks, she looked relaxed until Tia met her gaze. There was pain and fear behind a thin mask of feigned confidence. The woman was doing her best to put up a strong front.

"Hello, Tia." Bernice swung the door open. Her voice was strained and quiet. "Please come in and I'll get Sergeant Sawyer."

"Thank you, ma'am. I'm sorry to intrude.

Bernice seemed to find some strength in her voice. "No, no. You're not intruding. Someone has to do something to get this man—"

Bernice stopped when she heard the sound on the stairs. Both women turned and saw Jake halfway down at the landing. He was dressed in sweat pants and a well-worn Oakland Raiders T-shirt. Tia thought back to her last meeting with the boy and found herself at a loss for words.

Jake spoke first. "Have you seen my mom? Do you know when she can come home?"

Tia stuttered. "I-I haven't, Jake. I'm sorry. But your mom is tough. I'm sure she is hanging in there. But your dad has visited, right? You can talk to him about it."

Jake scoffed. "He can't do anything. They don't even listen to him."

Ben came down the steps and stood next to his son. He looked asleep on his feet. "What are you doing at home? Didn't you go to school?"

Tia listened as Jake responded in a tone of disrespect and anger. "I told you. I'm not going to school. No way."

Ben shook his head, then turned away from his son. He looked at the two women standing in the entry of the house, his face marked with distrust. "What's up?"

Tia took three steps toward the staircase. "I need to talk to you. It's about the case against Alex."

"What about it? I'm trying to get some sleep before visiting hours. Can this wait?"

Jake looked at his dad with a huff and then retreated back up the stairs.

Bernice took a firm tone. "I'm sure Officer Suarez wouldn't be coming by if it weren't important, Benjamin. You two need to talk."

"Really, Sarge," Tia said. "We need to talk. Now."

Ben cursed under his breath and came down the stairs with heavy steps. He walked into the living room and motioned for Tia to join him. Bernice left them alone. Ben dropped himself onto a couch and put his bare feet on a coffee table. Tia looked around and took a seat in an easy chair. She had been in the room only briefly during her last visit. Now she noticed the torn upholstery and the general shabbiness of the furniture. Ben picked up on her observations.

"Nice, huh?" His voice was heavy with sarcasm. "Our fall from grace out in California ended up being pretty costly. Not to mention the damn medical bills these days, but don't get me started."

Alex looked at the picture over the fireplace of the Sawyer family. Jake looked to be around five. Ben and Alex were younger too. The family was on a beach, wearing matching outfits and with bare feet. It was a beautiful portrait of the perfect family at what Tia figured was a much happier time. She looked at Ben and saw he was looking at the photo as well.

Tia sat forward in the chair and spoke. "I got hold of some useful intel from the murder. McKenzie is keeping everything under lock and key, but we can work around his dumb ass. I'm figuring if someone is out to frame Alex, we should start at the beginning, right?"

Ben chuckled slightly, and Tia realized from the sound of it that he was exhausted. "Framed, huh? Where do you get off thinking some crazy shit like that?"

Tia stopped. "What do you mean? You think Alex is good for it?"

"Who gives a shit, Suarez?" Ben shouted. He was closer to the edge than Tia had anticipated. "My wife kills a guy, or maybe she doesn't. Does it really matter? Have you seen the papers? I've got some experience in this kind of bullshit. Believe me, facts aren't all that important to the process."

Ben rubbed an open hand across his face, then went on.

"I got a call from a friend at the DA's office. Wanted me to know they'll give Alex one bite at the apple and that's it. After that, they're going to bring all they got. Like I said, it doesn't really matter if she did it or not. If she doesn't plead, they'll put her away for life."

Tia wasn't ready to give up, but she had to ask. "What's the offer?"

Ben stared back. "Murder two. Twelve to fifteen. Minimum-security facility. But they also want my resignation. Shit, they practically told me we have to leave town. The mayor, the Council, the DA—everyone wants the whole mess to just go away."

Tia knew there was a hard road ahead but didn't hesitate in her response.

"Okay. Listen up, Sarge. You got two choices. First one is Alex killed Louis Carson and then I guess that deal might not be too bad." Tia let the words sink in before she went on.

"The only other possibility is she's getting railroaded. Crazy, I know. But it's one or the other." Tia paused. "So tell me, Ben. You said you wished just one person had given you the benefit of the doubt, right? What about your wife? Don't you figure she's feeling the same way? Just hoping one person will stand up and fight for her?"

When Ben sat silent, Tia went on. "You don't think Doyle Mc-Kenzie gives a shit about the truth, do you? His case is solved. He's lining up media interviews. Probably working on a frickin' book deal."

"How could it be a setup?" Ben asked. "I mean, even I have to say that seems like a stretch."

"I've read over what they've got and none of it is hard evidence.

It's got the feel of a frame-up. Believe me, I know more about this stuff than I want to admit. You don't want to know how we worked people over in Afghanistan. If we needed to get rid of a drug lord or a local tribe leader who didn't want to play ball, we'd build cases for what they called 'cultural sins.' Stuff like fraternizing with Westerners or homosexual bullshit. We didn't spend a lot of time worrying about where the proof came from. Planting evidence, creating motive out of thin air. When it came time for the target to get stoned or his head to end up in a basket, we'd say, 'Mission accomplished,' and that was that. You can make anybody look pretty damn guilty if you put your mind to it."

Ben stared at her. "Keep talking."

"Most of what they got on Alex is pretty predictable. A weapon, blood . . . the bullshit pictures that are supposed to support the idea of an affair. It's really a pretty amateur job." Ben had never seen this side of Tia Suarez—the part of her that was a repository of subversive clandestine knowledge he was completely unfamiliar with.

"What we need to do is take it back to the beginning," Tia said. "Working on the assumption that this is all a frame-up, then the nine one one call from the anonymous person is bullshit." She looked at Ben. "In my mind, that makes it a pretty safe bet the caller is the killer."

"Has McKenzie followed up on it?" Ben asked. "Has he run the number down?"

"Yeah." Tia smirked. "To a pay phone a half mile up the road from the murder scene. Nobody saw anything. For his incompetent ass, that's as far as it goes."

"So? The phone location would be captured, but if it's a pay phone there's not much you can do with that, right?"

"Leave that to me. I've got some friends working on it."

Ben's voice was hesitant. "What are you saying? You need to keep it legit or Jorgensen will have your ass. You'll lose your job."

"I don't give a shit about Jorgensen," Tia said. "And believe me, this is old school for me. I can—"

Ben cut her off. "You've done enough. Really. I don't want you in the middle of this. Alex has an attorney. I'll light a fire under his court-appointed ass."

Tia sounded shocked. "Court appointed? You mean like a public defender?"

Ben's face went red and he answered, "I know. I'm working on it. The retainer to hire a private lawyer on a murder rap is pretty stiff. It's fifty K minimum. If you really want an adequate defense, it'll cost you six figures up front. For now, this guy is all we got."

"Sarge, I got ten grand stuck away in a CD. My family has a farm in Mexico. Let me make some calls and—"

"Knock it off," Ben said. "Don't even think about it."

"All right. But if this lawyer tries to blow you off, let me know. I'm telling you, I can find the guy who made the call, whoever he is and wherever he is. I'll throw him in the trunk of my Goat and drop him off on your doorstep. Give you a few minutes alone with him. You got some experience in that area, right?" Tia winked, trying to get Ben to show some life. He smiled but said nothing.

"Sarge, you aren't giving up, are you? I mean, you can't leave this up to McKenzie, Boyd, and some welfare lawyer."

"What am I supposed to do? I have a kid to take care of, Alex's dad is starting to lose it, and in case you forgot, I'm suspended with no paychecks coming in. I don't have access to a damn thing."

"You got me." Tia reached out and put her hand on his knee and squeezed. "Come on, Ben. Get mad. You gotta fight."

Ben held eye contact for several seconds. "You're a good friend, Tia. That means a lot to me right now."

Tia stood from the chair and headed for the door. Ben stood to follow. "Go visit your wife. Take some time with her. Make sure you tell her I said hello and not to worry. We're going to figure this out. She'll be home in no time."

Tia poked her head out the door and saw it was still clear. Heading for her car, she smacked the hood of the van of the sole media truck with her fist as she walked by. The driver jerked awake, and Tia got up close against the closed window and flipped him off, shouting out, "Get a life, you frickin' leper."

Tia had almost reached her car when the cell phone chimed in her pocket. The screen displayed "blocked number" and she knew who it was. "What's up?"

The voice was synthesized beyond recognition and didn't bother with small talk. "The guy you're interested in? He made a nine one one call to the police department in a place called Danville, Illinois, about forty-five minutes ago."

Tia waited. When the voice offered no more, she tried coaxing. "And?"

"And I'll play it for you one time. Then it goes away forever. You ready?"

Tia sat in her car with the doors and windows shut and the sounds of the world locked out. "Yeah. Let me hear it."

A recorded voice came over the line. Tia listened intently. The stressed tone struck her as an act from the start, but the content of the call was what took her breath.

The synthesized voice came back on the line. "That's it. You should go down there and ask around. Call was short, but it sounded like something you'd be interested in."

"No shit," Tia replied, already maneuvering her car into traffic. "Okay. You said Danville PD, right?"

"Yes, that's right. Danville. And Tia?"

"Yeah?"

"Hear me on this. I'm pulling the plug. That's all you're going to get, so make it work. You got it?"

"Yeah, I understand," Tia said. "I owe you. Thanks a million."

"You don't owe me anything. This never happened."

The line went dead.

Not much could be said over a cell, but what she'd just heard was damn intriguing and gave her plenty to go on. Everything Ben had said about keeping it legit was forgotten. Tia punched Danville, Illinois, into her dash-mounted GPS. A few minutes later she was southbound on I-94, pushing her luck and hoping that the Wisconsin State Patrol would look the other way for an off-duty cop doing 105.

THIRTY-THREE

Three people stood between Ben and the metal detector in the slow-moving line. Shuffling ahead, he pulled the coins and bills from his pocket and dropped them into the plastic dish; now off with the belt and shoes. Wait until called. Pass through the metal detector. Arms up for the wand. Spread your legs for the small area search. Sign the waiver. The routine was as aggravating as it was demeaning, but at least Ben's attitude had improved. After his talk with Tia, he had showered and even shaved. A fresh shirt made him feel almost respectable. He couldn't wait to see his wife. He needed to see her. He didn't know what he would say to her, but somehow he had to help her hang on.

At first, the person speaking to him didn't register.

"Hey, Sarge?" The voice was deep and commanding. "Sergeant Sawyer?"

Ben looked up to see a handsome uniformed guard with a disarming smile motioning for him to step out of line. The man wore a crisp short-sleeved uniform shirt over a V-shaped torso. Two stripes identified him as the corporal of the guard. His black hair was worn in a short military style, and the smooth dark skin of his arms covered muscles that stood out like thick ropes. Ben's first impression was the guy looked pretty squared away to be part of this outfit.

Great, Ben thought. *Now what? These rent-a-cops really got it in for me.*

Without giving up his place in line, Ben called back, feeling defensive, "What?"

"Sir, could you step around the counter, please?" He opened the swinging gate and motioned for Ben to come through, but he stayed put.

"I'll lose my place. Visitation starts in ten minutes, Corporal. Whatever this is about, can we take care of it after visiting hours?"

"Relax, Sarge. Just come around the counter for me."

Ben reluctantly followed the corporal away from the visiting line and through a nearby door. They entered a comfortable room that Ben figured the guards used for lunch breaks or to catch a nap on graveyard. There was a couch and chair along with a well-stocked counter with snacks, coffee, and bottled water. The coffeepot was full and smelled fresh.

"Make it quick, Corporal."

He looked young to be in charge but had an air about him that told Ben before too long he'd be more than a private company jail-house guard.

"I don't blame you for being put out," he said. His delivery was smooth and sincere. Ben reluctantly felt himself drawn in by the man's words. "What happened the last time you were here was uncalled for. I spoke to the officers. It won't happen again, Sergeant."

Ben remained skeptical but replied politely, "All right. I appreciate that. Now can I get back in line?"

"That won't be necessary, sir. Tia Suarez called me this morning. She and I served in the Marines together. Did some time overseas. She tells me you're a standup guy and that your wife is getting screwed. I don't know about any of that, but I know you're a cop and I'm not going to have you getting the shaft on my watch."

Ben allowed himself a smile, warmed by a sense of comradeship absent from his life the past few days. It felt good, even from a security guard who was a complete stranger.

"Thanks, Corporal . . . ?"

"Reynolds. Darnell Reynolds." The man stuck out his hand and Ben accepted. "Have a seat, Sergeant. I'll be right back."

The guard left through a rear door, and Ben sat down on the arm of the comfortable lounge chair. The Brewers were playing the A's on the television. Ben thought back to the night of steaks and beer. In another world, he'd be at that game right now, with Jake.

Ben looked at his watch and thought as nice a guy as Darnell might be, he had started to cut into his visiting time. A moment later Darnell returned along with Alex, uncuffed and without leg irons. Alex glanced around the room, confused by the break in routine. When she saw Ben, she stopped dead. Ben stood up straight but remained in place.

Corporal Reynolds stepped aside and spoke softly. "Go on, Sarge. Say hi to your wife. Give her a hug or something."

Ben finally understood. The rules had been lifted. *Tia Suarez, you are the man.*

Ben walked toward Alex, who was still standing stiffly just past the door. She looked baffled. He wrapped her in his arms, and after a brief moment of tension, he felt her body go limp against his. It had been nearly a week since he'd held her, the longest such stretch since junior high. She wept in his arms.

Darnell spoke in a quiet voice. "Again, Sergeant, Mrs. Sawyer, I'm sorry for the way things have been handled. Take all the time you need. I'll be right outside the door. The fridge is stocked with sodas and help yourself to some snacks. If you need to make phone calls, ma'am, just dial nine first, but you should be aware the line might be recorded."

Darnell turned to go. Ben pried himself six inches away from Alex and said, in a voice cracking with emotion, "Corporal Reynolds?"

Darnell stopped in the doorway and looked back. Ben saw the man was uncomfortable with the moment, but he had to say something.

"Thank you," Ben said. "I don't know what else to say."

"Don't thank me. Thank Tia. She's definitely got your back, Sarge."

"I know she does, but none of us can do anything alone, right? Not even Tia."

Darnell nodded and smiled as he left the room.

Ben held Alex as her body heaved with emotion. He rocked her gently and stroked her coarse hair, whispering in her ear in a low tone meant to soothe.

"I'm here now, baby. You're not alone." It came clear to Ben what he needed to say. What he knew to be the truth. He felt a growing strength in his body that had been absent for days. The words came easy. "I know you're innocent, Alex. I know you didn't kill Louis."

Ben felt Alex's arms go tighter around his neck and her sobs grew louder. "I'm sorry I doubted you. I was wrong. But we've got good friends, good people around us. We're going to fight this thing and we're going to win. It won't be long, Alex. I'm going to take you home."

THIRTY-FOUR

Her status as a fellow cop earned Tia access to Detective Anthony Seale, but not without a wait. She'd been sitting in the lobby of the Danville, Illinois, PD for forty-five minutes before Seale walked over and apologized for the delay, saying that the day had been hectic.

Tia was impressed with the small but bustling department. The building, the people, and the welcome afforded a visiting cop reminded Tia of the shortcomings of her own PD. All the same, Tia suspected that once she broached the subject of her visit, her favored-nation status might be in jeopardy.

In a few moments of small talk, Tia found that Detective Seale projected intellect and charm that were likely lost on most cops. Graying at the temples, dressed in a conservative high-quality suit, his appearance made him an imposing figure. The man sat at an ordinary government-issued metal desk in a gray sea of other desks, but he was not an ordinary man.

Detective Seale had spent twenty-five years on the Chicago Police Department, the last seven as a detective in the Organized Crime

Bureau. He explained to Tia he decided to finish his career in a place like Danville to remind himself that people are basically good. The detective struck Tia as a solid cop in every respect. When others passed by, Tia picked up on a sense of deference offered Detective Seale. He was like the big league star, headed for the hall of fame, who'd decided to finish his career in the minors. It made Tia all the more self-conscious of her thin police résumé. Tia was slow in opening up, but eventually Seale gave her a nudge.

"You're a ways from home, Tia. What brings you to Danville?"

The junior cop took a deep breath and dove in. "Have you heard about the murder up in Newberg? A guy named Louis Carson? Stabbed to death?" Tia gave the facts out piecemeal, waiting for Seale to acknowledge familiarity.

"Oh, yeah. I've seen the news coverage. Cop's wife is good for it, right?" Seale said matter-of-factly.

"Yeah, that's what everyone has pretty much decided. She's in jail. She and her husband, Ben Sawyer, Sergeant Sawyer, are good friends of mine."

Seale, sitting on the edge of his desktop, squirmed. "Sorry. That must be tough. Probably pretty much rocked the PD's world, huh?"

Tia answered, "Not as much as you'd think. Probably not as much as it should have. But anyway, I'm here on kind of a related issue."

Seale waited for Tia to continue.

"I've done a little behind-the-scenes work, off the grid, you might say. This morning, around eight fifteen or so, your PD got a nine one one call. Something about a guy putting something in his trunk. A rolled-up carpet? The caller thought it looked suspicious. Your front desk staff told me you caught the case. I wonder if you could tell me who it was that called?"

Seale cocked his head and after a moment asked, "Who did you say you're with? What's your assignment?"

Tia understood the implication. "Patrol, Newberg PD."

"You're a patrol officer on a small-town department in Wisconsin and you're hooked up enough to know who's calling nine one one in Danville, Illinois?"

"I know that seems strange, but I've got a source that—"

"Hang on." Detective Seale raised a hand in the classic *Stop* gesture. "I don't think I want to hear about your source. You're sticking your nose in on the middle of an ongoing murder case. I can't say I get a good feeling about that."

"Murder case? Here in Danville?" She looked at the ceiling and closed her eyes, realizing she had stumbled into a real pile of shit.

"Let me guess," Tia spoke plainly. "It came in from a pay phone and your caller hung up before he could be ID'd. Am I right?"

Detective Seale stared hard at the cop but gave up nothing. Tia realized the time had come to put her cards on the table.

"Look, I don't mean any disrespect. I know I've bent a few rules, but a person's life is on the line. Whoever made that call here in Danville might be a player in the murder in Newberg."

A detective greeted Seale as he walked by. Seale smiled and replied, then waited until the other man was out of earshot. When he finally spoke, Seale's voice was clipped, with an edge of anger.

"What do you mean, a player?"

"The call you got on whatever case you're working? It's the same person who called Newberg PD on nine one one and reported the murder *we're* working. The caller in Newberg hung up and was never ID'd."

Seale sat stone faced and Tia tried to coax something out of him. "Does that make any sense to you?"

Detective Seale spoke with some irritation. "Whether or not it makes sense doesn't mean I like some patrol cop monitoring my casework. Fact is, I'm wondering if I should even be talking to you about this."

Tia stared ahead and said nothing. Seale took a quick look around and stood.

"Let's get out of here. Get a cup of coffee. We'll take my car." Detective Seale took his jacket and a file from his desk and looked at Tia. "See if we can figure this out without getting you all jammed up on a half a dozen bullshit federal charges. Most of which, by the way, carry a minimum of five years."

Tia exhaled with relief. "Sounds fair. Thanks."

"Don't thank me yet. But you're damn sure buying the coffee."

The two cops pulled onto the quiet street in the unmarked police car, unnoticed save by one person. He fell in behind the large black sedan, wondering what the hell a cop from Newberg was doing all the way down here in the Land of Lincoln.

THIRTY-FIVE

Ben spent three hours with Alex before he finally left the jail through the staff entrance. Once their emotions had leveled off, Alex and Ben spent time talking about how to deal with the reality of their circumstances. They laughed about Marquette, the public defender, who could probably save them a hundred grand if Alex could just come to grips with the idea of spending a decade in prison. They agreed that Ben needed to level with both Lars and Jake, especially Lars. The man deserved to be told his daughter was jammed up on a bogus murder charge. Alex had been dumbfounded to hear Ben's news of her father—excited that he had spoken but frustrated she wasn't part of the moment.

Before he left, Corporal Reynolds told Ben to call ahead before his next visit and promised to make sure the on-duty staff was dialed in on the new arrangements. He also let Ben know that Alex would be reassigned to a more secure unit with a private cell. As a cop's wife, she rated increased security. When he left, Ben noticed that the attitude of all the guards had improved. The experience stood out as a single bright spot since the arrest, and he knew he had Tia to thank for it.

At Newberg Convalescent, Ben walked into Lars's private room and wondered how to break the news. *Easy,* he thought. *Tell the truth.*

"Hey, Lars. It's me, Ben." The old man's eyes fluttered open. Ben had never seen Lars look more gaunt and worn. *What does he know? What does he think has happened?*

Ben pulled a chair near the bed. "Lars, I need to talk with you about Alex. I need to tell you some things." Lars turned his head to face his son-in-law with a look that said, *It's about damn time.*

Ben laid out the story of Alex's arrest and the case against her. He told Lars that he knew beyond any doubt Alex was innocent and the only possible explanation was she had been framed. He spoke with conviction. The two men, the two cops, held eye contact with one another, and Ben felt a rekindling of the kinship they had lost years earlier.

"Lars, I don't know who would do this to her. The guy that got killed, Louis, they were friends. He was a good guy. But from what I can tell, he was just a guy with a coffee shop. Nothing else. None of it makes any sense. I can only figure—"

In a sudden and quick movement Ben would have associated with a man a good bit healthier, Lars grabbed Ben by his shirt. The grip was weak but meaningful. Lars opened his eyes wide and poised his mouth to speak. No words came, but Ben waited. The withered hand still gripped his shirt and Ben took hold of it.

"Take it easy, Dad. Don't get excited. Stay calm. We got plenty of time." Ben realized he hadn't called his father-in-law Dad since high school and saw that it had registered with Lars as well. The old man closed his eyes and steadied himself. Finally the sounds came. The pitch of the voice was strained.

"Harrr-leeee."

"Lars, who is Harley? You've got to tell me more. Does it . . . does he have something to do with Alex? With Alex getting arrested?"

Lars tapped lightly on Ben's chest.

"Harr-Leeee. Ben. Har-leeee."

Tears streamed from the old man's eyes as the grunting tones continued. "Alllll-lex. I'm soooorry." Ben watched as the man sobbed, rocking his head back and forth.

Alex was right. Lars Norgaard had the answer. The answer lay trapped in his mind, and the old man was fighting like hell to get it out.

THIRTY-SIX

The Danville Café was half empty in the midafternoon. The smells of chicken grease and freshwater fish left a permanent flavor in the air. A gray-haired waitress whose uniform was adorned with a button that read TIPS ARE SEXY ignored Tia and greeted Seale with a wink. The two cops followed the stout waitress to the seating area, and three more patrons greeted Detective Seale by his first name as he passed by. Tia stood off and watched Seale work the room, shaking hands and offering hellos like he was walking down a rope line. Tia figured the man should retire and run for mayor. After wrapping up a conversation about his recent performance in a local bowling tournament, Seale walked with the waitress to the back of the restaurant and Tia followed along behind. Seale motioned for Tia to take a seat across from him in a secluded booth. The waitress poured out two large mugs of steaming-hot coffee, gave Seale a final wink, and walked away. Facing her across the table, Seale turned all business.

"I got a call this morning," he said. "Came through nine one one and got forwarded to my desk. Anonymous. Fella said he wanted to report a body. Least, he thought it was a body. Told me he saw a guy putting a roll of carpet in the trunk of a car. Looked like a foot sticking out of the end.

"It was a convincing call. Definitely worth checking out. Said the car was parked on Lakeview Drive. Gave a description of the guy and the car. Even gave me the license plate. Everything. When I asked for his name, he hung up. I tried to the trace the number, but it came back to a drugstore pay phone." Seale looked at Tia and concluded with a note of sarcasm. "But I guess I shoulda called you, huh?"

Tia went straight to the truth. "I did some time in the Marines. Counterintelligence in Afghanistan. Still got a lot of friends. I got out and became a cop, but a few of my former coworkers . . . let's just say they're still in the business."

Detective Seale couldn't keep the intrigue out of his voice. "Go on."

Tia had meant to keep her methods to herself, but too much was at stake and she got a good feeling from Seale.

"I burned a copy of the Newberg nine one one call. Had a friend of mine download it into a satellite-based voice-recognition database. Kind of a legitimate government thing, but not really. I figured the guy would eventually make some more calls, public or private, Wisconsin, Illinois . . . hell, he could call from Mars, it wouldn't really matter. If he picked up a phone and said 'boo,' we'd know it." Tia sipped her coffee and looked at Seale to see if he was handling the revelation well enough that she should continue. The man was stoic and hard to read. Tia went on.

"My idea was capture a call, then set up surveillance on the guy. Then all I would need to do is wall off the source of the info and approach the guy from a blind. Some bullshit traffic stop . . . or maybe his car would conveniently get broken into and he'd report it to the cops. Then we'd get an ID on him. Start working it from there. Nobody would ever know the difference, and we could build a case independent of the all the illegal shit. Used to be normal ops for me."

She paused. "But I get it—that was a different rule book and I pushed the envelope a bit. I didn't mean to step on your work. Last thing I expected was to end up with a copycat of the case from Newberg."

A moment passed before Seale gave into a wry grin. "You might just end up in Leavenworth, but you are, without a doubt, the ballsiest and most interesting female cop I've ever met. And after twenty-plus years in Chicago, that's saying something."

"I appreciate the compliment, Detective," Tia said, "but I'm not much interested in the Leavenworth gig. You think we can work around that?"

"Yeah." Detective Seale said, his face gone dead serious. "I think we can work something out."

Tia prodded. "Can I ask? The info off the call, did it pan out?"

Seale took a long look at Tia and spoke slowly. "Yeah, you could say that. I took a couple of uniform guys and went to the address. A car that matched the description was parked right where he said it would be. The owner of the car was home and he was a dead ringer for the guy the caller identified as loading the carpet roll into the trunk. Sure enough, once we got in the trunk, we found a dead he-she whore. Probably missing from the city. Got its skull caved in with a ball bat. Little more brutal than most, but it happens now and then to men who pass themselves off as hookers. Your average guy can get pretty pissed once he realizes he just got head from another dude."

"So you've got a suspect ID'd. Let me guess," Tia said. "The case kind of just solved itself?"

"Yep," Seale said, "until you came nosing around with your secret agent shit. I knew the minute we opened that trunk this case was too good to be true."

"Where you at with it?" Tia asked.

Seale took a big sip of his coffee and looked at her over the top of the mug. "I was pretty far along. That's why you got stuck in the lobby. Spent most of the morning at the scene. Pretty straightforward. Once we got into the trunk, one thing led to the next. Recovered the murder weapon from the garage. Thirty-six-inch Louisville Slugger. Solid ash with, wouldn't you know it, a funny-looking red stain on the business end. We hooked the guy, and of course he lawyered up real quick; he's nobody's fool. I think he's probably been around the block a time or two at some point in his life. He's got a rap sheet, but most of it goes back quite a few years. Up in your neck of the woods, actually. Florence County."

Tia made a mental note of it. "Florence County? That's all the way up at the top of the state. Not much up there but forest and homesteaders. Real live-off-the-land types."

"Doesn't matter," Seale said, changing the subject. "I'll tell you what we'll do. We'll keep your extracurricular activities off the books for now. Keep it to ourselves. We can compare your Newberg case with the murder here in Danville. Something legit has got to match up. That way we can wall off your clandestine shit and give the connection a legal angle. With that, maybe we'll take another run at our so-called suspect. See if he gets a little more talkative."

Seale looked at Tia across the table. "Unorthodox as hell, Tia, but I gotta tell ya, it's hard to argue with the results. You're a hell of a cop."

Tia fought against the urge to stand and shout with the excitement of a heart that sensed vindication. She reached for her cell phone. "I need to get hold of Ben Sawyer. He'll want to know about this."

"Yeah, okay." Seale took a final taste of coffee and motioned the waitress for the check. "Don't go into a lot of detail over the phone, but tell him if his wife isn't home by dinner, her lawyer ain't worth a damn. I could get her out based on this crazy shit."

Tia began to search for Ben's cell number in her call history when she saw another man approaching the detective with a sense of apparent familiarity. Feeling the makings of an intrusion, she put the phone aside. "Hey, Tony. Don't look now, but here comes another member of your fan club."

THIRTY-SEVEN

Harlan had followed them from a distance and waited a full minute before entering the diner. He was glad to see the light crowd as he took a seat at the counter. The Danville detective and the female he recognized as a uniform cop from Newberg were laughing. A couple of old men were sitting nearby—nothing to worry about. The sole waitress finished with the cops and came over to greet Harlan.

"Good morning. What can I bring ya?" Her cheerfulness was wasted on him.

"Just coffee. Black." Harlan feigned a thick southern accent and did his best to avoid eye contact. He made sure to touch nothing. Looking toward the back of the restaurant, he shook his head in apparent disgust.

What the hell are you two talkin' about? he thought, wondering how the two cops had met.

Harlan had kept an eye on the Danville detective all morning, and the man had done everything Harlan had expected of him. Right after the call, the detective had headed out to the house with a couple of cops in uniform. Before too long, they'd discovered the body and arrested the obvious killer—the man who, years ago in a courtroom, identified Harlan as the one he'd seen fleeing the scene of a murder. All had gone according to plan, and that score was now nearly settled. Harlan had intended to leave Danville by nightfall and head north for good.

Now this bitch cop shows up, he thought. Harlan almost laughed at the thought of all the trouble the cop must have gone through to somehow end up here in Illinois. *Impressive, but all for nothin'.*

"Here you go, sir. Will that be all?"

Harlan remained pleasant and kept up his "southern charm." "Yes, ma'am. I believe it will."

The waitress walked away, and Harlan resisted the urge to sip the coffee.

Remember, he told himself, *they're cops. They'll be packin'. Hang back six feet or so. Spread it out even and be quick.* Harlan stood. For a moment he fumbled in his pocket, until he fixed his grip. Then he walked toward the booth shared by Detective Seale and the officer from Newberg. He pasted a corny smile on his face, doing his best to appear clumsy and disarming.

THIRTY-EIGHT

The words "fan club" still hung in the air when Tia heard the loud crack of two quick shots. For an instant Seale's expression turned to one of mild surprise, and then profound sadness. His eyes grew unnaturally wide just as he disappeared in an explosion of blood. Tia felt and tasted a warm sticky liquid spray out, getting in her eyes and covering her nose and mouth. Seale fell forward, and what had been his face settled unevenly against the Formica surface. Tia looked on in horror as the table turned into a growing sea of red liquid. There was a gaping round hole at the base of Seale's skull and most of the top of his head was gone. Two shots. Both lethal. Seale was most certainly dead, and the man who killed him stood less than three feet away.

Acting on extinct, Tia hunkered down to pull her 9mm from her ankle holster. As she bent low, her chest banged against the table-top and her fingertips touched the hard plastic grips that were just beyond her reach. Tia shifted her body but kept her eyes locked on the man who was now adjusting his point of aim. Tia continued to fumble for her gun even as the snub-nosed barrel swung her way.

The gun was poised inches from her face, and Tia could see down the length of the short barrel as though it were the opening of a train tunnel. She watched as the cylinder began to turn.

No time, Suarez.

Tia reached out with her arm and smacked the man's wrist just as the gun fired. A bright flash flooded her vision as the path of the bullet screamed past her ear along with the sound of patrons running for the exit. A dozen or more dishes crashed to the floor somewhere behind her, and Tia sensed the atmosphere of bedlam. Her ears rang from the gunfire, but as her vision cleared she could see the gun beginning to swing back her way. Tia pushed out of her seat while at the same time she picked up the mug of steaming coffee and flung it at her attacker. He screamed in pain and covered his face with his free hand. In that moment she was on him.

Tia broke free of the restricting table and positioned herself in front of the gunman. She grabbed his gun with both hands while delivering a knee strike to his groin. Tia knew by his forward momentum that she had found her mark. She pulled hard on the gun, but his grip remained firm. Keeping one hand on the gun, she pulled back her other fist to deliver a strike to his face, but his body suddenly pushed forward and forced her to the ground. He landed on top of her, and she felt the hard metal settle against her rib cage. Tia reached down and got both hands back on the gun. She grabbed the cylinder and squeezed her fist around it. Even as she held it, she could feel his finger against the trigger. She knew he too was squeezing hard as the cylinder turned slowly beneath her grip. She squeezed harder and still the cylinder turned. She looked toward his face and their eyes met.

Tia heard the explosion at the same time a burning sensation spread through her midsection. Her hand went numb and her fingertips slid off the cylinder. A second round was less painful, but somehow she could almost trace the path of the bullet as it nicked her spleen and exited out her back. Tia took a desperate breath, forcing herself to be calm and surrender to whatever her fate might be.

Lying flat on her back, searching for a last moment of peace, twenty-eight-year-old Tia Suarez allowed herself to drift away. The gunman pulled himself to his feet and stood over her. He pointed the gun at her face as she pictured her parents on their farm in Jalisco. She closed her eyes and conjured a mental image of the family she might one day have had. She heard the repeating clicks of the hammer as it fell on empty cylinders. Tia opened her eyes and a child appeared before her, calm and smiling as the gunman limped and stumbled away. A girl, Tia thought her to be four, maybe five years old was out of place in the café that was now deserted and quiet. Tia lay on the floor, and the little girl, ghost-like yet firm, pulled her close. Strength flowed from the child and Tia's pain disappeared. Her body now weightless, Tia watched the café drift away behind her.

"Come with me, it's not your time," the child whispered.

Tia sensed an intense familiarity, although the little one was unknown to her. "Where do we go, *mija*?"

"*No es tu tiempo. Ven con migo y te mostraré el camino a casa.*"

Tia took the small girl's offered hand. Together they walked down a path of shimmering shallow water, moving away from a distant brilliant light. Tia stood straight, overcome by a sense of wonder at the possibilities of what might come next.

THIRTY-NINE

B en sat at the kitchen table feeling invigorated by the events of the day. Having a real visit with Alex and then leveling with Lars had given him a sense of renewed hope. Bernie had spent the entire day with Jake and then stayed to cook dinner. Over pork chops and potatoes, Ben listened to Jake talk about the dinosaurs at the Geology Museum in Madison. Bernie had insisted if the boy wasn't going to go to school he needed to do something that was at least remotely educational. Jake's rare outburst of conversation ended when the phone rang, a harsh disruption of their pleasant evening. Ben immediately thought of Alex, imagining a jail assault or something worse. He practically jumped to answer the call.

"Sergeant Sawyer?" The sound of his name and title heightened Ben's fear.

"Yes." He could manage only the single-word response.

"Sir, this is Darnell Reynolds. Corporal Reynolds. You remember me?"

Ben's knees grew weak and his heart began to pound. *The jail guard.* He prepared himself for what he knew would come next. He caught himself praying for the first time in long memory: *Just don't let her be dead. Don't let her be dead.*

"Why are you calling?" he asked, his voice on the edge of panic.

"Sir, it's about Tia. Tia Suarez."

A rush of relief overwhelmed him even as his knees gave way and he sat. "Okay," Ben said with a sigh as he caught his breath. "What about her?"

"Tia's been shot, sir," the man said calmly, though now Ben could hear the edge of emotion in his voice. "She was shot down in a place called Danville, Illinois." Darnell pronounced the *s* and it came out as "Illi-noise," making what he said sound all the more ridiculous.

Darnell began to provide the details. "I got a call from a friend who works on Tia's shift. He said Danville PD called Newberg. Talked to the watch commander. Said Tia was with a detective in some café." Darnell's voice wavered between sentences, but Ben sensed the man was trying to be strong. "I'm at Newberg PD now. Everyone is talking about it. They say the other cop is dead and Tia's in a hospital down there. They say she might not make it."

Ben was shocked to the point of speechless, and the line was quiet until Darnell spoke again. "Hello? Sergeant Sawyer?"

"Yeah." Ben couldn't manage much more. "Yeah. I'm here, Darnell."

"Everyone is trying to figure out why Tia was in Illinois. I didn't know if you had heard. I mean, she's your friend. She really likes you." The man's deep voice finally cracked.

Anger began to build. *You're right, Darnell. A cop who works for me has been shot and I don't even get a courtesy call?* No time for that now, Ben told himself.

"Where are you right now?" he asked. "Who's there with you?"

Ben visualized the officer looking around as he spoke. "There's just a bunch of patrol guys. The sergeant is gone. But everyone is talking about it. She's in the hospital somewhere down there. In Illinois. What the hell was she doing in Illinois?"

Christ, this is frustrating, Ben thought. He knew that Darnell and Tia were friends and that the man was probably in some kind of shock, but Ben needed him to focus.

"I . . . I don't know what we can do. Everyone is just—"

"Stay at the station," Ben said, putting command into his voice. "In fact, tell everyone to stay there. I'll call dispatch and tell them to have the sheriff's deputies handle all calls within the city limits until further notice. I'll be there in five minutes."

Ben hung up the phone. A Newberg officer had been shot and was in critical condition. Ben was not going to sit this one out and watch from the sidelines. Especially when that officer was Tia Suarez. A small, scared voice broke the silence.

"Dad?"

Ben looked up to see Jake's fallen face staring back, as if he were preparing to brave some terrible news. Bernice had one hand to her mouth, expecting the worst. Her eyes had already begun to moisten. Jake spoke up. "What's going on? Is Mom okay?"

Bernice moved in behind Jake and put her hands on his shoulders. Ben pulled a chair in front of his son and sat. "Mom is fine, Jake. That was a friend of Tia's. You remember, Officer Suarez."

Relief flooded over the young boy's face. "Oh man, I thought—"

"Listen, Jake." Ben reached out and put his hand around the back of his son's neck. "Tia has been shot. She's down in Illinois. I've got to go into work and figure out what's going on."

Bernie and Jake both gasped in shock. The anguish in Jake's voice returned. "Shot? How? Is she dead? Who did it?"

"I don't know any of that, but it might have something to do with your mom. Like I said, I'm going to work and try to find out the details. You stay with Aunt Bernie, okay?"

"But you said you wouldn't work until Mom came home. You promised." Jake's voice conveyed a sense of betrayal.

"Did you hear what I said, Jake?" Ben expected his son to understand and didn't hold back on his frustration. "Someone shot Tia Suarez. Our friend. I need to go."

Bernice bowed her head and Ben stood from his chair, looking Jake in the eye. He did his best to convey the seriousness of the situation. "You need to understand. I'll be home as soon as I can and we'll talk about it, okay?"

"But Dad, what if—"

"Jesus, Jake. *What if what?*" The emotions boiled over. "Tia was probably trying to help Mom and somehow she got shot. I have to go."

Jake practically jumped from his seat and screamed in response. "What if something happens to you? What if whoever it was comes after you? Just like they did Officer Suarez?" Jake's voice finally cracked. "What then, Dad?"

Jake turned to run from the room. Before he could, Ben reached out and pulled his son close. At first Jake pushed back, but then Ben felt the boy's arms go tight around his back. They stood holding one another in a long moment of silence. Ben was the first to step back. He gripped Jake around the shoulders and held him at a half arm's distance. Jake swiped his moist eyes with the back of his hand, then dropped his arms awkwardly to his sides, embarrassed.

"Nothing will happen to me, Jake. I promise. I'm going to the department. I'm going to find out what happened. See if I can help. Before I do anything else, I'll come back here and tell you, okay?"

Jake stared back, his face blank. Ben knew the boy was near his limit. He couldn't take much more. His voice was hollow. "Yeah. Okay, Dad. I'll stay here."

"Don't worry, Ben." Bernice spoke up with a voice that conveyed more strength than either of the men in the room. Ben figured she knew not to ask questions now. Bernice was familiar with the crisis-driven nature of police work. She'd get the details later. "We'll be fine. Get to work and find out what's going on."

Ben looked back to his son. The emotional outburst was over, and he could see Jake had already drawn himself back in. *What the hell am I doing?* Ben wondered to himself. *Family comes first, Benjamin.*

"Listen, Jake. I'll call down—"

"No, Dad. I'm fine. You need to go. We'll be okay."

Jake looked at his father, and his careworn expression made Ben wonder how it would be when his son was an adult and dealing with the struggles of life. Would he be stronger because of all he'd been through in childhood, or would he be all used up? How would all of the turmoil ultimately shape his life?

Ben walked out the front door, his mind reeling. The well-being of his family, his wife, his son, his father-in-law, had consumed him for days. With barely any sleep and no interest in eating, at times he wasn't sure how much longer he could go on. Then, just when he had thought things might be looking up, the one person who had stood with him was shot and fighting for her life. Ben pulled the family van from the driveway knowing he had no choice. Now there was a new name on the list of people depending on him, and that name was Tia Suarez.

FORTY

Driving to the police department, Ben called Plate Boyd at home but got no answer. He remembered he had turned in the detective sergeant cell phone. He called the number. McKenzie picked up after the first ring.

"McKenzie, this is Ben Sawyer. Are you working?"

A long hesitation and static on the line indicated distance in Ben's mind.

"Yeah. I'm working, but you're not. What the hell do you want? You've been given some time off, remember?" Even now McKenzie couldn't resist a cheap shot. Ben ignored it.

"I heard about Tia Suarez getting shot. Is it true?"

"Yeah. It's true. About six hours ago in Illinois. Boyd and I are on our way down there right now."

"Boyd's with you? Put him on."

"This is none of your concern," McKenzie snapped. "We got it handled."

Ben heard Plate Boyd's voice in the background, demanding the phone.

"Yeah, Ben. It's Plate."

"Plate, what the hell is going on?"

Boyd sounded overwhelmed. "We don't know anything yet. I was going to call you, but can you at least give me time to drive down there?"

Ben shot back. "She worked for me, Plate. She's a friend of mine. I want to know how she is." There was a silence on the other end, and Ben wondered if he had lost the connection. "Plate?"

"It's not good, Ben. They say she's pretty shot up. They got to her quick; she's in surgery. I don't know any more than that. Shot down in Danville, southwest of Chicago. She was in a local diner with a detective from the PD down there. The detective is dead on scene."

Ben's hands were shaking. He forced his car to the side of the road. *Damn, Tia. What did you get into?*

"You still there?" Plate asked. "Sawyer? You there?"

"Yeah. Sorry. I'm . . . I'm just a little blown away."

"Now you know as much as I do. McKenzie and I will be in Danville in about an hour." Ben could sense a softening in Boyd's tone as the crackling of the line eased for a moment.

"Look," Plate said, "I know you two are tight. I know she respects the hell out of you. You should've got a call." Boyd paused. "When I find out more, I'll get a hold of you."

Ben held a short debate on whether or not to tell Boyd about the angle Tia was working. He decided against it, his gut telling him he could trust Boyd but no way was he giving the info to McKenzie.

"Okay. Thanks, Plate. I'll wait to hear from you."

The conversation over, Ben sat in his car and gave some thought to what he'd heard.

"What the hell happened, Tia?" Ben asked out loud. He remembered Tia talking about the nine one one call, saying something about a way to track down the caller. Now she was hundreds of miles from home, shot, and another cop was dead.

Ben put the car in Drive and headed for the Newberg Police Department. A cop on his department had been shot in the line of duty, and suspension or no suspension, he needed to be with other cops.

FORTY-ONE

By the time Ben arrived, every officer who worked for Newberg PD was in the building. For most, the experience of an officer being shot was something new, but Ben called on his years at Oakland PD and took a leadership role. He visited with his fellow cops and spoke of solidarity. No bad thoughts. Tia was strong. Others took solace from his words, and there were no references to the case against Alex or Ben's current suspension. The fact that Jorgensen was nowhere to be found was lost on no one. Ben could feel the rekindling of a connection. He moved to his old office that had been taken over by Plate Boyd. He gave some thought to driving to Danville himself but realized it would only hinder the investigation. He'd just have to wait. He sat for hours, talking with a few officers that stopped in. Trying to offer encouragement. Finally Boyd returned.

As soon as the older man walked in, Ben could see that the rotund sergeant was caving under the pressure of current circumstances. Plate willingly gave up the details of the case, and it seemed to Ben that Plate was looking for some guidance.

"This is a tough one. You doing okay?" Ben asked.

Plate sat in silence. Looking at Ben, he shrugged his shoulders as if to signal early defeat.

"If I were you, I'd let Danville do the work," Ben said, trying to sound encouraging. "Our guys should just work parallel. Multijurisdictional cases are always complicated; just try to keep everyone on the same page. I mean, obviously you want to be in the loop on everything, and if Tia was down there on a duty-related issue, we've got a responsibility to her. We need to make sure they do right by her."

Ben paused, then asked the obvious question. "Any idea what she was doing in Danville?"

"Seems like they were talking about a local case," Plate said. "Some hooker who got beat to death with a ball bat. The case file was found at the scene."

Plate looked at Ben with an air of nervous inquisitiveness. "You know anything about that? Why Suarez would be poking her nose around in Danville?"

Ben thought back to his conversation with Tia and decided to be up front about what he knew.

"Tia came by my house this morning." Ben looked at his watch and saw it was after one A.M. "Technically, yesterday. She wanted to talk about Alex's case; she was zeroed in on the nine one one call that came into the PD the night Carson was murdered. She wanted to try to ID the caller. I told her to hold off on it. Anyway, even if she didn't listen to me, why Danville?"

Boyd was shaking his head as Ben went on. "Something must have developed. Something got her down there. The detective she was with—I'm betting he was the one working the local homicide?"

"Yeah." Boyd seemed reluctant. "Real hot-shot guy. Worked Chicago PD for most of his career. Even worked lead on a couple of big-time mob cases. Made a lot of enemies. Transferred to this sleepy little town to get away from it all. Looks like somebody decided to track him down. From what everyone down there said, he was a hell of a cop."

"How bad was it?" Ben asked, not really wanting to know the answer but certain that he had to, in order to understand what had happened.

"They got caught flat-footed, that's for sure. Both their guns were still holstered. Whoever this bastard was, he went at 'em with what looks to be a three-eighty. No brass left behind, so we're figuring a revolver. Seale, the Danville detective, he took two at close range to the back of his head. I don't imagine he felt a damn thing." Plate paused, as if taking a moment to contemplate the idea of such an end. His voice grew louder when he went on. "Suarez, by the looks of it, she put up a hell of fight. The ER doc says she took one to the right side that shattered a rib and then got lodged inside somewhere. A second shot was a through-and-through in her gut. From what he said, her vital organs are okay but her blood loss was crazy. They got her to a hospital in about seven minutes. Somehow she was still alive. Last I checked she was hanging in there."

After a long pause, Ben said, "Tia got wind of something. Something about our case led her to Danville. Whatever it was, it got her shot and this other detective whacked."

Plate jumped all over the comment like he had been waiting for it. "Horseshit, Ben. This has nothing to do with the murder of Louis Carson."

"Come on, Plate. Someone is trying to keep us from making a connection between these two murders. What other explanation is there?"

"Like I said, this Seale fella worked the big time. This was a real hit. Even the shot to the face." Plate was working to dismiss a conclusion Ben could tell he didn't want to draw. "Well, not the face but the head. Same damn thing. That's what these OC types do when they want to show disrespect." The lack of confidence in his voice betrayed him. Ben figured Plate was repeating what he'd heard from someone familiar with the ins and outs of organized crime.

"Anyway, they're pulling guys in from his old unit in Chicago to work on it. Maybe even state boys from the attorney general's office. There's nothing for us to do but stay out of it and wait to hear about Suarez." Plate tried to put a finishing touch on the conversation. "I think Tia just picked a bad day for a road trip."

Ben didn't hold back. "You're wrong. Whoever shot Tia is the same guy who killed Louis Carson. I'll bet my life on it."

Plate's large body shot from the chair. "Goddamn it, Sawyer. Don't go making this into something it ain't."

"Plate, Tia was at my house, talking about the Carson case, two hours before she got shot. That means after she left my house, she hightailed it for Danville. You're going to ignore that?"

"What the hell do you want me to do?" Plate looked across the desk. "Ben, I'm sorry, but your wife's case is closed. It's headed for trial, and that's that. I know it's hard, but you need to come to grips with it."

Both men fell silent until Plate waived his hands in the air as if signaling surrender. "Hell, I need to get some sleep. This place is gonna be crazy in the morning. Jorgensen told me to handle the press and the investigation. He's not sure he'll even be in tomorrow. Can you believe that shit? A cop from his own PD is shot and that prick gets pissed about a wake-up call. I hate dealing with that asshole."

With his hand on the doorknob, Plate turned to look at Ben. "You gonna be okay? I know having to sit this out is hard. Believe me, I'd love to turn the whole mess over to you."

Ben stared at the older officer but said nothing. Plate pulled a single sheet of folded paper from his pocket.

"Here," Plate said. "Danville detectives put it together from witness statements. Something tells me you're gonna need it more than I will. I can always get another copy."

Plate tossed the paper onto the desk. Ben saw it was a black-and-white composite sketch. The face was all angles and bone. The eyes were set close, the features handsome but reeking of danger. WANTED FOR MURDER BY DANVILLE PD appeared in bold type across the top.

"But I'm telling you, Ben. You get caught poking around in this mess, Jorgensen will fry your ass. In case you don't already know, he ain't particularly fond of you." Plate left, closing the door firmly behind him.

Left alone, Ben stared hard at the face on the paper. The eyes took on a life and the mouth sneered in defiance.

Who are you?

Ben knew Plate was right. Alex's case was as good as decided, and it wouldn't be easy to stop a train that was running at full steam. The shooting of Tia Suarez would be dismissed as irrelevant. He needed more. He had to overwhelm the energy of the state's case, sink it with an indisputable knockout blow. Alex's words echoed in his mind: *I need you, Benny.*

Ben put his hands to his face and tried to rub away his frustration and guilt. His wife needed him. She didn't want anyone but him. With all that had happened in their lives, she still reached out to him and no one else. Rage forced Ben to his feet. He grabbed the sheet of paper from the desk and stepped into the hallway. Officers, still dazed from the turn of events, stepped aside as their sergeant stared straight ahead, acknowledging no one, and left the building.

In the car, Ben tried to focus. Wild ideas ran through his mind. Everything was a long shot. All of it fraught with risk.

Ben held the composite sketch and stared hard at the face looking back at him before folding the paper and putting it in his pocket. There would be no easy way, but Ben had never asked for that. *Any way. Any chance.* That's all he needed.

FORTY-TWO

Ben half jogged through the long, stark, harshly lit hallway of Chicago General Hospital. Doctors and nurses floated about as if they were somehow disconnected from the rest of humanity. Groups of family members clustered outside rooms, often huddled in quiet conversation. Some were smiling, their expressions reflecting relief and hope. Others dabbed at their eyes, their faces marked by disbelief and sadness. The oldest people Ben saw were very old indeed and, for the most part, alone. Invisible to everyone were the orderlies and cleaning staff, who were well represented not only by their presence but by the thick scent of Pine-Sol.

He'd left Newberg at daybreak, making the three-hour drive to Chicago in a little more than two. This was the first day Tia was being allowed visitors and Ben had to see her. Not just to see for himself that she was alive and how she was doing, but also to find out just what had happened after she'd left his house two days before.

Ben navigated through people, medical equipment, and food

carts. As he searched for Tia's room number, he saw two uniforms sitting in a doorway not far ahead. It was a pretty good bet, that was where he'd find her. He approached the officers, who stood. One put out a hand to stop Ben and spoke with polite authority.

"Official business only, sir."

The patch on his arm identified the man not as hospital security but as Chicago PD. Ben was impressed with the department's commitment of resources.

Looking first at the officer's name tag, Ben said, "How're you doing, Officer Woods? I'm her sergeant. Ben Sawyer. Newberg PD."

"No problem, sir. Could I just see your badge?"

Now, that was a problem. Still suspended, Ben's badge was back in Newberg, in Jorgensen's desk. "Uh, yeah . . . I . . ."

Suspicious of a man who said he was a cop but was unable to produce proof of it, Woods shifted to block the door. Ben admired the action even as he wondered how he was going to get past these guys. He hadn't expected Tia to be so protected.

The voice that called from inside the room was weak, but Ben recognized it immediately.

"It's okay, Albert. That's my sergeant. You can let him in."

Ben patted his pockets and turned sheepish. "Must've left it in the car."

The officer's defenses disappeared. "No sweat, Sarge. You want me to shut the door?"

"That'd be great, thanks."

Ben walked into the dim room, which was lit only by the midday sun leaking through the thick shades pulled down over the windows. The single bed was surrounded by beeping equipment; hoses and tubes ran everywhere. The enormity of it all—the shooting, the hospital, the near-death experience—seemed to have swallowed her whole.

Her head was turned toward the door. She raised an opened

hand a few inches off the bed, and Ben swooped in and took it in both of his own.

"Tia, what the hell did you do? I told you to stay out of it."

"Yeah . . . it's good to see you too."

Ben laughed. "Damn, girl. You're looking rough. How're you feeling?"

"Honestly, not bad. Between growing up in a migrant camp, going off to war, now being a cop, it's almost like I've been waiting half my life to get shot full of lead. I finally got it over with."

Ben couldn't hide his relief that Tia was alive and talking. He squeezed her hand. "I guess that's one way of looking at it."

Tia's voice turned lyrical as she switched to Spanish.

"*Papa, Mama. Este es mi jefe y mi amigo.*" Tia smiled as she gave the Spanish version of his name. "*Ben-ha-meen Sawyer.*" Ben had followed along with the basic introductions but was glad when Tia continued in English, "Sarge, I'd like to introduce you to my parents. Enrique and Consuelo Solis-Suarez."

For the first time Ben noticed the man and woman sitting quietly behind him and turned to greet them. Tia's father stood up. He was dressed in pressed jeans, a pearl-button shirt, and a bolo. Most men would have looked comical in such an outfit, but on this solid, compact man with a dark, weatherworn complexion, it worked. Enrique Suarez's leather boots were clean, but by the wear of them Ben bet more often than not they weren't. On the table next to his chair sat an aged Western hat that screamed with authenticity.

"*Ah, Señor Sawyer. Mucho gusto.*" The man's voice was reverent and he extended his hand. He continued, in accented English, "My daughter speaks of you often. And always with very great respect. My pleasure is to meet you."

"Likewise, Mr. Suarez. *Mucho gusto.* Your daughter . . ." Ben shook hands with Mr. Suarez, and was surprised by the wave of emotion that swept over him. "Your daughter is very special to me, to all of us at the police department. We were . . . we were sad to hear about what happened. But she's going to be okay."

Still seated, the woman bowed her head slightly and gave a polite smile. Ben returned the smile and added a nod of acknowledgment.

Enrique struggled for words. "My daughter. She tells me of your troubles. *Tu esposa. Yo lo siento.* My wife and I, we pray for . . ."

He looked to his daughter for help, *"Mija, como se dice interceder?"*

Tia looked warmly on her father; clearly the center of her world. "Intercede, Papa. You say intercede."

"We pray for God to intercede," Mr. Suarez said.

Ben, not big on prayer, was grateful anyway. "Thank you, sir. I think God must've sent your daughter to do just that, but he needs to keep up his end of the bargain and keep a closer eye on her."

Mr. Suarez translated for his wife. Mrs. Suarez covered her mouth in shock and crossed herself fervently. Tia spoke to her parents lovingly in Spanish. Ben couldn't follow a word of it, but Mrs. Suarez rose as her husband said, in a voice full of pride, "My daughter wishes to speak to you in private, sir. We will . . . uh, we will stretch out our legs, *sí*?"

Ben shook hands again with Tia's father and stepped away from the bed, letting her mother get closer. The women exchanged a few quiet words; Tia laughed softly.

Once both her parents had left the room, Tia took a deep breath. A look of intense pain flooded her face and Ben clenched his jaw at the sight. After a moment, the pain eased and Tia looked at her boss with the slightest glimmer of a twinkle in her eye.

"My mom said I forgot to mention my boss was an infidel."

"Oops. Sorry," Ben said. "Did I offend?"

"My mom prays before she crosses the street. That's her world. Don't worry about it." Tia's weak voice grew serious in tone. "How's Alex? How're you holding up?"

"Pretty damn good, thanks to you and Darnell Reynolds. Alex and I had a great visit last week, spent about three hours together.

I was able to see her again yesterday afternoon, and I got her up to speed. She was devastated at first, but I told her that you had pulled through and I was headed down here today for a visit. She sends her best."

"Darnell's good people. We go way back to Afghanistan. He saved my ass a few times." Tia frowned, changing the subject. "Ben, listen to me. You've got to get down to Danville. There's a case there . . ." She stopped and held her breath, wincing in pain.

"Take it easy," Ben said. "We don't have to talk about it right now."

"Yes, we do," Tia said, gasping after each word. "You need to get to Danville. Seale and I were going over the case against Alex when that guy opened up on us." Ben could see Tia's expression grow distant as her mind shifted gears, remembering the diner. "He just came walking up. I just figured him for some civilian. I never had a chance to . . ."

"Listen to me," Ben said. "I don't want you stressing about this right now. You need to stop talking."

"Goddamn it, Sawyer. You listen to me." Ben looked over his shoulder. She had almost been loud enough to be heard in the hall, and he didn't want the Chicago cops to come running in.

"There was a murder in Danville. Whoever pulled it also killed Louis Carson." Tia took a deep breath and went on. "There's no doubt about it. He'd duped nine one one calls on both cases. I confirmed it, and no, I'm not telling you how."

"What's that supposed to mean, Tia? How can I use the info if we can't talk about it? I don't care if you violated some search protocol. We'll get around it."

Tia grinned. "There you go again, thinking it's like the eye chart."

"Just fill me in, Tia. I can handle it."

"No, you can't and believe me, the U.S. government won't be too happy if they start getting more press for a database that doesn't even exist."

"Jesus, Tia. What the hell did you do?" Ben could hardly believe what he was hearing. "You reached out to your old crew didn't you? Your intelligence contacts?"

Tia was weak and the stress of the moment was heavy, but her head seemed clear.

"Don't worry about that. Just get to Danville and find another angle."

"All right. But at least tell me what I'm looking for."

Tia swallowed hard and spoke in a near whisper. "Get down there. Work around the nine one one. That connection will have to get made later and by somebody else. But I'm telling you, the caller is the same guy in both cases."

Tia took a couple of deep breaths. "Danville PD has a guy under arrest for the murder of a transvestite prostitute. I can tell you he is as innocent as Alex. Start there. The guy I was working with, Tony Seale, he was great . . ."

Ben squeezed her hand.

"I got a good feeling from him, Ben. I think he was probably a hell of a cop. I wish I could have—"

Ben knew she was getting worked up and cut her off. "Not now. Don't do that. There will come a time for that, but not now."

"All right," she said, nodding and closing her eyes for a moment. "But get down there. Find someone you can work with. That case is a copycat of the Carson murder."

Ben thought back to his badgeless condition. That would have to be fixed.

"Okay, I'm on it. Now get some rest. And no more getting worked up. I'm glad to know you got the uniforms at your door. I want your word you won't have any more to do with this."

Tia looked down at herself. "Yeah. I promise."

"I'm glad you're okay. You scared the hell out of all of us. We thought we lost you."

Ben watched a look of peace came over Tia.

"I was in good hands, Sarge. There was never a doubt I'd make it back. I still got a lot of life to live."

"What do you mean good hands? Back from where?" He was clearly clueless about such things.

"Just get to Danville," she said. "Start there."

Ben turned to leave, but Tia called his name. When he looked back, he saw that her face was contorted in pain, so he waited. When it passed, Tia said firmly, "You gotta hear me on this, Ben. The guy who shot me. Who shot Seale. He's your man. I know that's a leap, but he killed Carson. You find him and Alex comes home."

Ben practically ran from the hospital, filled with a new purpose. He got to the minivan, pulling out his car keys and cell phone from his pocket. He dialed the number from memory. He started the engine, waiting for someone to pick up.

"Bernie? It's me—"

That's as far as he got before she cut him off. He listened but jumped back in as soon as she took a breath. "Tia is fine. Well, not fine, but she's going to be. I saw her, Bernie. She's going to be okay."

Ben allowed Bernie to express her relief. He needed her undivided attention. When he felt she was ready, he changed the subject.

"Bernie, listen to me for a minute." His voice was serious. "I need you to do something for me. I hate to ask you, but I've go nobody else I can trust who could pull this off."

Ben paused and listened to the woman on the other end. "I know, Bernie. I know you would and I appreciate that. But this is different. You need to be careful. Here's what I need you to do."

Ben dropped the minivan into gear and pulled into traffic as he explained his plan to Bernice. After the conversation ended, he headed north. His mind was focused and his body energized. He couldn't help but think it felt damn good to have a plan.

FORTY-THREE

Doyle McKenzie walked past the desk of Bernice Erickson as if she wasn't even there. He knocked softly and walked into the chief's office, closing the door behind him. He began to speak without waiting for any acknowledgment.

"Chief, we need to talk about Plate Boyd. He's all over my ass on the Suarez shooting. Sawyer's got him all spun up, filled his head with all kinds of bullshit. He wants me to reopen the Carson murder. Compare it to Danville. Hell, he wants me to drive down there and follow up with the detectives."

Jorgensen looked up from behind his desk, and McKenzie picked up on the look of annoyance. The chief didn't hide his irritation.

"You know, Doyle, I'm starting to think you're in over your head. How is it I go out of my way to be sure you are the lead investigator on this case, and Sawyer, a guy who doesn't even have a badge, not to mention he is cut off from any official access, somehow does an end run around your ass? How does that happen?"

"I don't know, boss, I just know that there's no way Plate is coming up with this shit on his own."

"Who's feeding Sawyer information? He's got to have a source. Did you clean up all the historical bullshit like I told you?"

"Yeah, Chief. It's dealt with. Harlan Lee never existed in Newberg."

"Suarez?" Jorgensen asked.

"That's a problem. I know they're tight." McKenzie lowered his voice and proceeded more cautiously. "So, this guy they got hooked up for killing the he-she. He's hooked into Lee, right?"

"No shit. Is that just coming to you?" Jorgensen closed his eyes and turned away. "Jesus, we do have problems."

The insult stung, but McKenzie kept going. "What now?"

"Relax. Don't react. Sawyer is just throwing shit at the wall. Don't worry about Plate. He'll lose interest, and Sawyer can't put it all together on his own."

"Suarez?" McKenzie asked.

Jorgensen vented his anger.

"I'm tempted to reel that little bitch in. She's down there palling around with another agency, asking questions tied to an official department investigation. Feeding info to Sawyer. When she gets out of the hospital she'll be answering to me." The chief paused. "But the damage is done. Leave her out of it. Keep an eye on Sawyer. Pay a visit or two to his wife. She'll tip her hand if she knows anything."

"What about this attorney? This Petite character?"

"Handled," Jorgensen said. "Let's just say he saw the wisdom of going with the program. He's out of play now, and you make damn sure he stays that way. Under no circumstances does Sawyer get a chance to make that connection."

"All right, Chief." McKenzie headed for the door. "But you gotta know, this shit is a distraction. We're losing out on other opportunities, if you know what I mean. I don't care what happens to that broke-dick Norgaard or his bitch of a daughter. Seems like we could have just let this shit run its course and we'd have been better off."

"Let's be clear, Doyle." McKenzie knew the chief wanted his full attention.

"What's that, Chief?"

"You serve at my pleasure. All you do, all you *get* to do, flows from this office. If I say this case is a priority, that's all you need to hear."

McKenzie held the man's eye and wondered if the time had come for some push back. He answered his own question as he turned to leave.

"Whatever you say, Chief. You're the boss, but there's money on the street. Until we get clear of this shit, that's where it'll stay."

McKenzie closed the office door as he left. Walking by the desk of Bernice Erickson, he thought he caught the hint of a smile.

"Having a good day, Detective?"

McKenzie grunted in response but gave a last look over his shoulder on his way out the door.

FORTY-FOUR

ergeant Sawyer?"

The man approached as if in a rush, his long arm already out in front of him. Ben took the man's offered hand and did his best to come off casual, ignoring the jackhammer pulse that tripped in his neck. Since his visit with Tia two days before, Ben had known what he needed to do, but now that he was here it felt all wrong. From the moment he arrived at the small PD building with the flag at half-mast and quiet subdued hallways, he felt like he was committing some sort of terrible sin.

"Yeah," Ben stood as he answered. "Call me Ben."

"I'm Detective Dave Jensen." His large hand swallowed Ben's as he towered over Ben by six inches. "Sorry to keep you waiting."

Detective Jensen was dressed in a dark suit that hung on a lanky frame. His white shirt was pinched around his neck by a black necktie, and he wore his police shield clipped on the lapel of his jacket, a black band covering the badge. Detective Jensen explained the reason for the wait. His voice and mood were somber. "We're planning the funeral services for Tony Seale tomorrow. We never buried one of our own before. At least not like this. Getting killed on duty. Anyway . . . like I said. Sorry to keep you waiting."

Ben was sincere in his response. "It is the hardest thing to do in police work. I've been there. My heart goes out to all of you."

The detective remained grim faced. He looked at the thick file in Ben's hands. "I hope you had time to read over the file."

Ben tried not to sound sheepish. He thought about backing out, but he needed to do this. "Yeah, I did. I read it over pretty thoroughly."

"Good. Follow me, Ben."

As the two men walked down the quiet hallway, Ben sensed no distrust and again felt pangs of guilt. He reminded himself that the detective had no reason to doubt him. Thanks to the expert reconnaissance mission of Bernice, Ben had badge and credentials in hand. He had presented himself as Sergeant Ben Sawyer, Newberg PD, in Danville to follow up on the shooting of Tia Suarez. All perfectly true. Of course, Ben failed to mention his status as a rogue cop currently on suspension or that the badge had been recovered from his chief's locked desk.

"I understand you're here to interview Gerald Donaldson." The detective led Ben through a doorway marked POLICE ONLY. "We brought him over from the county lockup. I'm curious, though. What are you guys working on?"

"Not much, really." Ben tried to sound nonchalant. "My boss just wants me to hit the guy up about a case in Newberg. Officer Suarez may have been down here doing some off-the-clock follow-up. Looks like this guy Donaldson might be a witness in a case we're working."

"Really?" Jensen asked. "What kind of case?"

Ben tried to sound casual. "A homicide, actually."

The detective walked more slowly as he thought this over. "Wow, no shit? You're thinking Donaldson could be connected? I don't know much about his case, but he didn't strike me as the serial type. Seems more like a guy who overreacted to gettin' his junk sucked by a he-she. Almost falls into the category of 'can't blame the man,' if you know what I mean?"

"I'm just going at him as a witness. That's all. Like I said, boss's orders. Seems like Suarez had some reason to be down here talking to your detective about the case. We figured it might be worth following up on it."

"Yeah, weird coincidence, I guess." They stopped in front of a closed door. "Here's the interview room. Donaldson copped for a lawyer on our case, but if he's just a witness to you guys, you should be good to take a run at him for anything unrelated. These days, though, even the witnesses are lawyering up. Good luck."

"Thanks."

Ben walked in and found a lone man seated at the table. Dressed in a jail-orange jumpsuit, Donaldson sucked hard on a cigarette, his hands trembling. Smoke billowed in front of his face.

"Hello, Mr. Donaldson. My name is Ben Sawyer. I'm a police sergeant in Newberg, Wisconsin."

"What's this all about? What do you want? I told those other cops I'm not saying anything until I get a lawyer."

Ben took a seat at the interview desk and tried to sound disarming. "Relax, Gerald. I'm not here to jam you up on anything." From this point on, Ben knew, he would have to be careful with everything he said. If there was a case against Donaldson for murder, he didn't want to jeopardize it. "Gerald, I'm not here to talk to you about your problems in Danville. Do you understand me? I want to be clear on that."

"I don't care what you want. You're a cop, right? I'm not talking to any more cops. Just get a lawyer in here right now."

Shit, Ben thought. *I didn't want to have to play it this way, but he's shutting me down already.*

"Gerald, what if I told you I might be able to help you with your case?"

"I'd say bullshit. I don't talk to cops." The man sat up straight in his seat and looked over the top of Ben's head toward the door. Ben got the impression Donaldson was ready to shut things down and call for a guard. Ben knew he was going to have to give up more to gain the man's trust.

"Relax, Gerald. Just listen for a minute." Ben leaned in closer. A sense of guilty malfeasance drove his voice down to a low whisper. "My wife is up on a murder charge, but I know she's innocent. A friend of mine, another cop, was down here the day you got arrested. I'm sure it had something to do with my wife's case. My friend and the detective who arrested you got shot. That's what I'm looking into. I swear, I'm not here about your murder case."

The man looked at Ben, clearly puzzled. "What are you telling me all this for?"

"My friend, the one who got shot? She was nosing around because she was convinced my wife was being framed." The next words shot out of him before he could stop them. "Is that what's happening to you, Gerald? Is someone trying to pin a murder rap on you?"

Donaldson stopped looking at the door and stared straight at Ben. "I'm listening."

"Look, Gerald, I don't know what the connection is between your case and my wife's, or even if there is one, but I know for a fact my wife didn't kill anyone."

Suddenly Donaldson seemed to give in to a sense of desperate trust. "Mister, I didn't kill that hooker. I came back from Chicago like I do every week. I don't know anything about that gal, guy, whatever it was in my trunk."

"Okay," Ben said. "Then tell me this. Have you ever met Alexandra Sawyer?"

"Never heard of her." The man was no longer hesitant; he answered freely, though anxiety filled his voice.

"How about Louis Carson?"

"No. I don't know him." Donaldson buried his head in his hands. "Holy Christ. A dead body in my trunk? My prints on a baseball bat? Shit, that bat has been in my garage for two years. How did someone in Chicago get killed with it?"

"How about Newberg? You ever spend time in Newberg, Wisconsin?"

"No. I grew up in Florence," Donaldson said. "It's a long way from Newberg."

"Florence? Okay, you've got a tie to Wisconsin. You got friends there? Family?" Ben thought harder. "What about enemies, Gerald? You piss anyone off up there?"

Donaldson blinked several times in rapid succession and drew deeply on his cigarette. The break in eye contact meant something, Ben knew.

"What, Gerald? No big deal, I'm sure. You got baggage upstate?"

Donaldson studied Ben, sizing him up. Ben could see Donaldson was deciding whether or not to trust any cop no matter how high the stakes.

"What happened in Florence, Gerald?"

No answer. Ben reached for the composite drawing in his shirt pocket, but before he could pull it out, the door flew open.

"That's it, Sawyer. Donaldson, keep your mouth shut." Detective Jensen grabbed Donaldson and escorted him from the room. Jensen shot Ben an angry stare as Donaldson began to object.

"What the hell is going on? I want a lawyer right now, damn it. I know I get a lawyer."

Ben could hear Donaldson continuing to protest as he was dragged down the hall. A second man in a suit—a man with a greater air of authority than the detective—walked in, accompanied by a uniformed officer. Ben was suddenly filled with a sense of dread. It was clear to him the jig was up.

"I'm Lieutenant Gregory Isaacs." Ben could feel the anger rolling off the man's words. His fist was clinched into a black ball of bone and flesh. His sharp brown eyes penetrated deep enough that Ben felt laid open before him. "Jensen works for me. Told me about your visit. Thought that sounded pretty odd, so I shot a call up to Newberg. Got hold of your chief. He wants that badge back."

Ben wanted to explain. Wanted to tell the man it wasn't what it appeared to be, but words wouldn't come and he said nothing.

"*Mr.* Sawyer," the lieutenant said, "you are under arrest for interfering with an official police investigation. Officer Blake, take this man into custody. Keep him away from Donaldson."

"Yes, sir." The uniform pulled a set of handcuffs from the front of his Sam Browne belt and said, "Turn around and place your hands behind your back."

Without moving, Ben looked at the man in charge. His heart raced as it became clear to him what was occurring. "Lieutenant, please. Give me five minutes of your time and I'll clear this up for you."

"Five minutes, my ass." Ben could hear the seething anger in the words. "You come down here and stick your nose into a cop killing? *One of our own?* Pass yourself off as being on official business?"

"I didn't talk to Donaldson about the murder of your detective, Lieutenant." Ben wanted the man to know he hadn't stooped that low. "I wouldn't jeopardize your case."

"I talked with your chief. I know what you're all about, Sawyer."

"Wait a minute. Please." The cuffs were going on and desperation took hold. "Jorgensen's got his head up is ass. Let me explain."

"Sawyer, you're a disgrace to your department. Shit, you're a disgrace to the profession." A look of contempt accompanied the words. Ben felt horsewhipped. Isaacs directed his next words to the uniformed officer. "Get him out of here. Like I said, keep him away from Donaldson. Other than that, he gets no special consideration."

The uniformed officer snapped on the second cuff and spun Ben around, pushing him toward the door. Ben offered no resistance. At this point he figured he had it coming.

FORTY-FIVE

One night in jail had been one night too many. Back home, Ben looked at the papers on his nightstand and considered the mess his life had become. *The purpose of this correspondence is to inform you of your immediate termination from employment with Newberg Police Department.*

Arrested and booked for felony interfering, it had taken significant legal maneuvering by a court-appointed attorney to secure Ben's release on his own recognizance and passage back to Wisconsin. Now Ben had his own trial to worry about in addition to Alex's. His wouldn't take place for a month or two, and Ben had no idea what his life would look like by then. But the real salt in the wound had come in the form of the person who delivered the documents.

"So, Ben, let me see if I got this straight." McKenzie had glared through the bars of his jail cell. "You break into Jorgensen's office, steal your badge and police ID, then come down here and pass yourself off as being on official business. Gotta hand it to you, Ben, you got balls."

The half-dozen other men in the cell took note of the conversation. "Oh, sorry. Didn't your new friends know? No worry, boys. As of today, it's Mr. Sawyer." McKenzie held the envelope up high for everyone to see.

"Got some official correspondence from the department for you, Benny. I insisted Jorgensen let me make the delivery by hand. On a rush basis." McKenzie pushed the papers though the bars, and Ben watched them drop to the dirty cement floor.

"You're fired, you little prick. You're done." McKenzie turned to go, flinging his final sentences over his shoulder. "Interfering carries up to eight years in Illinois, Benny. But don't worry. You'll still be out way ahead of that murdering bitch wife of yours."

Fired. Arrested and jailed. Alex headed to prison. *What'll become of Jake?*

Though it was still early in the morning, Ben threw back the sheets and got out of bed.

On the brink of losing everything, Ben knew, beyond any doubt, that the answers he needed were locked inside the old man who lay doped up across town. He thought back to the old days with Lars Norgaard. The good years. What was it the old man always used to say back when Ben first started hitting him up about being a cop?

"It's like working in a sausage factory. People don't want to know how you make it. They don't even want to know what goes into it. They just want to buy it with no questions asked."

True enough. Police work could get ugly. Unconventional, even.

Ben picked up the composite sketch from Danville. He stared at the face of the killer, who had been seen by a half-dozen terrified witnesses. A detective, a good man, was dead. Tia Suarez had been shot to hell. Alex was going on trial for murder.

According to Tia, the man in this picture was the key to it all.

Ben would find him. He'd get answers by any means necessary.

He had tried to work within the system, to abide by the rules. But they had taken his badge and gun. They were destroying his family. At this point, all bets were off. Police work could get ugly alright, and at this point ugly was called for.

FORTY-SIX

Doyle McKenzie lolled on the couch in the officers' break room and watched as the door came open. Alex Sawyer entered cautiously, and he let his gaze travel the length of her body.

"Hello there, Alex," he said, cigarette in hand directly under the No Smoking sign. "I understand you're more comfortable in this room than the usual visitor area. I thought maybe you and I should have a little chat."

"What are you doing here? I've got an attorney now, remember?"

"So you have. Might work out okay for you and your husband to share, assuming your guy can practice in Illinois." He winked through the smoke.

"Sorry, McKenzie. If you're here to try to upset me, Ben told me about his arrest. He also told me about Officer Suarez. Shouldn't you be working on that instead of going over the same old ground with me?"

"Danville PD is working that case," McKenzie said, "and you and I never really got a chance to talk, what with you getting a lawyer and all. I just wanted to be sure you haven't changed your mind.

Sometimes memories get a little clearer when the trial starts getting close. You could still reach out for a plea."

Doyle stood and stepped closer. Alex backed away in fear. McKenzie worked to unsettled her further. He wanted to test the waters. He wanted to see if Alex or, more important, Ben had started to crack the protective layer he had placed over the truth.

"Look, Alex. I've known from the very beginning this was a case of self-defense, but I don't know the details. Only you know. Let me help you. Tell me what happened and then we can spin it the right way. You're a cop's wife. No one wants to see you go down for murder one."

"Save it. I don't need any help from you. Ben is twice the detective you could ever hope to be." Alex's voice cracked with emotion.

"Ben's working this for you, is he? Without a badge? He tried that already, you know. Ended up in jail."

"And I'd still take him over you," Alex said, raising her voice. "In fact, between Ben and my father, I don't even put you in the same category."

McKenzie knew he was getting to her. He kept pushing. "Your husband and your father? A fired cop and an invalid. You sure you know what you're doing?"

McKenzie waited as Alex stewed over his last comment. He watched as her anger boiled over and got the best of her. "So tell me, McKenzie. Does the name Harley mean anything to you?"

McKenzie played it off like a man with plenty of experience in being deceitful. He shrugged. "Not unless it's followed by Davidson."

"Ben and my father will figure it out, and that will clear up quite a few things up. We'll see you in court."

"That's fine, Alex. I just wanted to offer you a last chance to go on record with the truth. Juries in Wisconsin are made up of sensible, salt-of-the-earth kind of people. You get uppity with them, with all this right to remain silent bullshit, and they're likely to make you pay for it. I hope you know what you're doing."

Alex knocked on the door, signaling the guard she was ready to leave. "I can't wait to get this in front of a jury, McKenzie. Then everyone is going to see you for the horse's ass you are."

The door opened and Alex turned to leave. McKenzie called out. "Suit yourself, Alex. But don't go trying to saddle me up just yet."

FORTY-SEVEN

L ight snuck up from under the basement door, so Ben stopped to listen from the top of the steps. The *tap, tap, tap* of Jake's cell phone was all too familiar. Texting. California, no doubt. Like any kid these days, Jake could keep a half-dozen long-distance conversations going without ever saying a word. Ben walked down the stairs and found Jake slumped on the dilapidated couch off in the corner, legs pulled up high and elbows resting on his knees. Jake stared vacuously at the two-inch screen, totally absorbed by modern technology yet surrounded by relics from the Sawyer family past: an old television, several floor lamps, even furniture from Alex's childhood bedroom. It seemed odd Jake would prefer the musty air and cramped space of a cellar to his room upstairs. *But then again,* Ben thought, *anything to be clear of me.* Ben shuffled his feet until he was certain Jake must have heard him. When the boy still didn't acknowledge him, Ben spoke. "What's up, Jake?"

"Nothing." The voice was flat. "I just want to be alone, that's all."

Ben walked closer and hit Jake's feet to signal he wanted room to sit. Jake scrunched his face with annoyance but swung his feet high onto the back of the couch, pulling the phone closer without missing a keystroke.

"Who you texting?"

Jake made no acknowledgment and Ben playfully swatted at the phone. "You deaf?"

Jake looked up as he slid the phone into the front pocket of his sweatshirt, his eyes contemptuous. "Seriously, Dad. I just want to be alone. Is that all right with you?"

Ben couldn't take any more. "No, actually, it's not. I mean come on, Jake. This is pretty hard on me too. It wouldn't hurt if you—"

Jake cut him off. He sat up straight, swinging his feet to the floor almost kicking Ben in the head. "Are you kidding me? You think this is hard for *you*?"

Ben, shocked by the maturity and anger in the boy's voice, fired back. "Yeah, Jake. I do."

"Oh, man. Really, Dad. Just leave me alone." The tone sounded like a warning. "You don't even want to go there with me right now."

"Hey, no problem, Jake. Let's go." Ben decided the hell with it. He'd speak from the heart. "Let me hear why it is you act like such a dick. Treating me like I'm the goddamn enemy. I'm doing everything—"

That was as far as he got.

"Fine. I'll tell you why, Dad." Jake slowed down to enunciate each word and syllable. "*You—ruined—our—lives.*"

The words hung in the air, and Ben stared ahead as if he were rereading them to make sure he heard it right. Jake went on.

"You and your lousy temper. Trying to be the badass cop. What did you think would happen when you did that?" Jake stood up and looked down at his father. "All that stuff you told me. Cops are the good guys. Cops help people. All that . . . *bullshit*. You ruined everything. We had to run away from California. Now Mom's in jail." Jake flopped back on the couch so he was lying down again, and his voice went quiet. "All this is because of you."

Ben started to speak, then stopped. He groped for a response. The words cut deep. Words from his own son. He was ready to lash out, then he thought back to his fight with Alex.

"Ben, do you hear yourself? You sound like a damn child."

Deep down Ben could feel the first inkling of anger, but it got no farther. He sat quiet, realizing for the first time that Jake had his own perspective on how they came to this point. His mom was in jail because Ben lost it on a hot summer day in Oakland. It was all a chain reaction as far as Jake was concerned, and it started with Ben. It was hard to argue with the simple logic.

"You're right, Jake. I messed up. Big time. I can't undo it."

Jake's voice was quiet. "Why, Dad? Why did you . . . almost kill that guy? You were a cop."

Taken aback by the comment, Ben looked up. "I'm still a cop, Jake."

Jake mumbled, "Barely."

Another body blow. The insults just kept coming, and all from a boy who wasn't even a teenager yet. Ben and Jake had never talked about that day. Never once. Maybe the time had come. "I'd just had enough. At that moment, I couldn't take it anymore. A guy who thought he could kill a cop. Looking at me like he wanted to kill me. Like he hated me just for being who I was. I snapped. I blew it. Can you understand that, Jake?"

Father and son sat in silence, but then Ben spoke up. "I'm sorry, pal. I let you down. I messed up your life pretty bad. Mom's too. But I want to make it right. I want to fix it."

"Yeah, sure. Like I said, Mom's in jail, if you forgot. Now it's worse than ever. Even you went and got arrested."

"I was trying to get her out. To get her home to you."

"Well, she ain't out. And she's not getting out. I can read the paper, you know."

Ben rested his head against the couch, trying to empty his mind, but it was impossible. His wife was in jail, headed for prison. His son blamed him for all their trouble. His father-in-law was starting to lose it for good. Staring ahead, Ben tried to block it all out by focusing on the dozen or more boxes stacked neatly on shelves against the nearby wall. Most of it was junk still stored after their forced return from California. The rest was from when Alex packed up her father's belongings and moved him into Newberg Convalescent. Three of the boxes caught his eye, and he smiled in spite of himself.

"I'll be damned . . ."

"What?" Jake asked.

Ben felt the pull of nostalgia. It was a waste of time, but he could use a nice walk down memory lane. Maybe Jake could too. He stood and pulled one of the boxes marked OFFICER LARS NORGAARD from the shelf. The heavy box dropped with a thud onto the cement floor. "You think cops are all bad, Jake? That cops in Newberg are what? Posers? Isn't that what you guys say?"

Jake smirked. "No, Dad. Nobody has said that in like a million years."

Ben blew it off. "Say what you want about Newberg PD, but I'll tell you this. Your grandpa was a hell of a cop."

Ben pulled back the cardboard top of the box at his feet, knowing what he would find. Inside was a series of identical logbooks, the spines facing upward and stamped with the year in gold-embossed numbers. Twelve books stored in perfect chronological order, each one an inch thick. He picked up a volume at random and opened it, thinking it wasn't that long ago the world existed without laptops, cell phones, and iPads. Inside, he saw page after page of neat, handwritten entries. Dated and timed.

Jake stole a look, trying his best not to seem the least bit curious. His youth got the better of him. "What are those? They look like ancient scrolls or something."

It was Ben's turn to be the smart-ass. "Yeah, Jake. Right. Grandpa's ancient scrolls."

Both Jake and Ben laughed, and just for a few seconds it felt almost normal. It all came back. Ben remembered the days when he did his best to find any reason to hang around the Norgaard clan. "I haven't seen these things in years. I used to watch your grandpa when he got home from patrol. He'd sit and write down everything he did that day. Tickets, reports, arrests. Anything he did, he wrote it down. I'd sit with him and get some pretty good stories out of it." Ben looked at his son. "You know, I used to tell you stories too. When I would come home from work back in Oakland. You used to really like that stuff."

"Yeah, I remember. You had some good ones."

Ben pulled out the book from Lars's rookie year. The pages were stiff under his fingers and he turned them with care. Going back over thirty years, he found himself reading the entries not as a cop but more like a son. He was young again. Alex too. *Time's gone by,* he thought. Years and years of family history in his hands.

No. Ben leaned forward. Not family history. *Lars's* history. All of it. Right here. Ben sat and thought for a moment. He reached down and pulled out a more recent book, fanning through the pages like a deck of cards.

Lars had been trying to tell him something the other day, something about Harley. Could it be a name? Did it involve Alex somehow? *Anybody's guess,* he thought. Only Lars could know, but *what if?* What if the name was somewhere in one of these books?

"Jake, I think maybe we can help Mom."

"What are you talking about?"

Ben gestured to the box at his feet. "Grandpa might have written something in one of these books that will help us bring Mom home."

"Where? Which one?" Ben could tell that Jake wanted the answer immediately. He wanted his mother home tonight.

"I don't know yet. We'd have to look through all of them. Every book. We have to look for a particular name, but it could be here."

"Dad, there are like a hundred books." Jake sat up and used his foot to pull back the box top and looked inside. "It'll take forever."

"No. There should be about thirty of them and it doesn't matter how long it takes. We can do this, Jake. This could help Mom." Ben looked at his son. "Seriously. What do you say?"

Jake, still reluctant, leaned down and pulled a book from the middle of the box. His voice lacked conviction, but he opened the journal in his lap. "What're we looking for?"

"Grandpa has been trying to tell me something. I'm pretty sure it has to do with Mom. A name. Harley. H-A-R-L-E-Y. It's in here somewhere, Jake. I'm sure of it."

Jake gave Ben a sideways glance. "And if we find it, you're telling me Mom can come home?"

Ben took a book of his own. "It'll be a start. Let's find it and go from there. But one way or another, Jake, Mom is coming home."

FORTY-EIGHT

Ben woke, confused by his surroundings. He saw his son sleeping on the cot in the corner and stacks of logbooks at his feet. He remembered. He looked at his watch; he'd dozed off for twenty or thirty minutes.

Jake's face was relaxed in sleep, but Ben remembered his expression when he said, *"You ruined our lives."*

The words still stung. The truth has a way of doing that.

You and your lousy temper. What did you think would happen?

Ben slapped his own face as he forced himself awake. Quit feeling sorry for yourself. He reached for the next book—from seventeen years ago. *Jesus,* he thought. *We've spent hours on this and we're barely halfway through the collection. Stupid idea. Hopeless.*

Ben opened the book and began a rapid scan. To be safe, he finger-traced each page twice. No doubt about it, Lars had been diligent in his record keeping. The man must have noted every traffic stop. Ben had figured out that arrests were designated by stars. One star for a misdemeanor, two for a felony. Ben looked closest at the two-star notations. He didn't ignore the misdemeanors, but he figured that whatever it was they were looking for had to be something fairly serious.

Or maybe this bullshit is just a complete waste of time.

His finger glided down page after page after page. He forced himself to be patient, combating *Just get through this shit* with *Slow down, goddamn it, and look at each entry.*

Page after page. The names slipped by.

Hang on.

He'd already reached the bottom and turned the page before his mind caught up with his finger. He turned back and there it was again. A name with a one-star notation.

Traffic Stop/Car Search. Lee, Harlan. Arrested. Possession of Stolen Property.

Lee, Harlan. Harlan Lee. Harley. Harlan Lee.

Could it be? It made a kind of sense. Harley could be Har-lee, which could be Harlan Lee. A traffic stop over seventeen years ago that led to an arrest.

But come on, Ben thought. *Possession of stolen property? You're going to come back after seventeen years to even the score for a misdemeanor arrest?*

It didn't fit, but Ben couldn't deny the feeling that had come over him when he'd seen the name. A sixth sense kicked in as he looked at the words written with black ink in neat block letters: Harlan Lee. Seventeen years ago according to Lars's notes. The date and time of arrest were listed and, most important, Lars had written down the Newberg PD case number. The record of an incident from that long ago would be stored in the warehouse across the street from the PD. The warehouse for which he still had a key.

FORTY-NINE

Alex walked into the guards' break room and melted into Ben's extended arms. She rested her head on his chest and breathed in the scent of him. It felt good to be held by him, and she listened to the steady beat of his heart. She tried to just appreciate the moment, but the constant fear and uncertainty was too strong. Ben's arrest in Danville had left her rattled. She knew Ben was out there taking chances, trying to find a way to get her out of this mess, but she also knew that when her husband got riled up, he had a reckless side. Anything could happen. Up to this point, Ben had managed to stay on top of things, but what would she do if one day he didn't come back? If something happened to him? Or what if he just gave up? Stopped trying? Alex knew the truth. Ben was the only thing standing between her and a life in prison. He guided her to the couch and sat holding her hands in his lap. Was it excitement or anxiety that had him practically quivering?

"Darnell told me McKenzie was here yesterday. Said he stayed a while. Did you talk to him?"

"No. Of course not," she answered, perturbed and even disappointed by the question. "But come on, Ben. I've been locked in here for almost two weeks. I haven't seen Jake or my dad. A good friend has been murdered and everyone thinks I did it. The last thing I need right now is for you to come in here and start talking about that . . . that . . . *asshole* McKenzie."

"Alex, it's important." Ben's voice was patient and loving. He squeezed her hands. "You're represented by counsel. Darnell knows that. He knows no one, no cop, at least, is supposed to be talking to you."

Alex took a deep breath and told herself to calm down. The ordeal was starting to overwhelm her. She had overreacted and tried to recover. "That's nice of you both, but there's nothing to worry about. He tried to get me to talk. Still working that self-defense crap. I sent him on his way."

"Are you sure?" Ben asked. "Believe it or not, he can be cagey."

"I told him you and Dad are working the case, that you had some leads."

Ben looked pained. "Did you tell McKenzie what your dad said? Did you mention the name Harley?"

A sinking feeling came over Alex, and she lowered her voice and bowed her head, unwilling to meet Ben's eyes. "I might have."

"It's not Harley we're looking for, Alex. It's Harlan, Harlan Lee."

"Who is Harlan Lee?" Alex asked.

"You remember your dad's old logbooks? The ones in the basement? Jake and I went through them. Seventeen years ago your dad arrested a guy named Harlan Lee for possession of stolen property."

Alex, a cop's daughter and wife for her entire life, laughed. "Come on, Ben. A guy reaches out after seventeen years to settle a beef over getting hooked for stolen property? You do sixty days in county for that."

"But here's the thing, Alex," he said, speaking urgently. "I went to the warehouse to pull the report your dad would have filed for the arrest. It's gone."

Alex sat upright, pulling her hands out of Ben's grasp. "Mc-Kenzie?"

"Maybe. I don't know. But all the other reports from that time period are right where they should be. Just that one seems to have disappeared."

"Oh, Ben," Alex said now, realizing she had blown their best lead. "I'm sorry. How could I have . . . I was stupid." She buried her face in her hands.

"Don't beat yourself up," Ben said, putting an arm around her comfortingly. "Like I said, there's a cagey side to him."

"I should have seen it," Alex said. "I'm sorry."

"Don't worry. We'll deal with McKenzie. He ain't that smart." He drew a five-by-eight file card out of his pocket.

"What's this?" Alex asked, taking it and looking at the faded writing on one side.

"After I couldn't find the report, I started digging around for something else. I found thousands of these old booking cards. We had the same sort of thing out in Oakland, back before we started putting everything on computers. Officers filled out a card like this every time they arrested someone. I knew a case as old as this one must have a booking card, so I dug through a bunch of boxes. Took a while but, here it is."

Alex read the card as Ben explained it to her. She felt a sense of nostalgia as she looked at her father's neat handwriting from almost twenty years ago. She pictured him, a tough no-nonsense cop, booking a prisoner, filling out this very card.

"That shows your dad booked Harlan Lee into *this* jail seventeen years ago on a charge of possession of stolen property. Three days later this Lee guy was transferred to Florence County." Ben leaned in and pointed to the bottom of the card. "See right here?

The sheriff, a man by the name of Henry Lipinski, signed for custody. Harlan never came back to Newberg."

Ben looked at his wife. "The transfer charge was for murder."

"Murder?" Alex was shocked. "Who did he kill and what did Dad have to do with it?"

"I don't know yet, but there's more." Ben paused and Alex waited, wondering what could possibly come next. "I ran an Internet search on Henry Lipinski."

"And?"

"He was arrested last month for distribution of child pornography. It was all over the newspapers up in Chippewa Falls. His case was going to be transferred to federal court."

Alex, still scanning the card, looked up. "*Was* going to be?"

"He's dead. Hanged himself in jail."

Alex took it all in, trying to get her head around it. She thought it through out loud.

"My dad arrested Harlan Lee and I'm in jail. And the other cop involved in Lee's arrest is *dead*?"

Ben's expression was grim. "Yeah. That's what I'm telling you."

Alex sat back on the couch, trying to take it all in.

"We're headed in the right direction," Ben said. "But now we've got to be very careful. This is serious, serious shit."

"Ben, you said it was suicide, right? This guy Lipinski. He killed himself?" Alex was scared.

"No, I didn't say that." His voice was grim. "That's what the news reports said."

Alex stared at the card. The signature of a man named Lipinski. A dead man named Lipinski. She felt her heart begin to race. Her thoughts went wild with possibilities until Ben's voice brought her back.

"Don't worry. You're in protective custody. Darnell and plenty of the rest of the security team are on our side. You'll be okay."

Alex tried to sound confident. "If McKenzie comes back, I'll keep my mouth shut," she said firmly, promising herself that she would not be scared anymore.

"He won't be back. Darnell will see to that. And I'm going to make sure McKenzie doesn't bother your dad either."

"But how do we find out about this Harlan Lee? That must be the answer, Ben, but what do we really know?" Alex leaned in "We need more, Ben. I'm going to court in three days. This is good, but it isn't enough to get me out from under a murder charge."

"I'll confront McKenzie," Ben said. "Force his hand. He can't just ignore all of this. If need be, I'll get Plate Boyd involved. We've got to compare your case to whatever they had on this Lipinski guy. Then there's the case in Danville. I don't know what the connection is, but before they shut down my interview, the suspect said something about growing up in Florence."

Alex tried to keep the desperation out of her voice. "Will they listen? Will they do anything?"

"If Plate and McKenzie won't listen, I'll go to the DA. We're on to something. We could make them delay the trial. We could get a shot at a bail reduction. That way we can get you home while everything is sorted out."

Alex hugged him. "Oh, God, Ben. I can't even imagine what it would feel like to walk out of here. Can you really make that happen?"

"I'm going to make it happen. Just stay safe. Watch yourself and sit tight, you hear me?"

"Don't worry about me. You be careful. Don't take any more chances."

Ben squeezed her even more tightly and kissed her on the mouth. Before he left, he said, "I'll be back, Alex. And then you and I are walking out of here together. I promise."

FIFTY

McKenzie tossed the six-pack of beer on the counter and called out to the turbaned clerk who had his back turned.

"Yo, Slumdog, give me a box of Red 100s to go with the beer."

The man turned and stared at the detective before stepping forward and reaching over his head to pull a pack of smokes from the cigarette rack. He tossed the pack onto the counter, never taking his seething eyes off McKenzie.

"Beer and cigarettes. Will that be all?" The man's English was perfect, without a trace of an accent.

"That's it. Ring it up, Haji." McKenzie winked, knowing he had gotten under the clerk's dark skin.

"That will be twelve seventy-five."

McKenzie pulled out his wallet and flipped it open to display his detective shield. "What's the good-guy rate?"

"The price is the same for everyone, Officer. Twelve seventy-five, please."

McKenzie scoffed, throwing down a twenty. "Goddamn.

282 ■ NEAL GRIFFIN

Between owning every frickin' convenience store in America and the stranglehold on gas—shit, boy, why blow up buildings? All you fuckers are getting rich off us poor-ass Americans."

"I was born in Des Moines, asshole," the man shouted, slamming McKenzie's change hard on the counter.

McKenzie walked out, with the six-pack slung over his shoulder, his middle finger looped through the plastic ring and extended straight up at the clerk. He stepped into the dimly lit parking lot and stopped, staring at his car. Ben Sawyer sat on the hood as if resting in a favorite recliner, his back against the windshield, legs stretched out and crossed at the ankles. McKenzie approached slowly, set the six-pack on the hood, and busted out a cigarette from his fresh pack.

"Comfortable?" he asked sarcastically.

"Sure am, but one of those beers would be great right about now," Sawyer replied.

"Get your ass off my car, Sawyer," McKenzie growled, but the other man stayed put.

"Beer and cigarettes," Ben said. "Getting ready for another late-night stakeout?"

"What the hell are you doing here? Shouldn't you be home with the family?" McKenzie pulled a lighter from his pocket and the flame lit up his face. "What's left of it, that is."

Ben slid down the hood. "So tell me, Doyle. How's the big case coming along? I see you figured out the Harlan Lee connection. Nice work."

McKenzie didn't miss a beat. "Harlan who? What big case are you talking about?"

"You know exactly what I'm talking about. Harlan Lee and the connection to the Carson murder. My father-in-law arrested Lee seventeen years ago. A few days later, he was transferred to Florence County on a murder charge. You pulled the case from the warehouse."

McKenzie was careful to show no reaction. *Have to admire the sly little shit,* he thought to himself. He stepped around to the driver's side of the vehicle.

"Oh, you're talking about the murder case against your wife. Sorry. That shit is history to me. I've moved on."

"Where's the Lee file? I'd like to see it."

"The Lee file?" McKenzie feigned confusion. "Tell you what, I'll run a computer check, see what I can find, a favor from a working cop to a has-been. Will that make you happy?"

McKenzie saw Ben swallow hard, and he knew he was gaining the upper hand. He seemed to be winning this little mental chess game. He was determined to stay on offense.

"Hell, I'll even make a few calls. Where did you say the case was out of? Florence County?" McKenzie didn't bother even trying to hide his sarcasm. He recalled the name Jorgensen had given him. "The sheriff up there, Scott Jamison, is a good friend of mine. I'll have him take a look around. Seventeen years ago, you say? That's an old record. Might take some digging, but old Scotty, he'll do that for me."

McKenzie looked straight at Ben, narrowing his eyes. He wanted his meaning to be absolutely clear. "But something tells me, Sawyer, we ain't gonna come up with a damn thing."

McKenzie knew Ben was starting to see the truth. The great Ben Sawyer was getting his ass handed to him, and there was nothing he could do about it.

"How about Danville?" Ben asked. McKenzie thought he picked up on a hint of desperation. "How much do you know about the suspect in the murder of the transvestite?"

McKenzie laughed. *Very impressive,* he thought. "You mean the case where you got arrested for sticking your nose where it don't belong? The one where Suarez got her ass shot to hell? If you don't mind, I'll stay out of it. Those Illinois boys seem kind of sensitive to people meddlin' in their business."

"Come on, McKenzie. The suspect grew up in Florence County," Sawyer said.

McKenzie couldn't help but start to wonder how it was that Sawyer was putting this thing together, but he told himself it didn't matter. He shrugged his shoulders. "Wow. Strange coincidence. Thanks for letting me know."

"You know there's a connection in all this," Ben said. "You know it's going to come up at trial."

McKenzie did his best to appear confident. He cracked open a beer and replied, "Maybe it will. But you know what else is going to come up? Real evidence. Stuff like eyewitness accounts, the murder weapon, blood evidence, and a lot of information about how your wife was practically screwing the dead guy on the tables in that coffee shop. All things that make sense to the God-fearing Wisconsin citizens who sit on juries—unlike this crazy conspiracy shit."

McKenzie opened the car door. Ben slammed it shut. He looked McKenzie directly in the eye when he spoke.

"A missing case file you don't know anything about. A similar case two hours away you don't care about. Some sort of connection to Florence County that you're not interested in. Kind of makes me wonder what it is you're trying to keep quiet."

"You got a rich imagination, Sawyer," McKenzie said. "You wasted all those years being a cop. You should've made movies or some shit." He grabbed the door handle of his car. "Now step aside. I've got plans that don't involve standing around here jawin' with you."

"Tell me, Doyle, what happened to Henry Lipinski? You figure he killed himself instead of facing the music, or is that just what somebody wants us to think?"

"So you heard about that, huh? I gotta give it to you, Sawyer. You are pretty good at this detective shit."

McKenzie took a healthy hit off the beer. He couldn't resist rubbing Ben's face in it.

"Let me spell it out for, Sawyer. I don't give a shit about some ancient case out of Florence County, a ghost named Harlan Lee, a dead sheriff, or some fag that got its head caved in with a baseball bat. Truth be told, I could give two shits about that uppity bitch Suarez getting her ass shot to hell. Your wife is going down for murder. Get used to it."

Ben stared at him, openmouthed. "What the hell are you, McKenzie?"

"I think you're starting to get a pretty good idea of what I am. Of *who* I am and what I can do. That might be something you want to keep in mind. Now for the last time, Sawyer—back off."

"Goddamn, McKenzie," Ben said. "You're ass-deep in this. Harlan Lee, Lipinski, even this stuff out of Danville? Those were cops that got shot. One of them was from your own department."

Ben paused, then started to go on. "You won't get away with this. I'll—"

"You'll what?" McKenzie closed to within inches of Ben's face and lowered his voice. "Keep carrying on about some case from more than a decade ago that you got no record of and no documents? Talk about what was supposed to have been said during an illegal interrogation? An interrogation that got your dumb ass arrested and thrown in jail? Or maybe you should run and tell Jorgensen?"

McKenzie took another long swallow of beer. "No. Wait a sec. You can go tell Norgaard. How about that? Go ahead, Sawyer. Throw your weight around."

"Jesus Christ, McKenzie, how deep does this go? Just what are you into?"

"I'll give you some credit, Sawyer." McKenzie's voice flowed with complete confidence. "When you dragged your ass back here from Oakland, I figured you'd be happy just to have a job. Sit on the sidelines and collect a paycheck from your old man. It never occurred to me you'd come on like some supercop. But I'll be damned if you didn't come pretty close to figuring it all out. But you're done now, along with that bitch of a wife of yours."

McKenzie could see the clinched fists and heavy breathing. He knew Ben was right on the edge.

"Go ahead, Sawyer. I'll let you put a good hurtin' on me. I for sure got it coming."

"No, not here McKenzie. Not yet. We'll keep playing cat and mouse. Who knows? Maybe you'll even win. But get this—you and whoever you're working with are going to have to find another patsy. You try taking my wife down for a murder you and I both know she didn't commit, I'll kill you myself."

The two men were only inches apart, glaring at each other almost nose to nose. McKenzie blinked first. He pushed past Sawyer and opened the car door, leaving Ben with a closing thought.

"Your wife's going to prison, Sawyer. Get used to it. If anything happens to me, who do you suppose they'll look at? Might wanna ask yourself what becomes of a boy who's got two parents locked up for life."

FIFTY-ONE

McKenzie had sat outside Jorgensen's office for more than twenty minutes wondering just what the hell was going on. He'd been caught off guard when the chief's secretary called and told him to report to the chief's office. *Why did he have that old bitch call me? Why are we meeting here?* As he played out the possibilities in his mind, the door finally opened.

"Step in here, Detective," the chief called out from the doorway. "I need to speak with you about the Louis Carson case." McKenzie picked up on the wry smile from Bernice Erickson as he walked toward the office. The woman looked up and they exchanged stares. McKenzie was sure she was the culprit who had given Sawyer his badge and he didn't doubt she had something to do with this meeting.

McKenzie walked into the office and went for his usual chair, but Jorgensen stopped him with an upraised hand.

"Don't sit down. You won't be here that long. Plate Boyd stopped by a while ago. Said he found this on his desk this morning." Jorgensen jammed a piece of paper against McKenzie's chest. A copy of an old booking card. The name on the card was Harlan Lee. The words "Ask McKenzie" were written across the top of the form.

So that's it. Son of a bitch.

"Boss, I had no idea—"

"Did I tell you to clean this shit up? Did I tell you to be thorough?" Jorgensen's voice was harsh but delivered in a whisper. "Judas Priest, Detective. How have you survived as a cop all these years?"

McKenzie struggled for a response.

"Chief, we haven't used booking cards in over ten years. How the hell was I supposed to know this would turn up?"

"Because the case happened seventeen years ago, you stupid shit. Someone is sniffing around, McKenzie. Who the hell is it? Is it Sawyer?"

McKenzie blew out a breath. "It's gotta be." McKenzie pointed to the closed office door. "And I'll bet you he is working with that old bitch you've got for a secretary. You need to get rid of her, Chief."

"Oh sure, Doyle. And how is that going to look right now?"

It dawned on Doyle that was the reason for the official meeting. Jorgensen was worried and now he was covering his tracks. Separating himself from the whole mess. He needed to draw the chief back in. Let him know just how close the danger was. "Sawyer came at me last night, got in my face. He knows about Lee."

Jorgensen looked stunned. "And you were going to tell me when?"

"I'm taking care of it, Chief. I'm on it."

"I've heard that before, Doyle. I'm starting to think I fired the wrong damn cop."

McKenzie seethed in silence.

"Your ship is springing major leaks, Doyle." Jorgensen's voice went up an octave and his face was red. "This booking card is a formal link to the Lee case. You had better get a handle on this right now. Do you hear me?"

"Boss, I've got it under control. You told me to handle it. To keep everyone else away from it. I'm taking care of everything."

Jorgensen's voice dropped back to a whisper. "All this shit has got to stop. Sawyer cannot get to Harlan Lee. Do you hear me?"

"And what happens if he does? I'm in the dark here, Chief. Makes it kind of hard to know where the next move is gonna come from."

Jorgensen drilled two fingers into McKenzie's chest. "You don't need to know any more than what I've told you. I think maybe I should pull you off the case. I've still got some concerns about that body at the rest stop. Seems they've tied the boy into another local dealer, fella named Tyrone. Haven't I heard you mention an informant by that name?"

McKenzie knew he was in deep, deep trouble. "Okay, boss," he said, surrendering. "Point me in the right direction."

"There's no doubt in my mind that Sawyer is already halfway to Florence County," Jorgensen said. "When he gets there, he'll be asking a lot of questions. About Harlan Lee. And Henry Lipinski."

"I'll head up there and—"

Jorgensen cut him off. "Don't bother, McKenzie. I told you. I've got a good man in that area. A man I can damn sure depend on to get a job done. Sawyer ain't going to find shit. He'll have no choice but to turn his ass around and come home."

Jorgensen put his lips inches from McKenzie's ear.

"When he does, I want you to track his ass down. That son of a bitch is not to return to Newberg. And as for that old, broken-down piece of shit across town, he needs to be dealt with right quick."

"I'll take care of it, Chief." McKenzie's voice shook. "You can count on it."

"Stop with the ass-kissin' bullshit. If you had half the police sense Sawyer has, this shit would be history. Quit talking and get it done. Now get the hell out of my office."

FIFTY-TWO

Ben watched as the uniformed officer hopped into the cruiser marked FLORENCE COUNTY SHERIFF'S OFFICE and took off down the road. No doubt responding to a domestic violence in progress that had been called in clear across the county. *That should keep you busy for a half hour or so.*

After the late-night meeting with McKenzie, Ben had reluctantly driven two hundred and fifty miles to Florence County. He was certain McKenzie wasn't working alone, and Ben didn't know whom he could trust. He had copied the booking card and told Bernie to put it on Plate Boyd's desk. He could only hope that, in the end, Plate was still a real cop. Leaving Alex in Newberg with McKenzie on the loose had him worried, but what choice did he have? He hoped that she would be safe in jail—also not a particularly comforting thought. Ben had called Tia on her cell—she was still in the hospital, though her parents had gone back to Mexico—and they had come up with what they thought was a simple plan. Tia's stern directions had left Ben wondering who worked for whom.

"Don't be going all cowboy on this thing," she said. "Keep a low profile, be as quick as you can, and get your ass back down to New-berg. I'll take care of things while you're gone."

Once he had some proof of Harlan Lee's existence and some-thing that indicated that his murder conviction was somehow re-lated to an arrest in Newberg, he'd go to the courthouse and bang on the DA's desk. I'll bother her at home if I have to. *Hell,* he thought, *I'll take it to the media.* Somehow, he had to shed some light on the case, do something that would give Alex the benefit of the doubt.

The woman at the counter in the sheriff's office bought Ben's line about being a reporter researching an old murder case. She seemed to hope that maybe she would become part of the story. When she couldn't find anything in her computer, her apology sounded genuine.

"Sorry, sir. Are you sure it was Florence County? Do you have the name right?"

"Positive. The case was transferred up from Newberg. Harlan Lee. Can you check again?"

"I've checked three times. I searched through all the L's and H's just in case the name got messed up. We have no record of a trial, arrest, booking. Nothing. Nothing on a man named Harlan Lee."

Ben murmured under his breath, "McKenzie, you son of a bitch."

"Excuse me?" The clerk was beginning to look annoyed.

"Never mind." Ben's mind was turning. "Tell me this. Who were the key players back then? I know the sheriff was a man named Lipinski, but who else was here? Who prosecuted murder cases? Or a judge? Anyone still around?"

"Beats me. I was six years old." The girl shrugged, her hopes for notoriety dashed.

"That'd be Bill Petite," a new voice said. "He was the district attorney back then."

Ben turned around to see a white-haired man with tan leath-ery skin leaning against a mop. He wore an orange jumpsuit marked FLORENCE COUNTY JAIL and Ben figured his age at seventy-plus.

The clerk said, "Gus, be quiet and stick to your work. Don't be butting in on other people's conversations." The woman looked at Ben and rolled her eyes. "They send him over here every day and I end up babysitting him. He mops that same spot for eight hours."

"I see," Ben said, then turned to the man and encouraged him to continue. "What was that you said?"

"I said Bill Petite was district attorney back in them days. Hotshot lawyer. Came in for a few years, then lost his chair to another young buck. Headed out for greener pastures, or so he thought." The man snickered. He lowered his stooped shoulders and returned to his pressing duty of dry mopping the floor as if he hadn't said a word. Ben looked up and down the hall and saw no sign of a guard or other prisoner.

"You got a name, pal?"

The man took offense. "Name's Gus Walcowski, but that don't make me no pal of yours now, does it?"

Ben was willing to do what it took to gain the man's cooperation. "Sorry, sir. I didn't mean anything by it. But this is really important to me. Do you know where I can get hold of Mr. Petite? Is he still practicing?"

The old man laughed like he'd heard a good joke. "Practicing? Guess he could be practicing one thing or another."

"I'm not following you." Ben tried to hide his growing frustration. "Can you help me or not?"

"I can't help you with nothing other than to tell you Bill Petite was a district attorney who took a real pleasure in stickin' it to ya as hard as he could. I can also tell you he is easy enough to find these days."

"I'm still not following you, Gus." Ben gave a smile of encouragement.

"Petite went and killed his girlfriend and got his ass thrown in prison for it. No surprise to me. He always was a moody little prick."

Ben was stunned. "When, Gus? How long ago did this happen?"

Gus pushed his mop in long smooth strokes across the linoleum and spoke in a cadence. "Heard tell from an old partner of mine who finished up a hitch just as Petite was coming in. Wasn't much more than a few weeks ago, but Petite pled out quick. Cut himself the best deal he could. Serves him right. He was known to serve up a few deals back in the day."

When Ben was certain the man was finished, he double-checked the facts. "So the former district attorney of Florence County, William Petite, is in prison for murder?"

Gus looked at Ben like he thought the stranger was simpleminded. "Yep."

A district attorney had gone down for murder. A district attorney who might have prosecuted a killer named Harlan Lee. Ben's pulse raced and his mouth started to water. He asked a few more questions, but it was clear Gus knew nothing else. Knowing that the sheriff was probably headed back and might walk in at any moment, Ben prepared to leave.

He'd originally intended to make this trip a quick turnaround, but he couldn't take the word of an old felon from a county lockup. No one in Newberg would believe him. And if McKenzie found out before he got back, he'd figure out some way to discredit Ben's information. Ben knew he needed more. He turned to Gus and did his best to sound casual.

"Hey, Gus. You wouldn't happen to know where Petite is now, would you? Where he's locked up these days?"

"Course I know. He pulled the worst card a man can in this state." Gus never missed a stroke with his mop. "He landed at Red Cliff."

FIFTY-THREE

Doyle McKenzie walked into the quiet room and took a seat on the edge of the bed.

"Hello, Red." McKenzie smacked Lars twice on the face with an open hand, hard enough to get the old man's attention. Mc-Kenzie wanted Lars to know this was no social visit. "Damn, old boy. You have most certainly looked better."

Lars looked back with distrust in his eyes. McKenzie knew the former chief had never cared for him, and the feeling was mutual.

"You're probably wondering what the hell I'm doing here, huh? We sure didn't see much of each other on the job. Truth be told, Lars, I had every reason in the world to avoid your ass. But no hard feelings. Turns out Jorgensen's every bit the pain in the ass you were, just for different reasons."

Lars kept his eyes focused on McKenzie, and the detective kept talking.

"I imagine that son-in-law of yours has come by and filled your head with all sorts of bullshit, huh?"

Still McKenzie got nothing but a hard look so he kept talking.

"Yeah, Sawyer is a real piece of work. A fucking straight arrow if there ever was one. You ever have a sergeant like that? Meddling around in your affairs? I'm sure you can appreciate what a pain in my ass he is." McKenzie delivered the lines as if to say the two old cops had some shared history with by-the-book sergeants.

"I suppose you think I'm here to talk about your daughter, but that's old news. Sorry to be the one to tell you, but she's bought and paid for." McKenzie's tone was flippant. "Now, this ancient shit here, this we need to talk about."

McKenzie pulled yellowed papers from an envelope. "You remember this? Long time ago but, hey, it was a hell of an arrest. I seem to recall they made you Officer of the Year off of this, right? The big time comes to Newberg."

McKenzie held the report out where the old man could see his handwriting from almost twenty years ago. "But I got some bad news for you, Lars. Seems this old boy, Harlan Lee, might be out settling some old scores. Can you believe that shit?"

McKenzie waited for some acknowledgment and was certain he saw a look of understanding in the old man's eyes. "Problem is, Lars, Jorgensen's worried you might come around and get all talkative, about what I sure as hell can't say. Course, that don't seem to be much of a concern at present, huh?"

McKenzie waited as if expecting a response. After a long moment of shared silence, McKenzie went on.

"I told him, Lars Norgaard is a stand-up guy. Good copper. It's just . . ." McKenzie paused, as if what he had to say caused him personal discomfort. "There's a lot at stake, Lars. And with your little girl up on a murder rap, that shit has got to screw with your sensibilities."

McKenzie pulled a syringe from his pocket and removed the orange cap over the needle. He took hold of the plastic tube that ran food into Lars's body. "I'm just as sorry as I can be, old man. Hell, if you had something to live for, we could work through all the details. I'd be happy to somehow spring your daughter and figure out another way to take care of this mess. But that damn son-in-law of yours . . . It's best this way, Lars."

McKenzie lifted the syringe up to the tube and poked the needle through the plastic. His thumb pressed down on the plunger just as the old man somehow raised his arm. He cuffed McKenzie across the wrist, and the syringe fell to the floor.

"Goddamn it, Lars," McKenzie said. "Knock it off. Take this shit like a man." He dropped to his knees and cursed as he got down on his belly and low-crawled halfway under the bed.

"Excuse me? What's going on here?"

McKenzie recognized the voice and cursed under his breath. He shimmied farther ahead and saw the syringe clear against the wall and well beyond his reach. He stretched his full length just as the voice sounded again, this time with her usual tone of superiority. "Come out from under there this instant."

McKenzie struggled to back out from the tight fit under the bed. Frustrated and out of breath, he stood and turned to the familiar face of Bernice Erickson.

"Oh," she said, her voice full of contempt. "It's you."

McKenzie could barely conceal his own irritation. He knew there would be no fooling this one, but he had to play along as best he could. "Hey, Bernice. Paying your old boss a visit?"

Bernice walked deliberately to the bed, putting herself between McKenzie and Lars. She clearly wasn't buying it. "Get out, Detective."

McKenzie dug deep to put some authority in his voice. "Listen here—"

Bernice put her shoulders back and faced the much larger man. Her voice was firm. "I said get out. If you don't, I'll call security."

"I've got as much right to be here as you do, you old—"

McKenzie stopped when his cell phone chimed in his pocket. He pulled it out and saw the area code was out of Florence County. McKenzie glared at Bernice as he stepped into the hallway.

The two-minute conversation left McKenzie shaking his head wondering when he was going to catch a damn break. He hung up the phone craving a drink and a smoke. McKenzie needed to make arrangements for what he knew would be Sawyer's next move. *And his last one, if I have anything to do with it.*

McKenzie poked his head back inside the old man's room and saw Bernice Erickson had now pulled up a stool. The old bitch was already on the phone speaking to someone about an unauthorized visitor. Defeated for now, McKenzie scowled at Lars. The old man looked back with what seemed a sideways *fuck you* sort of glance. McKenzie headed down the hallway with pressing matters at hand. He'd deal with Lars Norgaard another time.

FIFTY-FOUR

The Gothic building jutted against the morning skyline. Seeing it, Ben thought, *Now, that's a prison.* Red Cliff State Penitentiary was the remotest of all Wisconsin's prisons, cut into the southwestern corner of Lake Superior. The severe structure would have looked forbidding even if you didn't know it was a prison—the whole building seemed to have a piss-poor attitude.

Built in the late 1800s, Red Cliff looked nothing like the campus environments of modern correctional facilities. The towering walls were thirty-inch-thick stone and topped with six feet of looped razor wire. Perimeter positions equipped with floor-mounted binoculars and industrial-grade air whistle alarms were built into the walls every fifty yards and on each corner. Inmates and visitors alike passed through thick steel gates that Ben estimated were thirty feet high. Ominous gray stone gargoyles stared down on all who entered, as did the flesh-and-blood guards who walked along the top of the wall, their high-powered weapons clearly visible. Ben drove through the gates with a sense of foreboding, thinking sarcastically that at some point in the prison's history someone must have decided to fill in the moat.

The night before, he'd driven across the top of Wisconsin, following the two-hundred-mile southern shoreline of the world's largest freshwater lake. When exhaustion overtook him, he'd pulled into a deserted rest stop and slept fitfully for a couple of hours, lulled to sleep by the lapping waves of Lake Superior outside the minivan. Alex haunted his dreams, calling out from a dismal jail cell, begging him to come back. At one point Ben woke to see Alex's face pressed against the window of the van. He screamed and sat up, and the image disappeared. Shaken, he'd driven to a nearby café, not because he craved food but because he realized it was either eat or stop functioning. He powered down a plate of eggs and a pot of coffee before resuming his journey, tracing long, winding roads through the virgin forest of towering pines.

The sun was halfway to its noon position when Ben arrived at the prison and took his place deep in a long line of would-be visitors that stretched a hundred yards or more along the exterior wall. Frustrated, Ben craned his neck to try and see the front of the line, without success. Soon enough, the guards announced that the number of visitors had reached the maximum permitted, and no one else was allowed to join the line. Ben felt a wash of relief as he watched the news fall heavily on late-arriving families, who, he assumed, had probably driven hours to spend time with a loved one.

"There's a Motel Six four miles up the road." The guard's voice was robotic. "If you want to come back tomorrow, you should get here by six A.M. to guarantee a spot."

"But visiting hours start at one o'clock," a woman said, sounding perplexed.

"Fine." The guard shrugged. "Show up at noon. See how much good that does you."

Ben stood in line outside for over two hours, then waited in a reception area for another forty-five minutes. He filled out the prison visitation request, using his real name and address with no mention of police affiliation. He endured a near strip search without complaint. He'd get in on his own merits or not at all.

Ben was certain McKenzie had made his search at the sheriff's office come up dry, but there was no way McKenzie could have anticipated Ben's conversation with Gus. Learning of Petite's existence and location was just plain old dumb luck, the cornerstone of any successful investigation. Ben figured he had a few hours at best before McKenzie learned of this development and figured out a response.

A guard entered the room and began to summon the next round of visitors.

"Jacobs, Allison, Myers, Diaz, Monroe, and"—the guard ran his finger down the page and Ben sat up, hoping—"Whitfield. Step forward for visitation."

The guard continued giving instructions, but Ben tuned him out, remembering his early visits to Alex in jail, before Tia flexed her muscle. Ben had spent years locking people up, and it had never crossed his mind to wonder what happened next. You throw a crook in prison for ten, twelve years and then what? The guy is going to have family, he's going to have folks who care about him. Those people, Ben thought, are right here. They've driven hundreds of miles, waited in line for hours, to have a chance to spend a few minutes with a loved one. What kind of system allows that? Ben answered his own question. *Your system. You spent your life in it.*

Alex. He tried to send good thoughts her way, then dozed fitfully until a voice said, "Are you Sawyer?"

Ben opened his eyes and saw the guard staring down. "Yeah," he said, straightening up. "I'm Ben Sawyer."

"You get forty-five minutes. Clock's ticking."

Ben got to his feet and fell in with his group as they were hustled through a series of tunnellike corridors lined with men in dark uniforms. Their footfalls echoed ominously against the hard surfaces of the floor, walls, and low ceiling. In the distance Ben could hear the loud voices of anxious men shouting among themselves. The vulgarity reminded him of the way cops talk when they're alone. From the changes in the sound, it seemed that the men were being shuffled along much like the visitors. Suddenly the voices grew louder, then stopped.

The guards guided the group of visitors through a door and into daylight. Ben was surprised to find himself in an open yard, surrounded on all four sides by walls three stories high. The walls were intersected by a "ceiling" of thick chain-link fencing that created a caged-in effect over the entire yard. The crisscross pattern was tight enough to keep anyone from squeezing through but loose enough for a sniper to track a target. Underfoot was hard brown dirt with short tufts of dead grass. Several chair-sized tree stumps served as evidence that nothing was allowed to interfere with a sharpshooter's line of sight. Several old wrought-iron park benches and two dilapidated, drab green picnic tables were the only furniture. Guards roamed the yard, tapping billy clubs in their palms or against one leg. Looking up and around, Ben saw rifle barrels extended from the highest windows, swinging in one direction, then another.

In the center of the yard stood about twenty men. All wore dark blue trousers and light blue collared shirts with a six-digit number stenciled over the right pocket. When the visitors arrived, the men cheered in unison and sought out their loved ones, hugging and kissing the new arrivals. Ben watched, happy to see that this simple pleasure was allowed. Alone in the middle of the yard stood an odd-looking character who looked to be a few years older than Ben and of slighter build. His clothes were much darker and crisper than those of all the other inmates, and his nervous energy was apparent. His skin was smooth with a deep tan, but he bore fresh bruises under both eyes and his lip was swollen with an ugly welt. His haircut was neatly feathered and looked like one of those two-hundred-dollar jobs from an upscale salon. He reeked of fresh meat. Ben walked straight over to him.

"Mr. Petite?"

"Who are you?" The voice was educated but nervous, the diction precise. Every bit the convict lawyer.

"Mr. Petite, I'm Ben Sawyer from Newberg. I appreciate your being willing to see me."

Petite's gaze roamed over Ben's face, his voice sharp with worry. "Newberg? I told your people I'm not going to make any trouble. Why are you here?"

Ben did his best to hide his confusion and play along.

"Uh . . . they sent me to check on you." Even he heard the bullshit in his voice, but he kept trying. "So how are you doing?"

"What do you mean how am I doing? How do you think I'm doing? I've been here less than a week. Somewhere around three thousand days to go. I was told I'd be left alone. Just do my time, right? Unless—" There was hope in Petite's voice. "Has something changed?"

"Changed?" Ben couldn't hide his confusion. "No. Everything is uh . . . everything is still like we planned."

Petite's pinched face hardened a bit. "Who did you say you were? Who sent you up here?"

Ben took a stab in the dark. "Doyle McKenzie sent me."

"Never heard of him." Petite looked around nervously. He turned and began to walk toward the door marked INMATES ONLY. VISITORS STAY BACK 100 FEET.

"I'm going back to my cell. We've got nothing to talk about."

"All right, Petite. I'm on my own. I want to talk to you about Harlan Lee."

Petite stopped. After a frozen moment, he turned slowly to look at Ben.

"Say that again? You want to talk about *who*?"

"Harlan Lee. Do you remember the case?"

"Why do you want to talk—" Petite shook his head as if clearing away a bad idea. "I don't know any Harlan Lee and I don't think we should be talking, so if you will excuse me . . ." He turned away again.

Ben called out, "Okay. I just thought the Lee case might be related to something going on down in Newberg. Damnedest thing. My wife? She's locked up on a murder rap just like you. She's locked up in a county facility. She's not in prison yet."

Petite stopped and looked back, a perplexed expression on his face. "What do you mean?"

"My wife, she's locked up on a murder charge, but I can guarantee you, she didn't kill anyone."

"Your wife?" Petite asked. "Murder?"

"Alex Sawyer. She's the daughter of Lars Norgaard," Ben said in a matter-of-fact tone. "He arrested Harlan Lee. Still don't remember?"

Petite turned his head in both directions, then reluctantly moved back toward Ben. When he was close enough, he whispered, "What do you mean, your wife didn't do it?"

Ben kept his voice low to keep from spooking the man. "My wife is being framed for murder. She didn't kill anyone."

"But what has that got to do with—" Petite caught himself. "With this person you mentioned. This Harlan Lee."

Ben knew he was getting to Petite.

"Because of another cop involved, Henry Lipinski. Don't tell me you don't remember him."

"What about Sheriff Lipinski?" Petite's interest grew.

"Mr. Petite, Lipinski was arrested for some very serious charges involving child pornography. A charge he denied, by the way. Then he was found hanging in his cell in the Chippewa County Jail. They're calling it a suicide." Ben shrugged and let the idea take hold. "Course you never know. Maybe he did kill himself."

Petite stood silent, staring into space.

"A man named Donaldson is on the hook for a murder down in Illinois. I'm betting he also played a role in the case against Harlan Lee. Does that help your memory, counselor?"

"Donaldson? Gerald Donaldson's been arrested for murder?" Petite sounded flabbergasted.

Ben continued. "Mr. Petite, I have information that says after being arrested in Newberg, Harlan Lee was transferred to Florence County and charged with murder. You were the district attorney in Florence County at the time. I checked. There were no other homicides that year." Ben leaned in for effect. "Here's the wild part, Mr. Petite. I went to the County Clerk's Office. There is no arrest record for Harlan Lee. No court record. I can't even find a booking photo. Nothing. How do you figure that?"

Petite stumbled to one of the nearby benches and sat, mumbling to himself. Ben joined him and spoke in a quiet but rapid-fire pace.

"My wife didn't kill anyone, Mr. Petite, but someone sure does want people to think she did. Donaldson? He says he didn't kill anybody either. We'll never know about Lipinski. How about you, Mr. Petite? Did you actually kill someone, or did you get set up too?"

"It makes sense." Petite stared at the hard dirt, his face white. "Of course, it makes perfect sense."

"Good," Ben said. "Then tell me. Tell me how any of this makes sense."

Petite looked up.

"I can't talk to you about this. I have a family." Petite laughed at himself. "I had a family . . . but I still have children." Petite's voice changed in tone. "I pled out quick and got manslaughter two. I'll be out in eight years. They'll still be young. I was assured that if I cooperated, they'd be taken care of. I'm not going to jeopardize that."

"Assured?" Ben asked. "Assured by who?"

"Never mind, Sawyer." Petite was firm. "I'm not going to talk with you about this. If you don't already know, that means you don't need to know."

"Did McKenzie put you up to this? I can handle him."

"I told you. I've never heard of this McKenzie."

"You're going to do eight years for a crime you didn't commit?" Ben asked. "What about Lipinski? What happens if you end up like that?"

"I don't want to talk with you, Mr. Sawyer. You don't know what you're up against."

"Look," Ben said, "just tell me about Lee and I'll leave you alone. I'll go back to the family of the victim. Just tell me who he killed."

"I'm not going to get into this with you, Mr. Sawyer. You want answers? Talk to Lars Norgaard. Let him tell you about how things work at Newberg PD."

"He can't, Mr. Petite. Lars had a stroke. Anything he knows is locked away somewhere I can't get at it."

"Then look beyond Norgaard. You got this far. Figure it out. But leave me alone. Please."

"Mr. Petite, I'm a cop. I can protect you. We can protect your family. You can't pretend none of this is going on."

"Yes, I can and I will," Petite said. "The last thing I need is more help from cops. Just leave me alone."

Ben pulled the paper from his pocket and held it out for the man to see. The composite sketch from Danville.

"Mr. Petite, this man shot two cops and ran off. I think he had something to do with the murder my wife is accused of. Maybe he knows something about your case. I also think he is somehow connected to Harlan Lee. Do you recognize him?"

Petite looked at the paper, studying the face. He seemed about to speak when a whistle sounded, followed by a voice ordering inmates back inside the facility.

Ben reached out and grabbed Petite by the arm.

"Mr. Petite . . . Bill. Please."

Petite stood and looked down at Ben.

"Get away from me, Sawyer. I'm going to do my penance in this hellhole. With any luck, I walk in the minimum and all this will be behind me."

"Who is he?" Ben knew, but he wanted to hear it. He wanted it said. "Just tell me that and I'll leave."

A long pause and Petite blew out a breath. "The man in the picture *is* Harlan Lee. Find him. I'm pretty sure he can answer all your questions."

FIFTY-FIVE

Ben drove the first twenty miles toward home with the accelerator smashed against the floor. He started to mentally string together the known facts so he could come up with a coherent plan. Get back to Newberg and find the district attorney. If necessary, go to her house. Show her Lars's log entry; brief her on the missing case file; tell her about Donaldson's arrest and how it ties into Tia getting shot. Explain the death of Henry Lipinski and McKenzie's possible involvement. Get Petite into protective custody. Ben was deep in thought until the red-and-blue light flickered behind him and the siren brought him back to the present. He pulled to the side of the road, hoping the squad car would pass him by, but no such luck.

The trooper approached, Smokey hat firmly in place. Ben had been doing over ninety miles an hour since leaving Red Cliff. *Nice going. Now just take your ticket and get moving.*

The trooper reached the van's window and leaned in. Ben picked up on the causal tone of voice.

"Good afternoon. Are you Sergeant Sawyer?"

Ben eyed the officer with caution. "Yeah, I'm Ben Sawyer. How did you know that?"

"Because you've got a law enforcement block on your tags." He looked at Ben, and when he saw nothing but confusion, he went on. "I ran your plates from my mobile computer. When you registered your car you used your police ID as part of the process, right?"

"Oh, yeah. Sorry, Officer. Guess I'm just kind of tired. Heading home after a long trip."

"You must be in a hurry. You've been doing over ninety for the last two miles." The trooper sounded like he'd had the same discussion with a thousand off-duty cops before Ben.

"Sorry." Ben did his best to look sheepish. "I'll slow down."

"I'm sure you will, Sergeant. Let's just see your badge and I'll get you out of here and on your way."

Ben tried to be casual. "I took off from Newberg in such a hurry, I left it behind." He shrugged. "Off duty business, you know."

"No sweat. Just let me run your license. Confirm your photo. Step back to my car for a sec." When Ben didn't budge, the trooper tried coaxing. "Come on, Sarge. I mean, I have to make sure you're not a wanted criminal or anything. Then you can be on your way."

"Sure, Officer. No problem." Ben exited the car and walked alongside the man as he returned to his patrol car.

"You shouldn't leave home without your badge," the trooper said. "Personally I take mine everywhere. You never know when you're going to need to talk your way out of a ticket, right?"

"You're right, Officer, I'll be more careful." Ben just wanted to be back on the road.

"Suit yourself. Left it at home though, huh? You sure you didn't leave it at Red Cliff?"

The words registered just as the trooper spun toward Ben and buried the short end of his baton in Ben's solar plexus. As Ben doubled over, he felt a second blow on top of his skull. His vision blurred. He lunged forward and grabbed the trooper around the waist. Baton blows rained down on his back, and Ben heard the man cursing, yelling for Ben to let go. Ben reached up and found the hard plastic handgrip of the officer's holstered weapon. It was the work of an instant to adjust his grasp to the correct angle and pull. It came loose easily and Ben fell back as he aimed and pulled the trigger without hesitation.

Two wires shot out and one of the fishhook barbs planted itself in the fleshy meat under the trooper's chin. The other punctured the muscle of his upper arm. A well-placed spread. The electric current began to cycle immediately and the baton flew from the trooper's hand. The man's body seized, and he gave a loud grunt of pain as he fell onto the roadway. The *clack-clack-clack* continued for five seconds—a brief enough interval that Ben was still on his knees, groggy from the baton blows. The trooper made as if to stand and Ben hit the trigger again, beginning another five-second fifty-thousand-volt ride accented by the *clack-clack-clack* and grunts from the trooper. This time, when it was done, Ben was standing over the prone officer.

"All right, asshole. What the hell was that all about? Who sent you?"

The trooper got to his hands and knees and reached for the semi-auto still holstered on his belt. His answer was short and sweet. "Fuck you, Sawyer."

"Oh, I don't think so."

He hit the trigger again, and the patrolman fell to the asphalt with a thud, splitting open his left cheek. When the cycle ended, the trooper lay stretched out and still, a trail of spit mixed with blood running across his face. Ben used his foot to turn the man onto his back and read the man's name tag.

"We can do this all day, Petersen. Who sent you?" When no answer came after several seconds, Ben spoke again. "I guess we're going to find out once and for all if one of these things can actually kill a man, aren't we? Ready for another ride?"

Ben held the Taser pistol up, making sure the trooper could see his finger on the trigger, and the man finally found his voice.

"McKenzie. Doyle McKenzie."

It's true, he thought. *McKenzie is behind all of this.* His thoughts turned to Alex and a sense of urgency overtook him. Ben nudged the trooper in the chest with the Taser. "Keep talking."

The trooper struggled to speak. "McKenzie called me. Gave me the description of your car. He knew you'd be at Red Cliff. Said from there you'd turn for home. Told me to find you."

"Find me and what?"

"Hold on to you. Let him know where you were. That's all, Sawyer. I swear it."

"And you did it? A guy calls you and says, 'Hey, nab an off-duty cop for me,' and you do it? How come I think you know more than that?"

"No. I don't, I swear to—"

The current sounded again, and the trooper let out a pathetic squeal. When the cycle was complete, Ben offered some cursory sympathy. "Was that number three or four? Either way, you've got to really be hurting by now, huh?"

"Jesus, Sawyer. You're going to kill me with that thing."

Ben held the Taser directly in front of the man's face with his finger poised over the trigger. "Maybe. Five seconds to start talking. Four, three—"

"McKenzie paid me." The trooper's voice started off sounding desperate, but when he saw Ben slide his finger away from the trigger, he fell into a slow, exhausted cadence. "I mean, he pays me to do special jobs for him. Usually it's just turn my back on some dope or something like that. He says it's undercover stuff. This time, though, he's crazy. He said you're working with a con named Harlan Lee and you've been out raising hell."

"Where is he? This Harlan Lee guy?"

"I don't know."

Ben held the gun in front of the trooper's face, and the man screamed. "Nobody knows, I swear! McKenzie thinks he'll head for Florence County; Lee lived there before he went to prison. In some homestead shack deep in the middle of nowhere couple miles from the Michigan border."

When the man went silent, Ben grabbed him by the shoulder. "Get your ass up."

The trooper struggled to his feet and Ben pulled the forty-caliber semiauto from the other holster on the Sam Browne belt and tucked it into his own waistband. He took the spare magazines from the trooper's belt and jammed them into the rear pocket of his jeans. He grabbed Petersen's police radio and flung it into the woods that lined the highway. Ben motioned the trooper to head to his patrol car, the barbs still buried in his skin and the wires running back to the weapon in Ben's hand.

When they reached the vehicle, Ben said, "Open the trunk and climb in, Petersen."

"What are you going to do, Sawyer?" the man said, sounding truly lost. "Don't kill me. I can help you. I'll tell you everything. We'll drive up to Florence and I'll help you find this Lee guy. I will. Just don't kill me."

Ben forced the cop into the trunk. "I'm not going to kill you, Petersen, but this is police work and you ain't a cop. You're just another crook. I don't work with crooks." Now that his adrenaline rush was fading, Ben noticed the feeling of moisture—blood—on top of his head and running down his shirt. He touched his fingers to his wounded scalp and blinked his eyes at the throbbing pain of the contact. He could feel the welts growing on his back.

"Asshole," he muttered and pulled the trigger one last time. The trooper's body seized and he thrashed around in the trunk's confined space as the electrical current played hell on his muscles and flesh. Ben threw the Taser in and slammed the trunk shut, with the trooper still a jerking mess inside. Ben heard the echo of the man's cries mixed with the sounds of his latest electrocution as he walked away.

"I guess we're about even."

Ben fought the temptation to steal the much faster police cruiser. If he was seen in the marked car with a state trooper locked in the trunk, he'd have the entire Wisconsin State Patrol chasing after him. As it was, they'd be after him soon enough. The odds were that before too long, someone would check on Petersen, who might tell a story that would put them on all Ben's trail. No doubt the crooked trooper would eventually alert McKenzie, and that spelled more trouble for Alex.

Alex was still on the hook for a murder she didn't commit, and in the morning she was due in court. Ben realized even with all he had discovered, McKenzie seemed to be hooked up enough to make it go away. If the trooper had been successful, it would have been over for Alex. Once the state got rolling, there would be no stopping it. Ben knew what he had to do. If he could get to Florence and find Harlan Lee, it would be over. That was the single blow that would destroy the case against Alex. He was sure of it.

He looked at himself in the mirror, his hair matted with blood, his shirt stained red and torn. He put the van in gear and rolled onto the road. A few miles to the south he'd pick up the state highway. His cell phone was dead, and he was headed into the remotest part of the state where not a single town had a population of more than five hundred souls. He hoped one of those souls was Harlan Lee.

FIFTY-SIX

McKenzie stood outside the bars and stared inside. Alex made sure to give it right back and lace it with steel hate. The isolation cell carried the thick smell of decades of nicotine being absorbed into the gray paint of the walls, mixed with human waste that sat in a covered bucket marked SUBJECT TO SEARCH. Alex figured the temperature in the cell hovered around eighty-five degrees, and she could smell that her visitor had already begun to sweat. McKenzie lit a cigarette as he began to speak.

"You can blame the new living arrangements on me, but you probably figured that out already."

When Alex said nothing, McKenzie went on.

"Thought you might want to know, your husband's a fugitive. He misrepresented himself to officials of the Florence County Sheriff's Office, then provided confidential information to a state convict. After that, he assaulted a state trooper. Nearly killed the man. Seems to me Ben must have just snapped. Every cop in the state is looking for him. As it stands now, he'll be lucky to survive the day."

Alex hadn't heard from Ben in more than thirty-six hours. In the middle of the previous night, male guards she hadn't recognized came to her cell and escorted her to the maximum-security isolation wing. She was confined in a space no bigger than a large broom closet, lit by a bare sixty-watt bulb. The only furnishing of any sort was a cement bench built right into the wall that also served as a bed. Her circumstances now seemed hopeless, but she'd choke on it before she let McKenzie get a reaction out of her.

"Anyway, I figured just in case that crazy son of a bitch got some idea about busting you out, we'd better put you in a bit more secure environment. I ran it by the DA. She was good with it. She's just wants to be sure you make it to the courtroom in the morning."

Alex tried to control her voice, but even she heard the tremble. "I'll be there, Detective. And so will my husband."

"Sorry, Alex. But I don't really think he's coming back. He seems to be having himself a hell of a time. Probably got a new Bonnie to go along with this Clyde Barrow image of his."

"He'll be back, McKenzie. You can count on it. And when he gets here, you're screwed. For Ben to be gone this long, he must have found out what's really going on around here. Something tells me you're in it up to your eyeballs."

McKenzie's eyes roamed up and down her body and Alex couldn't help but shiver, and she pulled her arms in tight around her waist. He seemed to pick up on her fear. "Tell you what, Alex. I got some pretty strong connections in the corrections department. Once you're locked up, maybe a year or two down the line, I'll stop by for a visit. We'll see just what you're willing to do for a square meal and a hot shower. See how sassy you are then."

"You are a vile degenerate, McKenzie." Alex nosed up to the bars and stood inches from his face. "On top of that, you're the ugliest, most pathetic excuse for a man I've ever laid eyes on. I'd spend the

rest of my life in this cell and eat the shit from that bucket before
I'd let you within a hundred yards of me."

"Yeah. You are something. That's really why I put you in here,
Alex. Just to fuck with you." McKenzie lowered his voice and leaned
his shoulder against the bars. "You wanna hear something that'll
really blow your mind?"

Alex offered no response, and McKenzie gave his yellow smile.
"I know you didn't do it."

Alex only stared ahead with a dumbfounded expression that made
McKenzie laugh out loud.

"That's right, sweetie," McKenzie said. "I won't go into any detail, but I thought you'd like to know that somebody out here knows,
shit-ass bitch that you are, you ain't a killer. Don't mean you ain't
going to prison for it."

"What are you talking about?" Alex shook her head in disbelief.
"You'd let an innocent person go to prison?"

"If it helps you to know, seems like your husband pretty much
has it all figured out. I gotta give it to him. Damn good cop."
McKenzie pulled on his cigarette and exhaled the smoke directly
at Alex. "Only problem is he's headed up to Florence, and there's
a hell of a welcoming committee waiting for him. When it's all
over, he'll just be seen as the loving husband who couldn't accept the obvious fact his wife was a cheating bitch who killed her
lover."

Alex felt an anger like none she had ever experienced. She thought
of her husband risking his life. Her son losing his mother. Her
father alone. Alex lunged forward; her hands shot between the
bars, and her fingernails connected with the flesh of McKenzie's
face. He sprang back, but not before she left a three-inch gouge in
his cheek. "You *bitch*."

McKenzie wiped the blood from his face. "I don't give a shit who
killed your boyfriend, Alex, but within a week you're going to be a

murder convict. I figure your old man will last about a month in a state hospital. And that boy of yours, what'll we do with him?"

McKenzie's loud voice grew maniacal, and Alex began to back away.

"Maybe I can line up a foster family down on the east side of Chi-town. One of those big-city arrangements, with fourteen rug rats runnin' around. He'll have three or four brothers named Leroy and a couple little girlfriends who go by Shanana. He'll be fine, don't you think?"

Alex put her hands over her ears and retreated to the corner of her cell. McKenzie gave a second swipe at the still oozing blood and once again approached the bars.

"You'll see, Alex. You'll come around. Then maybe if you treat me right I'll work out some special visiting arrangements for you and your boy." McKenzie grabbed his crotch and winked. "But re-member, degenerate piece of shit that I am, I don't do nothin' out of the goodness of my heart."

Alex sobbed, defeated. McKenzie threw his lit cigarette through the bars and headed for the exit. "Don't forget. Court in the morn-ing, Alex. I'll pick you up at eight."

FIFTY-SEVEN

S tanding in the darkness, Ben stared at the minivan's rear tire, which was buried to the axle—and sinking in thick, oozing mud. The rain had started falling hard two hours earlier, making the already difficult road leading into the Nicolet National Forest even more treacherous, and now that narrow track was swallowing the minivan whole. Nine miles down the road sat a modest parcel of land that, according to the records at the county seat, was all that was left of the one-hundred-sixty-acre homestead that had been owned by the Lee family for three generations.

The towering pines and hardwood trees of maple and hemlock were part of a vast forest that surrounded the roadway for thousands of acres in any direction. Looking again at the listing van, Ben realized he had no other alternative. He wrapped the forty-caliber and extra magazines in a sweatshirt, then tucked them into his backpack and strapped it on. He gingerly tested the leaf-strewn floor of a forest that had last been thinned by lumberjacks a hundred years ago and since then never altered in any substantial way. The surface felt slick, but he could keep his footing, and it seemed safer than the road. He patted the hood of the minivan as if saying farewell to a loyal horse, tightened the straps of his pack and headed into the forest at a fairly brisk pace, trying for a comfortable eight minutes per mile.

He soon fell into a good rhythm. Deeper in the forest, the canopy of trees served as a roof and his footing became more solid. Feeling strong, he opened up his gait. He'd left Newberg forty hours before and driven close to seven hundred miles. After his run-in with the trooper, Ben had made his way back to Florence County using less-populated roads. He'd snuck into the library, a stone's throw from the sheriff's office, thirty minutes before closing and convinced the librarian on duty to give him an extra half hour after that. The one-room country library didn't have computers, but Ben still knew how to work a microfiche.

In that hour he found a brief newspaper account of a drug-related murder, and that led to a good bit of information about a young man named Harlan Lee. Sure enough, nearly eighteen years ago Lee had pleaded guilty to murder and been sentenced to twenty-five years. With time off for good behavior, Ben figured Harlan could be out by now. Ben also found the obituary for Harlan's father, Jedidiah, who died several years after Harlan was locked away. County land records indicated there was a parcel of land a few miles south of the Michigan border that was owned by the Lee family. Ben imagined that would be the best place to look for Harlan Lee.

In two days Ben had slept less than two hours, but fatigue was not a factor. His mind was clear and he'd get plenty of sleep if he ended up dead. But until then, there was work to do.

An hour into his run, guided only by his instinct and the stars, Ben heard the sound of a revving engine. He stopped to listen more closely. By the sound of it, it was a truck, probably a four-by-four, and it was hard at work. The engine cut off. Silence, then the crack of gunfire from the same direction. One shot, a pause, then several more. Ben knew he was close to the scene. A few hundred yards away, maybe less.

This is it, he thought. The confrontation was at hand. Ben hunkered low to the ground and headed toward the sounds of the battle.

FIFTY-EIGHT

It had been thirty minutes since the exchange of gunfire. All man-made sounds had faded away, replaced by the night chorus of ten thousand types of wildlife and the residual rain hitting the canopy of trees a hundred feet over his head. Ben had been in the forest for over an hour, and his eyes had achieved a keen nocturnal dilation.

The small house of stone and timber stood dark. Ben imagined the builder had intended it to last, and though long ignored, the structure stood firm in the deep uncharted forest that probably predated Columbus. With only the waning moon to betray his position, Ben crept close enough to the cabin to peer through one of its many broken windows. It was hard to make out anything in the dim interior.

Ben climbed the three steps to the cabin entrance and pushed the door open, holding the trooper's forty-caliber handgun at the ready and surveying the part of the room he could see from the doorway. There seemed to be no signs of recent human activity or occupation.

He stepped fully into the small room and, in that instant, sensed movement behind him. Instinctively he spun to confront whoever it was, but the darkness was replaced by a brilliant light that burned away his night vision. A hard blow caught him in his chest, and Ben fell to the floor in a heap.

The blinding light remained in his eyes, and a voice came from somewhere in the brightness. "I don't know what the hell's going on out here, but drop the piece." The voice carried authority.

Ben peered into the light, trying to shade his eyes with one hand, and caught a glimpse of a large figure. He slowly lowered his weapon to the floor; the light followed the gun. Though his vision was still light dazzled, Ben made out the shape of a man in uniform, the glint of metal on his chest.

"Shove it away. Give it a good push."

Ben did as he was told. The gun skittered away and, by the sound of the impact, hit the cabin wall.

"Now what?" he asked.

"I'll tell ya now what," the man said. "You're going to tell me who the hell you are and what you have to do with this."

The flashlight beam shifted until it partially illuminated a dead man stretched out on the cabin floor. Ben's eyes still burned, but he could see that a good amount of blood covered the wood plank floor. The dead man, dressed in a flannel shirt and trousers, had been stoutly built and well muscled. In the dim gray light, he could tell little more about the scene. He turned back to the man currently in charge.

The man shifted and the white light once again shined in Ben's face. Ben raised a hand to shield himself.

"I'm Ben Sawyer. I got nothing on what happened here."

"Ben Sawyer." From the man's tone of voice, Ben felt that he was being studied. He knew he must look frightful—covered with fresh blood that still seeped from his head wound, soaked from old blood, sweat, and rain, pasty white with exhaustion. "You look like you've gone a few rounds. What brings you to the middle of nowhere?"

Ben studied the other man, picking up on the brown uniform of county law enforcement. He had few reasons to trust a cop. "Am I under arrest, officer?"

"Say what now?"

"I said, am I under arrest? If I am, I'd like to know the charge and you can get me to an attorney."

"You aren't from around here, are you, Sawyer?"

"Am I arrested or not?"

The voice turned serious. "Let me tell you how it is. I'll be damned if that son of a bitch right there, who by the way died at my hands in case you're wondering whether or not I mean business, ain't none other than Harlan Lee.

"Harlan ain't been seen around here for more than fifteen years. Last I heard he was doing life in the state penitentiary, but apparently there was a change in living arrangements and no one bothered to tell me. Then you come slinking in here armed with a hand cannon. I suppose I could probably just go ahead and oblige you, take your ass into custody until I figure it out."

Ben swallowed hard at the news that the dead man was Harlan Lee. Would he still be able to prove Alex's innocence? His better judgment and instinct still told him not to trust the cop, but sooner or later, Ben knew, he had to rejoin the world of law and order. He squinted into the dark, trying to see his captor. "You're a deputy, I take it?"

"Sheriff, actually. Sheriff Scott Jamison, Florence County."

Ben cringed, remembering McKenzie's reference to his friendship with Jamison.

"Sheriff Jamison." With his head, Ben motioned to the body. "You say you know this guy? This is Harlan Lee?"

"Don't work that way, Sawyer. I ask the questions. I know that comes off like TV bullshit, but it's true."

Ben ignored the comment. "But you say this man is Harlan Lee?"

Jamison didn't bite and waggled his gun barrel. "On your feet. My patrol truck is parked up the road. You can sit there while I get some deputies out here to sort through this shit."

"All right, Sheriff," Ben said. He decided to share a few more facts. "My name is Ben Sawyer. I'm a police sergeant out of Newberg down in Waukesha County. I've been investigating a string of murders that I think Lee was probably responsible for. One was a cop killed in Danville, Illinois. A second cop got shot. She works for me." Ben was hoping that would be enough.

"You sure you ain't the Lone Ranger? A cop from Newberg coming all the way out here to investigate crimes that occurred in another state?"

"You're right, that doesn't sound very good," Ben admitted. "A civilian was murdered down in Newberg, and my wife has been arrested for it. Long story, but I've got reason to believe Harlan Lee did the killing and is trying to put it on her. A friend of mine from the PD started asking questions. She wound up shot in Danville."

Jamison gave up nothing. "Go on."

"Bill Petite? You might know him—used to be the district attorney here in Florence County. He's locked up in Red Cliff for killing a woman, his girlfriend or something. I'm betting Harlan was good for that one too."

"Yeah, I heard about Petite. Did strike me as odd," Jamison said. "Especially when you put it in with everything else."

"Everything else?" Ben glanced away, then back into the light. He could barely make out Jamison, who seemed to be leaning casually against a wooden table, his gun held at the low ready.

"I mean not only Petite but also Henry Lipinski. Former sheriff of Florence County. My predecessor, you might say. Lipinski is the one who ran the scam on Harlan all those years ago."

Ben stared blankly at him. His dumbfounded expression must have amused Jamison, who gave a short laugh and continued.

"Damn, Sawyer, I thought you were the hotshot Lone Ranger. Don't you even know what this shit is all about? If you want to put all this on Lee, you need to get your facts straight."

"Sorry, Sheriff," Ben said. "Fill me in."

"Back about twenty years ago, Jedidiah Lee owned a hundred sixty acres of land in the big woods. This cabin sits right about in the middle of what was the Lee homestead for more than a hundred years. I guess you could say old Jed took advantage of the remoteness of his surroundings.

"He was known to cultivate a crop that was in very high demand by some of the folks around the state. The law—that would be the fella named Lipinski—didn't have a problem with what Jed was growing, but he didn't like that Jed wouldn't cut him in on it. Time came when Lipinski and some of his crooked friends decided Jed needed to be brought to heel. They decided to hit Jed where it would hurt him the most."

Jamison's demeanor had changed when he'd begun the story. Ben heard strong emotion in his voice, slowly building anger.

"Lipinski waited until Jed's son, Harlan, took a load of product downstate, then got into cahoots with some of his ass-bag associates down in your neck of the woods. Newberg PD pulled Harlan over on a traffic stop and planted evidence on him from a homicide case—the weapon used to kill some small-time dope dealer from just outside of Tipler, more than a hundred miles away."

Jamison snorted. "As if Harlan would give two shits about how that boy worked his crop. Anyway, they used that trumped-up bullshit to search the Lees' cabin, where they found more so-called evidence, not to mention a hundred-plus acres of mature marijuana plants."

Ben asked, "What happened after that?"

"Lipinski burned the grow and arrested Harlan for murder. The boy said he'd take his chances on a trial. But when Lipinski threat-

ened to charge the old man in federal court with drug manufac-
turing, cultivation, distribution . . ." Ben heard pity in Jamison's
voice.

"Suffice it to say the old man would've died in prison. Harlan
took a plea, got twenty-five to life."

"And Jedidiah?"

"Sold off most of the homestead trying to buy off Lipinski. Trying to get his boy an early out. Tried up until the day he died. Here
in this cabin."

Ben studied the face that remained a shadowy outline. "So what
about Lipinski?"

The sheriff laughed. The force of it shifted the light to the ceiling for a moment, allowing Ben his first good look at the man. "He
got himself arrested. Just like Petite. Turns out he was a freak for
kiddie porn."

It struck Ben as interesting the sheriff didn't know of Lipinski's
alleged suicide.

"Wasn't there some guy down in Danville?" Ben asked. "Named
Donaldson?"

"Yeah. If memory serves, Donaldson was the snitch who claimed
Harlan confessed to the killing while they were locked up together.
It was just more bullshit the cops came up with to make sure Har-
lan didn't weasel out from under the murder rap.

"So you say your wife is hooked up for a killing down in Newberg. Is she related to that lying sack of shit Lars Norgaard? Word
is that old bastard stroked out."

"Mind if I stand up, Sheriff?" Ben asked, stroking the back of
his swollen scalp.

The voice came out of the light smooth as polished metal. "Why
not? Nobody here but us cops."

Ben stood, wavering on his feet, and reached for a heavy wooden
chair to steady himself. "Whew. Feels like I've been run over by a

truck. Talk about your crooked cops, I didn't even tell you about the run-in I had with a Wisconsin state trooper. I tell you, Sheriff, it's been a hell of a day."

"Yeah, I'll bet." Jamison's voice tightened. "Tell me, Sawyer. What led you to Harlan? How'd you figure he was good for all this?"

Ben's pulse picked up; he let adrenaline flood his body but took measures to give no outward signs. He allowed himself one last look at the body laid out nearby, not surprised to see that the man who had been identified as Harlan Lee, wore green uniform trousers and an unbuttoned flannel shirt.

"Funny how that came about, Sheriff," he said, then dropped his voice and added, "Guess I'd better sit down. Still feeling a little groggy."

He pulled on the chair as if to sit, then swung it into the light.

Gun and light both fell to the ground. Ben heard the glass bulb break. Blackness swallowed the room so suddenly that Ben felt a wave of vertigo and tilted on his feet. The other man was unaffected and leaped onto Ben, propelling him into the sharp corner of a beam. Hot pain shot through his body and he would have fallen if not for the other man's boxer's grasp.

Ben pushed off and tried to ready himself.

Two stinging blows struck his jaw; a third went to his cheek, and when Ben tried to strike back he caught nothing but black air. A fist smashed his ear, knocking him to his knees. A kick to the side of his head grounded him, and Ben struggled to remain conscious. He made out the shape of a boot coming toward his head. He managed to deflect the blow and heard his opponent hit the ground. Ben was on him in an instant.

Unseen hands and fists smashed hard against his body and head. Ben pressed himself against his opponent's chest; the awkward angle made the man's blows glance off and largely ineffective. Ben's thumb found his opponent's eye socket and dug in deep. Both the man's hands grabbed at Ben's arm, but he managed to push deeper and felt the eye muscle grip and moisten his thumb.

Ben took two more blows to the chin, but he kept working the man's eye, pushing his thumb deeper. He used his other hand to deliver a blow to his enemy's mouth, then struck him repeatedly about the face and head. Sure now of their relative positions, Ben used both hands to clamp down on the neck, concentrating on his windpipe. The ridges and the circular muscles were pronounced under the pressure of his grip.

He squeezed harder, compressing it completely. The blows directed at his body and face grew weaker, became nothing more than flaying slaps of a desperate and dying man. This was it. This was his moment. Ben bore down, held tight, and did his best to strangle the life out of Harlan Lee.

FIFTY-NINE

At one minute past eight A.M., McKenzie strode into the county jail intake area. He let his hand drift to his pocket as reassurance. Yep, still there. The handmade shank was fashioned from a toothbrush, tape, and a blade from a discarded box cutter. McKenzie had made it himself and felt proud of the authentic nature of the weapon. The shank, plus the testimony of an inmate who would swear she sold it to Alex Sawyer earlier in the morning, was all McKenzie would need. He just had to be sure to get it deep enough into his gut that everyone would agree he had no other option but to shoot the fleeing murder suspect. It would be one Sawyer down, two to go.

"Open up, turnkey," McKenzie called out, waving the transport orders he held. "I'm here to drive Sawyer to the courtroom."

McKenzie recognized Corporal Reynolds when he looked up from his position in the control booth. He'd dealt with him a few times before. Uppity black bastard was his recollection. Word had it he was the one who had arranged for Alex to be placed in protective custody. McKenzie also heard this Reynolds stud was tight with Suarez. *Go figure,* he thought. *Dark meat goes for its own kind, I guess.*

"Have a seat, Detective," he said politely enough. "The prisoner is already being brought to the control booth for transportation."

"Thank ya, son. I'm much obliged." McKenzie bowed dramatically and used a southern drawl.

Darnell glared through the Plexiglas. "I said, have a seat."

A few moments later a uniformed guard emerged with Alex Sawyer handcuffed and in leg irons.

McKenzie looked Alex over with indifference. "You can take off the cuffs. I don't think Mrs. Sawyer is going to give me any trouble, are you, Alex?"

When she saw McKenzie, Alex stopped walking. "I'll go you one better, McKenzie. I'm not going anywhere with you."

Corporal Reynolds looked at Alex from the control booth. He picked up a phone and spoke briefly, then turned to McKenzie.

"The cuffs are standard, Detective," he said. "Inmate Sawyer is to be cuffed at the wrists and leg irons applied anytime she is not in the facility."

McKenzie snapped, "I know the procedures. I'm just telling you we don't need the cuffs. Take them off her. Now."

Corporal Reynolds was calm but firm. "The cuffs stay on, Detective."

Alex repeated, "I'm not going anywhere with him." She looked at the man in the control booth. "Corporal Reynolds, I want to see your boss. This man has come to my cell; he's threatened me. I will not go anywhere alone with him. I refuse."

"Oh, knock off the drama, Alex," McKenzie said. He had to get moving. "Fine, I'll take her cuffed." He wrapped a hand around Alex's elbow and pulled her toward the jail exit.

"Please, Darnell. Don't let him do this," Alex called as he towed her along.

"Wait a minute, Detective," Darnell said, but McKenzie ignored him. He struggled toward the exit, the gate begin to slide shut on its metal rails. He tried to make it through the gate before it closed, but Alex dug in, slowing their progress.

"Goddamn it," McKenzie seethed. He turned and looked through the Plexiglas of the control booth. "Listen here, turnkey. Open that door right now or I'll have your black ass for lunch."

"Calm down, Detective. We've already made transportation arrangements for the inmate. She will be delivered to the courtroom and released to the bailiff."

McKenzie growled. "What kind of arrangements?"

Tia Suarez stepped through a door behind the control booth. She walked down into the sally port area, dressed in her Newberg PD uniform. She moved slowly and her face was an expressionless mask, but her tone was pleasant when she said, "How're you doing, Detective? Long time no see."

"Suarez?" McKenzie stared. "What the hell are you doing here? You aren't supposed to be back for months."

Tia looked at Alex and winked. "I owe it all to my youth and clean living, Doyle. Great recuperative powers."

McKenzie was unimpressed and highly annoyed. "Yeah, whatever, but you can leave. I'm transporting Sawyer to court."

Tia stepped between McKenzie and Alex. "No," she said, "you're not."

"Tell you what, Suarez," McKenzie said. He could see the pain in her eyes and knew she was still in pretty bad shape. "You step aside or I'll put you aside. I don't figure you'll be too hard to handle, now, will you?"

McKenzie looked back at the control booth and shouted, "Open this damn gate, now." He turned to Tia again and said, "Step aside, Suarez. That's your last warning."

McKenzie took a step toward Tia but then saw her face flood with relief as she looked past him and over his shoulder. McKenzie heard a familiar voice from behind, and he turned to look.

"You heard the man, Corporal Reynolds. Open the gate."

McKenzie looked on in disbelief. Sawyer stood just outside the thick gray bars, three feet in front of him. He was towing a hand-cuffed prisoner who looked beat to hell, and Plate Boyd was standing alongside. Like the prisoner, Sawyer looked as though he had gone a few rounds. His face was bruised and battered. His nose and jaw were swollen and appeared fractured. Dried blood caked his face and clothes. He looked like hell and yet here he was. McKenzie could only stare ahead, and Ben stared back.

"Thanks, Tia," Ben said, never taking his eyes off McKenzie. "I'll take it from here."

"You got it, Sarge," Tia said. "Welcome home."

Ben turned to his wife. "Sorry, Alex, it took a little longer than I thought. I got back as soon as I could."

McKenzie looked on as Ben and Alex seemed to reconnect. The two exchanged looks of satisfaction, and even McKenzie could feel their affection for one another. Ben looked back to McKenzie.

"Corporal Reynolds. Sergeant Ben Sawyer, Newberg PD, booking a prisoner. Request permission to enter."

Reynolds hit the control pad and the door began to open. "Permission granted."

Ben walked in, along with his prisoner and Boyd. McKenzie saw that the man in handcuffs wore the disheveled uniform shirt with a shoulder patch out of Florence County. One eye was screwed tightly shut and his throat bore a savage deep purple bruise. The air about him was that of a proud champion prepared to admit he had been bested. Ben had hold of one arm while Plate Boyd held the other. McKenzie saw that the name plate said "Jamison." His mind reeled with confusion, but then Ben cleared it all up.

"Corporal Reynolds," Ben said, "Sergeant Boyd and I are booking Harlan Lee into this facility on multiple charges of homicide and attempted homicide, most notably the murder of Louis

Carson and the shooting of Tia Suarez. Other charges are forth-coming."

Harlan Lee? McKenzie thought. How is this happening? McKenzie gave a nervous laugh and tried to think his way through the storm descended on him.

"What the hell are you talking about, Sawyer? You come walk-ing in off the street beat to shit, every cop in the state looking for you, acting like you got the authority to book a prisoner on my mur-der case? We've got our killer, Sawyer. Tell him, Plate."

"It's over, Doyle." Plate spoke with a resolute firmness Mc-Kenzie hadn't thought him capable of. "Ben called me on the way down from Florence. Told me everything. You've got a lot to an-swer for."

McKenzie worked hard to respond calmly. "I don't know what the hell you're talking about."

"Is that right?" Plate asked, then went on. "After talking with Ben, I got a little curious about the old booking card somebody left on my desk. I think Chief Jorgensen might have mentioned it to you, didn't he?"

McKenzie saw a knowing glance pass between the two cops, and he thought back to his meeting with Jorgensen. McKenzie couldn't keep up with the growing mess, but then Plate made it worse.

"Anyway, it got me to thinking, so I decided to drop in on my old friend Lars Norgaard. It took a while, but we got to communi-cating."

McKenzie watched as Plate opened his jacket and pulled a clear plastic bag stamped EVIDENCE from his pocket. "I recovered this from under his bed. It's loaded with pure morphine. Enough to kill a man. Your thumbprint was lifted off the plunger, Doyle. It all fits in pretty well with what Mrs. Erickson was able to tell us. You re-member. Your visit to Chief Norgaard's room?"

McKenzie stared at the syringe. He tried to speak, but his voice faltered. "That? I don't have any . . . I don't know . . ."

"Save it, McKenzie. You're under arrest for conspiracy to commit murder." The authority in Plate's voice continued to grow. "Corporal Reynolds, we'll be booking a second prisoner. And initiate release papers for Mrs. Sawyer. The charges against her are dropped."

McKenzie watched as Ben passed Harlan off to an arriving deputy in exchange for a handcuff key. Ben's hands were shaking as he pulled his wife free of McKenzie's grip. Ben fumbled with the cuffs around her wrists. A moment later her arms were around his neck. He pulled away and dropped to his knees to free her from the leg irons. When Ben got the second iron snapped open, he stared at McKenzie, flinging the chains hard across the floor where they rattled against the bars of a holding cell. McKenzie stared back in stunned silence until Boyd pulled him by the arm.

"Let's go, Doyle. It's over. You're under arrest."

McKenzie threw an elbow and pulled away from the old man. He bolted toward the still-open door and started thinking of his escape plan. His car was in the lot. He'd have to get to his cash, but then he could disappear easy enough. He took two steps toward the door before an explosion of pain in his leg dropped him to the ground. He screamed in agony and looked up. Darnell Reynolds stood over him still clutching his police baton.

"Not so fast, *Detective*. We've got a cell that just came available in the isolation wing. You should be very comfortable."

Reynolds pulled McKenzie to his feet and to the hallway where the cells were located. The pain in his leg was excruciating and McKenzie limped along.

"Goddamn, man. I think you broke my leg."

McKenzie looked back over his shoulder, and just before they rounded the corner he knew led to the isolation wing, he saw Ben

Sawyer. The man was on his knees, his eyes closed hugging his wife around the waist.

He looked on as Alex Sawyer stood over her kneeling husband, and spoke in a hushed voice.

"I knew you could do it, Benny. I knew it all along."

SIXTY

Nearly a week passed before Ben returned to the county jail. The trip had a surreal quality. His wife had recently been an inmate here, and passing through the iron gates would always remind him of that. The last time he had walked through this door, it had signaled the end of a desperate journey. He'd rescued his wife and imprisoned a cop. When he'd left the building that day, he'd delivered Alex to her son and father in what was the proudest moment of his life.

In the hours and days that had followed her release, he had not left her side. They ate, slept, and bathed together. It was the stuff of storybooks, and Ben had never felt more alive, especially during their private homecoming, after Jake was finally in bed. But there was unfinished business to attend to. Ben found Corporal Reynolds again on duty.

"Good morning, Sergeant Sawyer. He's waiting for you in the interview room."

"Thanks, Darnell." Every head turned and every jailer greeted him as Ben passed through the series of gates that led to the interview room. Of all the publicity the story had gained, none of the experience was more important to him than to be back in good standing as a cop and to have the unqualified respect of his peers. He walked into the interview room and found the man there waiting with the patience only an experienced con can display. A patience that acknowledged that time was not a factor in his life.

"Heard you wanted to see me, Sawyer," Harlan Lee said in an emotionless voice still raspy from his injury. "I thought I'd pretty much filled you in on what you needed to know driving down from Florence." He snorted in what seemed to be admiration, then said, "You done good. You ain't gotta rub my face in it. I'm gonna do my time, but it'll be time I earned. I got no beef with that."

"I appreciate your willingness to see me, Harlan. Then again, you really should get yourself an attorney."

Harlan's smile was thin and cold, and Ben felt a chill run down his spine. This was a dangerous man; the black patch that covered one eye added to his air of menace.

"Sawyer, I admitted to killing a half-dozen folks, including a cop. I'll admit it again in open court. Ain't no lawyer gonna get me a better deal than life. And as long as I can keep myself in a Wisconsin courtroom, I ain't looking at the chair. Gotta love the bleedin' hearts in this state, don't ya?"

A very strong though strange connection had grown between the two of them in the hours they had spent alone in the sheriff's four-by-four, driving back from Florence County. After Ben made the conscious decision not to kill Harlan, he'd declared the man under arrest and driven straight to Newberg. During the four-hour drive, Harlan had been handcuffed and seated in the backseat behind the wire mesh as he told Ben his story. Ben was here to review part of that tale.

"I wanted to let you know," he said. "I looked into that murder in Florence, eighteen years ago."

Harlan's one eye showed only the slightest interest, but Ben knew he had the man's attention. "Whaddya mean? That case is off the books."

"Doesn't mean I can't look into it. One thing struck me as odd. You said the gun they pulled out of your car was reported stolen, right?"

"So?"

"It *was* stolen," Ben said. "But it was stolen in Newberg. I got to wondering why a kid from Florence steals a gun in Newberg, goes back to Florence to use it in a homicide, then ends up with it back in Newberg."

"Seems unlikely, don't it? But maybe you oughta ask that father-in-law of yours."

"Yeah, maybe I will ask around a bit. But I just thought I'd let you know that I believe you. I don't think you killed the fella up in Florence. You should have taken it to trial. All this"—Ben waived his arms in a wide circle—"all this could have been avoided. It just took a little police work."

"Is that how you see it, Sawyer? All it took was *police work*?" Harlan's voice was bitter and held more emotion than Ben had heard in their extensive conversations. "And who was I gonna get to do this police work, Sawyer? Lipinski? Norgaard? How about you? If your wife hadn't been locked up, would you have crossed the street to help my convict ass?"

Harlan turned his head and spit into a corner of the room, then locked his one eye on Ben's face. "You all stuck me in prison and were set to leave me there. You finally took the time to figure out what really happened all those years ago, but it's too damn little and too damn late."

"Okay, Harlan, you got every reason to be mad as hell at Lipinski, Petite, even Lars Norgaard. But all those others, Harlan. Why?"

"What do the bigwigs in Washington call that shit, Sawyer?

'Collateral damage,' right? I don't hear you taking a high-and-mighty tone with them."

"I thought you deserved to know, Harlan."

"What about what's his name? McKenzie?"

"Attempted murder. Conspiracy. Half a dozen other charges. He's right down the hall from you. He's going to end up doing near as much time as you. Maybe you two will run across one another."

Harlan scoffed. "He'd better hope not. I'd kill him on general principles. I got nothing to lose."

After a short pause, Harlan spoke again. "And your woman. How's she?"

Ben tried to imagine the circumstances that could've led him to having a near intimate conversation with a man soon to be a convicted of multiple homicides. It still seemed altogether unreal. Even more so when he found himself answering the question without hesitation.

"She's good, Harlan. She's home. Where she belongs."

Harlan grunted, "Norgaard?"

Ben looked at Harlan with honest conviction. "He knows, Harlan. He knows the part he played in all this."

Harlan looked away. Ben wondered what he was thinking.

"So, Harlan. Are you sorry? Any part of you sympathetic to the people you killed? The victims?"

Harlan thought for a moment before answering. "Sympathy is one of them reciprocal kind of emotions. Kinda get a little, give a little, but not a lot has ever been thrown my way, and I don't lay much out for other folks. Regret, though? Now, hell, Sawyer. That's a whole different creation. I might sense a bit of regret."

The men sat in silence for several minutes. Then Ben said, "All right, Harlan. I'll leave you alone now."

"Yeah. All right, Sawyer."

The two men looked one another over. Neither extended a hand or offered a parting word. Ben banged on the door as Harlan stood. A guard arrived and both men turned and walked away. One returning to his life, his home, and his family. The other to his private cell.

SIXTY-ONE

Ben walked into the office of the Newberg chief of police unannounced and uninvited. Jorgensen looked up and broke into what was for him a wide grin.

"Ben Sawyer. The conquering hero returns." Jorgensen stood up in greeting and, with a bit of flair, waved Ben forward. "Do have a seat."

Ben dropped into the chair centered in front of the chief's desk. He slumped, set the bottoms of his shoes against the expansive mahogany surface, and balanced the chair back on two legs. Jorgensen looked a little put out, but Ben knew the man had no choice. At this point, no one was going to mess with Ben Sawyer.

Jorgensen sat down and said, "I guess you've come for this?" He reached into his desk drawer and pulled out Ben's badge and police ID. The chief held the items as if to tantalize.

"Keep it. I'd rather the new chief reinstate me."

"Oh, you heard wrong, Ben. I'm not going anywhere. Granted, it was quite a shit storm you stirred up. But remember, once I learned of the Lee connection, I was on it. I couldn't have known the crimes McKenzie was involved in. I have nothing but respect for you, un-covering McKenzie's graft and corruption. Tell me, how's Lars holding up? Does he realize what was going on? It's unfortunate that all this will leave a real blemish on his administration."

"Forget about my father-in-law," Ben said. "McKenzie puts most of this shit on you, says you were pulling the strings. Hell, he's even said Lipinski's death was actually a murder. He gave you up as a coconspirator. I hear Chippewa County is reopening the case. Seems Doyle McKenzie's had a come-to-Jesus kind of moment."

"Nah, nothing that noble. McKenzie is a desperate man, not to mention a lying son of a bitch. I think my adamant denials will make good copy in the papers, don't you?"

"Bill Petite might be a little more convincing."

Jorgensen laughed.

"Try again, Ben. Bill Petite knows better. He's just happy to be out from under a murder conviction. He's already busy trying to reinvent his law career. Believe me when I tell you he won't be too interested in rehashing ancient history."

Ben kept pushing. "The stolen gun Lars planted on Lee? It was from a Newberg burglary. The report was taken by a patrol officer. Fella by the name of Walter Jorgensen."

Jorgensen licked his lips, and Ben saw the slightest twitch in the chief's eyes.

"Touché, Ben, well done. But what of it?"

"I pulled the report, Jorgensen. The gun was stolen along with some credit cards. The crook was caught with the cards the next day. He confessed to the burglary and to stealing the plastic but said that was it. He didn't know anything about a stolen gun."

"Crooks lie, Ben." There was the slightest tremor in Jorgensen's voice. "Is that news to you?"

Ben kept going. "Then, a week later, Lars somehow pulls that

342 ■ NEAL GRIFFIN

gun from a car driven by Harlan Lee. A gun that two days before had been used in a killing up in Florence."

"What are you implying?" Jorgensen asked.

"I'm not *implying* anything. I'm drawing a pretty obvious con-clusion." Ben dropped the chair onto all four legs and sat forward. "You stole the gun from the burglary. That way the gun could be reported along with the stolen cards. Two days later that weapon was used to kill a dealer in Florence County."

Ben stared across the desk at Jorgensen. "Tell me, Walter. Did you do the killing yourself? Or was it Lipinski? Who actually pulled the trigger? How did you get Lars to agree to the plant? What story did you tell him?"

"That's quite a theory, Ben." Jorgensen's voice was shaking now; Ben wondered how much longer the chief would be able to hold it together. "Very impressive. But what makes you think Lars needed convincing? If you want to come up with a list of suspects for your wild tale, his name better be on it."

Ben made no response. Jorgensen seemed encouraged by his si-lence, and his voice rose with fresh conviction.

"That's right. You want to stir all this ancient shit up, go ahead. It'll be quite a show. But remember this: As far as all the shenani-gans that were perpetrated against that innocent boy, Harlan Lee, I never signed any report. I never raised my hand and swore to any-thing. As far as the crimes . . . the *sins* . . . that were committed, I can only say I'm ashamed to have been that close and not have fig-ured it out what was going on. I most certainly should be held ac-countable for my shortcomings. I suppose I could lose my job over it. But old Lars, that's a different story altogether."

Jorgensen stood and stepped around his desk. He towered over Ben and went on. "It was always easy to motivate Lars . . . under certain circumstances. He was never one to take so much as a free meal. But if you told Norgaard that a crook might beat the rap, the rule book would fly from the window like it had sprouted wings.

"Personally, I'm not comfortable prosecuting an invalid," Jorgensen said. "But maybe that's only because of my close personal affection for the accused. The public might feel differently. Tell me, Ben. You've been the subject of a media feeding frenzy. How well do you think old Lars is going to hold up? Criminal charges for perjury? Filing a false police report? Allowing an innocent man to sit in a prison cell for near twenty years? Hell, maybe they'll even want to revisit the murder in Florence. You gotta wonder how Lars came to have that gun."

Jorgensen stepped back behind his desk.

"You have to ask yourself if the old boy will even survive it. How about his daughter? That little grandson of his? Course they've been through it before, haven't they?"

Jorgensen reclaimed his seat and took his turn to prop his feet up. His cotton sky blue dress shirt with a satin tie was a perfect fit around his massive neck, but Ben could see that a ring of sweat had begun to form.

There was some truth to what he said. Any case against Jorgensen would be tough sledding, but Lars was pretty much bought and paid for. Right now, Lars would welcome his day in court as a chance to confess his sins and admit his involvement.

Hell, it seemed like Lars wanted to go to jail. He had allowed an innocent man to spend nearly twenty years in prison for a crime he had not committed. Lars might feel like he had it coming, but Ben knew better.

The fallout would never end, and it wouldn't just be Lars who paid the price. His family would be labeled for life. As would every member of the Newberg Police Department, past and present. Everyone would pay a price and nothing would change. Harlan would still have lost two decades of life and the dead would stay dead.

344 ■ NEAL GRIFFIN

"Here's what's going to happen, Jorgensen," Ben said, meeting the other man's gaze. "Pack your shit because you're retired. You walk away from Newberg PD and you don't even sniff around another cop job. Your days of scamming the public are over."

"And if I decide to stay?"

Ben stood. Staring into Jorgensen's eyes, he took a step forward, placed his hands flat on the desk.

"I can live with you walking away, Jorgensen. But I won't have you wearing a badge. Lars will welcome the chance to put the truth out there. My wife and son, they'll understand that. But you're right. It won't change a thing and I'm really not up for it."

"Good to hear, Ben," Jorgensen said. "I figured with your own history, you'd see the wisdom of keeping this all in house. Now if you'll excuse me, I have—"

Ben reached out and slapped Jorgensen's feet from the desk. Jorgensen was caught off guard and leaned forward to regain his balance. Ben took the opportunity to reach out and grab Jorgensen by the tie. He pulled hard and the man stretched across the desk. Ben leaned in and spoke in a low voice.

"Yeah, I get it, Jorgensen. Here is what we're going to do. You walk away and that's the end of it. But if you stay?" Ben hesitated for a moment, pulling harder on the chief's necktie. "Stay and we all go down together. And I promise you, you'll do time. Hard time."

Ben tightened his grip even more, and the man gagged. "And know this, Walter. You make me do that to my family? You'll do time, all right, and I'll see to it you don't survive it."

Ben pushed off with both hands and Jorgensen fell back, landing hard in his leather chair. Jorgensen's hands went to his throat, and Ben waited for a response. After several moments of silence, Ben turned to walk out, leaving Jorgensen seated at his desk, disheveled and breathless. "Clean out your desk and get out Jorgensen," he called out as he left. "Either that or plan on joining your boy McKenzie in a jail cell."

EPILOGUE

Ten Weeks Later

B en took a seat beside Alex on the porch swing. The warm summer weather had lured several neighbors into their yards, all
enjoying a splendid evening. Ben nuzzled Alex's neck and handed
her a glass of cranberry juice, then took a long pull from his bottle
of Leinenkugel's.

"Very funny." Alex looked away.

"Don't worry. Seven more months or so and you can have one
yourself." Ben patted her stomach, still flat and giving no hint of
what was to come.

"Not if I breast-feed. Unless, of course, you want an alcoholic
toddler in the family." She grinned at him. "You know, most
modern-day husbands consider themselves pregnant along with
their wives. Shouldn't we both give up beer for the duration?"

Ben didn't answer, just took another swig and looked through the
window into the house, where Lars sat in his wheelchair. Jake was
close beside him, reading to his grandfather.

"Dad had a good day," Ben said. "The speech therapist said he
has shown real progress this last couple of weeks. We practically

had a conversation today. He thinks the Packers will go all the way this year. Course he always says that."

Alex's voice held pure contentment. "Thanks for working with him. I don't think he'd let anyone else see that side of him. He's still reluctant to talk to me."

"Just the pride thing, Alex. Don't make anything out of it. He can't wait for the two of you to sit down and catch up." Ben knew Lars's desire to talk with Alex was the old man's main motivation in therapy. Lars wanted to explain to Alex what had happened all those years ago. He wanted to be the one to tell her the role he had played in bizarre events. But Ben knew something that Lars didn't. Alex had long since figured it out for herself what role Lars played in the entire episode and she had already forgiven him.

"I think he just looks at me as another cop. Makes it easier. Less personal that way."

"No, it's very personal," Alex replied. "He looks at you as his son. He'd be proud if you'd take the chief job."

Ben rolled his eyes. Alex wouldn't stop bringing it up.

"What, Ben?" she said. "Everyone wants you to take it. You want them to bring in someone from the outside? How will that go over?"

"I told you, I'll think about it. There's no rush."

"I think you should talk to Dad about it."

He and Lars had been spending a good deal of time together. More in the past few weeks than in the past ten years. Lars knew that if Ben put his mind to it, he could blame Lars for all that had happened to his family. After all, it had been the sham Lars ran on Harlan Lee that had begun the entire series of events. *Another one of those chain reactions,* Ben thought.

Lars had tried his best to discuss it with Ben, to explain how the everything had gotten out of control. How it seemed like the right thing to do at the time. How police work had changed. Most of all, how he now understood that no one ever knows how his actions today might affect events years, decades down the road.

The two men had been sitting alone on the porch of the convalescent center looking out over the pond surrounded by grass grown long over the summer months. "It's over, Lars. What happened then has nothing to do with us now. From now on, we look ahead."

The old man reached out just the same and put his hand on Ben's cheek. The words were coarse but clear. "I'm sorry, Ben. Sorry for everything."

Alex's voice brought Ben back to the present.

"What do you hear from Tia? How's she coming along?"

"I talked to her this morning. She said it felt good to speak English. She plans on staying on with her parents for a couple more weeks, but Jalisco isn't Newberg and she's just about ready to get back to work. She told me to say hello."

"And the case against McKenzie. Is Dad going to have to testify?"

"Naw. McKenzie's not that stupid. He's going to cop a plea."

Alex shook her head. "Could've been me, Benny. A life in a prison cell."

"But it isn't you." Ben put his arm around his wife. "That isn't your life. This is." He gazed out past the quiet backyard to the warmly lit houses nearby. "We could do worse, right?"

Alex looked at her husband, tears welling in her eyes. "Thanks, Benny. I'll never stop thanking you. I could've . . ." Her voice broke.

"Alex, we go through this every night. You've said enough. I know. I—"

She cut him off with a hand to his lips. She caressed the jagged red scar that trickled down his forehead and breezed the back of her hand across the uneven rise that marked the healing fracture of his cheek. The subtle changes to his expression served as physical testimony to his trial and victory.

"No. You don't know, Ben. You'll never know."

He knew better than to argue with his wife. He understood her gratitude and it meant the world to him. He lightly touched her stomach and thought of the life growing inside her. He put his arm around her and looked into her eyes until she lowered her head onto his shoulder. Alex nuzzled his neck, and he breathed deep to smell her hair and skin. They sat together on the porch swing of their home, and his focus fell on the billion stars of the clear Wisconsin sky. He held his wife and thought again of all they had been through, everything that had brought them to this place. To this point in their lives. He decided that when all was said and done, he wouldn't change a thing. And with that, he pulled his wife a little closer, held her a little tighter, and enjoyed a moment of silent perfection.